A *"Witch's Brew"* *of* *Betrayal, Deception, and Love*

The Websters of Columbia, Maryland appear to have a lot going for them. Larry is a highly respected scientist; Vivian is a homemaker and part-time real estate agent; and their daughter, Rachel, is awaiting word on applications to some of the nation's best colleges. But beneath their veneer of normalcy lies a hidden family tragedy. Although many years in the past, this tragedy still dominates each of their lives and their relationships – much more so than they realize.

"The Other Part Of Me" is a story of interwoven family secrets, the darkest of all possible family secrets.

Ronnie Kinsley

The Other Part Of Me

Ronnie Kinsley

Published by: Instant Publisher
Instant Publisher
P.O. Box 985
Collierville, TN 38027

ISBN: 1-59196-043-6

Printed in the United States of America.
Second Printing May 2003

The Other Part Of Me

Chapter 1

Just enough muted light filtered through the curtains from the street lamp to reveal hairline cracks in the swirls of the textured ceiling. He studied the cracks, straining to make out the face of an old man. The nose and eyes were easy; he couldn't miss the eyes glaring down at him. But the mouth was wrong, he couldn't visualize a normal looking mouth. The best he could do was an angry slit of a mouth, a ghoulish mouth. He rolled his head to the side searching for a less threatening mouth from a different angle, but the face disappeared as the cracks faded into a jumble of incoherent lines. When he twisted his head back to its original position the eyes came back. But they weren't the eyes of an old man any longer, they were much younger eyes, and they were feminine eyes. And now there was a different mouth, a soft mouth with delicate lips.

It had been a sleepless night for Larry Webster, one that seemed to go on forever. Finally, the welcomed thud of the newspaper tossed onto the driveway provided the first hint that this miserable darkness was about to end. He turned toward the nightstand next to the bed, straining to bring the clock into focus through bleary eyes. Despite having been awake practically the entire night, he hadn't allowed himself even one glance at the clock, until now. His body stiffened as the numbers on the clock took hold of him, not the time, 5:48 a.m., but the date, 12/4/93. He just kept staring and staring at that date, finally shutting his eyes tightly to break free from the clock's hypnotic clutches.

He gingerly crept out of bed, careful not to disturb his wife who lay curled in a ball next to him. Leaving the

1

warmth of Vivian's body caused him to shudder as he confronted the coldness of the room on this December morning. He bent over and pulled the covers up snugly to her chin. It was important that this day be as short as possible for Vivian, the fewer the number of waking hours the better. He reached for the light switch, but then thought better of it – shouldn't take the slightest chance of waking her even though the sedatives would likely keep her asleep for several more hours. She took them often enough that he had pretty well calibrated the effect they would have on her.

In the darkness of this early Saturday morning his hands fumbled through the chest of drawers grabbing for his running clothes: socks, jock strap, shorts, tee shirt, and a long sleeve turtle neck. More than enough for a thirty-degree run he reasoned. But then a blast of chilly December wind whistled through the old wooden windows causing him to dig deeper in the chest for a heavy sweatshirt.

Tiptoeing out of the bedroom his jaw tightened at the sight of the thin line of light coming from beneath the door of the adjacent bedroom. The bedroom belonged to his seventeen year old daughter, Rachel. Up until two years ago Rachel always slept with the light on, but only did so now when she was especially upset. He inched the door open, careful to deaden the sound of the squeaking hinges as much as possible. The room was littered with clothes, magazines, and stuffed animals and smelled of sickeningly sweet perfume. Rachel lay crunched up on the bed with a blanket in her arms, dressed in the jeans and sweatshirt she had worn the day before. In sleep her face appeared peaceful and innocent, contrasting the harshness of her short, black hair and the semi-circle of earrings adorning her right ear. He shook his head in silent frustration as he noticed the natural blond roots in the part of her hair. Ninety-nine percent of the female population would kill to have hair as beautiful as Rachel's, but what does she do – gets herself a buzz-cut and dyes her hair an unbecoming and unnatural jet-black. Thankfully, her hair was beginning to grow out and just yesterday she said she intended to let it return to its natural color. He leaned over and carefully untangled the blanket from her arms and gently laid it over her, his eyes moistening as he kissed her cheek.

At the bottom of the stairs he sat down on the next to last step to lace up his Nike running shoes. Just above and directly in front of him was an oil painting hanging on the wall next to the front door. The painting was of a young man laden with a fully loaded backpack, standing in front of a waterfall. He wore a blue tee shirt and a pair of khaki walking shorts. Thick, droopy socks fell below muscular calves and rested on the tops of rugged hiking boots. A darkened, sweat soaked area running down the center of the tee shirt revealed how hard the young man must have had to work to get to the base of the waterfall. But you could tell from the excitement in the young man's eyes and from his smile that it had been well worth the effort. You couldn't help but feel the love the artist felt for this young man. She had signed her name in the lower left-hand corner, "Vivian Webster."

Larry stretched his arms behind his back as he headed to the kitchen to guzzle orange juice directly from the carton, something he would never do in front of Vivian. Vivian was obsessively clean and obsessively neat, just the opposite of him and Rachel. It was but one of many tensions that filled the Webster household.

"Shit," he hissed at the heavy frost covering his 1992 Ford Taurus. Scraping off the windshield he glanced up and down the street, Eaglebeak Row, of his Columbia,

Maryland neighborhood. It was still dark so he couldn't see the Mercedes and BMWs, but he knew they were there. Columbia was a nice place to live and he liked the people, but too many of them were struggling to claw their way up the social hierarchy. Why else, he reasoned, would they pay almost twice as much as they needed to for a car?

Larry suffered no illusions about his own place on the social ladder, despite his rather lofty academic credentials. He had received an undergraduate degree from Princeton and a Ph.D. in Physics from Johns Hopkins University, but chose not to be included among the social elite for which his academic and professional accomplishments most certainly qualified him. He was born in the hills of Kentucky and had moved to Baltimore with his parents in 1958 when he was in the fourth grade. His father, who left Kentucky to get away from the coal mines, died of black lung disease less than three years later. Larry's mother would often recount to him how she and his father had debated leaving for years, and then, with tears filling her eyes, how his father might still be alive had he not been so "hard-headed" and left the mines sooner. "Dag-gum-it Larry," she would plead, "when the right thing to do is starin' you in the face, don't pretend you can't see it."

Closing his eyes, he could still hear her sweet Kentucky twang, just as if she were right next to him. Her last words haunted him, simple words spoken as she lay in her hospital bed on that June morning in 1975, less than a week after he had received his doctorate degree. "Your daddy would be real proud." When Larry Webster was down, feeling blue and reveling in his own despair, he could send himself to still greater depths of depression. All he had to do was to think of that precious lady who had thrown her body and soul into being both mother and father to that little boy from Kentucky.

At first, the city kids loved to make fun of Larry's clothes and especially of his accent. But Larry followed the advice of his father, "Remember, you can give just as good as you can get." Those city kids quickly figured out that he was the smartest among them as he cleverly deflected their cruel remarks back at them with increased venom. The teasing stopped within weeks and Larry's hillbilly characteristics became subjects of admiration rather than subjects of ridicule. Over the years most of Larry's "Kentuckyisms" vanished as he blossomed into a full-fledged "Baltimorean." But that first month in the strange and terrifying big city had shaped and molded the inner being of Larry Webster forever. The failed attempts of the city kids to demonstrate social superiority over the little boy from Kentucky poisoned Larry's attitude toward status seekers for the rest of his life. To emphasize the point he'd often say to Rachel only half-jokingly, "I'd rather run around the bases naked at Memorial Stadium during the middle of an Orioles game than be seen driving a Mercedes Benz."

As he continued scraping the windshield, Larry gazed up at the cold, cloudless December sky. Despite the glare of the street lamp he quickly located the constellation Ursa Major, or, as he simply preferred to call it, the Big Dipper. In this one respect Larry was lucky. The one uncontaminated love of his life was his work. He was an astronomer, a senior scientist at the National Science Foundation in charge of the astronomy department. While he had spent most of the last ten years of his career in management, he remained one of the world's leading experts on the theory of galaxy formation and evolution. He worked hard to remain scientifically active, performing original research whenever the opportunity presented itself. Unlike his colleagues, Larry didn't feel his intellectual talents anointed him with an inherent right to pursue scientific curiosity at taxpayer's expense. Instead, he just felt incredibly fortunate to be getting paid to do something he truly enjoyed.

Larry loved astronomy, but there was something he loved even more. He loved to run. He didn't run in races, or rarely even with other people. He ran by himself. Columbia was one of the first "planned communities" in the country, replete with a marvelous network of beautiful bike paths throughout its neighborhoods and parks. Even though one of these paths ran directly behind his house, Larry preferred to run where he could find greater solitude. So on this cold December morning he hopped in his car and drove out of his neighborhood.

Ten minutes later he pulled into the parking lot of an old elementary school converted into the Howard County Center for The Arts. Larry discovered this departure spot for his "trail runs" when Rachel had taken ballet lessons at the Center as a little girl. It was 6:50 a.m. and the first signs of daylight were creeping through the early morning darkness. Hiding his keys under some leaves, he slipped on the headset of his Sony Walkman, pushed the play button, and was off to the sounds of the Beatles singing "I Should Have Known Better."

Larry had short black hair, tinged slightly with gray at the temples. A strong chin and a nose that was a little crooked from the time he broke it playing basketball in the high school championship game provided a touch of ruggedness to offset his baby blue eyes. His lips were full, but a little lopsided. Rachel loved to tease him by saying he could imitate Elvis without even trying. Naturally athletic, broad shouldered and very trim, he weighed 165 pounds and was just less than six feet tall. When he was asked how tall he was, he always answered, "five-eleven." It wasn't his way to exaggerate.

He jogged slowly away from the Center through a neighborhood of small houses with faded bricks, bleached from years in the sun. The houses were surrounded by neatly trimmed shrubs and large leafless oak trees, and about every third house came outfitted with a barking dog that seemed to take exception to his presence in their neighborhood. The branches of the oak trees made dark cracks in the early morning pink sky. The air felt cold against his face and bare legs as he quickened his pace and passed a large colonial, a house that seemed out of proportion with the rest of the neighborhood. An unleashed German shepherd lounging in the front yard, unlike his canine neighbors, seemed oblivious to Larry, as he didn't so much as turn his head as Larry hustled by him. Just past the large house he came to a seldom-used gravel road that led into Patapsco State Park. He followed the road for about a hundred yards and turned right onto one of the Park's rugged hiking trails. The strengthening rays of the rising sun provided the needed light to see the trail, rutted with roots and rocks, and overgrown with bushes and tree limbs. Being able to see the trail was important, one misstep could result in a sprained ankle or worse. The trail quickly turned into a roller coaster of up and down hills. Feeling energized, he steadily increased his pace. Charging over the crest of the first hill, he began his first steep descent. He wasn't jogging anymore, but running at full tilt instead. The effects of the cold wintry air were more than offset by the self-generated heat of his body's internal furnace.

Sprinting down the trail Larry was no longer forty-four; he was eight years old again, running through the Kentucky woods. He felt completely alive, a sensation that could be fleeting and hard to come by. He sang along with the Beatles as his mad downhill rush followed the pace set by their music - smooth and effortless with "Nowhere

Man" and "The Long and Winding Road", then flying completely out of control to the sounds of "Help."

Two miles and about sixteen minutes later he came to River Ridge Trail, the path with the final half-mile descent to the Patapsco River far below. Just as he started down the steep trail John Lennon shrieked out the opening lyrics of "Twist and Shout." As he sang along with Lennon a feeling of pure childish delight engulfed every molecule of his being. Not running now, but jumping from rock to rock, he grabbed every available tree trunk to control his descent. A startled deer sprang out in front of him and bolted down the trail. Increasing his speed in an attempt to keep up with the deer proved fruitless. He galloped the final fifty-boulder-strewn yards of the trail and blasted out of the woods on to a steep embankment leading up to railroad tracks.

He turned left and jogged north alongside the tracks. On his right, the Patapsco River gurgled noisily as it made its way toward the historic town of Ellicott City just a couple of miles downstream. In just a few minutes he came to the quarter-mile long tunnel carved beneath Route 40, a major east-west highway leading into Baltimore about ten miles to the east.

The entrance to the tunnel was an ominous black void filled with coldness and loneliness. Glancing back over his shoulder the dull light from the tunnel entrance grew more and more faint with each stride. The force of the tunnel pulled him in deeper and deeper. His strides became short and tentative as he was consumed by the blackness. He punched the off-button of the Walkman and listened to the sounds of his labored breathing and of his running shoes shuffling awkwardly against the uneven gravel floor of the tunnel. Now there was nothing but complete blackness everywhere. It was a terrible place to be, but the proper place for the horrible feelings that began to take hold of him. He crumpled to the ground, leaned his back against the painfully hard and frigid tunnel wall and began pounding the back of his head against the wall. Finally the pain was sufficient to bring tears to his eyes. But it was a good kind of pain, much better than the other kind of pain, the kind that crushed his heart and smothered his soul.

Chapter 2

Seeking the warmth of the sun, Larry hurried out of the tunnel, his personal demon exorcised.... until the next time. Sometimes he could go for weeks, even months, dealing with the pain as if it were nothing more than a dull ache to be ignored and forced to the back of his consciousness. But then it would come back, building to an intensity that could not be withstood. And then he would return to the darkness of the tunnel and let it out.

Running south along the railroad tracks he turned on to River Ridge Trail and began the steep climb back up the hillside as the sound of the river faded behind him. The melting of the morning frost made the rocky trail especially slippery. After several slips and near falls he reached the top of the hill and stopped for a moment to fill his burning lungs with deep breaths of cold air.

Thirty minutes later, slowing to a walk, he approached his car, soaked with sweat, but with a sense of renewal that hopefully would carry him through this day. A hooded sweatshirt provided warmth for his now chilled body. The car radio was tuned to 105.7 FM, the local "oldies station." Just as the engine kicked in Steve Rouse, Baltimore's most popular DJ, shouted enthusiastically, "What better way to get your morning going than 'This Magic Moment' by Jay and The Americans." The song brought back memories of backpacking with Vivian in West Virginia during the summer of 1973, the two of them hiking along a mountain trail singing this very song together, sharing their own magic moment. The memory was so intense he could smell the mountain rhododendron, taste the wild blueberries, hear the muted roar of a distant waterfall, and feel the frigid water of a stream crossing. Even more significantly, he could visualize the loveliness of Vivian's form a few feet in front of him laboring under the weight of her pack, and feel the anticipation of making love with her beneath a canopy of stars at the end of a tiring day. But the memory was quickly discarded, it was hard to sustain happy thoughts, such thoughts would only make him sad in the end.

Opening the front door he was immediately overwhelmed by the scent of burnt pancakes coming from the kitchen. "Who's trying to burn down the house?" he yelled jokingly.

Rachel, wearing fresh jeans and a University of Virginia sweatshirt, came marching out of the kitchen with a box of pancake mix in her hand. Her short black hair with blond roots was wet from a morning shower. Her face was flooded with anger.

"Damn it! You tell me I should help out more around the house, take more responsibility. And then I get up early to make you breakfast and you're all over my case because one pancake gets a little burned. It's not my fault the directions on the box are fucked up."

Larry, not expecting and certainly not wanting a confrontation, took several deep breaths and suppressed the urge to strike back. "Rachel, I didn't mean anything. I was trying to be funny. I wasn't being critical. But I don't appreciate your foul language."

"Foul language! You don't like my language. Well here, make your own fucking breakfast!" Rachel screamed as she threw the box of pancake mix directly into her father's face from point blank range.

His heart thumped inside his chest as Rachel sprinted past him to the stairway, then stopped and turned to face him. Calming her demeanor and concentrating all the anger she could summon up, she hissed, "How could you go running today?"

Larry dropped his head, closed his eyes, and winced at the pounding of Rachel's footsteps up the stairs and the thud of her bedroom door slamming shut. With his eyes still closed he rubbed his hands up his face and over his head, smearing his hair with pancake mix. Feeling numb and with a sickening sourness in his stomach, he trudged upstairs to his bedroom. Thankfully, Vivian was still sound asleep. His body shook with frustration as he washed the pancake mix from his eyes and hair. A hot shower helped restore his composure, at least a little.

It was already an uncomfortable day and he expected it to get even more uncomfortable so he dressed in the most comfortable clothes he owned, a pair of well-worn jeans and an oversized flannel shirt with frayed sleeves.

He raised his fist to knock on Rachel's bedroom door, but changed his mind. After cleaning up the kitchen and gobbling down a large stack of Rachel's surprisingly good pancakes he heard footsteps in the foyer. Thinking it was Rachel, he crept down the hallway, but stopped before turning the corner as he spied Vivian standing in front of the grandfather clock, unaware of his presence. Dressed elegantly in a gray wool skirt, a pair of low black pumps, and a long sleeved white silk blouse, she opened the door of the clock. Her hands trembled as she pulled the chains to raise the weights. Her movements seemed awkward and almost painful as she closed the door, bowed her head and brought her hands up to cover her face. She stood very still, almost as if she were reciting a silent prayer.

"Vivian, is something wrong?"

Despite the softness of his voice Vivian was startled as her eyes met those of her husband. Rather than putting on weight like most women her age, Vivian was five pounds lighter than she had been on her wedding day. At

5' 6" and 110 lbs she was delicate, almost frail. Surprisingly, on this day she wore bright red lipstick, almost always choosing more subtle shades instead. Gray hair blended with a smattering of youthful blond and fell softly on her shoulders. She was quite striking and always attracted the glances of men wherever she went. She had large blue eyes, a small perfectly straight nose, large full lips, and beautiful teeth she rarely revealed. But despite her beauty, her face looked drawn and tired. She was 43 years old, one year younger than her husband, but she looked older than him.

Larry reached out and took hold of her hand. "Are you okay?"

She shook her head up and down and gave his hand a reassuring squeeze. "I'd like to get out of the house. Let's go have brunch and then do some Christmas shopping?"

"I just had some pancakes, but okay, sure. Give me a few minutes to get changed."

Larry thought for a moment, started to ask if he should invite Rachel, but quickly concluded it wouldn't be a good idea even if she had calmed down. He had no idea what was apt to happen, or what Rachel or Vivian might do on this day. It would be best to keep them apart as much as possible.

Having changed into a pair of gray wool slacks, black penny loafers with dimes in them, a beige turtleneck, and a blue blazer, he knocked on Rachel's door. "Rachel." He waited several seconds and once again whispered, "Rachel."

"Yes, Daddy," Rachel replied meekly from behind the closed door. Larry leaned against the door and spoke softly. "Your mom and I are going shopping. Are you doing okay?"

"I'm sorry Daddy. I'm ashamed of the way I acted."

"It's okay."

Rachel tentatively opened the door revealing eyes red from crying. "I haven't done anything like that for the longest time. It's just this day..... Daddy, it's so hard," she sobbed.

Larry took his daughter in his arms and rubbed the back of her head reassuringly. "I know. It's hard for all of us."

"I tried to pretend like it was just any other day, but I couldn't and then I just went crazy. I won't do anything like that ever again, I promise. "

"It's okay. When I get back we can talk if you want."

"Thanks Daddy. I love you."

"I love you too."

Rachel pressed herself tightly against her father's chest. "Daddy, please don't tell Mom."

Larry assured his daughter he wouldn't say anything. But as soon as he reached the bottom of the stairs Vivian immediately confronted him. "What was that about? Did you and Rachel have a fight?"

"We just had a little discussion about a mess she made making pancakes. It's no big deal."

"Are you sure she's all right?"

"She'll be fine. Come on, let's get outta here."

As they started to leave Larry opened the front door and a package, a little larger than a shoebox, with a UPS label addressed simply to "Webster," plopped onto the floor. It had been left between the entry door and the storm door. As he started to tear the box open Vivian said, "Just open it when we get back. I'm hungry." He complied and set the unexpectedly heavy box on the foyer floor next to the grandfather clock.

Larry held the front door open for Vivian and dejectedly glanced up the stairway in the direction of

Rachel's bedroom. Just as the door closed behind them, rap music began blaring from inside the house. Even though he despised the music it was a relief to hear it. When Rachel was depressed she would sink back into herself, shutting out the rest of the world. Playing music was a clear sign she was feeling better.

As he started toward his Taurus, Vivian chirped, "Let's take my car, I feel like driving for a change." Larry opened the right side door of their two-car garage; Vivian always kept her 1990 silver Toyota Camry in the garage.

"So where are we going to eat?" Larry asked as he fastened his seat belt.

"I don't know, what do you feel like?"

"You're the hungry one, you decide," Larry countered.

"Hey, I know, let's go to Mrs. Z's."

Larry's stomach knotted up as he unconsciously clutched the armrest with white-knuckle intensity.

"What's wrong?"

Without success, he tried to drive the emotion from his voice. "Vivian, Mrs. Z's burned down in the 70's."

After what seemed an eternity of silence Vivian meekly replied, "I meant wouldn't it be nice to go to Mrs. Z's like we used to."

"That's not what you said."

Again there was a prolonged silence.

"Well Larry, even you ought to realize that's what I meant. Do you remember how good their breads were, how cozy it was, how everyone was so friendly? And those desserts, I loved their desserts."

"Yeah, I remember," Larry mumbled in an obligatory manner.

Vivian smiled sheepishly. "Oh well, since some idiot decided to burn down Mrs. Z's, we'll just have to go to Clyde's instead."

Vivian's attempt at humor worked. Larry eased back in his seat and felt the knot in his gut loosen. She had drifted off into her own little world displaced in time and reality, something she used to do with regularity. But what was important, he realized, was that she knew it as well and had dealt with it. She had bounced back to the here and now and was even able to make fun of herself. This was far better than years before when she would turn to alcohol for weeks at a time, and insist, "I'm just a little tired."

"Smoking or non-smoking?" the Clyde's hostess asked Vivian.

"Non-smoking please. And could we have a table next to the window? We'd like a view of the lake."

Clyde's was located in Columbia's "Town-Center," sandwiched between Lake Kittamakundi and the Columbia Mall. Town-Center was the hub around which the "new city" was constructed. Having celebrated its 25th anniversary the previous June the new city wasn't all that new anymore. Never looking or feeling like a city, Columbia could more aptly be described as suburban sprawl, but with a measure of forethought and taste.

Larry recalled how insistent Vivian had been that they buy in Columbia when they had done their house-hunting back in 1975. At that time he had preferred housing developments closer to Washington D.C. in order to shorten his commute to work, but Vivian wouldn't budge on the subject. With its family-friendly atmosphere, she was absolutely convinced Columbia was the best possible place to raise kids.

"When was the last time we rented a boat?" Vivian asked, as she looked out on the little boat dock at the edge of the lake.

"It's been a long time. Rachel couldn't have been more than eleven or twelve." Larry paused to rub his hands up his face. "I'm so worried about Rachel. I know she's doing much better, but my goodness, she's a senior in high school and getting ready to turn eighteen."

Vivian held up two pairs of crossed fingers. "She should begin hearing about her college applications pretty soon."

Larry consciously tried to relax himself when he felt his facial muscles tighten, but it didn't work. "With her grades I can't imagine she'll accepted anywhere other than Howard Community College. What a crime, an IQ of 148 and until this year all she ever got was C's."

Vivian clamped her hands together with interlocked fingers. "It's my fault. I wasn't there for her during the most important years of her life. I wasn't a mother; I was just someone who lived in the same house."

Vivian looked at Larry for some sort of reassuring response, but when it didn't come she went on. "And now that I'm trying as hard as I possibly can, she won't let me into her life."

Larry reached across the table and took Vivian's hands in his, knowing it was time to come to her rescue from this self-inflicted flagellation. "She's gotten so much better. And it's because you have been there for her these past three years. Maybe she's not ready to acknowledge it, but you're the reason she's turning her life around. You started turning your life around three years ago, and because of that she's finally doing it too."

"But she has so far to go. For God's sake, she began experimenting with sex and drugs when she was fourteen years old. She was just a baby. She's still just a baby."

"She does have a long way to go, but she's not a baby anymore. She's made so much progress over this past year. And now that she's taking her schoolwork seriously she's getting straight A's. A little late, but ...."

"I just wish I had .... " Vivian interrupted, but stopped to keep from losing her composure.

"Vivian, it's good that you're talking about these things. If you and I can keep working together we can help Rachel get better."

Vivian squeezed Larry's hands even more tightly. "You're right."

Larry puffed out his cheeks and slowly shook his head from side to side. "I don't think she's ready to leave home, she needs some more time. I think she should go to Howard Community College for a year or two. I know it's a terrible thing to say, but I hope she doesn't get accepted by any of those out-of-state schools."

Vivian nodded her head in agreement. "I know you're right, but she thinks she's ready. And her boyfriend, Vinnie, has done wonders for her self confidence."

"I don't trust him," snapped Larry.

"But he's such a nice boy."

"Seventeen year old boys are interested in only one thing."

"I think you're wrong about him. I'd hate to think what it would do to Rachel if they split up. I think he's the reason she's doing so much better."

"Trust me Vivian, you're the reason."

They ate their meals in silence, consumed with their own thoughts. After neither of them had uttered a single word for over five minutes, Vivian locked on to Larry's eyes. "Why did you stay with me? Why did you never leave me?"

"What do you mean?" Larry asked unconvincingly.

"You know what I mean. I made our lives a living hell. You could have left me and could have taken Rachel with you. Any divorce court in the world would have ruled in your favor. Why did you stay with me?"

Larry's throat tightened. He felt dizzy. He chose the right words, but made them sound hollow. "Because I love you. I'm your husband." He coughed awkwardly. "Why are you asking me these things?"

Without moving her eyes from his, Vivian replied in a shaking voice, "I've always felt there was something else, some part of yourself you keep hidden."

"I don't know what you're talking about."

Vivian stayed right in his face, trying to peer beyond his eyes into his thoughts. Larry stared back, fighting to achieve a standoff in this contest of wills, a contest for which he was ill equipped. The convenience of the approaching waitress provided the relief valve he so desperately craved. Turning in the direction of the waitress, Larry asked for the check.

"Let's go. I'm fired up to do some serious Christmas shopping," Larry said, mocking his extreme dislike of shopping.

"I'm not ready to leave yet," Vivian replied sternly.

Larry tried to get comfortable in his chair, but it was impossible. He settled on just trying not to reveal his level of discomfort.

Vivian dropped her hands to her lap away from Larry's sight and anxiously rubbed them together. "You said Rachel made a mess. Was that all that happened? Is she upset because today is the fourth of December?"

"Yes, she was upset, but she's okay now."

"Are you sure?"

"I'm sure. Can we go now?"

They strolled up the hill past the Columbia People Tree, a thirty-foot metal sculpture in which the limbs and branches of the tree are fashioned from people with outstretched arms. From there they followed the walkway over the Little Patuxent Parkway to the Columbia Mall.

They spent the afternoon making the entire circuit of the mall, first the upper level and then the lower level. In their pattern developed over many years, one would enter a particular store and the other would dutifully follow, waiting patiently until the interested party had satisfied his or her curiosity. Their combined interests led them to browse in about one out of every four stores. With over 100 stores in the mall this made for a long afternoon. Larry chose only the two bookstores and the two sporting goods stores. He enjoyed looking, but almost never bought anything in the mall, choosing to do his real shopping at the discount warehouse stores exiled to the outskirts of Columbia.

Vivian chose all of the specialty shops, the women's clothing stores and the mall's two large department stores, Woodies and Hecht's. She bought a sweater and scarf combination, a bracelet, and a very expensive bottle of perfume, for several of her friends. Larry bought a $50 gift certificate for his secretary.

Their sole collaboration was in the selection of a gift for Rachel, a major source of tension between them years before. In the past, Vivian would approach the Christmas season feeling tremendous guilt over her alcoholism and disregard of Rachel's needs. She would insist that she take responsibility for buying Rachel's gifts. To make up for her lack of motherly nurturing over the past year, she would shower Rachel with an orgy of gifts.

While Larry watched Vivian browsing in one of the mall's most popular stores, an eclectic jewelry shop, he remembered seven years earlier how Vivian was unable to choose between two styles of bicycles for Rachel, so she bought both. He recalled how that year and every other year Rachel would slowly approach the Christmas tree on Christmas morning, methodically open each gift, place it back in its box, stack the boxes neatly under the tree, and say, "Thank you Mommy. Thank you Daddy. My gifts are wonderful." The gifts would remain undisturbed for days, and sometimes weeks, long after the tree had been taken down. Rachel would then secretly, usually in the middle of the night, come and take her gifts to her room. This pattern repeated itself every year until 1990, when Rachel was fourteen. After waiting until eight o'clock on Christmas morning for Rachel to come downstairs, he had gone to her room to find that she was gone. Several hours later, after having called every child from her school and the neighborhood, Vivian called the police. At seven o'clock that evening, well after dark, Rachel walked in the front door, cold and hungry. He remembered so clearly how she shivered uncontrollably for almost twenty minutes; and how she refused then, and ever since, to say where she had been.

Later that evening Vivian asked Rachel when she was going to open her gifts. He wished he could forget what Rachel had said in reply, but he couldn't forget those angry words coming from such a tiny voice: "Go to hell Santa Claus. You must be Santa Claus because you aren't my mother. You've never been a mother to me and you never will."

Rachel never did open her gifts that year. Nearly a month after Christmas, he asked if she would like to donate the gifts to Goodwill. She said yes and did so, without ever knowing what they were.

But Rachel was wrong, that Christmas changed Vivian forever. After years of half-hearted attempts, she joined Alcoholics Anonymous and stopped drinking. She started taking care of herself and then she started taking care of Rachel. It took many months for Rachel to realize Vivian had changed, that she was trying to become a real mother to her. But the emotional damage from years of uncaring behavior could not be undone quickly, if ever.

21

He thought about how the next Christmas the gift giving ritual changed with he and Vivian picking a single item for Rachel.   They bought her a stuffed animal, Garfield-the-Cat with an ear-to-ear grin. Rachel opened the box, wrapped her arms around Garfield, hugged him to her chest, slowly rocked back and forth, and cried softly.

Vivian's excited voice pulled him away from his memories. "This will look beautiful on Rachel. What do you think?" She was holding a delicate gold necklace.

Chapter 3

It was very late in the afternoon when Vivian and Larry left the Columbia Mall. Vivian's feet ached from all the walking so she asked Larry to drive home.

"Hungry?" asked Larry as they pulled out of the mall parking lot.

"Yeah, but I'm too tired to cook. Let's stop and get some of those really good sandwiches from the Bagel Bin. I'll call Rachel and see what she wants," Vivian said as she punched the number on the "hands free" car phone.

After six rings an authoritative Rachel answered. "You have reached the Calculus Command Center of the Starship Enterprise. Please provide your password."

"Rachel, what's going on?" Vivian asked.

"What is your password?" Rachel demanded.

"Is someone there with you?"

"I must have your password." Rachel insisted once again.   And then in a commanding voice directed to someone else she ordered, "Spoc, contact security, I believe we have an attempted illegal entry into the Calculus Command Center."

And then a new voice, a male voice, responded, "Aye, aye Captain, sir, I mean madam. Recommend we maintain contact with the intruders to get a fix on their location coordinates."

Hysterical laughter came from the other end of the phone. Vivian and Larry stared at one another with a look of annoyance, but also of amusement.

And then more orders from Rachel. "Spoc, I have their coordinates. Arm the lasers!"

"Excellent, Captain. Where are they?"

"They're at the Dorsey Search video store. No, wait, wait..... I have a more precise location. They're in the back room of the video store, the room with the X-rated videos. Fire lasers! Fire lasers!"

Then Larry joined in with the banter for the first time. "Very funny guys, and quite creative. Rachel, I assume that's Vinnie there with you."

"Yes Dr. Webster, it's me."

"We've been doing our calculus homework. We just finished when you called," Rachel added.

"We're going to stop and get some take-out food from the Bagel Bin. Vinnie, do you like the Bagel Bin?" asked Larry.

"I'm a huge fan of the Bagel Bin," Vinnie replied enthusiastically.

"Well, would you like to stay over and have dinner?"

"That would be excellent Dr. Webster. That is, if it's okay with Mrs. Webster," Vinnie answered politely.

"Of course it's okay with me," replied Vivian.

Larry and Vivian stopped at the Bagel Bin in the Wilde Lake Village Center and arrived home a few minutes later. Vinnie's beat up 1980 Ford Maverick was parked on the right side of the driveway blocking the entrance to the garage. Larry parked the Camry behind his Taurus, annoyed that Vinnie had disrupted the natural order of traffic flow in the Webster driveway. Upon walking in the front door they found themselves in the midst of a heated argument.

"Touchdown, I win!" screamed Rachel.

"No way!" countered Vinnie. "Dr. Webster, is this a touchdown? No way it's a touchdown," Vinnie shouted as he shook his head from side to side causing his long black curly ponytail to whip back and forth.

The Other Part Of Me

Larry put a large bag of bagel sandwiches on the counter and moved toward the kitchen table to make the crucial ruling that would determine the outcome of this obviously hard fought game of match-pack football.

The game consisted of flicking a pack of matches back and forth across a table in an effort to score a "touchdown" by having the pack stop in a position overhanging the edge of your opponent's side of the table. If you flicked the matches too hard and they fell off the table, your opponent was given an opportunity to "kick" a field goal through goal posts constructed by aligning your index fingers and holding your thumbs upright. Larry had taught the game to Rachel when she was five years old. For years he dutifully performed his fatherly role, letting Rachel win. However, she had now become so proficient at the game Larry no longer had to concern himself with letting Rachel win. In fact, he was rarely ever able to beat her anymore.

Larry stared at the pack of matches hovering at the edge of the table. It was truly a difficult call. The top edge of the oak table was rounded and the matches were definitely hanging over the rounded edge. But were the matches overhanging the flat vertical edge of the table necessary for a touchdown? Larry looked directly from above then bent over, bringing his eyes to table level, and looked along the edge of the table.

"I'm just not sure. This is too close to call, I need to make a measurement." Larry excitedly scampered from the kitchen to his study. He quickly returned with a "right-angle" ruler. He placed one edge of the ruler underneath the table. The other edge of the ruler, pointing straight up, was pushed against the flat vertical edge of the table. He began to slowly slide the ruler along the edge of the table toward the matches. If the ruler slid past the matches without touching them it would not be a touchdown.

Vinnie began a whispered chant of "defense, defense, defense..... ," as he bobbed his thin muscular body up and down in anticipation.

Everyone held their breath as the ruler approached the matches. The matches moved ever so slightly as the ruler slid past. Larry quickly thrust both arms straight up and shouted, "Touchdown!"

"Yes! Yes! Yes! Nobody beats me on my home field. Nobody," screeched Rachel as she ran around the table pumping her fists in the air.

"You cheated!" shouted Vinnie.

"I did not."

"Did."

"Not."

"Did."

"Not."

Vinnie struggled to get out another "did" but he couldn't, he was laughing too hard. Rachel ran to his end of the table, threw her arms around him and kissed him passionately. As an embarrassed Vinnie wriggled to free himself from her grasp Rachel exclaimed, "I love you Vinnie!" Rachel slowly released Vinnie and turned to face her parents who stood staring at her in stunned silence. Tears dripped slowly but steadily from Rachel's eyes. "I love him. I really do. He's been kinder, more caring and nicer to me than anyone has ever been."

Rachel had surprised everyone including herself. She had felt this way about Vinnie for months, but was afraid to say so, afraid it would scare him off. But now the Jack was out of the Box and there was no reason to hide her feelings any longer.

The four of them stood around the table like ice sculptures, frozen, not moving and not knowing what to do or say. Vinnie finally blurted out, "I need to go to the bathroom," as he bolted from the kitchen past the hallway bathroom, and down the stairs to the bathroom in the basement.

Vivian set her jaw and demanded, "Do you know what you're getting yourself into?" Rachel glared back at her mother defiantly, but Vivian pressed on. "You two are having sex, aren't you?"

Rachel shot back, "Are you and Dad having sex? When was the last time you made love to your husband?"

"Damn it Rachel, I'm your mother."

"Since when have you been my mother?"

Larry tried to keep the situation from getting further out of control. "Rachel, that's not fair. For a long time we weren't very good parents, but for these last few years your mother and I have......"

Rachel interrupted. "I'm not talking about you Dad. I've always had a father. It's the mother department where I have a problem. Maybe she hasn't had a drink in a while, but she'll start up again. I learned a long time ago not to trust her. And she'll say that horrible thing to me again, the way she used to say it when I was a little girl! I know she'll say it again!"

As Vivian slumped onto the table and buried her face in her arms, a noticeably pale Vinnie hesitantly walked back into the kitchen.

"Vinnie, I think it would be best if you went home now," Larry said.

"Okay. I mean, yes sir," Vinnie stammered.

As Vinnie turned and headed to the front door, Rachel rushed to him. "I'm sorry. I shouldn't have said it. I'm really sorry."

"No, I'm glad you said it. You're the only girl I've ever cared about. I just need time to think. I'll call you tomorrow."

Rachel watched through the living room window as Vinnie backed his Maverick down the driveway into the street. They waved to one another as he drove away. Rachel's thoughts raced a mile a minute. She had thought about her feelings for Vinnie for quite some time, but they had always been just silent thoughts not shared with anyone. Having now brought a voice to those feelings and having shared them with Vinnie, not to mention her parents, strengthened her feelings even more. She had led a very unhappy life, but none of that mattered anymore as long as Vinnie was a part of her future.

Larry eased up behind Rachel and placed his hands on her shoulders. "Your mother needs you. She's been trying for so long to earn your love. What you saw in there was just her frustration. You need to let her into your life. Maybe it's asking too much for you to love her, but can you just forgive her?"

Rachel's emotions swung wildly back and forth. One part of her ached for her mother's love, another part ached from the pain her mother had inflicted on her. She continued to stare blankly out the window away from her father. "I'll go back in there and talk to her, but Daddy you've got everything backwards. I do love her. I don't know how or why, but I do. Someday maybe I'll tell her. But forgive her? I don't see how I could ever forgive her. She hurt me too many times." Rachel turned around and searched for understanding in her father's face. "Why did she take everything out on me? I was just a little girl."

Larry knew there was nothing he could say that would lessen her pain, knew there was no salve he could apply to heal a wound so deep.

Rachel continued to search her father's eyes for understanding. "I hate this day, it brings back all the hurt I feel inside."

Larry put his arms around his daughter and held her close. "It brings back everybody's hurt."

As Rachel sobbed, they slowly rocked back and forth in each other's arms for several minutes, both of them reminded of a father and daughter dance they had gone to many years before.

"Daddy, I know it's cold outside, but could we go for a walk. I feel like I can't breathe in here."

"Okay, you get our coats from the closet and I'll go grab a flashlight."

Larry lit the way down the hill in their backyard. There was no need to discuss which way to go – it was always the same whenever they went for a walk. When they reached the firm footing of the bike path Rachel said, "Turn off the flashlight, the moon's bright enough for us."

They snaked their way through the woods along the twisty path. The moon was only bright enough because they knew each turn by heart. When they reached the kid's playground they sat on swings next to one another, and gently swayed back and forth.

"When did you decide to become an astronomer?"

"When I was a little boy in Kentucky."

"Way back then?"

"Well, it wasn't that I decided to become an astronomer; I didn't even know what an astronomer was. I just remember fallin' in love with the night sky. And that never changed... so somehow I ended up bein' an astronomer. How 'bout you, what do you wanna be?"

"I'm still thinking about it."

"Like my mom always said to me, do something you love."

"Okay, I will" Rachel said as she began kicking her legs back and forth, picking up momentum, until she was able to slice large arcs in the night. Larry couldn't resist and did the same, each of them swinging higher and higher. But when the old wooden swing began making a threatening squeaking sound they dragged their feet until their arcs became smaller and smaller and finally they stopped.

"Why did Mom quit painting?"

"I think it just became too stressful for her."

"I thought things like that were supposed to be relaxing."

"Maybe for some people, but not for your mother. For her painting is a very emotional experience. I used to encourage her to start back up, but it never worked. I don't think she'll ever paint again"

"That's a shame, she's so good at it," Rachel said.

"I know."

"I feel badly about the things I said to Mom when she accused me of having sex with Vinnie. I know it hurt her very much. I'll tell her I'm sorry as soon as we get home."

"Good."

They walked slowly along the bike path and up the hill in their backyard. Just as they opened the front door they were startled by the sound of shattering glass coming from the kitchen. They instinctively rushed in the direction of the sound.

Vivian, her back turned towards them, was reaching into the kitchen pantry. She slammed the door with all her might and turned to face them as she braced herself against the kitchen counter. A nearly empty bottle of scotch waved about unsteadily in her hand. Her face was contorted and streaked with mascara, bringing back awful memories for Rachel and Larry.

In a raspy and ugly voice Vivian slurred, "Larry dear, the quality of liquor in the Webster household is rather poor since you assumed responsibility for its purchase. I do believe I shall relieve you of that job. Henceforth, I will buy my own damn liquor!"

"Vivian please don't do this. You can't do this to yourself. You can't do this to us," Larry implored.

"Just watch me," Vivian sneered as she gulped down the last ounce of scotch.

Rachel clamped her hands together like a beggar pleading for a handout. "Mother, please don't do this. I'm sorry."

Vivian's entire body shook as she stuck her face only a few inches from Rachel's. "You're sorry! I'm sorry too! I'm sorry those bastards didn't take you and leave my precious little Karen! She was a much better daughter than you!"

As soon as the words had come out of her mouth, a look of horror coursed across Vivian's face. She hated herself for what she had said. Wanted to suck those words out of the air and back down her throat. Would give anything to be able to do it.

Rachel covered her ears, turned towards her father as she stomped her feet on the floor, and screamed hysterically. "I knew she would say it again! I knew she would say it!"

Larry leaped at Vivian, grabbed her by the shoulders, and pounded her against the kitchen cabinet, as she offered no resistance. "You swore you would never say that again! How could you say that to her? How could you?"

He released her and let his body crumple to the kitchen floor. Without looking up and with no hint of real concern in his voice he asked, "Are you hurt?"

Ignoring him, Vivian tentatively reached out and touched Rachel's arm, but Rachel immediately jerked away and turned her head, refusing to look at her mother. "Rachel, I didn't mean it. I'm so sorry." When Rachel once again covered her ears with her hands Vivian lowered her head, and wobbled down the hallway and upstairs to her bedroom.

Rachel slowly rocked from side to side and looked down at her father. "Was she?"

"Was she what?" Larry replied with a look of confusion.

"Was Karen a better daughter?"

Larry patted the floor beside him. "Minnie, sit down here."

Still towering above her father crumpled on the floor, Rachel puzzled, "Minnie? Who's Minnie? Is that me?"

Larry shook his head up and down. "I can't believe I said that. I haven't called you Minnie since you were a baby. I don't know why I said it now, it just came out."

"Don't call me that again. I'm not a baby anymore."

"I won't. I'm sorry. But please sit down next to me."

Rachel dropped to the floor and leaned her head against her father's shoulder. "Was Karen a better daughter than me? I've always wanted to ask, but I've been too afraid. Was she?"

"My goodness Rachel, you and Karen were identical twins. The two of you were only nine months old when she was taken. You looked so much alike and acted so much alike that most people couldn't tell you apart. It took me six months before I stopped looking at the bottom of Karen's foot to see her birthmark to make sure which of you was which. You were both wonderful little babies, how could one of you possibly be a better daughter than the other?"

Larry saw the same hurt in Rachel's face he had seen when she was a little girl. "I don't know why your mother did the things she did and said the things she said.

She was just never able to deal with Karen's abduction and death, and in some crazy way she took it out on you. She went to so many shrinks. Each one of them had a different theory, but none of them helped her."

"What's your theory Daddy? Why do you think she did the things she did?"

Larry tilted his head back as if he were searching the heavens for divine guidance. "My theory? From the very beginning she was petrified about becoming a mother. I remember when she found out she was pregnant with twins she totally freaked out."

"What did she do?"

"She cried a lot and she kept saying she wasn't going to be able to handle it. So I just kept reminding her that I'd be there to help her."

"Did she have a difficult pregnancy?"

"Yes, she had a very rough time. Her blood pressure went through the roof, and her body was retaining fluid. She had to spend five months confined to bed because the doctor was concerned the placenta was going to tear away from the uterine wall before she reached term."

"But Karen and I did reach full term?"

"Yes, March 10, 1976, only twelve days before the official due date."

"During delivery she had a problem with bleeding?" asked Rachel.

"Yeah, she lost so much blood they had to rush her to intensive care. She was there for two days, and didn't even see you and Karen until she came out. Then two weeks later when she finally did get home, she stayed in bed for another six weeks. You know, I've never said this to anyone before, but I think she could have gotten out of bed much sooner. I think she didn't want to because she doubted herself as a mother."

"That must have really been hard on you."

"I thought I was gonna go nuts. I had expected to be pretty much of a spectator when it came to taking care of the baby. But here I was having to do everything for two babies, three if I count your mother," he chuckled. "I was completely exhausted. I almost never slept and I lived off of pizza deliveries. I once went five days without a shower. At the time it seemed like it would never end, but you know what?"

"What?"

Larry sobbed gently as he covered his face with his hands. "I wish I could have that time back. In some ways it seemed like I was in a torture chamber, but I would give anything to have that time back. I didn't realize it then, but that was the happiest time of my life."

Rachel snuggled up closer to her father's side.

"Even after your mother did get up and around, she was useless at first. You or Karen would start crying over something and she'd immediately go to pieces. By that time I'd become a real pro at taking care of the two of you and I would jump in and fix whatever the problem was. But that only made your mother feel even more incompetent. It finally dawned on me that I was the problem. I was preventing your mother from building up her self confidence."

"So what did you do?"

"I just backed off. If one of you started crying I let your mother deal with it. Even if I knew what the problem was I wouldn't say anything, I'd let her figure it out. Slowly she took on more and more of the responsibility for caring for the two of you. And a wonderful thing happened."

"What? What wonderful thing?"

"Well, I don't want to sound like a male chauvinist, but mothers are better at taking care of babies than fathers.

While I did a good job caring for the two of you, your mother was much better at it than I. And when she realized that, it did wonders for her self-confidence. She started trusting her own instincts and she became a truly wonderful mother. I know you find that hard to believe, but she really was a good mother before Karen was taken."

"I do find that hard to believe."

"Well, it's true. When I went back to work, I was so afraid she wouldn't be able to handle things by herself. And then she wanted to have this big cookout for the neighbors who had helped us out. I thought she was crazy; we always had so many things to do. We never had time for anything so it seemed like insanity to me for us to be putting on a big social event, but she handled it so well."

"It sounds like that was a happy time for you and Mom."

"It was."

"But you just said the happiest that you ever were was when Mom was still in bed and you were doing everything. Why wasn't that summer after Mom had gotten better, and things were more like a normal family...... why wasn't that the happiest time for you?"

Larry thought very carefully before he replied. "That was a happy time."

"But not the happiest," Rachel persisted.

"I'd been through a lot. I guess I wanted someone to take care of me, but your mother was too busy trying to be super mom."

"Were you having sex?"

Larry's back stiffened. "That's one thing I agree with your mother about. I don't think we have to answer questions from you about our sex lives."

"I think you just did," Rachel responded knowingly. "I'm sorry Daddy. I shouldn't have said that. I'm sure a new baby, in your case two new babies, puts a strain on the sex lives of every young couple."

Larry continued to sit quietly.

"But if Mom turned into such a wonderful mother, why did she take everything out on me?"

Larry scooted closer to his daughter. "When Karen was abducted, your mother went to pieces. The confidence she had built up, which seemed so strong, was really very tenuous and it was gone in a flash. She turned to alcohol and tried to forget, but she couldn't forget."

Rachel's chin quivered. "But when one of her babies was taken, why didn't it make her want to take care of me and protect me even more?"

Larry squeezed his daughter's hand. "That's what I did, that's what almost anyone would do. But the combination of depression and alcohol robbed her of self-confidence and reason. When she drank, every time your mother looked at you she saw Karen. Had you and Karen just been sisters, and not twins, I think she would have been able to deal with things better."

"That doesn't make sense to me."

Larry shifted his body around so he was sitting on the floor yoga-style directly in front of Rachel. He rubbed his hands up his face and through his hair. "You know that your mother was raised by her grandparents."

"I know that. Her parents were killed in a hotel fire."

"No, just her father was killed. Her mother got out without being hurt."

"What!" Rachel screeched incredulously.

"Vivian's mother became an alcoholic and abused her."

"Mom was an abused child?" Rachel replied in a disbelieving groan.

"It became so bad her mother was committed to a psychiatric hospital. Your mother was ten then, that's when she moved in with her grandparents."

Rachel folded her arms around her knees and rocked back and forth. Several times she started to speak, but no words would come out. Finally, she did speak. "Are you saying the reason my mother became an alcoholic and abused me is because that's what her mother did to her? Is that what you believe?"

"I'm not sure what I believe, but one psychiatrist said that when Karen was taken, Vivian responded the same way her mother did when her husband was killed."

"By taking it out on her daughter?"

"Yes."

"Why was I never told about this?"

"Your mother doesn't want you to know."

"She thinks I'll do the same thing, doesn't she? Since my grandmother and my mother did it to their daughters, she thinks I'll do it too." Rachel stopped to take several deep breaths and then continued, her voice choked with emotion. "If I ever get to be a mother, I hope I have a daughter. I'll take wonderful care of her. I would never hurt her, you can trust me."

"I know I can," Larry said as he moved even closer and held his daughter tenderly.

Each seeking comfort from the other, they stayed wrapped in each other's arms. After many minutes Larry slowly released his daughter. "It's very late. Let's go to bed."

"Please not yet. I know you don't like talking about the abduction, but there's one thing I've always wanted to know."

Larry wanted to respond with "what is it" but he couldn't get the words out.

"Why was there confusion at first over which one of us was taken?"

"Oh my goodness Rachel, how did you know that? I never thought you knew about that."

Rachel wiped the tears from her eyes with her sleeve. "When I was twelve, I went to the library and read all the old newspaper articles. One of 'em said you were confused about which daughter was taken and at first told the police your daughter Rachel had been abducted."

Larry couldn't stand the pain building up inside of him and started crying, choking out his words between gasps for air. "Rachel, I'm so sorry. I never thought you knew about that part of it. If that was bothering you why didn't you ask me before?"

Squeezing her father's hands she said, "I was afraid to ask, because I knew it would hurt you to talk about it. I don't have to know. I'm sorry, I shouldn't have asked about it."

"That's not why I'm crying. I just feel terrible this has been bothering you for so long and you've been afraid to ask me. I want to tell you."

Larry filled a glass from the kitchen faucet and drank it down. Then he and Rachel moved to the kitchen table, and sat across from one another, holding hands on top of the table.

"Daddy, tell me everything that happened."

Larry released his daughter's hands, rubbed his hands up his face and back over his hair, and then leaned back in his chair and closed his eyes. "It was the fourth of December, seventeen years ago today. It was warm for December, almost seventy degrees. I took you and Karen to Lake Elkhorn to feed the ducks. The two of you loved to throw Cheerios to the ducks. I pulled our van right up to the dock. You and Karen were in the side-by-side stroller in front of the van. I went to the back of the van to fix the two of you something to eat and get some juice. When I came back to the front of the van Karen wasn't in the stroller."

"How long were you behind the van?"

"Just a couple of minutes. I mixed two kinds of baby food together the way each of you liked it. Then I filled two baby bottles with apple juice from a large bottle."

"Why did you think it was me who'd been taken?"

"You had a Minnie Mouse doll and Karen had a Mickey Mouse doll. When I came to the front of the van you were holding Karen's Mickey Mouse doll. My mind went completely blank; I saw Mickey and assumed you were Karen. I went totally crazy, picked you up and started running around like a mad man. A woman saw me and came out of her townhouse, one of the ones near the dock. We went into her house and called the police. Then I called your mother and told her you'd been taken. She got there in just a few minutes, still wearing her nightgown. She came running at me screaming, 'Thank God you found my Rachel.' For the first time I realized it was Karen who had been taken."

"Mom knew it was me right away?" Rachel asked in a whisper.

"Yes, she could always tell the two of you apart, even from a distance. I don't know how and she could never explain it." He let go of Rachel's hand, looked up at the ceiling to collect his thoughts, and then continued. "I've always wondered how much damage that horrible roller coaster of emotions did to her. Being awakened with my call, hearing you had disappeared, driving five miles and then experiencing the relief of seeing you safe in my arms. And then being told I had made a mistake, that it was Karen who had been taken. She became completely hysterical, and it was almost an hour before she calmed down enough to understand what happened."

"No one at the lake saw anything or anyone out of the ordinary?"

Larry shook his head sullenly.

"What about the boy who saw a woman in a green sweat suit running away? I read about that in one of the newspaper articles."

"He saw a woman on the bike path on the other side of the lake. The police could never find her and concluded she was just a jogger."

Larry got up, filled his glass, and took another gulp of water. He looked up at the clock; it was past midnight, no longer the fourth of December. "Rachel, honey, I'm so tired and so are you. I think we should go to bed and get some sleep."

"Not yet Daddy, please. Was my nickname Minnie because of my Minnie Mouse doll?"

"Yes."

"Why don't I remember having a Minnie Mouse doll? What happened to it?"

Larry reluctantly answered, "Your mother threw it away on your second birthday. She said if Karen couldn't have her Mickey Mouse doll, then you weren't going to have Minnie. She was drunk and I felt like killin' her."

"Daddy, I'm so glad this day is over."

"Me too."

Chapter 4

The next morning Rachel awoke to the sound of wind and sleet against her bedroom window. The clock read 7:35a.m., but she always kept it set twenty minutes fast. She had done so to address a past problem of habitual lateness. She was never late to anything any more, having received a stern lecture from her father as to how lateness was a sign of inflated self-importance demonstrated through a lack of consideration for others. She didn't see it that way, but knew it was hopeless to argue the point with him. She reached for her compact stereo system, pushed the play button on the CD player and flopped back on the bed to the sounds of Boyz 2 Men singing, "In The Still Of The Night." Even her father, who despised rap singers, admitted he liked the Boyz 2 Men version of this song, but he would always add, "Of course it's not as good as the original by 'The Five Satins.'" – "What a lame name for a group," she thought.

Competing with the harmony of the Boyz, Rachel heard Gizmo and Gadget, the next-door neighbor's two tiny Yorkshire Terriers, barking furiously. She yanked back the curtain from her window and watched as her father walked his bicycle down the hill in their backyard with Gizmo and Gadget yapping at his feet. She couldn't help but chuckle as both dogs tucked their tails and ran when her father turned and snarled back at them. When he got to the bike path behind the trees, he hopped on his bike and peddled away. How he could enjoy going for a bike ride on a day like this she would never understand, but then there were many things about her father Rachel didn't understand.

Larry headed south on the bike path alongside a tiny tributary of the Little Patuxent making its way toward the Chesapeake Bay. The sting of small pellets of sleet against his face felt good as he peddled through a stand of enormous beech trees. Through the trees and out into the open he quickly covered the distance around Jackson Pond and continued south. Back into a heavily wooded area, he peddled hard until he reached the section of Columbia's Owen Brown Village that had once been Sewell's Orchard. The orchard had been suitable for a Norman Rockwell painting - a wonderful place to pick apples, peaches, and strawberries, and buy fresh produce from the old farm store. Now it was only a memory.

He stopped on the bike path and looked up the hill at the endless ribbons of three and four bedroom homes that wound their way through what had once been the orchard. For years he tried to visualize exactly where the farm store had been located before the dozens of houses had been built; but he just couldn't do it, everything was different, all the old land marks obliterated. Last summer he and Vivian had gone for a bike ride. Vivian rarely ever took her bike out of the garage anymore, but for some reason on that warm July evening she was "in the mood to go for a ride." They had stopped at this exact spot on the bike path, and Vivian pointed up the hill toward a gray two-story colonial and said, "That gray house up there, that's the spot where the farm store was located." He was sure she was wrong, but chose not to argue the point. Now, as he looked up the hill through the clouds of his breath and through the light but persistent sleet, he could visualize the farm store with its adjoining barn exactly where Vivian had described. What he couldn't see on that July evening he now saw clearly.

He jumped back on his bike and continued on for another mile, peddling furiously. He stopped, glanced at his watch, dismounted his bike and looked both ways on the path. Not surprisingly, no one else had ventured out on this cold, miserable Sunday morning. He quickly darted off the path and pushed his bike through a small stand of apple trees, one of a very few remnants of the original orchard. Peeking out of the apple trees he saw the backs of three houses that sat at the end of a cul-de-sac. His view of each house was partially obscured by large pine trees scattered throughout the backyards of the houses. He moved quickly towards the middle house, a large two-story colonial with light green aluminum siding. Now less than fifty feet from the back of the house the view of the two neighboring houses was completely blocked by the pine trees.

Although it had been daylight for a good while, the lights in the house were still on. The house was undistinguished in every way with the exception of a beautiful hand-carved wooden duck hanging in the kitchen window. He carefully studied the duck, thinking how appropriate for the duck to be flying southward on this cold day. He then turned his attention to the basement sliding glass door exiting onto a brick patio.

The steady beat of music blared from the basement. He leaned his bike against a pile of firewood at the edge of the patio, and quickly glanced in the directions of the two adjacent houses to assure himself he could not be seen. He quietly crept up to the sliding glass door and looked in.

Not more than ten feet in front of him was a woman methodically moving back and forth in unison with a television set full of aerobic dancers. Long black hair pulled tightly back into a ponytail bounced wildly atop a lean and unusually muscular body. She wore tight fitting black spandex shorts beneath an equally tight fitting red and white leotard. Strutting to the left, pumping her arms vigorously, and then repeating the same orchestrated sequence of motions to the right without a hitch didn't look easy. Suddenly, she shifted into a Charleston-like dance, moving back toward the sliding glass door and then forward toward the television. As the Charleston dance grew more energetic she backed closer and closer to the sliding glass door, so close he could see the beads of sweat on the back of her neck. He was mesmerized as the narrow thong of her leotard became more and more wedged in the crack between her shapely buttocks. He could feel the heat building inside of him as he moved closer and closer to the glass door. His deep breaths against the glass now clouded his view of the tantalizing creature. Again he stole a glance to either side, reconfirming that the pine trees totally obscured the view from the neighboring houses.

With his palms against the glass door he felt the vibrations of the base tones from the blaring aerobic dance music. He pressed himself against the glass feeling its coldness against his aroused body. As the woman swung her leg to the side in time with the music, her body twisted just enough to provide a fleeting glimpse of the contour of her bouncing breast beneath her outstretched arm. Larry Webster was feeling flushed and out of control. As he leaned harder against the glass door it unexpectedly slid to the side.

Surprised to find the door unlocked he flung it open and lunged into the basement. Startled and knocked off balance, the woman turned to face her intruder. She instinctively thrust both arms toward him and screamed, "You son-of-a........." only to be stopped by his right hand clamping down forcefully over her mouth.

With his left arm locked behind her back he pulled her forcefully against his body, keeping his right hand pressed firmly over her mouth. With their eyes only a few inches apart he hissed, "Don't make a sound".

He lifted her off the ground and carried her in his powerful grasp, knocking over a lamp as he forced her down onto the sofa. He pressed the full weight of his excited body against her rigidly tense body. As he began to slowly grind himself into her, he raised his head and again warned, "Don't make a sound."

He removed his hand from her mouth and buried his face into her neck, sucking and licking its entire length. Feeling the tenseness in her body, he lifted some of his weight off of her and undid the snaps of her leotard. Rising up over her he yanked the leotard up to her armpits exposing large, well-formed breasts. With his hands on either side of her waist he grabbed her shorts and jerked them down her legs and over her sneakers. He stared down, awe struck by her beauty, momentarily pausing to ponder his exciting options. She lay there as if petrified, looking up at him without expression.

Still fully clothed he lowered himself onto her motionless body. He began softly licking her neck and then started moving down. He lingered at her breasts and began slowly rubbing his hand between her legs. Moving further down he licked her stomach, letting his tongue go around and around her navel. Covering the last few inches he could sense her wetness and began to feel her ever so slight rhythmic thrusts. Reaching up with both hands he stroked her nipples in slow circular motions. He did everything slowly, very slowly.

As the intensity of her pelvic thrusts increased he paused momentarily, looked up, and mused, "Why I do believe you're enjoying this."

She responded only with a low whimper, grabbing the back of his head and forcing his face back down between her legs. Clamping her thighs against the sides of his head, she pushed harder and harder against him. She gasped for air as her thrusts became violent and uncoordinated. As the pressures building inside her body erupted she arched her back, clamped her thighs against his head even tighter, and let out a long guttural wail as her body convulsed over and over in orgasmic ecstasy.

As her body went limp, he scolded her, "I thought I told you not to make a sound."

"Screw you," she spat, covering her face with her hands.

"What an excellent idea. I was just thinking of that myself."

Quickly shedding his clothes, he chuckled as she kept her hands over her face, brought her thighs tightly together, and pulled her knees up against her chest. Placing his hands between her knees, he forced her legs apart, lowered himself onto her, and began to slowly thrust himself deep inside of her.

Removing her right hand from her face, she grabbed a handful of hair and jerked his head up. "You asshole, you scared the shit out of me."

"Sorry," he muttered, without interrupting the rhythm of his movements.

Having not released his hair she again lifted his head, only gently this time. "Please don't ever scare me like that again."

Again without losing a beat he replied, "I won't. I'm sorry."

This time he didn't put his face into her neck, but instead kissed her lovingly on the lips. She wrapped her arms and legs tightly around him as they continued to kiss passionately. Enjoying the warmth and electricity of this woman's body he felt himself falling into an almost dream-like state, only to be interrupted as she again grabbed a handful of hair and yanked his head.

"You know, I'm getting a little tired of you pullin' my hair," he said before she could say anything.

"I just thought I should tell you something."

"Tell me later."

"I think I should tell you now."

"Whatever," he grunted in time with an especially energetic thrust.

"My husband's going to be home this morning."

This seemed to get Larry's attention as he stopped and propped himself up on his elbows. "What! You said he had a west coast flight today and wouldn't be back until tomorrow. And what about the duck, the duck is flying south!"

"His plane had mechanical problems and the flight was delayed. He wasn't feeling well and didn't want to hang around the airport all day, so he swapped schedules with one of the other pilots. He's on his way home now from Dulles."

"But what about the duck?"

"I'm sorry. I was going to flip it to the north after I finished my aerobics tape. I mean, I really didn't expect you to show up at seven-thirty on a Sunday morning."

Still perched on his elbows Larry cautioned, " The duck's important, don't ever make that mistake again."

"I won't," she said, knowing a miscommunication on the duck's direction could produce very serious consequences.

"When is he going to be here?"

"Not for at least an hour, we've got plenty of time."

Their eyes just a few inches apart, he whispered, "When I was standing at the sliding glass door looking in at you, I felt it again."

"Felt what again?"

"Chills running through my bones like an electrical current. The way I felt it the very first time I ever saw you. No other...."

"Please Larry, don't start that," she pleaded.

Ignoring her he continued, "No other woman in the entire world could make me feel the way you do."

She rolled her head to the side, choosing not to look at him. He gently licked her ear as he said, "I don't know how or why, but I know you're the one. The one woman, the only woman in the world capable of possessing my soul." With his hand he gently turned her head so she was once again looking into his eyes. As he slowly moved in and out of her he said, "You know you possess my soul, don't you?"

She gazed into his eyes, but didn't say anything. As he slowly moved his mouth toward her lips, she placed her hand on the back of his head and redirected his lips to her neck. As Larry Webster hungrily buried himself into Barbara Reilly, she stared blankly at the ceiling with moist, sad eyes.

Chapter 5

Larry yanked up the garage door he left unlocked earlier that morning. As he pushed his bike inside he thought about hanging it from the ceiling hooks to make more room for his car, but didn't feel like going to the effort. Instead he leaned the bike against the lawn mower, figuring that would leave just enough room for his car should he want to park it in the garage. Vivian kept her car in the garage every day, year round, but Larry did so only during the winter and then, only on nights he expected a heavy frost. Scraping frost off a windshield on a cold morning was high on his list of pet peeves.

Shivering uncontrollably, he stepped into the laundry room from the garage as the ten o'clock chiming of the grandfather clock echoed through the house. The early morning sleet had changed to a pouring rain during the ride back from Barbara Reilly's house. He peeled off his soaked clothes and laid them in a pile next to the washing machine. Dressed only in a jock strap, he anxiously tiptoed through the family room to head upstairs for a hot shower. Hearing voices coming from the kitchen, he peered around the corner and was surprised to see Vivian and Rachel sitting at the kitchen table having coffee and talking quietly.

Catching a glimpse of her father, Rachel offered cheerfully, "Dressed for success, huh Dad."

The best Larry could do was to muster up an embarrassed grin, and cover his jock strap with a pair of hands.

"What could possibly possess you to go for a bike ride on a day like this?" asked Vivian.

"Biking in conditions like this builds character," Larry replied, but immediately wished he hadn't, his guilt was already sufficiently acute.

After a clumsy about face, he darted up stairs and showered. Twenty minutes later Vivian and Rachel were still sitting at the kitchen table. Unnerved by their seemingly civil discussion, after being at one another's throat the night before, he started down the stairs to the basement as Vivian called out to him, "Larry, please come in here and join us".

Larry poured himself a glass of orange juice and sat down at the kitchen table, trying to act natural and appear relaxed in spite of the fire inside his gut, a fire stoked by two separate fuels. First, it felt as if his morning activities were written all over his face. It always seemed that way after being with Barbara Reilly, as if somehow the pressing of her flesh against his had left an implicating imprint. Second, it was upsetting to see Vivian and Rachel behaving as if they had a normal mother-daughter relationship. Every time he got his hopes up that they were making progress towards normalcy, towards ending their mutually vindictive and destructive behavior, those hopes were destroyed. And after what had happened last night, how could one ever think them capable of sustained civil behavior toward one another.

After seconds of strained silence Vivian cleared her throat and spoke up. "Rachel and I have reached an important agreement. It's a simple agreement, but it's going to let us get on with the rest of our lives."

Instinctively not believing them, not trusting them, Larry replied sarcastically, "Yeah, so what's the agreement? And how long does it stay in effect? Until this evening? Tomorrow? Next week? "

"We're dead serious Dad. The agreement stays in effect forever," Rachel said.

"Okay, tell me about it," Larry said with a forced modicum of calmness in his voice.

Vivian spoke slowly and carefully as if she were reciting a prepared speech and wanted to get every word just right. "I know we've dashed your hopes in the past, but this time we really mean it. Neither of us ever wants to go through another night like last night. We're so tired of hurting one another. We're never going to let something like that happen again. That's the first and most important part of the agreement, neither one of us is ever going to intentionally do anything or say anything to hurt the other."

"We've intentionally hurt each other in the past, and we did it again last night, " Rachel said.

"And now the hard part," Vivian said, her voice cracking and uneven.

"It gets harder?"

"Yes, it gets harder because both of us must accept some of the responsibility for the problems between us. I'll go first." Vivian paused to take a deep breath. "I admit that because of my addiction to alcohol I'm guilty of neglecting Rachel when she was a little girl." Fighting to keep from crying she kept going. "I don't deserve her forgiveness and I have no right to ever expect Rachel to love me."

"Now it's my turn. I admit that Mom stopped hurting me three years ago. She's been so good to me for a long time, but I've refused to acknowledge it. Last night was my fault; I pushed and pushed until she had no choice. I'll never do that again." Rachel took a long sip of coffee to organize her thoughts. "I've been using my neglect as a child as an excuse for not facing up to my responsibilities. This is an important point in my life and I'm gonna stop screwing up. I've been improvin' in school, but I can do even better." Rachel looked directly into her mother's eyes. "Now Mom, you've got to say it."

Vivian covered her face with her hands.

"Please Mom, you've got to say it. Unless you say it we can't go forward from this point, our agreement doesn't mean anything unless you say it."

Vivian hesitantly uncovered her face and grabbed the edge of the table with such force one would think she had hold of a narrow ledge above a great precipice. Squeezing the table tighter and tighter, she said, "I accept the fact that my other daughter, Karen, is ...... I'm sorry, just give me a second." Vivian released her grip on the table and closed her eyes. Then she said it. "I accept the fact that Karen is dead."

Larry's body wobbled as he reached for the table to steady himself. "What?"

With her face flooded with tears, but in a strong and forceful voice, Vivian answered, "I said, I accept the fact that Karen has been dead for a long time."

Larry rolled his eyes back in disbelief. "After all these years, why would you finally admit it?"

Vivian folded her hands on the table in front of her. She took an inordinate amount of care in doing so as if she were posing for a portrait and wanted to appear as relaxed as possible, even though she wasn't at all relaxed. "I've known it all along, at least I've known it for the last three years since I've been sober enough to think straight, but I could never let myself say it. It was as if by saying it I was deserting her."

"But what made you say it now?"

"Until this morning I never realized how important it was to Rachel. And I never realized it was keeping a wall between us." Vivian's eyes finally overflowed and her tears splattered on the table.

Larry swept his arm across the table and sopped up Vivian's tears with his shirtsleeve. "But what about your drinking? You hadn't touched a drop for over three years and then you got drunk last night."

"It'll never happen again. I didn't drink last night because I wanted to. I had to choke it down. I did it to hurt Rachel, because she hurt me. I'll never take another drink again, not for Rachel, but for me. But oh, how I hate the thought of ......"

Rachel reached across the table and took hold of her mother's hand. "What is it Mom? What do you hate the thought of?"

Vivian dropped her head as tears splashed onto the table once again. "My next AA meeting. Those people have stood by me, and now I've let them down."

"Just don't tell them Mom. You're never going to do it again."

A hesitant smile formed on Vivian's face. "Being honest with one another is what holds us together. I have to tell them."

"Would you like me to go with you?"

Vivian put her free hand on top of Rachel's. "I'd like that very much."

Larry looked at Rachel. "I don't understand. How did this happen? The two of you spent years together in therapy and nothing really changed. What happened this morning?"

"I couldn't sleep last night after we talked about Karen's abduction. I kept seeing this image of Mom running toward you with me in your arms. She thought everything was okay, but then she found out that it wasn't. I always knew it was terrible for Mom, but I don't think I ever truly realized how terrible it was until last night. And,......"

"And what?"

Rachel's reply came in between breathless gasps. "I never knew Mom was abused when she was a little girl.

She told me about it this morning. What happened to her was much worse than what happened to me. I never knew, I never knew."

"Are you saying you forgive your mother?"

"I'm not exactly sure what I'm saying. I just understand things more clearly. Mom treated me badly when she drank, but I now realize it wasn't because she didn't love me."

"You can't imagine what a shock it is for me to hear you and your mother say these things. After all these years, for the two of you to..... I just can't believe this is happening."

"When Mom came downstairs this morning I asked her about Karen's abduction. I hadn't brought up the subject with her for years, because she'd never talk about it with me, but today she did."

Vivian leaned back in her chair and wiped the tears from her eyes. "I was so upset about last night, but when she asked me about the Minnie and Mickey dolls all I wanted to do was to hold her as tight as I could. All those therapy sessions, all those doctors, they couldn't get it out of me. But when she asked about those dolls it was like the dam broke, everything started pouring out of me. I heard myself saying things I never thought would come out of my mouth."

"Daddy, while you were out riding your bike in the sleet and rain, Mom and I connected, we really connected for the first time. We're never going to hurt one another ever again."

Larry linked hands with his daughter and his wife. "What can I do to help make this work?"

Vivian said, "It's up to us. You don't have to do anything, you've already done enough."

Chapter 6

Larry Webster sat at his desk at the National Science Foundation's office in northern Virginia strumming his fingers against the side of his head. The Gateway computer emitted a steady low frequency hum as he studied the budget data on the screen and jotted down key numbers in his day-timer notebook. Satisfied he had the needed information he sprang to his feet, jabbed the computer off-button, tossed his notebook and three magazines - Sky and Telescope, Physics Today, and Outside - into his briefcase.

He slung his coat over his shoulder and walked briskly through the bullpen of modular cubicles that housed his staff of scientists, budget analysts and clerical support personnel. Just as he turned a corner, he jumped to the side to miss a young man with long curly red hair barging down the hallway.

"Whoa Dr. Lynch. Trying to break the office speed record?"

"Oh, you know me Dr. Webster. Hardworking, dedicated, never a moment to waste," replied the young man.

Larry brought his hand to his face and rubbed his chin with mock thoughtfulness. "And don't you look especially nice today. Double-breasted pinstriped suit." Then he paused and changed the tone of his voice for effect. "Lynch, look around you. How many other people do you see wearing double-breasted suits? That's right, you don't see any. This is a government facility. You're a civil servant, not a cast member of L.A. Law. If you want to move to the top of this organization you should dress like me."

The young man tilted his head at an angle as if in deep thought. "Well Dr. Webster, you present me with a very difficult decision. Let me see, I can either get myself a nice baggy, wrinkled, lime-green, corduroy suit from Sears like yours and watch my career skyrocket. Or I can dress like this, meet some hot babe in Georgetown this evening, and spend the night at her place getting laid four or five times."

Jerry Lynch looked skyward as if calling on guidance from above. "This is really a tough decision. My career is important to me. Maybe I should go to Sears right now." Then after a few more seconds of deep concentration he purred, "Naaaah, I think I'll stay with getting laid. But thanks for the career counseling."

"Four or five times?" Larry questioned.

"Well, I'm a dedicated employee and I want to come to work tomorrow well rested, so, yeah, I'll limit it to only four or five."

Knowing he had lost this round of verbal jousting Larry mumbled, "I see," and walked away.

"Hey Larry," Jerry yelled out.

Larry looked back over his shoulder and replied, "What is it now?"

"When do I get a racquetball rematch? "

"Thursday at six is good for me."

"Okay, Thursday it is," Jerry Lynch replied.

Larry began to walk away then turned back to face his youthful adversary. "Oh Jerry, after the third or fourth time you've laid this babe tonight, tell her how your boss, who happens to be seventeen years older than you, routinely kicks your ass in racquetball." When there was no retort, Larry mentally declared victory and jubilantly marched away, stopping at the desk of his secretary.

"Kathy, I'm going out to the University of Maryland to meet with Dr. Bramwell. He's going to show me some new images of Andromeda from his Kitt Peak observations. Thinks he can talk me out of cutting the budget for his grant."

"Have a good evening Dr. Webster."

"Thanks, you too."

Within a few minutes Larry was in his Taurus heading through the heart of Washington D.C. and then north on New Hampshire Avenue to the Maryland suburbs. It was 1:30 in the afternoon when he turned onto the University of Maryland campus from the south entrance on Route 1. He drove another half mile, coming to a stop several times to avoid legions of jaywalking students, and then parked in a visitor's space behind the Glen L. Martin Building, a mammoth brick building housing the University's math department. The building had a large open marbled lobby with a massive pendulum suspended from the center of its dome ceiling. Hordes of chattering students scrambled in all directions through the lobby, like a frenzy of ants swarming randomly about picnic litter. Larry dodged and jostled his way to the stairway, climbed to the third floor and entered the math library.

The stillness and quiet of the library, almost empty except for a few students with their faces buried in textbooks, was in sharp contrast to the chaos two floors below. The smell was a bit musty, but not offensively so. Heads lifted as the leather heels of Larry's penny loafers slapped against the oak flooring as he passed a series of small study cubicles and opened the door of the fifth cubicle. Barbara Reilly, sitting at a small wooden table covered with computer printouts, looked up in surprise.

"Hi," she said as she gathered the printouts into a neat stack, her movements touching off a blizzard of dust particles in the shaft of sunlight blazing through the small window of the cubicle. Her black hair was combed straight back and fell softly on her shoulders. Alternating between contacts and glasses as the mood struck her, she was wearing a pair of thin-framed "granny glasses" that made her already large dark-brown eyes look even larger. Her black eyebrows were so thick and so beautiful they didn't look real. Other than a slight hint of lip-gloss, she wore no make up. A gray knit sweater with an oversized turtleneck collar fit her chest snugly. A pair of faded jeans and Nike running shoes made her indistinguishable from the co-eds twenty years younger.

"So what are you up to?" Larry asked as he flopped down into an unusually small wooden chair that seemed more appropriate for an elementary school than a college.

"Trying to balance the University's budget for next year. Looks like we're gonna have to cut employee benefits. I'm looking at different options. You know, health coverage, sick leave, retirement, everything."

"Why don't you just raise student tuition instead?"

Barbara blushed as she changed the subject. "That was quite a surprise you sprung on me Sunday morning."

"Liked it, huh," Larry replied with a devilish grin.

"Not really.... Well maybe a little bit, but don't ever do it again. Now, what did you ask me?"

"I said why don't you just raise tuition. Tuition here is still way below most state universities."

Barbara rocked her chair onto its back legs, and leaned it against the wall behind her. "You're preaching to the choir. Of course I'd rather raise tuition, so would the Chancellor, but the politicians in Annapolis won't let us. They're protecting their asses, can't piss off the voters in an election year."

"Yeah, I know how that works."

A smile spread across Barbara's face as she leaned forward - the front legs of her chair smacking the floor with a thud – then stretched across the table, and kissed Larry with a soft, open mouth.

"Why'd you do that?"

"Cause I wanted too. Is that all right?"

"Any time at all, all you gotta do is call, and I'll be there..." he sang Beatle lyrics in reply.

"So what brings you out here today? "

"Why, that kiss. I drove all the way out here for that kiss."

"Bullshit, it would take a bit more than a kiss to get you out here."

"Well, I do have a meeting with a professor from the Physics Department."

"What about?"

"Same thing you're doing. I have to cut his research grant by fifteen percent. Small world, huh?"

Showing no further interest, Barbara crunched her shoulders together, instantly looking more like the forty year old she was. "What happened on Saturday, we didn't have a chance to talk on Sunday?"

"Sunday, liked it, huh?"

"It was stupid. No more surprise visits, understand? Now tell me what happened."

With mock frivolity Larry chirped, "You know the Webster household. We're in final negotiations with CBS on a new sit-com, The Websters: America's Dysfunctional Family."

In a whisper, but with gritted teeth Barbara demanded, "Dammit Larry, what the hell happened? Are Vivian and Rachel okay?"

"I really don't know what okay means in my family."

"Just tell me what happened," Barbara pleaded.

"Well, the whole weekend seems like a blur," Larry said as he ran his hands up his face and over his head.

Barbara sat perfectly still as he began to recount the highlights and lowlights of the Webster's attempt to deal with the anniversary of the abduction.

"Rachel threw a tantrum and started a fight with me to start the day off."

"Over what?"

"Over nothing. It was going to be a bad day for her, and she was going to make it a bad day for everyone else."

Barbara quickly brought her right index finger to her lips and in an exaggerated whisper cautioned, "Shush. I know this is hard for you, but these walls are like paper."

"Okay, I'm sorry," Larry whispered back. "When I came back from running, Rachel was making pancakes and I kidded her about burning them. She just went crazy, throwing things, using foul language. It only lasted a minute or so then she ran up stairs and locked herself in her room."

"What did Vivian do?"

"Thankfully, she was asleep. I didn't tell her about Rachel's tantrum, I didn't want to upset her. When she got up, we went out for brunch and did some Christmas shopping."

"What about Rachel?"

"I checked on her before we left. She had calmed down, told me she was sorry."

"So you spent the day with Vivian?"

"Yes, we had a pleasant day, a wonderful day by Webster standards. We had lunch at Clyde's and spent the afternoon at the mall."

Barbara lowered her eyes and fumbled with the computer printouts on the table, as she stammered, "Did you and Vivian talk about ...., you know, that it was the anniversary of the abduction?"

"No, not directly. But we were very open with one another. Neither of us tried to act like we didn't know what day it was. But we mostly talked about Rachel." Larry paused for a moment as he heard several students shuffle down the hallway outside their cubicle. "We got home around seven. Rachel's boy friend, Vinnie, was there with her. They had supposedly spent the day studying."

"Vinnie? Isn't he the one that Rachel really likes?"

"Yeah, he's the one. He's a little weird, but really bright. Takes all advanced courses and pulls straight A's, runs on the cross-country team. Rachel says he wants to go to Duke and major in biomedical engineering."

"Sounds like the ideal boyfriend, too good to be true."

Larry straightened his back and raised his eyebrows, causing wrinkles to crease his forehead. "He's too good to be true all right. It's the screwing my daughter part I have a little problem with. "

"Are you sure?"

"Vivian and I don't have any proof, but we're pretty sure – which brings me back to Saturday night. We get home. Rachel and Vinnie are having a great time fooling around. The four of us are in the kitchen and out of the blue Rachel runs over to Vinnie, throws her arms around him, and gives him one of the most passionate kisses I've ever seen, then says 'I love you' to him. Me, Vivian, and even Vinnie are blown away."

"So what happened then?"

"I'm honestly not sure. I think Vivian accused Rachel of having sex with Vinnie. It was the wrong thing to say at the wrong time. She has a real knack for that."

"Did they get into a fight?"

"Vivian didn't want to fight, but Rachel said every cruel thing she could think of."

"Did you stop them?"

"I got them separated, then Rachel and I went for a walk.... But while we were away, Vivian was in the kitchen downing half a bottle of scotch."

"Oh no, I can't believe it," Barbara moaned.

Larry continued, speaking in the present tense as if reliving Saturday night all over again. "Vivian starts throwing things and Rachel and I run into the kitchen to see what the hell's going on. Vivian looks Rachel directly in the eyes and says she wishes the bastards who took Karen had taken her instead. I completely lose it, grab Vivian and start pounding her against the cabinet." With his face covered with beads of sweat, he stared straight at Barbara, but looked through her, not at her. When he refocused on Barbara's face he saw tears welling up in her eyes. "I'm sorry I upset you, but you asked what happened. That's what happened. I no longer feel responsible for either of them. I've tortured myself for too long. I have nothing left to give, I've got to get away from both of them."

"What do you mean?"

"I'm going away for a while. The Europeans are building four large telescopes in Chile. They've offered me a Visiting Scientist position on the team overseeing the construction and I'm going to take it. I'll spend a year in Chile, after that I'll be guaranteed observing time twice a year for as long as I want."

Barbara glowered at him with obvious disapproval.

"What?" asked a befuddled Larry.

"How can you leave now? What about Rachel, are you going to let her go away to college without being here?"

Larry glanced at his watch. "Barbara, I need to get going. I'm already fifteen minutes late for my meeting with Dr. Bramwell."

"Fuck Dr. Cromwell, you're not leaving this room."

"It's Bramwell, not Cromwell."

"Fuck him too."

Larry performed his thought organizing habit of rubbing his hands over his face and back over his hair. Fully understanding the seriousness of the discussion and the extent of Barbara's emotional investment in the topic at hand he relented, "Okay, I'll be back in five minutes. I'll call him and reschedule the meeting."

He left, made his call, and was back in fifteen minutes instead of the five he had promised. When he opened the door Barbara was sitting in the same position, looking as if she hadn't moved a muscle during his absence. With not one dust particle floating in the shaft of sunlight, he suspected she really hadn't moved.

"I'm sorry it took longer than I expected. He's very concerned, I had to answer some pointed questions."

"Fuck Dr. Bramwell."

"Barbara, I know I've dropped a bombshell on you, but please just try to listen to me."

"I'm listening," she snapped.

"When I got home Sunday morning after being with you, Vivian and Rachel said they had reached an agreement. I can't remember their exact words, but they basically said they were going to stop hurting one another."

Unable to look Barbara in the face, he stared sullenly down at the table and mumbled, "Then Vivian said she accepted the fact that Karen was dead."

Barbara instinctively jerked her head back as if she had taken a George Foreman uppercut. "Oh my God!"

"I asked how I could help them work things out, and they told me there was nothing I could do, it was up to them. Maybe my going away will actually be good for them. But it doesn't make any difference whether it helps or hurts; I've got to go. I can't stand it anymore."

Locking her hands together to keep them from shaking Barbara asked in a desperate whisper, "What about us?"

"Is there still an us?"

Barbara choked out her reply. "My God, we've been together forever. How can you ask, is there still an us?"

"I'm sorry. I thought things were getting better between you and your husband. You said he was trying to make your marriage work. And I hardly get to see you anymore; you volunteer at the shelter almost every evening. I just thought you felt things were different between us."

Barbara grabbed fist-fulls of hair on both sides of her head, as if she were considering pulling it out. "Different between us, I can't believe you said that. All these years you've told me I was the one woman meant for you, the one you wanted more than any other, it was only our circumstances that kept us apart. And now you're going away and leaving me."

"I'm sorry, I never meant it that way. I just thought my being away wouldn't be that important to you."

"How in the hell could you possibly think that?" Barbara whimpered as she let go of her hair.

With an anguished expression, Larry rolled his head back and looked up at the ceiling. "You always hold everything inside. I never know where you stand on anything. I guess I just thought this whole thing had just become......."

"Had just become what?" she replied with forcefulness returning to her voice.

"That it had just become a sexual thing to you."

"What!" she screeched, as she jumped out of her chair, banging her knee on the bottom of the table.
Towering above him, she rubbed her knee with one hand and clutched the table with the other.

"Barbara, sit down."

She just glared down at him.

"Please sit down."

"Damn you," she moaned as she slumped back into her chair.

"When we got back together two years ago you said you were sexually frustrated. You told me your husband didn't satisfy you."

Barbara turned her head in the direction of the window, catching a glimpse of the twitching tail of a squirrel in the overgrown pine tree just outside. She closed her eyes for a moment to think, then turned to face Larry. "I love you, I've loved you for so long I can't remember not loving you. I've never really loved John. I married him because I was lonely, not because I loved him."

Larry let out an exasperated sigh and shook his head back and forth. "I love you more than I ever thought it possible to love anyone, and I tell you all the time. But you never say it to me. That's why I asked you if there is still an us, because you never tell me that you love me," his voice faded as he fought to get the words out.

Barbara reached across the table and took hold of Larry's hand.

"I never say it, because it hurts too much for me to admit it," Barbara confessed.

After more than a minute of silence Larry said, "Two times you asked me to leave Vivian, in '81 and in '90 before you got married. You didn't ask me, you begged me. Both times I wanted to. I wanted to more than anything in the world, but I didn't because of my guilt. Those were the two biggest mistakes of my life. You gave me two chances and I blew it both times. Are you saying I have a third chance?"

"I didn't think you would ever want a third chance."

"Come to Chile with me."

"Just like that?"

"Yes, just like that."

"How would it work, we're both married?"

"I don't know, but we'll figure it out."

"When would all this happen?"

"I have until the first of February to accept the position. The assignment starts in March or even earlier if I want. I'm going down a couple of weeks before that to make my living arrangements." He paused and held his breath to emphasize what he was about to say. "Please come with me. We can be together forever."

A look of panic spread across Barbara's face as she began to rattle off her concerns in rapid-fire succession. "My God Larry, that's barely two months away. What would I tell John? I know our marriage is on the rocks, but how could things get resolved that quickly? And my job, I just can't up and quit on them, they've treated me so good. Then there's my work at the women's shelter. I don't see how I could deal with so many things in just two months."

"Slow down, okay. Now look, as for your husband, just bite the bullet and tell him you're leaving him. It's not like he hasn't been through this before."

She glared at him. "Is that what you're going to do to Vivian, just tell her you're leaving her."

"My situation is different and you know it."

The softening of her expression indicated she wasn't going to argue the point.

"And as for your job, ask them for a one-year sabbatical. They grant those for faculty members all the time, don't they? With what you've done for this place, don't you think you deserve some time off as much as some bullshit philosophy professor?"

"Yeah, I guess so. But what about my work at the women's shelter?"

"For God's sake, do something for yourself for once. The shelter can survive without you."

"The work I do for the shelter is more for me than it is for them."

Larry continued to press the attack. "Think about it, we're going to be in Chile. It's not a wealthy country. There will be endless opportunities for a professional do-gooder like you to work herself to a frazzle. Come on, don't over analyze this, just go with your gut......I mean your heart."

"I need some time to think about it."

Larry relaxed and smiled. "I was just thinking. I've got the rest of the afternoon off. We could.... you know.... go some place and get comfortable."

"Sorry, I can't. John is picking me up in about an hour."

"As in the case of Dr. Bramwell, fuck 'em," Larry smirked.

"I think that's exactly what he has in mind."

"I'll see you next Tuesday," Larry said as he got up to leave.

Chapter 7

It was December 11, and Larry Webster was on his regular Saturday run through Patapsco State Park. It was a cold damp morning with the sun fighting its way through heavy clouds, trying to show itself for the first time after several days of torrential rains. He was on the very last section of River Ridge Trail, the steep section heading down to the river. Running at a much faster pace than normal despite the muddy conditions, he pushed himself to keep time with Bruce Springsteen's "Born In The USA" tape playing on his Walkman. Emerging from the woods at the bottom of the trail, he wobbled up the embankment to the railroad tracks and stopped to catch his breath. Burning lungs and a pain in the lower right portion of his abdomen caused him to bend over and grab his knees.

He couldn't remember the last time he had to stop to catch his breath during the middle of a run. It must be due to the fatigue of the past few weeks, sleepless nights brought on by a general state of anxiety. First, there was the dread leading up to the anniversary of the abduction, followed by the gut wrenching events of that day, and then the inner turmoil of his decision to go to Chile, a decision he had shared with no one other than Barbara Reilly. Could he really go? When would he tell Vivian and Rachel? How would he tell them?

And what about Barbara? He hadn't even considered the possibility of her going with him until the words "come with me" jumped from his lips without warning, without thought. Did he really want her to come with him? What he told her was true, he regretted not leaving Vivian when she had pressured him to do so in 1981 and then again in 1990, but things were much different then. If he hadn't done it back then, how could he do it now? Back then, Vivian was barely functional, a full-fledged alcoholic, and was hell to live with. Rachel was younger and would have benefited greatly from the love and nurturing she would have received from Barbara compared to Vivian's abuse. But now Vivian had conquered her problem with alcohol, Rachel was no longer a little girl, and most importantly mother and daughter had just agreed to peacefully co-exist. Had he left Vivian before, he could have taken Rachel with him, no judge would have ruled in favor of an abusive, alcoholic mother. But if he left Vivian now, he would also be leaving Rachel. And, oh yes, there was one other complication now - Barbara was married.

After a few deep breaths the pain in his abdomen lessened and he started jogging along the tracks. The Patapsco River, normally a gentle stream, surged past him, a deep chocolate brown, swollen out of its banks, and clogged with logs and debris. The roar of the river's rapids overpowered Springsteen's remorseful rendering of "My Hometown" as he approached the entrance to the tunnel, especially ominous looking on this day.

It seemed as if he were running down a steep hill, as if he were falling into the tunnel, even though he knew the ground to be perfectly level. Somehow the tunnel exerted a force, not explained by the normal laws of physics, that Larry Webster was incapable of resisting. The light faded to grayness and then to blackness, and the sound of the rapids gradually went away as he was pulled deeper and deeper into the tunnel. And then the sound of the rapids was completely gone leaving only Springsteen's music, the crackle of gravel beneath his feet, and the whistling of air rushing in and out of his lungs with every heavy breath.

But from somewhere deep in the emptiness of the tunnel the sound of the rapids started to return. But how could that be? In the darkness he fumbled to turn down the volume of the Walkman, as the rapids grew louder and louder in explosive bursts that engulfed the tunnel. He yanked the headphones from his ears, letting them girdle his neck and fall to his shoulders.

Oh my God, it wasn't the sound of the rapids at all, but that of a train barreling towards him! Its angry roar consumed the tunnel, the blackness and the sound were everywhere, the entire universe was nothing but blackness and sound! Unable to separate the sound from the blackness, he froze. He knew he was screaming, but he couldn't hear his screams. And then with the stabbing realization that this was really happening, he tried to remember how to run. What he always did without effort, without even thinking, now seemed impossible. The gravel floor of the tunnel, normally firm and level, was slippery and rutted; each awkward stride jarred his insides. He yanked at the cassette headphones, which bounced annoyingly around his neck, and hurled them against the tunnel wall. The sound of the train grew even more consuming as he tripped and fell forward in the darkness, instinctively thrusting his arms outward to break his fall. Even the angry roar of the train couldn't mute the horrible snapping sound as the full weight of his body slammed onto his left arm.

Normal sensory functions were completely askew, he felt no pain, just the blackness and the train's thunderous roar. He didn't see blackness, he didn't hear the roar, he felt them. Crawling wildly to get to the side of the tunnel, he hit something hard and cold on his right side, then something hard and cold on his left side. It was the rails! He was in the middle of the tracks! All of a sudden, instantaneously, he was blinded by white! Not gradually, but all at once the blackness was replaced by a burning white as the headlights of the on rushing steel monster rounded a bend in the tunnel, not more than a hundred feet away! Fifty feet, twenty feet, ten feet....... Screaming, he lunged to the side and rolled over and over, his face and damaged arm pounded hard into the gravel with each revolution, and then he felt the wonderful pain of smashing against the tunnel wall, free from the path of the rushing monster. He lay perfectly still as the monster raced past, the sound of its raging fury setting off cannon blast after cannon blast just a few feet away. He tried to cover his ears, but with a useless arm one ear was all he could protect. After an eternity of sound, a sound that dwarfed all others he had ever heard in his life, the sound mercifully began to change. It changed from a high frequency thunderous roar to a low frequency rumble. Without any sensation of time, was it minutes or was it hours, the rumble became lower and lower and then it was gone. Now there was nothing but blackness once again, and the awful cold of the ground and of the tunnel wall.

The blackness and the cold carried Larry Webster away. Taken from the tunnel, he could feel himself falling down, down, down, into the deepest, darkest crevices of his memories. And when he stopped falling, he was in a different place, a different time.

Her mouth was soft and warm. He cradled the sides of her face with his hands as their kisses went on and on, feeling the wonderful kneading of her hands on his bare bottom pulling him into her. Forcing himself to slow down again and again he accepted her pleas to, "Make it last, not yet, not yet, please make it last." But then with an urgency neither could restrain, their sexual energies boiled over as they erupted into one another. They lay still as she held him and pulled him tight against her. He lifted his head up, looked dreamily into her eyes, and gushed, "You've been a part of my life for less than a year, but I can't imagine living without you. I'm never going to let go of you. Never, ever." Again, they kissed deeply as she gently ran her hands along his naked back.

Startled, he sprang up, lifting his torso above her.

"What is it? What is it?" she asked nervously.

"I don't know, I thought I heard something. Here put on your clothes," he urged as he handed her a green sweatshirt.

He reached down and hastily pulled up his jockey shorts and Levi jeans that had been left partially draped around the bottom of his left leg during this rather unexpected lustful tryst. Slipping on his penny loafers and quickly pulling a hooded sweatshirt over his head, he slowly cracked open the rear door of the van and stuck his head out. With relief in his voice he turned to the woman, who was now hurriedly tying the laces of her running shoes, "I don't see anything, I don't think anyone's there."

"Good," she replied gratefully.

Quietly stepping out, he crept to the front of the van and cheerfully asked, "Okay ladies, what are you two up to?"

"Where's Rachel?" he queried without excitement or emotion.

And then he froze, unable to move, unable to think. He stared in disbelief at the sight he now began to comprehend. In front of him was the twin's double stroller, with a beautiful little baby girl holding a Mickey Mouse doll sitting in one seat, but the other seat was empty and a Minnie Mouse doll lay on the ground beside it.

"Oh my God, oh my God!" he wailed as he ran around the van searching in every direction.

"What's wrong?" the young woman said as she jumped in front of him to stop his maddening laps around the van.

"Rachel's not here! She's not here! Someone has taken her!"

Again he began racing around the van, then rushed off on the road heading away from the lake, only to immediately turn around and sprint back to the van. "Run over to those townhouses and call the police!"

"Larry, I can't be here when the police arrive. Your wife will find out about us!"

"I don't give a shit about...... No, no, you're right. Wait a minute, let me think, let me think," he gasped breathlessly. "Okay, okay, you run around the bike path...... and look for Rachel....please look for her."

"Larry, this is terrible. I love you. Please call me as soon as you get a chance." With that, Larry's twenty-three year old lover, Barbara Serelis, who would one day marry a man named Reilly, turned and ran away.

Larry yanked the baby girl out of the stroller and started sprinting toward the townhouses, the weight of the baby causing his left arm to ache with each jolting stride. He ran with all his might. But he was running in quicksand. Sinking deeper and deeper. Instead of getting closer, the townhouses drifted further and further away and began to fade in blackness. The pain in his left arm became unbearable, and the blackness of the tunnel became unbearable, and he felt the cold of the tunnel wall cutting through him like a knife.

Worst of all, he felt the horrible shame he had carried deep within his soul for seventeen years.

Chapter 8

Park Ranger Roger Gamble cranked the car window down as Ranger Debbie Marin raced up the hill holding her hand on top of her head to keep her brand new park service hat from falling off. "This man's hurt. I'm taking him to Howard County General. Call the hospital and his wife. He's too shook up to remember his phone number so you'll have to get it from the operator. Says his name is Larry Webster and he lives in Columbia."

"Larry who?" Ranger Marin yelled out as she fell to the ground from skidding on a patch of mud.

"Webster. Larry Webster. Got it?

"Got it," shouted Ranger Marin as she wiped her muddy hands on her pants.

Larry shivered uncontrollably in the back seat of Ranger Gamble's car as it sped west on Route 40, then south on Route 29. Ranger Gamble had used a flannel shirt to fashion a temporary sling for his left arm, then eased him into the car and covered him with two wool blankets. Still, he was cold, colder than he'd ever been.

He had been sprawled out in the tunnel for almost an hour drifting in and out of consciousness, shaking from fear and cold. Were it not for a few precious drops of water seeping through a mortar joint in the ceiling of the tunnel splashing on his face and bringing him to his senses, he would have frozen to death. When his thoughts became sufficiently coherent to realize his predicament, he struggled to his feet and stumbled out of the tunnel. Once outside the daylight provided a shot of rejuvenating energy allowing him to make the steep, rocky, one-mile ascent to the ranger's station. Normally jogging and climbing that mile in about fifteen minutes, it took him almost two hours, as he held his left arm against his body and struggled with every step up the slippery trail. Running shorts, tee shirt, turtleneck, and knit hat were fine for a normal run in thirty-degree weather, but proved totally inadequate for the events of this day.

With the insulating warmth of the blankets and the car's heater going full blast he began to recover from the early stages of hypothermia. Still he shivered viciously, jarring his arm despite every effort to hold it still. The ride to the hospital was like a visit to the proctologist, it only lasted twenty minutes but it seemed like an eternity.

"We're here," Ranger Gamble shouted over his shoulder as he pulled up to the entrance door of the emergency room.

Two orderlies, an emergency room doctor, and a nurse rushed through the door with a stretcher to meet the car. The doctor, a young Oriental man, cautioned, "Don't move him until I've determined the full extent of his injuries."

"He's got a broken arm," Gamble replied matter of factly.

"A broken arm? That's all?"

"Well, he's got a bump on his forehead and he's kinda cold."

The doctor leaned into the car and asked, "How ya feeling mister?"

"I'm cold and my arm hurts like hell."

The doctor raised Larry's eyelid, looked in his eye with a small flashlight, repeated the procedure on the other eye, then turned to the nurse and snapped, "Come get me when the X-rays are ready."

Ranger Gamble looked at the nurse quizzically. "What's his problem?"

"Dr. Cheung's tired as hell, been on duty for over twenty hours. We got a call from Ranger Marin, she was nearly hysterical. Said you were rushing a man here who was seriously injured. She didn't give us much info, but sure made it sound much worse than a broken arm." The nurse helped Larry out of the car and muttered, "I wish I hadn't woken Dr. Cheung."

"I'm sorry. She's only been on the job for a week, but she's a good kid. I'll talk to her. It won't happen again."

The ranger turned to Larry. "You know those trails are intended for hiking, not running."

"I'll remember that. And thanks for all your help," Larry replied through clenched teeth as the two orderlies carefully lowered him into a waiting wheelchair. He wasn't about to admit he had fallen inside the tunnel running from an oncoming train, a much bigger "no-no" than just running on the hiking trails.

About twenty minutes later, Larry was being wheeled out of the X-ray room as Vivian came running down the hallway, her hands pressed against the sides of her face. "Larry! Larry!"

It was obvious her level of concern was way out of proportion with the situation. "Vivian, I'm fine. I fell and broke my arm; that's all. Really, I'm fine. Hurts like hell, but I'm fine."

Vivian placed her hand over her heart. " This crazy woman called me, and made it sound like you were dying."

"That would be Ranger..... aaah....., I forget her name. It's her first week on the job. Guess she got a little carried away."

"Someone ought to talk to her."

"Someone will. Now why don't you go home; it's probably going to be a while before I'm ready to be released. I'll call you to come pick me up."

A devilish grin spread across Vivian's face. "No way I'm leaving you. I'm embarrassed to admit it, but do you know what kept going through my mind on the way over here?"

Larry grimaced as he gingerly tried to reposition his arm. "I don't have the slightest idea."

"I thought about not being able to make love to you anymore."

Larry cocked his head to the side. "Huh?"

Vivian dropped to one knee and kneeled next to Larry's wheelchair. "After that woman called I thought for sure you were going to die. While I was driving over here I kept thinking about how we almost never make love anymore, and I just started crying. Things are going to be different now, just wait 'til I get you home!"

Looking up, Vivian was surprised to see the elderly orderly standing quietly and politely behind Larry's wheelchair. "Oh, I'm sorry sir, I didn't mean to go on like that. I don't know what got into me."

The orderly, a black man who looked to be in his early sixties said, "No need to apologize miss. Why as soon as I get your husband, I assume he's your husband, as soon as I get him back to the doctor's station I'm gonna go and break my arm, see if it has the same effect on my Ruthie. Now if you'll excuse me."

Vivian stood up and stepped aside. "Can I go with him?"

"No, you'll have to stay in the waiting room. Someone will come get you, shouldn't be too long." And with that the orderly wheeled Larry down the hall.

Remembering, Vivian called out, "Oh sir." The orderly stopped and turned around. "He is my husband."

The orderly smiled and just strolled away, smoothly steering the wheelchair down the hallway. Vivian started toward the waiting room, but having rushed out of the house without explanation after receiving the ranger's call, she wanted to let Rachel know what was happening. The phone rang seven times before a shaking voice answered, "Hello."

"Rachel, is that you?"

"Yeah, it's me."

"Didn't sound like you, thought maybe I dialed the wrong number..... wanted to let you know your dad broke his arm, but don't worry, he's going to be fine. I'm at the hospital, they just x-rayed his arm and should be putting it in a cast soon."

Vivian paused expecting Rachel to ask where and how her father got hurt, to ask for further assurances he was okay, but Rachel didn't say a word. Instead Vivian could hear Rachel's labored and uneven breathing on the other end of the line.

"He's okay. There's nothing to worry about."

"Okay Mom."

"Are you all right? Is something wrong? I can come home now, then come get your father when he's ready."

"No, stay with Dad."

Vivian glanced at her watch; it was 1:35 p.m. It would be quite a while before she got Larry home and he wouldn't have eaten since early in the morning. She thought about asking Rachel to get something for dinner from the grocery store, but then realized that neither of the cars was at home. Rachel was obviously upset about something, something other than her father's accident. Giving her an errand to do might help get her mind off whatever was bothering her.

"Would you walk over to Highs and get some lunch meat and make some sandwiches for us? Your father is probably going to be really hungry when he gets home."

"Mom, could you just get something? I really don't want to leave the house today."

"Okay, I'll see you in a little while. Are you sure you're okay?"

"Just take care of Dad. I'll be fine."

It was 3:45 p.m. when Larry shuffled out of the hospital to Vivian's Camry. The cast covered his left arm from slightly above the elbow to the hand, just his fingers protruded. One of the blankets the ranger had used to cover him in the car was draped around his shoulders.

"How do you feel?" Vivian asked as she started the car.

"Much better, feels so good to be warm again."

"How 'bout your arm?"

"It's weird, feels like it's not there. They gave me some pain killers half an hour ago, must really be working."

He pulled his right arm from under the blanket and handed her a prescription slip for pain medication. "Get this thing filled soon as you get me home."

"Generic, okay?" Vivian asked with raised eyebrows, mocking Larry's almost religious preference for generic drugs.

"No, get the name brand," Larry moaned pathetically.

Just like a man Vivian thought, when it's someone else don't spend an extra dime, but when it's his pain.....

Larry felt dizzy as soon as he stood up getting out of the car. He wobbled to the front door, feeling like he'd just gotten off one of those stomach turning amusement park rides.

"Want something to eat?" Vivian asked as she held the door open for him.

"No, just some juice. I feel really light headed and just want to lie down for a while."

Vivian took hold of his right arm and helped him up the stairs to the bedroom, propped two pillows against the headboard, pulled back the covers and lowered him onto the bed. She bounded down the steps feeling a strange sense of satisfaction from her husband's helplessness, deriving pleasure from knowing he was dependent upon her, even if just for a little while.

"Anything you need before I go to the drug store to get your prescription filled?" she asked as she set a glass of orange juice on the nightstand next to the bed.

"Another blanket, I don't want to get the least bit cold again anytime soon."

Vivian headed to the spare bedroom to get a blanket. Passing Rachel's room she stopped and knocked lightly on the door. "Rachel, are you in there?" Hearing no reply she continued down the hallway.

Seconds later Larry heard a panicked scream, "Oh my God! Rachel! Rachel! "

Larry struggled out of bed and rushed, as best he could, to Vivian who was banging her fists on Rachel's locked door. "Rachel, honey please open the door. Please…."

"What's going on? What's wrong?" Larry implored as he leaned against the hallway wall to steady himself.

Squeezing the sides of her head with her hands, as if shielding her ears from a loud noise, Vivian whimpered, "Sleeping pills are all over the bathroom floor. I think Rachel has…." Vivian stopped in mid-sentence as the door swung open.

Rachel stood there wearing only panties and a bra, hair in disarray, eyes red from crying, and face streaked with makeup. "I didn't take the pills. I thought about it, but I didn't take any."

Vivian and Larry slumped in unison, as if they were balloon people who had been simultaneously deflated. Larry, now leaning against Vivian for support instead of the wall, pleaded, "My goodness Rachel, why would you think about taking sleeping pills?"

Before Rachel could respond, Vivian put her arm around her. "Here, slip your robe on first."

Helping with the robe, Vivian cinched the belt firmly about Rachel's waist, as if doing so would help hold her together, keep her from coming apart. With Rachel between them, Vivian and Larry guided her to the bed where the three of them sat down; Rachel secured snugly in the middle.

"Rachel, what happened?" Vivian asked softly.

"I don't want to talk about it."

"You've got to talk about it. Your father and I want to help you, but we can't unless we know what happened."

Rachel rubbed her hands up her face and back over her hair, only Vivian recognizing the gesture as one learned or maybe inherited from her father. "On Thursday I got a rejection letter from Duke. I was so embarrassed I didn't say anything about it. And today I got........ two more. Hopkins and Virginia."

Both parents blurted out responses at the same time, with each being drowned out by the other. Vivian nodded to Larry to go first. "Rachel, college is important, but it's not that important. Nothing is important enough to make you want to take your own life."

"I only thought about it for a little while and I didn't do it. I didn't take any pills."

Vivian hugged Rachel tightly. "But honey, you can't ever think that way, not even for a few seconds. Suicides, especially by kids, can be impulsive acts. So you can't let thoughts like that creep into your head. I know you've experienced some horrible things....." Vivian paused, nervously clearing her throat. "And I know it's my fault. But you've got your whole life in front of you."

"I've been a screw-off my entire life, but now I'm working hard and want to go to a good college. I could make it at those schools. I know I could."

Larry brushed his right hand softly against his daughter's cheek. "I know you're smart enough for those schools, but you've got to be realistic. Schools of that caliber take three things into consideration - grades, SAT scores, and extracurricular activities. Let's face it, you did great on the SAT, but that's it. Until this year your grades haven't been good, and you don't have any outside activities...... But don't worry, you'll get accepted by Maryland, and then there's Howard Community."

"Damn it Dad, I don't want to go to Howard Community College and I'm not sure I want to go to Maryland either."

"You don't have a whole lot of choices. I think Howard Community College is the way to go; after two years, if you do well, you can reapply to some of the same schools. Plus by then you'll have decided what you want to major in and you can pick the best school for that field. Anyway, your mother and I think another two years at home would be good for you."

"Well, I don't. I'm not going to Howard Community College. I want to go away to school.... I guess I'll go to Maryland." And then Rachel added dejectedly, "If I get accepted."

"You'll get accepted," replied Larry with less than complete confidence.

"Dad, I know everything you said is true, but it still hurts anyway."

Vivian seized the chance to distract Rachel from her self-pity. "Speaking about hurting, I can tell from your father's face he's not feeling too well right now."

"Your mother's right. I think I'm going to need some medication for the pain pretty soon. And I'm starting to get hungry. Would you make me some soup?"

"Oh Daddy, I'm sorry. All I've been doing is thinking about this stupid college stuff and you're sitting here with a broken arm. What kinda soup do you want?"

"Chicken noodle would be good."

Rachel started to get up, but flopped back down between her parents. "Vinnie heard from Duke."

"He did?" Vivian said.

"He got accepted, I'm really happy for him. Now let me up so I can make that soup."

Larry and Vivian remained sitting on the bed as Rachel left the room only to poke her head back in and say, "Thanks for listening.... Oh, you know there's one other school I applied to."

"Yeah, which school is that?" Larry asked.

Rachel averted her eyes from her parents, sticking her bare foot out and rubbing her big toe back and forth on the carpet, as if she were writing a message in the sand at the beach. "Harvard."

"Harvard!" Vivian and Larry both squealed in harmonious disbelief.

"I guess I wasted my fifty bucks on that application, didn't I?"

"Yes, I'm afraid you did," replied Larry.

Chapter 9

Larry Webster had a miserable, sleepless night. The medication had taken the sharp edge off the pain in his left arm, but a dull, steady throbbing remained. Unable to sleep he spent the night thinking about his wife and daughter, and about his lover, Barbara Reilly. And while he tried not to, he couldn't help but think about the events of the past week and of that day at the lake seventeen years ago.

Tossing and turning all night long, a troubling question swirled relentlessly through his head. He remembered opening the door when leaving the house this past Saturday with Vivian. He had picked up a UPS box and laid it on the floor in the foyer, intending to open it when he got home. Until this sleepless night he had forgotten about the box. He hoped, no he prayed, Vivian had taken the box, that it was nothing of interest to him so she never said anything about it. But if Vivian didn't take the box that meant Rachel did. That terrifying possibility filled his mouth with cotton, burned his eyes, and turned his stomach sour.

The low point in Rachel's relationship with her mother had come three years earlier when she was fourteen years old, in the ninth grade. In what, according to her psychiatrist, was an attempt to strike back at Vivian, Rachel had become sexually involved with a nineteen year-old college sophomore. When he discovered what was going on, he threatened to report the young man to the police – Rachel was well under the legal age of consent. That's all it took, the guy wasn't a problem anymore.

During that period he discovered a cardboard box in the garage attic, a box with UPS markings very much like the one he had left in the foyer a few days ago. The box contained sexual devices and implements, many intended for use in sadistic and masochistic activities. Initially, Rachel denied any knowledge of the box, but ultimately she confessed about her relationship with the young man. She explained how he had encouraged her to "try new stuff so we can keep things interesting." The whole incident scared the hell out of him and Vivian – Vivian had stopped drinking only two months earlier and this more than sealed her commitment to remain sober.

Still dark outside, but with no hope of falling asleep, Larry lay there with the throbbing in his arm, torturing himself with the possibility that his daughter might once again be allowing herself to be degraded and abused. It had always been the age of the guy, five years older than Rachel, which he found especially despicable. If she were involved with Vinnie in that way, a young man her own age, maybe that wouldn't be quite so bad. No, no, that didn't make any sense, being involved with any man in that way would be a horrible thing.

Maybe he was worrying for no reason, maybe Vivian had ordered the box and it was full of dried flowers; she loved dried flowers. No, whatever was in the box was heavy; maybe the box was full of books. Yes, perhaps the box contained books, books that Vivian had ordered from one of those book clubs she always got suckered into. He should wake Vivian so she could rescue him from this self-inflicted torture. No, let her sleep, she needed as much sleep as she could get; he would wait until she woke up to ask.

But there was something that couldn't be put off, a quick trip to the bathroom. He stumbled out of bed, painfully bumping his left arm against the wall before finding the light switch. Somehow, the act of relieving himself lessened the throbbing in his arm. If it could only lessen the knot in his gut caused by the UPS box, he'd trade another broken arm to make the box go away. He crawled back into the warmth of the bed, but his movements were awkward and uncoordinated, the full weight of his body flopping onto the bed.

"Honey, are you okay?" Vivian said as she stretched her arms and let out a big yawn.

"Yeah, I'm fine."

"Does your arm hurt?"

"It's not too bad....... I wanted to ask you something," Larry said in an unconcerned tone, not wanting to upset her. He would just ask if she had the box. She would say yes it was a box of books, or a box of whatever, and he wouldn't need to subject her to the memory of that horrible experience three years earlier.

"Ask me later," she purred, rolling her surprisingly nude body on top of him and kissing him with an open mouth.

Her writhing body was full of energy, her hands moved smoothly over him. She wedged her hands under his back and wrapped her arms around him pulling him anxiously against her forceful, undulating pelvic motions. She momentarily broke off their kiss and panted heavily, sucking in oxygen to fuel her desire. Then her tongue was in his mouth moving wildly about, the seal of their joined lips only being occasionally broken to accommodate her labored breathing and muted moans.

He was erect almost immediately and could feel himself fully exposed through the open fly of his pajamas. As she pushed against him he could feel her wetness, wetness so extreme it seemed unnatural. She slithered higher on his body, spread her legs, pressed her crotch into his stomach, and then pushed down bringing him inside of her. Lifting up, she came to a kneeling position atop him, grabbing the bed's headboard for balance, sliding up and down his full length, first slowly, but then with a sense of boiling urgency. Again and again she rose up on her knees, and rammed the full weight of her body onto him, forcing him further into her than he thought possible. He coordinated his movements with hers, not only for pleasure, but also to better absorb the impact of her thrusts.

"Don't let me hurt you," she wailed as she incongruously increased the intensity and speed of her motions. He could no longer keep pace with her, and she was hurting him. This was a level of sexual excitement he had never before experienced. He reached up with his right hand and grabbed one of her gyrating breasts, trying to gain control of her body, but it was no use. It was as if he had hold of a wild animal gone berserk; the splash of her spittle sprayed his face with each gasping moan. Ready to explode he begged, "Slow down, please. I can't last." Increasing the intensity of her gyrations to levels that seemed impossible she groaned, several octaves deeper than her normal voice, "Go ahead baby, it's okay, it's okay."

As he erupted inside the creature that had taken control of his wife's body, he instinctively jerked his hands up to cover his face. The pain in his left arm was unbearable. He screamed in agony and his body lurched to the side. But the strange being on top of him, just now reaching a state of complete physical ecstasy, paid no attention to his pain. The creature maintained its rhythm for a few more savage thrusts, then convulsed uncontrollably as its head rolled back exposing the full length of its neck bathed in a thin shaft of early morning sunlight coming through the window. The being, now strangely calm, straightened up and peered down on him, as if surveying its wounded prey, and then collapsed on top of him.

After several minutes of shared exhaustion and stillness, Vivian lifted her head and gently kissed her husband on the cheek. "Oh, Larry," she sighed.

"Vivian, Vivian, Vivian," he moaned softly.

Still inside of her, but no longer fully erect, he could tell by her measured breathing she was falling asleep. Her breathing was hypnotic; he was asleep even before her.

He dreamed about the first time they made love, dreamed about being hard inside of her, only to awaken to find her still on top of him sliding smoothly up and down. This time it was different, her movements more gentle and loving, his pleasure her only concern. With no sense of urgency, their shared climax was slow and easy, physically timid in comparison to the explosion they experienced earlier, but emotionally more fulfilling.

With their depleted bodies still interlocked, Larry puzzled, "What in the world has gotten into you?"

"I'm not sure. I guess I'm just letting out what's been trapped inside of me for all these years."

They lay there in each other's embrace without speaking for many minutes, thinking their own thoughts; she regretting so many lost opportunities with him and with Rachel, he worrying about the box.

He couldn't wait any longer. He had to ask. "Viv, did you open that UPS box we got last Saturday?"

"No, I completely forgot about..... You didn't get the box?"

As Larry shook his head no, lines of worry and concern instantly engulfed her eyes. His fear was now her fear. Why did he have to ask her now, he should have just waited. It had been eighteen years since she had experienced anything like this morning, why did he have to take it away from her?

"Oh God, no," she whimpered.

Larry hugged her tightly with his right arm. "She's downstairs. I'll go ask her."

"Please don't upset her, heaven only knows how she'll react. Maybe you shouldn't even mention the box. I know if she is back into that sadistic stuff we've got to deal with it, but not now, not after what she almost did to herself yesterday."

"I won't accuse her of anything, but I have to ask her, we can't ignore this."

They dressed quickly and hustled downstairs to find Rachel sitting at the kitchen table eating a bowl of corn flakes, her school backpack on the table in front of her.

"How are you this morning?" asked Vivian with forced cheerfulness.

"Better. I'm still disappointed, but I realize it's not the end of the world. I over-reacted yesterday, it won't happen again."

"Where you going with the backpack?" asked Larry in an unconcerned tone.

With ever so slight a smile, a smile she didn't even know was there, Rachel answered, "Over to Vinnie's to study."

Larry swallowed hard, recognizing her habit of smiling that smile when she was nervous or when she was being less than candid.

"Vivian would you like some cereal?"

"Not right now, but I wouldn't mind some OJ."

Larry made himself a bowl of Cheerios and poured a glass of orange juice for Vivian, his ability to do things with one hand improving quickly with practice and concentration. After a few spoonfuls, milk dripping down his chin, and his mouth crammed full of Cheerios to make his question seem ever so nonchalant, Larry casually remarked, "Oh Rachel, did you see that UPS box that was delivered here on Saturday?"

The telltale smile reappeared and her eyebrows arched high on her forehead. "A box?"

Larry consciously relaxed his locked jaw. "Yeah, a cardboard box, a little bigger than a shoe box."

"No, I didn't see any box."

Vivian clutched Larry's right hand beneath the table and gave it a hard squeeze, sending the message not to push Rachel any further. Concerned he wasn't going to comply, she decided to turn the conversation in a different direction. "Have you taken your pain pills this morning?"

Convinced Rachel was once again involved in some form of disgusting and degrading behavior, Larry wanted to reach across the table and shake the living daylights out of her, but he agreed with Vivian. If he pressed the subject, the situation might rapidly spiral out of control and might result in Rachel harming herself. He was glad for the excuse to get away from her.

"No, not yet. I better go do that."

When he returned, Vivian was still sitting at the table, only now with her hands covering her face, Rachel having just gone out the front door. "She's lying," Larry growled as he plopped down on to one of the kitchen chairs.

"I know it, but after yesterday we've got to give her some time."

"You're right, but it's hard to sit back and do nothing."

"Maybe the box is something else, something totally innocent," Vivian said.

"God, I hope you're right....... Do you believe what she said about not being accepted to those schools, that it's not the end of the world?"

"I don't know when to believe her. I think she meant it when she said it, but what will she do when the next big disappointment comes along, whatever it might be?"

Larry hunched his shoulders and shook his head in exasperation as he ate the last few spoonfuls of cereal, then peeked up at Vivian, seeking permission.

"Go ahead, drink the milk from the bowl."

"Are you really sure that it's not going to bother you?"

"It doesn't seem very important to me right now."

Larry lifted the bowl to his lips with his right hand and slurped the milk down as noisily as possible, let out an exaggerated "Aaaaahhhhh," then wiped his mouth with the back of his shirt sleeve. "You're full of all kind of surprises this morning, aren't you? What's going on?"

"Do you really want to know?"

"Of course I want to know."

"This is going to be hard. It's a good thing, not a sad thing, but I'm afraid I'll start crying."

"Don't worry about crying."

"But I don't want to cry. I want to celebrate what I'm feeling now."

Larry tilted his head at an odd angle. "So just tell me what you're feeling."

"Okay. You remember that before I got pregnant I liked sex, I liked it a lot."

Introducing some levity to help lessen Vivian's nervousness Larry rubbed his chin thoughtfully. "Now let me see. Yes, I do seem to remember that."

It worked momentarily as Vivian laughed, but seriousness quickly returned to her expression. "When I became pregnant I got myself all screwed up - no pun intended - sex was the last thing on my mind. And after the babies were born I got sick, really sick. You think I exaggerated my health problems, but I didn't. I felt awful all the time. When I did begin to feel better my interest in sex started to reawaken, but you seemed so distant and I didn't know how to get things started again. I thought you didn't find me attractive anymore."

Vivian paused to gulp the last of her orange juice. "It was Thanksgiving evening and the girls were asleep, I told you there was something important I wanted to discuss. It had taken me a long time to get up my courage, but then the phone rang. It was your aunt. Your uncle had slipped on some ice and hurt his back and she had to tell you every last detail. When you finally got off the phone you forgot I wanted to talk. You were tired so I decided to wait until another time..... Do you remember that Thanksgiving?"

Vivian looked at him expectantly. "Well, do you remember?"

"I'm sorry, I... I don't remember," Larry stuttered as visions of an early Thanksgiving morning rendezvous at Barbara Serelis' apartment flashed on and off inside his head like an x-rated movie illuminated with a strobe light.

"Well, I decided to give it a little more time, but a week later Karen was taken. Nothing meant anything to me after that, sex certainly didn't...... I'm sorry; I need a drink of water, that orange juice left a bitter taste. Want one?"

"No."

Vivian filled a glass with water, drank it all, then sat back down. "I don't know how to say this."

"Just say it."

"Okay, I'll try," she said as she placed the palms of her hands on the table in front of her, like a magician trying to prove she didn't have anything up her sleeves. "For all these years when ever we had sex I never let myself enjoy it. Those times when I couldn't hold back and did climax it felt good, but afterwards I would feel so guilty."

"Guilty over what?"

"Guilty over feeling that kind of pleasure when I should have been mourning Karen's death."

"That's not a logical way of thinking."

"Sitting here now hearing myself say it, I know it isn't, but that's the way I felt."

"Did you ever tell this to any of the psychiatrists?"

Vivian shook her head back and forth ever so slightly, her embarrassment painfully obvious.

"No wonder they were never able to help you."

Larry reached across the table with his right hand and wiped the tears from beneath her eyes with his thumb. "I don't understand what happened this morning?"

"When that ranger called, I thought you were hurt very badly, maybe dying. All of a sudden I realized something. I realized I had finally stopped mourning Karen's death. I don't know exactly when I stopped, maybe when Rachel and I had our talk. And then yesterday, I thought I might lose you...."

"I'm sorry, but I just don't understand what you're trying to say."

Vivian leaned across the table until their eyes were only inches apart. "When I started worrying about you, some very sad thoughts crept into my head. Then it dawned on me that I hadn't had a sad thought for an entire week. I never thought admitting Karen was dead would change anything, but it did, it changed everything, it changed me."

Vivian's eyes opened wide, so wide she looked like a little kid about to open a present. "I feel alive for the first time in seventeen years. I want to do things I've never done, go places I've never been. It's like I just stepped into a beautiful garden bright with flowers after having spent a lifetime trapped in a dungeon."

Larry smiled. "I can't tell you how good it is to hear you say these things."

"Guess what I feel like doing?"

He shrugged his shoulders.

"I want to start painting again."

"That's absolutely wonderful. No, that's beyond wonderful."

"I'm gonna go to the craft store and get supplies tomorrow," said Vivian.

"No, let's go right now."

"Naaah, there's one thing I feel like doing even more than painting."

"What's that?"

"I want to screw you like crazy for the rest of my life. As a matter of fact, I want to right now."

"I don't know what to say."

"Don't say anything, just come upstairs with me."

Chapter 10

It was 8:45 a.m., Tuesday, December 14, and Larry Webster, normally punctual to a fault, strolled into his office an hour late. His regular routine was shot to hell - up past midnight making love with Vivian, going at it again this morning, then promising not to be late so they could get "an early start this evening." Seven times in less than forty-eight hours and already looking forward to getting home, how long could he maintain such a pace? Who knows, just enjoy it while it lasts.

There was only one little problem, a scheduled meeting with Barbara at the Day's Inn in Silver Spring after work. During their on-again, off-again affair of almost eighteen years he had canceled planned meetings with her no more than three or four times, certainly never to have sex with his wife. He punched the first four digits of Barbara's number, but stopped short, needing a bit more time to get his story straight before placing the call. Slouching in his chair, he considered the irony of viewing Vivian with greater excitement than Barbara, and thought about his relationships with these two women.

His love for Barbara was all consuming and unrelenting. His love for Vivian was genuine, but had grown quite tenuous over the years. Deep down inside it was only the guilt over Karen's abduction that kept him from leaving Vivian for Barbara.

He met Vivian at a lodge in Killington, Vermont, in April 1971, he a senior at Princeton and she a junior at Penn State. Both were on spring break ski trips, Vivian with three other girls from Penn State, and he with his roommate from Princeton. One evening he walked into the lodge's game room only to find it crawling with screaming kids. As he turned around to leave, out of the corner of his eye he caught a glimpse of a shapely rear in tight purple stretch pants leaning over a pinball machine. Drawn to that rear-end like a moth to a light bulb, he offered advice about the finer points of playing pinball, a subject about which he knew absolutely nothing. The pinball discussion led to dinner later that evening, then three days of skiing together and more dinners, and on their last night a passionate good bye in his room - his accommodating roommate exiled to sleep on a sofa in the lobby.

They didn't see one another again until June, after Larry's graduation from Princeton. Vivian's grandparents lived in York, Pa., only about an hour drive north of Baltimore where Larry had returned after graduation. At first, they dated once a week or so, but as the relationship heated up Larry began making the drive every couple of days. In August, Vivian's grandparents went away on vacation and Larry moved in, commuting to his summer job at the Applied Physics Laboratory southwest of Baltimore. Driving the hour and a half each way seemed a small price to pay to spend the night with the girl he loved.

They got engaged on a muggy Saturday night in September when Larry proposed as they crested the first hill of the Comet roller coaster at Hershey Park. Vivian screamed "yeeeessssss" in reply as the coaster made its heart-thumping descent. Their rain soaked wedding took place the following June after Vivian graduated from Penn State with dual degrees in Business Administration and Art, and Larry had completed his first year of graduate school at Johns Hopkins. After a honeymoon in upstate New York they moved into an apartment in Baltimore, and Vivian took a job with a stock brokerage firm.

For the next three years Vivian was the primary breadwinner as Larry pursued his PhD in Astrophysics. It was a carefree life with low budget trips to the beach in the summer and weekend backpacking trips to West Virginia in the fall and spring. It was on one of the West Virginia trips that Vivian had taken the photograph of him standing in front of the waterfall that she used as a model for the oil painting that now hung on the wall next to their front door. During this period they discovered every inexpensive restaurant in Baltimore and frequented the Sunday matinee bargains at the local theaters. Life was full of happiness and totally stress free until June 1975, when everything changed and changed abruptly.

So much happened during the first two weeks of June, starting so wonderfully, but ending so horribly. He received his PhD from Hopkins, they moved into a new house in Columbia, and then his mother's car was struck by a drunk-driver. She died three days later.

Scheduled to begin his new job as a staff scientist with the National Science Foundation the day after his mother's accident, Larry was emotionally devastated and unable to start working until August. One week into his new job, Vivian discovered she was pregnant despite her meticulous use of a contraceptive diaphragm. On Halloween, serious complications with her pregnancy began. The toddler at the door dressed in a skeleton costume screamed hysterically as Vivian doubled over with cramps and bled profusely. She was confined to bed for much of the next seven months, the five months until the twins were born in March, and then two more months while she recovered.

From the carefree bliss of a year earlier, Larry and Vivian now knew nothing but stress. Vivian had to deal with health problems, and terrifying self doubts about her fitness for motherhood born from her traumatic childhood experiences. Larry, who had grown up poor, but spoiled nonetheless, was for the first time in his life confronted with enormous responsibilities: his first permanent job, a physically ill and emotionally frail wife, and two beautiful, but outrageously demanding baby girls. He had long since assumed responsibility for all household and family matters, filling his life with one crisis after another. One particularly irritating chore was keeping the health insurance claims organized and up to date. At one point there was a major dispute, with more than a thousand dollars at issue, with the health insurance carrier. Unable to resolve the matter after countless letters and phone calls, he sought help from the National Science Foundation's personnel department. A young benefits analyst, Barbara Serelis, handled his case.

On Good Friday he limped - having twisted his ankle slipping on a soiled diaper that morning- into Barbara's office burdened with a folder of disorganized hospital and doctor bills, pharmaceutical receipts, canceled checks, improperly filled-out insurance claims, and a tangled web of correspondence with the insurance company. Barbara's back was to him as she filed casework papers in a cabinet behind her desk. He dropped the folder on her desk with a thud to get her attention. A chilling tingle, not an imaginary tingle, but a real tingle, flashed through his body the instant she turned around to face him. The attraction was immediate and of such intensity he stood mesmerized unable to move or speak. After several awkward seconds he broke free from the spell and clumsily flopped into the chair in front of her desk. He tried to explain his insurance situation, but it was no use. He was so taken by the young lady he couldn't think clearly, much less speak coherently, and had to excuse himself, remarking he had forgotten an important meeting and would have to come back at another time.

Completely flustered and with his face beet red, he returned to his office, locked the door and tried to clear his head, but all he could think about was Barbara Serelis. His body struggled for a sense of equilibrium as beads of sweat peppered his forehead while chills coursed through his bones at the same time; his senses were overwhelmed like never before. He remembered how in junior-high he and his friends had played the juvenile game of rating girls on a scale from 1 to 10. He had given out 9s like handing out jelly beans on Halloween, but had always reserved his one "10," joking to one of his buddies, "There's only one of 'em out there." His buddy asked, "What does she look like?" With dead seriousness he had replied, "Beats me, but I'll know her when I see her." Years later as he had sat at his desk at the National Science Foundation, as an adult, as an up-and-coming scientist, and as a new father with enormous responsibilities, he realized he had just seen his one and only "10." He knew she was the one. He didn't know how or why; he just knew it.

With large brown eyes peeking out from beneath jet-black bangs and unusually thick eyebrows, soft full lips, and a well-formed figure, she was attractive, but not outrageously so. This just didn't make sense. With all his problems on the job and especially at home, idling at his desk consumed with desire for a woman he had just seen for the first time in his life was insane. He had a beautiful wife, in fact more beautiful than this woman, at least she would be more beautiful once she got back to looking like herself, pregnancy had been very hard on her. He loved Vivian dearly and wasn't the least bit interested in having another woman in his life, not now, not ever, not even if she was a "10" – what the hell was he thinking of, he wasn't in junior-high anymore.

By the next day he felt things were under control, but when he went to see Barbara Serelis his knees wobbled and he became so clammy and light headed he feared he might faint. He wanted this woman so badly it made his insides hurt, but a steely determination and a legitimate need to deal with his insurance situation overcame the strange attraction and allowed him to concentrate on the problem at hand.

The health claims situation was so complicated, involving several doctors and two hospitals, that its resolution required many meetings with Barbara over a period of weeks. Throughout this time he worked hard to suppress his attraction, and was reasonably effective in doing so. But his life consisted of a constant struggle to keep up with problems on the home front and at the office, and he had no emotional outlet to discuss his burdens that at times were overwhelming. Vivian's grandparents lived out of town, which was just as well since they drove him absolutely crazy. His co-workers would occasionally inquire about how things were going at home, but such interactions rarely extended beyond polite chitchat. As a result, almost without realizing it, he began turning to Barbara Serelis for emotional support.

The time spent meeting with Barbara involved in-depth discussion and analysis. She proved to be extremely helpful, not only straightening out his claims situation, but in advising him on alternative health care strategies. She was unusually dedicated, almost maniacal in her work habits. At her suggestion, he switched insurance options, obtaining better coverage and saving several hundred dollars in the process. When the insurance claims were finally resolved, he invited her to lunch to show his appreciation, confident he had contained his attraction for her. While having lunch at Mrs. K's in Silver Spring, he met her eyes for just a moment, impulsively leaned across the table and kissed her lightly on the lips. Embarrassed, he immediately tried to apologize, but before he could utter a word she returned his kiss with a much more sensuous one of her own. She confessed to finding him irresistible and wanting him desperately, then suggested that they go to her place.

In less than five seconds his world had been turned upside down. Having gone without sex for six months because of Vivian's complications with pregnancy and delivery, his ability to resist Barbara's advances was paper-thin. He tossed two twenties on the table for their half-eaten lunch, knowing he'd paid way too much, but not wanting to waste an extra minute waiting for the check. Less than twenty minutes later, after running two red lights and parking illegally in front of a fire hydrant to shorten their walk by fifty yards, he was making love with a "10", the "only one of 'em out there."

Afterwards, his guilt was unbearable. For the next month he avoided seeing Barbara and didn't return her persistent phone calls, but ultimately physical desire overwhelmed his guilt. On the morning of July 26th he stopped by her office and ended up spending the evening in her bedroom. In September, he had sex with Vivian for the first time in almost a year. By that time it was too late to end the affair, he was way beyond just being in love with Barbara Serelis, she had become an obsession. They had sex on a regular basis, usually twice a week and sometimes more often.

On Saturday morning, the fourth of December, he met Barbara at Lake Elkhorn under the guise of taking the twins to feed the ducks. He had no intention of having sex; Monday after work would be their first opportunity for that. She had been away for a week visiting relatives, and he missed her terribly and just wanted to be with her for a little while. Getting baby food from the cooler in the back of the van, he didn't see her come up behind him, and wasn't expecting her tap on the shoulder. When he turned to face her, she wrapped her arms around him and kissed him wildly. Their physical desires spiraled out of control and the next thing he knew he was on top of her in the van.

After the abduction he went through a prolonged period of deep depression, blaming himself, and immediately breaking off the relationship. It took almost a year to come to terms with the grief of his daughter's death, but his obsession for Barbara never went away. Ten months after the abduction he approached her, but she rebuffed his advances, saying she was terribly sorry for what had happened, but needed to get on with her life. She had recently started dating again and made the point that she would never get involved with another married man. To add emphasis to her intent to move forward with her life, she was about to leave the National Science Foundation and start a new job at the University of Maryland. Unexpectedly, a month after starting the new job she called and they resumed their love affair.

Four years after that, before Christmas in 1981, Barbara pleaded with him to divorce Vivian. Her arguments were persuasive, but he couldn't bring himself to leave his wife; Vivian's problems - the alcoholism, Rachel's mistreatment - were of his doing. Their affair continued over the years, cooling off occasionally, only to heat up again with renewed passion. In November of 1990, Barbara met John Reilly, an airline pilot, who proposed marriage six weeks later. Again, Barbara begged him to seek a divorce. As before he refused. With shameless selfishness, he pleaded with her not to get married, a plea she ignored. Ironically, her marriage brought her closer, at least geographically, since her husband's house was located in Columbia just three miles down the bike path from where he lived. Barbara broke off their affair two days before her wedding, but she called five months later and they started up again, neither of them ever able to break free from the hold of the other. Only now the ground rules were a bit different, for the first time he was having an affair with a married woman.

He had long ago capitulated in trying to analyze the situation, and just accepted his interwoven relationships with the two women in his life. His lover knew almost everything about his wife, but his wife knew nothing of his lover. He was not honest and open with his wife, the woman with whom he shared his life, but was always honest and open with his lover, the woman with whom he shared his soul. Now for the first time ever, he was about to lie to Barbara Reilly.

"Hi Barb, it's me."

"We all set for this evening?"

"Well, that's what I'm calling about. We're having some new problems with Rachel and I have to cancel out."

"Can we get together tomorrow? You know John gets back in town on Thursday."

"I'm sorry......... this thing with Rachel is going to take several days to straighten out. I'll call you when things are under control."

"Well, okay."

"Love ya Barb. Bye."

"No Larry, wait! I've got to tell you something. I really wanted to do this in person, but I can't wait any longer."

"Okay, what is it?"

"My answer is yes!"

"Your answer is yes? What's the question?"

"Yes, I'm gonna go to Chile with you!"

Chapter 11

It was the afternoon of December 21. Larry was in his car heading to the University of Maryland to see Barbara. His personal life had never been so complicated. He had been struggling for days to sort things out in his mind, but it wasn't easy. He prided himself on being decisive. When a difficult decision presents itself, one collects and organizes the relevant facts, identifies the available options, assesses the likely consequences of each option, then selects an appropriate course of action. Simple as that, there is no place in today's world for indecisive people. Considering every last detail, indecisive types allow their thought processes to become paralyzed and most often their decision is to make no decision, letting events control them rather than taking action.

Now for the first time in his life, the shoe was on the other foot, his foot. The idea of accepting the position in Chile seemed so perfect a month ago. It would get him in on the ground floor of one of the world's premier astronomical facilities and guarantee him research opportunities for years to come. Desperate to get away from the bureaucracy of his government job, he doubted an opportunity such as this would ever surface again. None of this had changed, going to Chile would be the best possible thing for his career, but from the perspective of his personal life the decision had become much more complicated.

Years of trying to deal with his guilt and years of putting up with Vivian's and Rachel's mistreatment of one another had beaten him into submission. But that was a month ago, so much had changed in these past few weeks.

Vivian was becoming a new person, unshackled from the dual burdens of keeping alive the memory of a daughter who had been dead for many years, and of hopelessly seeking the love of her living daughter. She was at peace with herself for the first time in seventeen years and functioning with a level of confidence and independence unlike ever before. She was exercising regularly and knocking off projects one by one, like wall-papering the first floor bathroom, a project she had talked about for as long as he could remember. He had come home from work one evening and the entire job was finished: measurements made, materials bought, and the paper hung, all in less than ten hours. She had jumped back into her part-time job as a real estate sales agent with a vengeance: in less than one week she reorganized her files, printed new flyers, and listed two houses for sale. And on top of everything else she had begun working on a new painting, but insisted she wasn't ready to let anyone see it just yet.

But the biggest change in Vivian was in her attitude toward sex. While her appetite had diminished somewhat from those first few outrageous days, her cravings remained strong, and even more significant than the sheer frequency of her desires was the depth of emotion she put into her love making.

Rachel was another story. She bounced back from the depression of the college rejections and seemed happy about acceptance letters from Howard Community College and the University of Maryland, but he continued to be concerned about her. He hadn't brought up the subject of the box again, but he knew she lied about it; she was being evasive and dishonest about something. She often disappeared and was frequently away, "studying with Vinnie." Vivian had tried to talk to her about birth control, but she became confrontational and Vivian was forced to drop the subject. Hopefully, she and Vinnie had enough common sense to take the proper precautions, and hopefully, they were engaging in a normal relationship between a boy and a girl, not a one-sided abusive relationship like that with that college punk.

He hadn't seen Barbara in over two weeks, not since the day they talked in the math library, the day he impulsively asked her to go to Chile. Since their phone conversation several days later when she answered "yes," he had canceled planned meetings with her on three separate occasions, in each instance choosing to be with Vivian instead.

Now, after several agonizing days and sleepless nights he had made up his mind. He had given up on his normal analytic approach to making a decision since he was getting nowhere doing that; instead, for one of the few times in his life he was going to follow his heart. And he was ready to tell Barbara what he had decided.

He turned into the University of Maryland campus from Route 1, the campus nearly deserted, semester break having begun a few days earlier. He steered his Taurus around a nasty blob of road-kill in the middle of the main campus drive, and parked in a garage behind Cole Field House.

He hustled around to the front entrance of the field house, a cold wind stinging his ears. Ahead of its time when it was constructed in the 1950's, the field house had aged remarkably well, and remained an outstanding facility. On this afternoon, the 14,000 or so seats were almost all empty except for a few people sprinkled here and there. Far below on the gymnasium floor, basketball players dressed in red shirts and shorts were practicing passing drills. Even from the top of the stands the players looked tall and skilled, must be members of the varsity basketball team he thought, although there were no coaches or other signs of a formal practice.

Continuing to watch the players below, he walked around the top level of the field house until he was even with the mid-court line, and then shuffled down the steps to about the tenth row above the court and took a seat. Formless from above, at this distance the players looked like kids, very tall but also very young, probably eighteen to twenty years old, all but three were black. Their shouts of encouragement to one another and the dribbling of the ball against the floor echoed throughout the cavernous field house. Larry whistled a silent "wow" in admiration when one of the smaller players soared high above the rim and jammed the ball through the basket.

"With these freshmen and sophomores, we're going to have a powerhouse in a year or two, " Barbara Reilly predicted as she stood in the aisle looking down at him.

Larry glanced up and patted the seat next to him. "I saved this for you, almost got into a fight with a big burly guy who couldn't find an empty seat."

Barbara sat down, but looked forward toward the basketball court, purposely avoiding his eyes.

"I know you're upset with me."

"You're damn right, you've been lying to me and I know it. What the hell's going on?"

"Barbara, please look at me."

"What's that?" she asked with concern as she turned to face him.

"It's a cast."

"No shit, I know it's a cast. What happened?"

"I fell jogging and broke my arm."

"You fell jogging?"

Not wanting to lie, but also not wanting to go into the details of the train and everything else he replied, "I was running alongside the railroad track in Patapsco State Park and tripped."

She softly placed her hand on his thigh. "You idiot. When did this happen?"

"About a week and a half ago."

"Why didn't you tell me?"

"It's no big deal. The times we've talked on the phone since then, I just didn't remember to say anything." With a wry grin he joshed, "Actually it's not really broken, I just had this cast put on my arm for sympathy 'cause I knew you were going to be mad at me."

"You're right about that. Now, what the hell's going on?"

"It's pretty complicated," he forewarned.

"I can handle complicated."

In an absurdly rapid cadence Larry began recounting recent events, like a nervous teenager trying to camouflage a piece of bad news within a barrage of information. "Rachel got turned down by three colleges. She almost tried to kill herself, then she ordered some porno equipment."

He took an exaggerated deep breath and continued at the same ridiculous pace. " And Vivian has turned into an over-achiever, pumping iron, doing aerobics, wall papering the house, selling houses.... And, oh yeah, she's turned into a nymphomaniac."

Tightening her jaw, Barbara was not amused.

Larry clenched her left hand with his right as seriousness returned to his voice. "Things have gotten crazy. Everything I just said is true, but I'm confused about when things happened. I can't remember what I've told you and what I haven't."

In a quiet voice, but boiling with anger she fumed, "Well, let me refresh your memory. The last time we spoke was two Wednesdays ago in the math library. I seem to recall you asking me to leave my husband and go to Chile with you. Now, do I have it right so far?"

"Yes," he replied meekly.

Squeezing the arm rests of the seat so hard her knuckles turned white; she choked out her words, fighting not to cry. "And then we were supposed to get together three different times and you put me off each time. The first time I believed your excuse, but the last two times I knew you were lying. Now why don't you give me your little story again, only this time cut out the bullshit."

"Okay, I'm sorry........ Rachel got rejection letters from Duke, Hopkins and Virginia all at once. She took it very badly, admitted she thought about killing herself. It scared the hell out of us."

"Is she okay now?"

"She says she's okay."

"What's this porno stuff about?"

"Remember when she got involved with that college kid?"

"How could I possibly forget that?"

"Well, back then she bought this collection of porno stuff from a mail order outfit, dildos, vibrators, leather straps..... Hell, I didn't even know what half the stuff was."

"So what are you saying, did she buy some more?"

"Yeah, I think so."

"What do you mean, you think so?"

"I didn't actually see the junk, but I don't need to see it. A UPS box was delivered to our house. I didn't think anything of it at the time and put the box aside, but then it disappeared. We know that Rachel has the box, but she denies it."

"So?"

"The box was identical to the one the porno stuff came in the first time."

"Maybe it was something else."

"If it was something else she wouldn't have to lie about it."

"So what did you do about it?"

"We're afraid to do anything..... Hell, she thought about killing herself because she got turned down by a couple of colleges."

"You've dealt with tough situations before with Rachel."

"I know, but she's been doing so much better lately. I hate the idea of her back sliding."

Barbara turned away and looked down at the basketball court. "So Vivian has become a nymphomaniac."

"I don't know how else to describe it, she's all over me."

"And what caused this little miracle to take place?"

"Barbara, please look at me." She reluctantly turned to face him as he continued. "For the longest time she hasn't been able to enjoy sex, but now that she has accepted Karen's death her sexual desires have come back."

"I don't get it."

"I don't get it either, but she said when she heard herself actually say the words that Karen was dead it changed everything."

Barbara dropped her head disconsolately. "So where does that leave us?"

Detecting the unmistakable hint of jealousy in her voice, he replied, "I am married to the woman. I've always had sex her, I don't see what's different."

"I'll tell you what's different. I've never heard you talk about her like this..... and you never skipped a chance to make love with me to stay home and screw your wife. That's what you did, isn't it?"

Larry lowered his head. "Yes."

"What are you saying to me? Are we finished?"

He clasped her knee with his right hand and squeezed as hard as he could. "What the hell are you talking about?"

"Damn it, you haven't given me many details, but it's pretty obvious you and your wife have been trying to screw each other to death."

He tried not to laugh, but he couldn't stop himself. "Well, you've got that part right, but you've got everything else ass backwards."

"What do you mean?" she asked, now genuinely confused.

Releasing his grip on her knee he gently took hold of her hand. "What I'm saying is that it's you I want, not my wife. I want to be with you."

Her eyes brimmed with tears. "I don't understand."

Picking up a scarf lying on her lap and softly wiping the tears from her eyes, he said, "It all makes perfect sense to me. I admit I've enjoyed having sex with Vivian over the past couple of weeks, but that's not what's important. What's important is all the years you've been there for me: when she was so drunk she couldn't stand up, you were there for me; when she was horrible to Rachel you were the one who helped me figure out what to do. You're the one I can talk to; I've never been able to talk to my wife. I've always tried to convince myself that I love both of you, but the truth is that I love only you. If I did love my wife, I loved her out of guilt." Momentarily distracted by a chorus of loud screams from the basketball court as one of the players made an especially difficult shot, he paused. "And as far as the sex goes, there's nothing she can possibly do that can make me feel the way you do when we're making love. I could stop having sex with Vivian today and never miss it, but the thought of never making love to you again is something I couldn't deal with."

"If that's true, why did you cancel out on me to have sex with her?"

"After seventeen years of my wife not being interested in me, it sorta threw me for a loop. I hate to admit it, but I think it was an ego thing."

"I practically drool all over you every time I'm with you. Don't I make you feel sexy?"

Larry ran his right hand along the inside of her thigh. "Of course you do, I love the way you make me feel, but it's such a downer when you live with a woman and she approaches sex like it was a household chore."

"So you mean nothing is going to change between us."

"That's not what I mean at all. Everything is going to change......... I'm going to leave Vivian; I want to spend the rest of my life with you. I want that more than I've ever wanted anything.... That's what I've always wanted, I just never admitted it to myself."

Barbara tried to speak, but the words wouldn't come out.

"The only thing that has kept me with her all these years was the guilt. I didn't think she could function without me and I felt responsible, but these past couple of weeks have convinced me she can make it on her own."

Barbara flung her arms around him, kissing him long and deeply. They became lost in the kiss, oblivious to their surroundings; it went on and on..... Then as if from the bottom of a deep well, a distracting sound grew louder and louder. Becoming clearer now, the sound rose to a steady chant, "Go! Go! Go! Go! Go! Go! Go!..........." Breaking off their kiss, they were startled to see the basketball players, not on the court, but at the edge of the stands looking directly at them and being urged on in their cheers by a young black player with a shaved head. With the kiss over, the players screamed and yelled exuberantly, exchanged congratulatory high fives and returned to the court.

They sat stiffly in their seats, with red faces, smiling at one another, Larry finally saying, "That kiss was just like the very first one you ever gave me, the one at Mrs. K's more than seventeen years ago."

Barbara instinctively started to lift her hand to her chest, but stopped herself. Her expression was different than he had ever seen; it was an expression with a meaning of which he was unsure.

"I didn't mean to upset you."

"It's okay, I just need a few minutes to let all this sink in." She gently stroked the side of his face and reminisced, "I hadn't thought about that first kiss for a long time."

Chapter 12

Larry had just returned to his office from a lunchtime meeting with several of his staff. They had gotten wind of a rumor that NSF had just received a fifty million dollar budget augmentation that had not yet been allocated to any specific program. If true, there would be intense competition for the funds from programs as diverse as Larry's astronomy department to geological studies of Antarctica.

During the meeting Larry and his staff had developed some ideas on how best to argue that the astronomy department should be allocated a sizable share of the money, but he was disappointed, none of the arguments were all that persuasive. As he sat at his desk going over his notes from the meeting, Jerry Lynch, the young staff member with the penchant for double-breasted suits, burst into his office.

"Larry, I just thought of another angle we might play."

"What's that?"

"I was thinking that with all the good press NASA is getting after fixing the Hubble telescope, maybe we can make that work to our advantage. If we can develop a program of coordinated ground observations with the new and improved Hubble, maybe we could garner some of that favorable press for ourselves. And if we convince upper management we can make NSF look good, I think they'll give us some money."

Larry scratched his chin thoughtfully. "For once in your life, I think one of your half-ass ideas makes sense. In fact, I think...." he stopped in mid-sentence as his phone

rang. "Wait a minute Jerry, let me get rid of this call......
Astronomy Department, Larry Webster speaking."

An extremely excited Vivian was on the other end
of the line. "Larry, the most amazing thing has happened."

"Vivian, I'll call you back in a few minutes, I'm in
the middle of something."

"No Larry, please, I need to talk with you now."

With a sneer of mild disgust Larry replied, "Okay,
okay, just give me a second." He covered the phone's
speaker with his hand. "Jerry, I think that's a great idea, a
real winner. I need to take care of this call now, so go
ahead and get in touch with the NASA people on the
Hubble project and set up a meeting. I'm sure they'll be
interested in working with us. They're always looking to
hype their programs."

Jerry Lynch looked up at the ceiling and held his
hands aloft. "He likes my idea." With his hands still held
skyward he turned and marched out of the room, again
triumphantly proclaiming, "He likes my idea."

"Vivian, I'm back. Now what's so important?"

"You're not going to believe this."

"Try me," he barked.

"Rachel has been accepted by Harvard!"

Her scream was so loud Larry jerked the phone
away from his ear, but quickly brought it back. "What?"

"I said Rachel was accepted by Harvard!"

"Where did you hear this?"

"I didn't hear it anywhere, I have the letter in my
hand right now."

"Are you sure you're interpreting the letter
properly?"

"For Christ sakes, I think I know how to read!"

"What does it say?"

"It says she got accepted."

"Vivian, this can't be. What does the letter say, exactly."

"It says, Dear Ms. Webster. It gives me great pleasure to inform you the admissions board of Harvard University has ruled favorably on your application for enrollment. Then it says some other stuff, and at the bottom it says, I congratulate you on your acceptance to Harvard University." Vivian began speaking faster and faster and louder and louder.   "And it says she'll receive further information about...., hell, I don't know about what. I can't read it my hands are shaking so much. There's some kinda form for her to sign and return."

"Who signed the letter?"

"Let me put it on the table so I can hold it still, here, that's better. It's signed by a Dr. Reginald Devonshire, Dean of Admissions."

"Is it on Harvard letterhead?"

"Of course it is. Can't you get it through your thick skull this is the real thing. It's a real letter from Harvard and she's really been accepted."

After a long pause Larry replied somberly, "Vivian, it has to be a mistake. She couldn't possibly get into Harvard."

"But she scored 1490 on her SATs."

"I know that's a great score, but those kind of scores are a dime a dozen at Harvard. You've also got to have the grades and the outside activities and she doesn't have either. Believe me, you don't get turned down by Duke, Hopkins and Virginia and then get accepted by Harvard. I wish to God it was for real, but it has to be a mistake."

"But how could they make a mistake like this?"

"Maybe it's a computer foul up or something, I don't know. What made you open her mail?"

After a long silence Vivian confessed. "Because I assumed it was a rejection letter and I didn't want her to see it, at least not yet. I guess you're right. What are we going to do?"

"Let me get on the phone to Harvard and see what I can find out. How long before Rachel gets home from school?"

"She's going to be late 'cause she's having dinner at Vinnie's."

"Again?"

"He's a good kid and you know it."

"I keep hearing what a great guy he is, even find myself saying it. I just hope we're right. Listen don't say anything to Rachel about the letter. I've got to check this out. I'm going to call this Dean guy. What's his name again?"

"Reginald Devonshire. Sounds very Harvard, doesn't he?"

"Is there a phone number?"

"No, it just says Admissions Department, Harvard University...... Wouldn't it be fantastic if it were somehow true? It would do so much for Rachel's confidence."

"Viv, don't let yourself get so worked up over this. I wish it were true too, but its just gotta be a mistake."

Vivian exhaled so hard through her teeth it sounded like a burst of static over the phone. "All right, but I'm not going to give up hope until we find out for sure."

"Fine. Just don't say anything to Rachel."

Larry ran his right hand up his face and through his hair. It felt strange to do it with just one hand; he couldn't wait to get the cast off. Rocking back in his chair he caught sight of Jerry Lynch standing in the doorway of his office.

"Still trying to unlock the mysteries of the universe, huh Dr. Webster?"

"Yeah, something like that."

Ronnie Kinsley

"Hey, I just got off the phone with the NASA people. They really like the idea and want to meet with us over there in an hour. If we don't do it now, the Hubble Project Scientist disappears for a couple of weeks over the holidays."

"Go ahead without me. I have some things to check out this afternoon, you can handle this."

Jerry Lynch looked skyward, raised his arms high, turned and pranced away. "He likes my idea..... and now he trusts me."

After a quick call to the Massachusetts information operator, Larry was on the phone with Harvard's general information receptionist. "I would like to speak with Dr. Reginald Devonshire, Dean of Admissions."

"One moment please."

Larry punched the speaker button on his phone, put the receiver down, and proceeded to strum the fingers of his right hand on the desk as a female voice with a heavy New England accent answered, "Harvard Admissions."

"Hello, this is Dr. Larry Webster of the National Science Foundation. Could I please speak with Dr. Devonshire?"

"Dr. Devonshire is off for the holidays and won't be back in the office until the third of January. Is there anything I can help you with? I'm Mrs. Alderman, Dr. Devonshire's assistant."

"Is there any way I can get in touch with Dr. Devonshire?"

"Not unless you can figure out how to find his sailboat somewhere in the Gulf of Mexico."

"Okay, maybe you can help me. My daughter just received her acceptance letter from Harvard and I'm afraid you've made a mistake. I'm sure her acceptance is an error."

118

"Dr. Webster, I'm sure you must realize how difficult it is to get into Harvard. We have to be extremely selective. There are many, many outstanding candidates who are not accepted. Given that your daughter has the self confidence to have applied..."

Larry interrupted. "Excuse me please, I don't think you understand..."

"But Dr. Webster I do understand what a disappointment this can..."

"Please be quiet and listen to me. I apologize for being so abrupt, but you don't understand. My daughter did get accepted. I repeat, she just received a letter of acceptance from Harvard. I believe you intended to send her a rejection letter, I think you made a mistake."

"Well Dr. Webster, we get plenty of calls from disappointed parents of children who don't get accepted. But this is the first call we've ever received from a parent, whose child did get accepted, who insists that we made a mistake. Now, what's your daughter's name?"

"Rachel. Rachel Webster."

"Give me a few minutes to retrieve the file from our computer and I'll call you back. What's your number?"

"I'd rather just hang on."

"Suit yourself, but it's going to take a while, I just shut the system down right before you called."

He tried to go through the mail in his in-basket, but it was no use, he couldn't even focus his eyes well enough to read, so he just sat there, closed his eyes and tried to relax. Although it seemed an hour, it was less than five minutes when Mrs. Alderman came back on the line. "Dr. Webster, are you still there?"

"Yes."

"Well, I pulled up your daughter's file. She is Rachel Webster of Columbia, Maryland, social security number 214-04-9919?"

"Yes."

"Well, she's been accepted to Harvard."

"Mrs. Alderman, if we tell Rachel she's been accepted to Harvard and then she finds out it's a mistake, she'll be devastated."

"You mean she doesn't know? The letter was sent to her, not you."

"The letter came in the mail today and my wife opened it a few minutes ago. Rachel isn't home from school yet."

"You tell her that Maggie from the admissions department says congratulations."

"Isn't there any way I can speak with Dr. Devonshire?"

"Dr. Webster, I've worked in this department for twenty-three years. We have never, I repeat never, made a mistake of this nature. Our process is as close to foolproof as it can get. I checked your daughter's file, and everything is in order. The approval of the evaluation panel, reference checks, interview summaries, the independent review and certification, and Dr. Devonshire's personal approval."

"But Mrs. Alderman, I mean Maggie, is the evaluation process always the same? Does Dr. Devonshire always..."

"Dr. Webster, I'm sorry, but I have to go. I've got to get out of here and finish my Christmas shopping. I suggest you and your wife take that daughter of yours out this evening and celebrate. It's not every day someone in the family gets accepted to Harvard. Now good bye."

Chapter 13

Larry shoveled the last of his Cheerios into his mouth when he heard what sounded like a buffalo stampede charging down the hallway. Looking up from the Baltimore Sun sports page he caught a blur of Rachel bounding towards the refrigerator. Despite a wrinkled black turtle neck sweater and faded jeans with a large gaping hole over one knee, she somehow looked neater than normal.

"Hi Dad. Where's Mom?"

"She went to the office for a few minutes to pick up some blank contract forms. She's showing a house tomorrow, and thinks she might make a sale."

Rachel scrunched up her face and tilted her head at an angle. "She's showing a house on Christmas day?"

"Got my days mixed up, this is Christmas Eve isn't it? She's showing the house on Sunday, the day after Christmas."

"Mom's really looking good lately, isn't she?"

"Yeah she is, and I'm sure you know why. When the two of you aren't at each other's throats, it's as if the weight of the world is off her shoulders. I hope you can keep it up."

Rachel opened the refrigerator door, took out an opened carton of orange juice and slurped down a big mouthful. "We can and we will," she replied as she retrieved a glass from the cabinet and filled it with juice.

"Why would you take a drink from the carton and then pour the juice in a glass?"

Rachel plopped the glass on the kitchen counter and ran her hands up her face and back over her hair. "I wanted to make sure it tasted okay before I went to the trouble of getting a glass." She picked up the glass and guzzled it empty. "What did ya think of my imitation?"

"Your imitation of what?"

"Of you."

"What imitation of me?"

"When you do this." With an exaggerated flair she once again rubbed her hands over her face and back over her hair.

"I do that?"

"Only about a hundred times a day."

"Do I really?"

"Yes, you really do."

Larry smiled. "Your mother isn't the only one who is looking good."

"I've been jogging with Vinnie for the past month or so. I've lost eight pounds and I feel great."

"I didn't know you had started running."

"Vinnie says I have natural endurance."

"He does, does he."

"Gotta roll, see you this evening," Rachel said as she hoisted a backpack over her shoulder.

"Wait a minute, where are you going?"

"Over to Vinnie's, we're gonna study."

"It's Christmas Eve, I know damn well you're not going to be studying."

"Well, it's not exactly studying, I gotta help him with a project he's working on."

"What kind of project?"

Ignoring his question she replied, "Bye," and darted down the hall and out the door.

Larry propped his right elbow on the table, rested his chin in his palm, and said aloud to himself, "Is it possible she could really be going to Harvard next year? No, it's not possible, it has to be a mistake."

He rinsed off his cereal bowl, and placed it in the dishwasher. Then he peeled off a yellow sticky from its pad and scribbled, "Vivian, Gone to do some last minute Xmas shopping. Back around noon. Love, Larry." Glancing up at the kitchen clock and noticing it was 9:15 a.m., later than he thought, he scratched out noon and wrote one o'clock.

Driving up the hill on Little Patuxent Parkway, the Columbia Mall came into sight on the right side of the road. Going past the entrance to the mall parking lot, he turned left into a lot behind an office complex across the street from the mall.

Keeping his head down, avoiding the eyes of the young couple coming toward him, he made his way through the lobby of the Columbia Inn to the elevator. Stopping at room 344, stealing a glance in both directions, he bent over and ran his fingers under the edge of the door and picked up a key.

Barbara Reilly, decked out in a red lace bra and matching panties, was stretched out on the bed, eating a blueberry muffin and watching television. She invited him to her with outstretched arms as he clicked off the television with the remote. Still fully clothed he awkwardly lowered himself onto her, not quite sure of what to do with his immobile left arm, but somehow managing to lick the muffin crumbs from her chest.

"How's this going to work with that arm of yours?"

"I'll figure out what to do."

"Oh yeah, I forgot, you've been getting lots of practice," Barbara mocked in obvious reference to his wife's newly resurgent interest in sex.

He lifted his head. "Hey, knock it off."

"Any more orders?"

"Yes, one more order. I want another kiss, like the one at Cole Field House and the one at Mrs. K's." She pulled him to her and carried out his order.

For the next two hours they blocked out the rest of the world. Over the years they had developed a special rhythm and harmony to their lovemaking, not a rhythm in the sense of movement, but a rhythm in the sense of a shared state of mind. Their lovemaking benefited from the advantages of a physical relationship sustained over an extended period of time: each totally at ease with their shared intimacy; each precisely attuned to the physical intricacies and proclivities of the other's body; and each capable of giving completely of themselves for the pleasure of the other. The limitations in their relationship also provided advantages. Unable to have each other as often as they wanted, and constrained from sharing other aspects of their lives, they never took one another for granted. Their encounters were always imbued with a sense of youthful excitement, an excitement that didn't diminish with time.

Their lovemaking was especially energetic on this morning, the level of sexual energy always seeming to be proportional to the amount of emotional tension between them, and with recent events that tension had been very high. In the afterglow, lying on their sides, breathing deeply in unison with one another, her back against his chest, their knees bent at the same angle, they fit perfectly together like two spoons.

Barbara nuzzled her butt even closer, squeezing away any empty space between them. "What time do we have to be out of here?"

"Check out time is at noon."

She grasped his right hand, guided it across her body and pressed it between her breasts. "What do you think it's going to be like when we're together all the time?"

"What do you mean?"

"We've been seeing one another forever, but almost never for more than a few hours at a time, and now in about two months we're going to be living together, twenty-four hours a day."

"It's not like we don't know each other," Larry said.

"Do we? Do we really know one another?"

"Of course we do. Why would you ask that?"

Barbara didn't say anything.

Larry said, "I lead this double life and no one but you knows the real me. The only time I can be me is when I'm with you. Sometimes when we're apart I think I'm going to explode because there's no one I can be honest with. Isn't that the way that you feel too?"

Barbara shook her head up and down in agreement, and then brought his hand to her lips and kissed it. "When are you going to tell Vivian about us, about me going to Chile with you?"

"When are you going to tell your husband?"

"I don't know. I need to know when you're going to tell her."

"I haven't even mustered the courage to tell her I'm going to Chile yet, much less tell her another woman is coming with me."

She rolled over, bringing her eyes just a few inches from his. "You are going to tell her about me, aren't you?"

"Yes, I'm going to tell her. I know I can't wait until I'm walking out the door, but I don't want to tell her before I have to."

"And when's that going to be?"

"I'll tell her about Chile soon, after Christmas sometime. But telling her about you, that I'm leaving her, that's going to be devastating for her. I'll wait until about two weeks before we leave, that should be enough time to get things worked out."

"Things? What things?"

"I haven't thought any of this through, but I guess we should split up the finances, everything is in both of our names. I just can't walk away from Vivian and Rachel, they're going to need a lot of financial help. Vivian barely made ten thousand dollars this year selling real estate."

"But she hardly worked. It's going to be her responsibility to support herself."

"Listen Barbara, I know she's capable of making a lot more, and I expect she will based on what she's accomplished these past couple of weeks. But Vivian and Rachel have never had to worry about money."

"I'm sorry, you're right. It's just that I'm a nervous wreck over this whole situation."

"I know what you mean," Larry said, stroking the side of her face with his unencumbered right hand.

Barbara decided to change the subject. "What are you going to tell Rachel about Harvard?"

"Vivian wants to go ahead and tell her, but the more I think about it the more I'm convinced they made a mistake. Vivian has agreed we won't say anything until I've spoken personally to the Director of Admissions. That won't be until after the New Year."

"What if they didn't make a mistake and she really has been accepted?"

"Look, I've been through this a dozen times with Vivian. They made a mistake! If by some miracle the world has been turned upside down and she really did get accepted, then, yes, I guess she'll be going to Harvard."

Barbara sat upright leaning against the headboard of the bed. "It's just that...... I'm sorry I brought it up."

"We can't tell her she's been accepted only to find out it's a mistake, that's a disappointment Rachel just couldn't handle."

Larry twisted the clock on the nightstand so he could see the time. "Damn, it's ten of twelve, I wish we had another hour," he whined as he ran his hand up her thigh and rubbed suggestively. "I know you're nervous because we have a lot of things to work out. When do you get back in town?"

"We'll be flying back from John's parents on Sunday the second."

"All right then, let's get together on Tuesday the fourth. We can meet at Union Station for lunch and start figuring out what we need to do and when to do it. Okay?"

"Okay."

Larry hoofed it across the pedestrian overpass spanning the Little Patuxent Parkway to the Columbia Mall and went into Hecht's department store. Hastily, he picked out Christmas presents for Vivian: a sweater, a necklace and matching earrings, and a bottle of perfume. Everything was finished in less than half an hour. Of course if asked, his story would be that he spent the entire morning at the mall agonizing over gift selections.

Leaving the gifts in the trunk of the Taurus, Larry eased in the front door and down the hallway to find Vivian with her back to him bent over the kitchen table, gathering up papers and stashing them in her briefcase. Hearing his approach she spun around.

"Oh my God!" Larry shrieked.

With a smile that would light up several Christmas trees, Vivian swished her hands alongside her head. "I had it done this morning. Do you like it, it's not too blond is it?"

With bulging eyes, Larry couldn't help but shout, "You look great, it makes you look....."

Vivian swung her head around, her rejuvenated blond hair waving about gracefully. "Go ahead, say it. It makes me look ten years younger, doesn't it."

"Fifteen," countered Larry incredulously.

Vivian giggled as she danced about the kitchen. "Fifteen, all right! That's what I feel like, like I'm fifteen years younger."

As Vivian twirled about, just for an instant Larry saw the face of the girl playing the pinball machine at the ski lodge. Almost unconsciously he remarked, "My God, you look just like......"

"I look just like what?" Vivian asked excitedly.

"Just like your original color. It looks just like your original color."

"I was so scared it was going to look stupid."

"It looks fantastic," Larry replied as calmness returned to his voice.

"Thanks. Where have you been all morning, anyway?"

"Shopping. Didn't you see my note?"

"What note?"

He picked up the yellow stickie from the counter and stuck it on his nose.

"It says you'll be back at one o'clock. You're late, it's twenty after one."

"Sorry, I'll do better next time," he replied as the note fell from his nose and fluttered to the floor.

"Where's that daughter of yours?" asked Vivian.

"Where else, she's at Vinnie's. You'd think they would give it a rest once in a while."

With her eyes brightening and her smile widening Vivian chirped, "Speaking of not giving it a rest, why don't we go upstairs and get comfortable."

Not yet recovered from his morning session with Barbara, he suggested, "Why don't we go get the groceries for dinner now and then we can take our time when we get back."

With a look of mischief Vivian countered, "How about just a quickie and then we can go to Safeway?"

"Let's wait 'til later so we're not rushed."

"Hmmh," she relented, snapping her fingers to emphasize her disappointment.

Christmas Eve was always the highpoint of the holiday season for the Websters; Larry and Vivian grocery shopping and preparing dinner together, and Vivian and Rachel obeying an unwritten rule to be civil to one another. It was Christmas day when things usually went to hell, but hopefully, with Rachel and Vivian having reached equilibrium in their relationship, this year would be vastly different.

The grocery store was less than two miles from their house. Vivian was hot to get home, keeping the shopping cart on full throttle as she zoomed down the aisles grabbing items from the shelves - steamed clams for an appetizer, fresh vegetables for a salad, grilled salmon steaks with rice and green beans for the main course, and Ben & Jerry's Cherry Garcia ice cream for dessert. Fortunately for Larry, the store was mobbed with last minute shoppers, forcing them to wait in the check out line for almost thirty minutes, his libido strengthening with each passing moment.

By the time they got home he was able to make love to Vivian enthusiastically. How many more times would they make love? Should he gradually cool off the sexual firestorm raging between them or just go cold turkey once he told her about Chile, about Barbara? Her renewed youthful look certainly wasn't a motivator to cool things off just yet. She snuggled close as he draped his arm across her body, and she purred, "I can't remember the last time I was this happy."

It was almost two hours later, after another round of lovemaking, that they finally rose from bed, showered and dressed casually, Larry in jeans and a green flannel shirt, Vivian in jeans and a black turtleneck.

Larry couldn't help but watch as Vivian brushed her wonderfully blond hair. "You look beautiful."

The chiming of the clock diverted his thoughts. "Damn, six o'clock and Rachel isn't home yet."

"She called while you were in the shower, said she and Vinnie would be here at seven."

For the next hour they busied themselves preparing dinner. Without clearly defined responsibilities they constantly bumped into one another and playfully argued about the precise oven temperature, the right thickness to slice the cucumbers, and the correct amount of seasoning for the fish.

Watching Vivian flit around the kitchen and back and forth to the dining room reminded Larry of what had attracted him to her in the first place, not just her beauty, but also her spirit and enthusiasm, personal attributes she had kept hidden all these years. He recalled a summer day long ago when some friends had invited them out on the Severn River for a day of water skiing. Vivian had never skied before and the boat's motor was underpowered making it very difficult for a skier to be pulled to the surface, an almost impossible situation for a first time skier. Vivian persisted repeatedly in her efforts, exerting herself to near exhaustion, but was unable to get up. With everyone scolding her to call it a day, she pleaded for just three more tries. On her last attempt, with darkness setting in, she made it to her feet and skied for almost an hour by moonlight.

Despite these sentimental thoughts, the truth of the matter was he loved Barbara Reilly more than he had ever loved Vivian. Soon he would have to tell her, but not now.

It wasn't until after eight o'clock that Rachel and Vinnie barged through the front door, with Vinnie stamping his feet and rubbing his hands together. "It's freezing out there," he said to no one in particular, then catching sight of Vivian he let out a piercing, "Wow!"

"Vinnie, what was that all about? Oh my God Mom! Is that you?" screeched Rachel.

"Yes, it's me."

"You look like a fox! Doesn't she look like a fox?"

Vinnie hunched his shoulders, glancing first at Rachel and then Vivian, but opted to remain silent.

Vivian laughed. "It's okay Vinnie if you don't think I look like a fox."

Vinnie tilted his head forward, his eyes looking up at a steep angle. "Actually, I think you look like a mega-fox Mrs. Webster."

Vivian blushed, her face turning flamingo pink. "I'm going to assume that was a compliment. Now let's get this show on the road, you two are late, big time."

Larry was crouched in front of a kitchen cabinet retrieving salad bowls when he looked up to greet Rachel with muted sarcasm. "I imagine you've had an exciting day."

Fighting through the frustration of her father's constant jibes Rachel replied, "As a matter of fact I had a wonderfully exciting day, I'll tell you all about it sometime."

Raising his eyebrows, Larry continued to needle his daughter, "Oh yeah, I bet you'll tell me every last detail."

Vinnie, still rubbing his hands for warmth, interjected, "Hi Dr. Webster..... and Merry Christmas."

Everyone's attention immediately turned to Larry in anticipation of his returning Vinnie's greeting, but he made them wait, staring at Vinnie's long black pony tail. "Don't call me Dr. Webster, I prefer to be called Larry."

Since the comment had been delivered in a seemingly unfriendly manner, Vinnie simply said, "Okay."

Rachel tapped Vivian on the shoulder. "Can I see you for a minute in my room? I want to show you something."

"Of course."

They were gone for only a few minutes, Larry busying himself with the last of the salad preparations and not even acknowledging Vinnie who stood stiffly leaning against the wall painfully aware of the silence, but unable to think of any offering to assuage the tension.

Vinnie was grateful when they returned, and Vivian, sensing that things were heading in the wrong direction, broke the ice. "Since you guys are a bit late and none of us drink alcohol, we can get right to the food."

Larry just wouldn't let up. "Is that right Vinnie, you don't drink?"

With Vinnie becoming flustered, Rachel shot back. "That's right, he doesn't drink, he doesn't smoke, and he doesn't do drugs. Anything else you need to know about the boy I love? If not, I suggest we eat. Vinnie and I are hungry, we didn't have lunch today."

Pressing his assault Larry replied smugly, "Oh, you were too busy to stop for lunch."

Tears welled up in Rachel's eyes as she awkwardly cleared her throat. "Daddy, I want you to stop it!" she screamed. "I know what you keep insinuating and I don't like it. I'm almost eighteen years old and I've taken control of my life for the first time. When I was a basket case you always helped me, but now that I'm feeling better about myself you act like you resent me for it."

The maturity of his daughter's words made clear the immaturity of his own. Not fully understanding why he was acting as he was, but knowing he had to stop, Larry simply apologized, "I'm sorry. Please forgive me."

Vivian put her arm around Larry. "Rachel's right darling, but this is hard on you, so much is changing in this family and it's happening so fast. " Then nodding to Rachel and Vinnie she said, "Let's go eat that fish, even though he did put too much seasoning on it."

In an effort to lessen the tension he had created, Larry protested, "It's got just the right amount of seasoning."

With that they sat down to eat. For several minutes there was a painful silence, each overly concerned about not saying the wrong thing. It was Vinnie who finally spoke up. "This is really an outstanding meal, Mrs. Webster."

"Thank you, I'm glad you like it."

"Mom's hair looks great, doesn't it Dad?"

"Yes it really does."

After another extended silence Rachel blurted out, "Vinnie just got accepted to Stanford. Duke and Stanford, that's really something. I'm so proud of him."

The flamingo pink from Vivian's face earlier in the evening made its way to Vinnie as he hid his face in his rice, not looking up even when Vivian asked, "Did you apply to any other schools?"

"I applied to Maryland as a back-up, but I guess I don't need that now," Vinnie replied, immediately turning to Rachel. "I'm sorry, I didn't mean it that way."

"That's okay, Maryland was my back-up too and I'm glad I have it. It might not be Stanford, but it's a good school," Rachel replied with forced enthusiasm.

"But you still haven't heard from Harvard," Vinnie reminded as he placed his hand on top of Rachel's.

"That's such a long shot...... I've just about given up hope."

Larry, afraid Vivian might spill the beans, gave her a quick kick beneath the table and met her eyes sternly. Vivian glowered back, sending the message she didn't agree with him on not telling Rachel about the letter from

Harvard. While he was very much at odds with Vivian on this point, Larry was beginning to see what Vivian had already seen, the genuine feelings and consideration Vinnie had for Rachel. Maybe he was being too judgmental about his intentions, maybe he should give this young man a chance. "What is it again that you want to major in Vinnie?"

"I haven't absolutely decided, but I'm leaning towards biomedical engineering. I think it's an exciting field."

"How's the money in that field?" Larry blundered, immediately feeling stupid he had done so.

"I really don't know, I guess it's okay. I just think its something I'll enjoy doing."

Rachel's pride in this young man was obvious and Larry began to see that it was deserved. "Duke or Stanford - that's a tough choice. Which one are you leaning toward?"

"I haven't made up my mind yet. Both schools have excellent biomedical programs and both are offering some limited financial aid... Duke's offering the most, if I commit to running cross-country. I just have to sit down and make an apples to apples comparison. But I guess I'm leaning toward Duke."

Rachel then added her two cents. "Of course Duke's a lot closer. It's only about a six hour drive from Maryland."

Larry deduced, "I think my daughter wants you to choose Duke."

"So does my mom and dad."

Vivian added, "You can't go wrong with either school, but I hope you pick Duke too."

"Thank you, Mrs. Webster."

"Now who wants some Cherry Garcia?" Vivian asked.

"Why don't we wait until later? Is that okay with you Dad?" Rachel replied with a sense of excitement building in her voice.

"Yeah, that's okay."

"Can I do it now Mom?" Rachel asked, bouncing in her seat like a five year old.

"Yes, I think now would be a good time."

"A good time for what?" Larry asked.

"Daddy, I want to give you your Christmas present. Follow me, we're going down to the basement."

"Shouldn't you wait until Christmas morning to give me the present?"

"No, it's not a morning kind of present. Now come on."

With that, the four of them got up and traipsed down the stairs to the basement.

"Let's pick up the pace," Rachel said excitedly as she led them to the sliding glass door, which opened to the patio in the backyard.

"Everyone put on their coats," Rachel ordered as she pointed to the coats she had obviously smuggled into the basement.

"We're going outside?" Larry protested.

"Now who was it that said I didn't have a smart father?" Rachel mocked with obvious enjoyment. "Dad, there's one other thing you have to put on," she said as she handed her father a blindfold.

"Are you really going to make me wear this?"

"Yes."

Rachel clasped her father's hand as Vivian adjusted the blindfold over Larry's eyes. Vinnie opened the door, pulled out a flashlight from his coat pocket and lit the way as Rachel led her father slowly across the patio, Vivian following close behind.

"It's beautiful," Vivian said.

Caught up in the excitement and literally feeling as curious as a kid on Christmas Eve Larry shouted, "What is it? What is it?"

Rachel continued to lead her father slowly across the patio. "Be patient, you're about to find out. Now take two more steps. That's it, stop."

"Can I look now?"

"Not yet, take one more step..... Okay good, now don't take any more steps."

"Here Mrs. Webster," Vinnie said as he handed her the flashlight. "Shine it right here."

Rachel took over again. "Now Dad, we want you to slowly bend over. Vinnie and I are going to help guide your head."

"I don't have the slightest idea what's going on."

"Good, that's the idea. Now move your head just a couple more inches." Larry felt his forehead lightly bump against something hard and cold. "Okay stop. Now I'm going to move your head just another smidge...... That's it, perfect."

Vinnie provided the final instructions. "Now Dr. Webster, I'm going to remove the blindfold. I want you to keep your left eye closed but open your right eye. Okay, now!"

Larry did as instructed. His head bobbed and what he saw didn't register, but then he steadied himself, holding on to Vinnie's arm for balance. And then there it was, the Andromeda Galaxy. He was looking through a telescope.

With childish glee he shouted out, "It's M31. Wow, it's spectacular."

"What's M31?" Vivian whispered into Vinnie's ear.

"That's the scientific designation for the Andromeda Galaxy. Its about two million light years away."

Larry could clearly see the galaxy's spiral shape, its dark band of dust and many of its individual stars.

"Dr. Webster can you see Gamma?"

"Perfectly!"

"What's Gamma?" Vivian asked excitedly.

This time Rachel answered. "It's a double star. The primary, the big star, is a golden yellow color and its companion is a smaller blue star."

Now Vinnie was having trouble controlling his excitement. "Can you see Pi? That's another double star, Mrs. Webster."

Larry was unable to answer because his body was shaking so much.

"Daddy, what is it? What's wrong?"

Larry struggled to get words out of his mouth, pausing for several short breaths. "Nothing's wrong...... I've looked at this galaxy a hundred times. I've seen it through the world's greatest telescopes, I've seen images from satellites...... But it has never looked so beautiful to me."

He stepped back and took the flashlight from Vivian. "Now let me take a look at this thing..... This is a cassegrain telescope."

"Yes it is," replied Rachel.

"It's huge. What is it, an eight inch aperture?"

"Nine inch."

"How could you possibly buy me this telescope? It had to cost three or four thousand dollars."

"I didn't buy it, I made it. I mean Vinnie and I did. We've been working on it for almost four months. All those times I said we were studying, we were really working on the telescope."

"You made it," Larry declared in astonishment.

"Well sort of. We had a machine shop in Baltimore make the tube and the light baffle. I bought a used equatorial mount from an ad in the newspaper. I ordered the optics from a small company in Russia. We did make the tripod from scratch. Then we assembled everything and did all the optical alignments in Vinnie's basement."

"You did all this by yourselves? That's unbelievable."

"Well we did get some help from Dr. Paul Ryland, he's an astronomer like you. We were having trouble aligning the optics and he helped us solve the problem. He spent the whole day with us a couple of Saturdays ago."

"Who's he and where did you meet him?"

"He interviews students from this area who apply to Harvard. He came to school to see me back in October and I told him about the telescope. He has a Ph.D. from Harvard in Astronomy and offered to help. I didn't want to ask anyone for help, except Vinnie of course, but when we got stuck I called him and he came right out and fixed the problem."

"I don't know him. Where does he work?"

"I forget the name of the company. They do contract work for NASA."

Vivian tried not to sound too excited. "Rachel you were interviewed for Harvard. Why didn't you tell us about that?"

"I don't know. I guess I didn't want to make a big deal of it."

But Vivian couldn't control her excitement. "Do they interview everyone who applies?"

"I don't know, but I don't think so."

"Well what did he say to you?"

"About what?"

"About your chances of being accepted?"

"He just said Harvard was the most selective university in the country. He wished me luck, that was about it."

"What about when you saw him a couple of weeks ago, did he say anything then?"

"He asked me if I had heard anything yet, I told him no..... Mom, would you like to look through the telescope? Vinnie and I have already used it quite a bit the past few nights."

"Yes I would, but first I want to clear off some of the dishes from the table. Want to give me a hand?"

"Sure."

Larry couldn't contain the miser in himself any longer. "Rachel I've just got to ask. How much did it cost you to make the telescope?"

"Five hundred and twenty-six dollars. Of course we put a lot of labor into it," Rachel stated concisely and with obvious pride.

"That's fantastic for an instrument of this quality."

"The most expensive thing was the optics. They cost over three hundred dollars. Remember that UPS box you asked me about, that was the optics."

"The UPS box," Larry mumbled, feeling as if the air had been sucked from his lungs. He felt light headed and had to steady himself against Vinnie to keep from falling, and winced with pain as Vivian gave him a solid kick on the shin.

"Mom, why did you do that?"

"Oh, it's just a little inside joke between your father and me. Come on inside and help me with the dishes."

Vinnie waited until Rachel and her mother were inside. "Dr. Webster, I need to talk to you about something."

Larry stood motionless, his mind tumbling out of control - incredible relief over the UPS box and incredible regret over his attitude toward Rachel and Vinnie.

"Dr. Webster."

"Huh?"

"I want to talk to you about something."

"I told you to call me Larry."

"With what I'm about to talk about sir, I'd prefer to call you Dr. Webster."

"Okay, what is it?"

"This is not easy for me to say."

"Whatever it is, just say it."

"Okay, I'll try..... I know you think Rachel and I are having sex, but you're wrong..... I've never......." Vinnie stopped to clear his throat. "I've never had sex. I love Rachel. I'd never make her do anything before she's ready." Vinnie waited for a response, but there was none. "Sir, I know what happened to Rachel when she was fourteen and got involved with that guy. I know you're worried she could be hurt like that again, but I swear to God I would never hurt her. Please believe me, and have faith in Rachel, she's a wonderful person." Again there was no reply. "Dr. Webster, please don't say anything to Rachel about this, she'd kill me."

Larry took a step toward Vinnie and extended his hand. "Thank you, that took an incredible amount of courage. And don't call me Dr. Webster, or sir, ever again, call me Larry, no matter what you want to talk about."

Before Vinnie could reply, both men were startled out of their skins as the basement sliding glass door was jerked open with a loud bang. Rachel came screaming out of the door. "Oh my God! I can't believe it! Oh my God! Oh my God!"

As she ran around and around the patio Vinnie tried to stop her. "Rachel, what is it? What is it?"

"I can't believe it! I can't believe it! "

"What is it? What's going on?" shouted Vinnie.

Completely oblivious to Vinnie's frustration, Rachel continued to run about and scream incoherently.

"Dr. Webster, I mean Larry, do you know what's going on?"

"Yes."

"Well, what is it?"

"I think her mother just told her she's been accepted to Harvard."

"Holy shit!" Vinnie screamed as he joined Rachel in chaotic laps around the patio, their paths finally intersecting, forcing them to stop and face one another. "Is it really true? You've been accepted to Harvard?"

Maniacally running in place, her feet pounding the patio, Rachel squealed, "Yes! Yes! Yes! I've been accepted to Harvard!" She vaulted into Vinnie's arms, wrapping her legs about him as he spun around and around with her glued to his body.

"Watch my telescope!" Larry shouted as he could no longer prevent himself from enjoying the moment.

Vinnie dropped Rachel back to her feet and yelled, "Don't worry Larry, if we break it, we'll just build you another one."

Rachel called back over her shoulder, "Don't wait up for us," as the two of them raced off into the night.

Larry turned to Vivian, standing in the doorway, a smile on her face, and the letter from Harvard in her hand.

"So you had to tell her."

"Yep."

"I hope to God it's not a mistake."

"It's not a mistake."

"You better be right."

"I'm right."

"Well, we won't know for sure until I talk to that Dr. Devonshire."

"Don't bother."

"What do you mean?"

"Rachel said she was interviewed personally by Dr. Devonshire over the phone, two different times."

"Oh, my God!   This guy knows Rachel?   He's interviewed her himself and he's the one who approved her acceptance!   Then it's not a mistake!"

"Nope."

Larry rushed to Vivian, kissed her, turned and ran into the darkness. "Rachel! Rachel! Rachel! "

Chapter 14

Rachel awoke early on Christmas morning, the dull grayness of an overcast day barely penetrating the curtains. Groping in the darkness, she found the phone on the nightstand, pulled the covers over her head and wrapped herself into a tight little ball, safe and warm inside her makeshift cocoon. Closing her eyes she visualized the configuration of numbers on her phone - certain about the locations of 1 through 9, but unsure about 0........ in the middle of the fourth row that's where it had to be. Counting and feeling with her fingers she carefully punched in seven digits.

It rang only one time. "Hello."

"Can you talk?"

"Yeah, my parents are still asleep."

"You sure answered the phone awful fast."

"I have it in bed with me. I started to call you, but thought you might still be asleep."

Rachel pulled the covers even tighter around her. "Vinnie, you were wonderful."

"You're just saying that."

"No I'm not, last night was the most wonderful night of my life."

"I guess so, you found out you were accepted to Harvard."

"I'm not talking about that part. I'm talking about the you and me part."

"Are you sure?"

"If you don't stop it I'm going to get angry. I mean didn't you like it?"

"Of course I liked it. I was just so scared I might not be doing the right things."

"Trust me, you did the right things."

"You didn't mind that it was in the back seat of my car?"

Rachel could feel the smile on her face, could feel the warmth flowing through her body. "I love that car."

"You always say you hate my car."

Rachel pressed the pillow against her face to dampen her laughter. "Not anymore, from now on a 1980 Maverick will be my favorite car of all time."

"I always told you it was a great car...... Rachel, don't get mad, but I have to ask. The reason you wanted to do it......, was it because you got accepted to Harvard ?"

"That had nothing to do with it."

"What was it then? After all this time, what made you finally want to?"

"Last night at dinner, you were talking to my dad about college, I don't know what it was, but I just knew I wanted to."

"Is your dad home now? I could come over and talk to him some more."

"Don't push your luck, buddy."

"You know what was weird?"

"What?"

"For me it was like it wasn't really happening, like in a dream. When I woke up this morning, at first, I wasn't sure we had actually done it."

"I sure made an impression on you."

"You know what I mean, don't ya?"

"Yeah, it was like that for me too."

"Rachel, I'm glad you made us wait...... so how long are you going to make us wait until the next time ?"

"Like I said, don't push your luck buddy..... I gotta get going. I want to surprise Mom and Dad with a fancy breakfast."

"Wait a minute, when are we going to talk about Harvard? We didn't talk about it last night, we're not talking about it now, is this not a big deal or what?"

"Would you have preferred we talked about Harvard last night instead of doing what we did?"

"You have a point there."

"Of course I want to talk about it, but I need to let it sink in first. What time are you coming over to exchange our gifts?"

"Sometime after lunch, maybe about two o'clock. But as far as gifts go, you already gave me the best Christmas gift I'll ever get."

"I love you Vinnie."

There was dead silence on the other end of the line.

"Vinnie, are you there?"

"I love you too."

"Oh my God! I can't believe you said that."

"Neither can I. Bye."

Much too warm now, she yanked the covers off and uncoiled her body, stretching her arms over her head and pointing her toes - the room now made much lighter by the brightening sun squeezing its way through a crack in the clouds. Was it all a dream? Harvard? Last night? Vinnie saying he loved her?

"Ooooh," she felt a burning tenderness between her legs as she stretched further. Wait, that meant last night with Vinnie was real, everything had really happened, nothing so uncomfortable had ever felt so good. So how was it possible that just a short time ago she had held a handful of sleeping pills, had almost.......

Bounding from the bed, she was dressed and downstairs in a flash. "Good," she mumbled as she rummaged through the refrigerator, quickly selecting her ingredients. Her hands moved like a blackjack dealer as she diced chunks of ham, green peppers and onions, mixed it all with milk and eggs, and poured everything into the frying pan.

In less than twenty minutes everything was ready - the table neatly set with plates of western omelets and home fries, grapefruits sliced in half, and glasses of orange juice next to steaming cups of coffee, and a Nat King Cole Christmas album, her mother's favorite, on the stereo. With absolutely perfect timing Rachel placed the last knife and fork on the table just as Vivian came downstairs.

"Is Dad awake?"

"He'll be down in just a minute. Something smells good, what is it?"

"I made you and Dad breakfast."

"Great, I could eat an elephant," Larry bellowed as he seemed to appear from nowhere.

"What a lovely breakfast," Vivian said as she took a seat at the table.

Larry was immediately at Vivian's side, attempting to attack his breakfast. "I've discovered another thing that can't be done with one hand," he grunted as he tried unsuccessfully to remove one of the grapefruit sections with his spoon.

"Here, Dad let me do that for you," Rachel offered as she quickly harvested a pile of triangular shaped sections from her father's grapefruit.

"Thanks. I can't wait to get this thing off."

"Does it still hurt dear?" Vivian asked.

"Not really, but it's such a pain trying to do everything with one hand."

"Well, aren't you going to ask me what time I got home last night?" Rachel smugly asked her father.

"Nope, I think you set me straight on that subject. From now on I'm going to trust you to do the right thing. However, if you wanted to tell me what time you got home I would certainly be interested."

"Two-thirty."

Larry tried to ignore Rachel's reply. Two-thirty was way the hell too late for a seventeen year old, but he wasn't about to get into that now. He gobbled down a large chunk of omelet and turned to Vivian. "You know you're right, this is an excellent breakfast..... I don't know about you, but this is the first time I've had breakfast prepared by someone from Harvard."

"You know", Vivian scratched her head thoughtfully, "I don't think I've ever had breakfast prepared by someone from Harvard either."

Larry rocked his chair back on to two legs. "I don't like this two-thirty stuff.... but I can't begin to tell you how happy I am for you, and how proud I am of you."

"Thanks Daddy, but why didn't you want me to see the letter?"

"I was afraid it was a mistake. I just wanted to make sure before you saw it."

"You don't think I'm smart enough to go to Harvard?"

"Don't be ridiculous, I know you're smart enough. It's just that the people who make the decisions about who gets accepted and who doesn't just have a bunch of data from an application to go on. They don't know what you're capable of the way I do. And to be honest, I don't understand how your application could have been up to Harvard standards."

Larry bore into Rachel's eyes searching for a reaction, maybe the slightest hint of an explanation, but he saw nothing.

He took a big swig of orange juice. "So tell me, how did you get accepted to Harvard?"

"I guess they must have looked past the data."

"Why?"

"What do you mean, why?"

"You know what I mean. You were turned down by three schools not nearly as selective, why did Harvard look past the data?"

Vivian fidgeted uncomfortably, not liking the direction the conversation was heading. "I'm sure when Dr. Ryland came to see Rachel, and when Dr. Devonshire spoke with her over the phone that made all the difference."

"I'm sure that did make a big difference, but for the life of me I can't figure out what got the Dean of Admissions to take an interest in our daughter in the first place? I can't imagine him getting personally involved in very many cases unless there are exceptional circumstances."

"Well, we have an exceptional daughter."

Larry zeroed in again on Rachel's eyes. "I know we have an exceptional daughter, but how would he know that?"

"Daddy, you're upsetting me. You act like I did something wrong."

"I don't think you did anything wrong, but something is missing, you're not telling us everything."

Rachel got up and walked around the table, stopping at the kitchen window, her arms folded in front of her with her back to Larry and Vivian. "All right, I'll tell you." She executed a military-like about face, had she not been wearing bedroom slippers her heels would have made a clicking sound. "It was the essay I included with my application, that's what got me accepted. The essay got me the interview with Dr. Ryland and the phone interviews with Dr. Devonshire."

"You wrote an essay? What is it about?"

"It's about me."

"That's wonderful. Can your mother and I read it?"

"Daddy, I'm sorry, but I can't let you read it. It's very personal."

Larry snapped back, "My God Rachel, I'm your father. What could be so personal that you can't share it with me? And let me remind you who's going to be paying your way at Harvard." He quickly held out his uninjured hand in front of him, like a crossing guard stopping traffic. "I'm sorry I said that, forget about the money, that has nothing to do with this. But I'm your father and I think I deserve to know what this essay is about."

"It's about what I'm like on the inside. It's about my feelings. It's about a bunch of different stuff. I could never let anyone read it. I'm sorry."

"Well, you decided it was okay to let a lot of strangers at Harvard read all about your feelings."

"I knew it was my only chance to be considered by Harvard. Writing that essay was the hardest thing I've ever done...... And as far as a lot of strangers at Harvard reading it, that's not the case. Dr. Devonshire assured me that only five people have read it, he and Dr. Ryland and the three people on the evaluation panel."

Vivian felt a sense of enormous relief, realizing Rachel would maintain the secrecy of her essay. She knew the essay must be filled with painful memories from Rachel's childhood and she was the cause of those painful memories. "I think this is an issue of privacy, it's Rachel's decision."

But Larry just wouldn't let go. "I disagree, this is absolutely unacceptable. If you won't show me the essay, I'm going to call Dr. Devonshire and insist he send me a copy."

"You'll be wasting your time. He assured me my application and my discussions with him were confidential and would never be revealed to anyone under any circumstances."

"What is this deep dark secret you're carrying around?"

"There is absolutely nothing for you and Mom to worry about. There's just this part of me on the inside that I can't share with anyone, not with you or Mom, not with Vinnie, not with anyone. Last night I asked you to trust me and I'm asking you again."

Larry shook his head in disgust. "I guess I don't have any choice, but this is something I'll never be able to understand."

"I don't know why this should be so hard for you to understand. Isn't there some part of your life you keep to yourself, some part that I don't know about, that Mom doesn't know about?"

Vivian searched Larry's face for a reaction to Rachel's question, looking for some hint of an answer, but his expression remained blank. His face didn't reveal any secrets, but on the inside his heart thumped so wildly he thought his chest might explode.

Chapter 15

Despite the turmoil in his life, the New Year came in uneventfully for Larry. Four days off from work between Christmas and New Year's Day allowed time to begin laying out his game plan for Chile, what needed to be done and when. The hardest part - so much so it was causing him sleepless nights - was figuring out when and how to tell Vivian.

A New Year's Eve trip to WhiteTail, a ski slope just west of Hagerstown Maryland, with Vivian, Rachel, and Vinnie provided a needed temporary mental escape. With his arm still in a cast he was restricted to spending the day in the lodge in front of the fireplace while the others skied, but catching sight of them hopping on a lift and heading up the mountain was just too much for him to bear. Draping his mountain parka over his left arm to hide the cast, he bought a lift ticket and rented ski equipment. Two trips to carry the skis, boots, and one pole out of the crowded rental hut turned out to be an ordeal; putting his boots on with just one hand was a task of even more enormous proportions.

Crouching in the snow, muttering curses of frustration beneath his breath he heard a voice from above. "Hey man." A young kid of about sixteen, a snowboard propped on his shoulder, watched as he struggled with his boots. One side of the boy's head was completely shaven, the other half adorned with shoulder length blond hair.

"Holy shit man, you gonna ski with a broken arm?"

"I'm going to give it a shot."

"Man you must be forty or something, that's totally freaking awesome. Want some help with those boots?"

Not one to normally swallow his pride, he had no choice in this situation. "Yeah, I think I could use some help."

His first few runs down the mountain were an adventure as he adapted to the imbalance of his left arm being held against his chest. But by the fourth run he was in a groove, skiing with one arm like he'd done so his whole life, and ready to hook up with the others.

Getting off the lift just a few minutes later he spotted the three of them about a hundred yards below, poised at the top of a particularly steep slope summoning their courage. Zooming past at full tilt, missing them by only a couple of feet, the left sleeve of his parka flapping in the breeze, he let out a piercing rebel yell. He laughed with childish glee as Vivian screamed from behind, "Larry, you stupid asshole!"

Rachel was the first one to catch up as he waited at the bottom of the hill. "Dad, are you sure you should be doing this?"

"Doing what?"

It was obvious her father was going to make light of skiing with a broken arm. Knowing there was no way he was going to be talked out of it, she countered with, "Why skiing without sun block, on a bright sunny day like this you'll get a sunburned face."

"Oh my goodness, you're right," Larry replied with mock concern.

Rachel reached in her coat pocket, pulled out a small tube of Coppertone and offered it to him.

Disappointed she wasn't going to play along with his little game he entreated, "Do you think you could put it on for me? I have this broken arm and it's so hard to do some things with just one arm."

She complied, glopping an overly generous layer on his face. "Think that's enough?"

"Yeah, that's enough," came his less than appreciative reply.

Rachel completed the process by squeezing and then pulling his nose between her index and middle fingers, the way he had taught her to imitate the Three Stooges when she was a little girl.

Just as he demonstrated his Curly imitation, "Why, thank you," the slower skiing Vivian arrived on the scene.

"Have you lost your mind?"

"Vivian, I'm fine. I'm skiing very conservatively."

"Bullshit! Every time you put on skis you act like you're fourteen, and the way you skied past us, it doesn't seem to make any difference whether you have a broken arm or not."

"I'll slow down. I promise."

Vivian shrugged her shoulders in disgust and started to lay into him once more only to be bowled over as Vinnie crashed into her.

"Yikes, I'm sorry Mrs. Webster...... Did I hurt you?"

"I'm fine," Vivian replied as she got to her feet.

"I'm kinda having a little trouble getting the hang of this," confessed Vinnie.

Rachel slung her arm around Vinnie's shoulders and jostled him comfortingly. "Nonsense, you're doing better than any first time skier I've ever seen."

"She's right, you're a real natural," said Vivian with a smile as she carefully brushed the snow from Vinnie's hair.

Larry couldn't help but notice Vivian's growing affection for Vinnie. It was clear she was granting him a level of trust that he just wasn't ready to relinquish.

The rest of the day was relatively mishap free; everyone skied into the evening and had a great time. Larry did give the others cause for concern when, late in the day, he had to turn sharply to avoid another skier and fell hard on his left side, but without consequence. On the hour and a half drive home they all sang along to Beatles' songs playing on the car's tape deck. Larry was pleasantly surprised to discover that Vinnie knew all the lyrics. He had pegged Vinnie as somewhat of a nerd and had expected him to be a lover of Mozart, not a fan of the Beatles. The more he found out about this young man, the more he liked him.

They phoned ahead for take out pizzas from the Pizza Hut on Route 108 near their house. After stuffing themselves in front of the fire place, they spent the rest of the night bundled up in the back yard with Larry's new telescope, taking turns star gazing, holding the flashlight, and fetching cups of hot chocolate from the kitchen. As Vinnie peered through the telescope at Iota, a triple star formation in the constellation Cassiopeia, a series of loud bangs went off.

He jerked his head up. "What was that?"

"The neighbors celebrating the start of 1994..... It must be midnight," Larry deduced.

From out of the darkness Rachel made a prediction. "I have the feeling 1994 is going to be the most awesome year of my life."

Several days later Rachel's words echoed in Larry's head as he dashed out of NASA Headquarters in southwest Washington, D.C., having just sat through a tedious meeting with NASA scientists arguing over plans for cooperation between NSF and NASA. Running late for lunch with Barbara at Union Station, he jogged a block and hopped on the down escalator at the Federal South Metro station. After descending just a few feet he spun around and ran back up the moving steps, bumping into an elderly woman who gave him a dirty look. "Sorry," he yelled over his shoulder, scampering up the last few steps. It was a chilly but pleasant day, a good day for a walk he decided. He could make it in twenty minutes going at a good pace, as opposed to waiting who knows how long for a train.

The mile-long rectangular mall running from the Capitol on the east to the Washington Monument on the west was deserted except for a few government workers out for a lunchtime stroll. He double-timed it past the reflecting pool behind the Capitol and then up the hill to Union Station. The bells of a local church chimed twelve times just as he stepped inside the entry area of Union Station with its six-story high arched ceiling, sculptured fountains, and marble floor. He rushed through a horde of jabbering elementary school students - probably from Mississippi or Alabama from the sounds of their accents - to the main ticketing area that overlooked restaurants and eateries on the floor below.

Leaning on the brass railing, he scanned the crowded tables below, finally spotting Barbara at a small two-person table placed discreetly against the wall and partially obscured by a decorative display of large plants. Even from this distance she looked striking, her long black hair and beautiful thick eyebrows highlighted by a light blue sweater.

Gazing upon her he felt a tingling sensation in his body, the same sensation he felt the very first time he saw her. It was crazy: Vivian's remarkable turnaround, Rachel's acceptance to Harvard, the wonderful Christmas they shared for the first time in seventeen years - all the things that should be so important in his life - paled in comparison to his feelings for Barbara. Never able to understand the inexplicable pull this woman exerted on him, as hard as he might try to resist, he could do nothing but give in to it. While beautiful, she certainly wasn't the most beautiful woman he had ever known. In fact, when comparing Barbara to Vivian, which he tried not to do, he always concluded that Vivian was the more attractive of the two. For the longest time he had assumed the attraction was strictly based on sexual chemistry, but had long ago discarded that notion. It was more than that, something beyond sex, something beyond love, something that took hold of every molecule of his very being.

"Hungry?" he asked.

Barbara looked up from the Washington Post. "As a matter of fact I am."

Barbara remained seated - open tables being hard to find during a crowded lunchtime - while Larry bought sandwiches, French fries and lemonades from a New York style deli.

"How was your holiday?" Larry asked as he spread the food on the table.

"I've had better. How 'bout you?"

"Mine was good. The big news is Rachel really was accepted by Harvard."

"No kidding, that's fantastic. I guess you talked to the head of admissions to confirm it?"

"No, I didn't call him. Turns out he personally interviewed Rachel, the letter wasn't a mistake."

"What about all of your concerns, they certainly seemed valid?"

"Seems she wrote an essay."

"That must be one hell of an essay. What's it about?"

"I don't know exactly. Vows she'll never let anyone see it."

"Huh?" Barbara mumbled with her mouth crammed with a big bite from her turkey sandwich.

"I was angry at first when she wouldn't let us see it, but after I calmed down I pretty much figured out what the deal is. Rachel had a torturous childhood, emotionally neglected by Vivian, sexually taken advantage of by an older boy...... It's a minor miracle she turned out to be an intelligent and competent young lady."

"You think that's what her essay is about?"

"Yeah. By understanding what she's been through and how she's been able to deal with it, I think the admissions people developed an appreciation of her potential. I think they accepted her on the basis of that potential. They certainly didn't do it on the basis of her high school grades."

"Is that what Vivian thinks?"

"I think so. We haven't talked about it, but I can see it in her face. She doesn't want to read the essay, and now, neither do I. It served its purpose; it got Rachel into Harvard. All it would do now is tear open old wounds."

"That's pretty amazing, writing that essay must have been hard for Rachel."

"Said it was the hardest thing she ever did.... But enough of that, we have some important things to discuss ourselves."

Barbara put her elbows on the table and rested her chin in her hands. "Let me go first..... I moved out on John yesterday."

"You're joking? No you're not. I can tell by your face you really did it."

"Sunday evening after we flew back from his parents, I told him about Chile and I told him about....... about us."

Larry's jaw dropped and his whole body seemed to shrink as he sunk down into his chair, looking like a shriveled up piece of fruit.

"I hadn't planned to tell him yet, but I started talking and it just came out. And guess what? He didn't take it very well, told me to get out. I spent Sunday night in a motel, and I scrambled around all day yesterday trying to find a place to live. I ended up with a furnished apartment north of Laurel, a real dump, but they're letting me rent month-to-month. It'll do 'til we leave for Chile."

"I can't believe this is happening," Larry whispered, almost as if he hadn't intended for Barbara to hear him.

"You better believe it. This morning I told the Chancellor I wanted a one-year leave of absence. He didn't like it, but he approved it. And guess what else?"

Larry shrugged his shoulders. "What?"

"We are going to be living in the town of Santiago, aren't we?"

"How did you figure that out?"

"I did some research and found out where your telescopes are going to be built. And when I checked a map, it looked like Santiago was the only place within about fifty miles, so I just put two and two together."

Larry smiled and said, "Beautiful and brilliant, aren't ya?"

Barbara winked in reply to the compliment. "There's more. Last week I dropped by the Chilean embassy in D.C. to get the scoop on Santiago. And after my pleasant little discussion with the Chancellor this morning, I spent an hour on the phone with a wonderful lady who runs an orphanage for girls in Santiago. And I got myself a job."

"You got a job?"

"Well, sort of. This woman, her name is Guinevere Gabor, like Gza-Gza. She's a missionary from France. Went to Chile twelve years ago and has been there ever since. She started the orphanage all by her self nine years ago. At first we were speaking in Spanish, but when I told her I was an American she began speaking in English. But wait it gets better." Barbara paused to take a bite of her sandwich, but was so excited she began speaking with her mouth still half-full. "About thirty minutes into our conversation, Guinevere starts telling me about herself, and tells me about being from France. So I begin speaking in French and she gets so excited she starts bawling. She can't wait for me to get down there, and neither can I." Barbara stuffed the last of her sandwich in her mouth. "She's going to pay me ten dollars a day, can you believe it. I'll be doing a little bit of everything, teaching and counseling the girls, helping her with the finances, doing anything and everything. She was telling me about some of the girls she has there..... they sound so precious. I tell ya, it's a dream come true, working with kids, and using my Spanish and French for the first time. At ten dollars a day I'll be taking about a 95% pay cut. But hey, you can't have everything."

Larry shook his head back and forth in bewilderment. "You are absolutely amazing."

She took a sip from her drink and bore directly into his eyes. "No, I'm not amazing, but I am ready to go to Chile. What about you?"

"You're a tough act to follow.......I formally accepted the position in writing and I've coordinated everything with NSF upper management. The official assignment starts on the seventh of February. The date was moved up."

"And?" Barbara prodded.

"And what?"

"You know exactly what I mean. What have you told your wife?"

"Well, I haven't said anything yet, but don't worry I'm going to."

"Are you having second thoughts about this? It's too late for second thoughts, I just left my husband!"

"I admit this whole thing scares the hell out of me, but I'm going to do it. I can't help but have second thoughts at times, but..." He paused to point back over his shoulder at the brass railing above them. "Before I came down here

I stood up there watching you. For the millionth time I tried to decipher your hold on me, and for the millionth time I failed, I'll never figure it out. All I know is - and pardon the quote from an old Sonny and Cher song - you got me babe."

Relief flooded Barbara's body. "Now that I'm an unattached lady with my own place, we can up the frequency of our romantic encounters. You can get there in about ten minutes from Columbia, and the duck will always be flying south. How about tonight?"

Larry pondered the question for several seconds and then with his most thoughtful expression, demurred, "But you said your place is a dump."

She reached across the table and grabbed his tie and yanked him to her, kissing him long and sensuously.

"Tonight sounds good."

Chapter 16

Late on Friday evening, the seventh of January, Larry climbed out of his car, tired, hungry and with a splitting headache. As he fumbled for his key in the darkness, Vivian opened the door. "Did you get caught in that traffic jam on I-95?"

"How'd you know about that?"

"It was on the news."

"Good, maybe you can tell me what happened. Traffic was backed up for miles. When I finally passed the accident there were so many rescue vehicles and flashing lights I couldn't tell what was going on."

"The newscaster said a tractor trailer jackknifed and started a chain reaction pileup, nine cars involved, four people killed. They think the truck driver was drunk."

Larry rubbed the back of his neck with his right hand. "Three hours to get home, what a shitty way to start off the weekend."

"It could have been worse, you could have been in the accident."

"You've got a point there."

Larry dropped his briefcase at the foot of the hallway stairs, tossed his overcoat across the railing and wobbled into the kitchen like someone who had just been mugged.

"Hi Dad," Rachel said cheerfully as she placed a large bowl of salad on the kitchen table, neatly arranged with three place settings of spaghetti with meatballs and fresh bread.

"Why haven't you guys already eaten?"

161

"We were pretty sure you were caught up in that traffic jam so we decided to wait. We wanted to have a nice dinner with just the three of us," explained Vivian.

"Just the three of us, no Vinnie?" Larry questioned with feigned disbelief.

Ignoring her father's histrionics Rachel replied, "Vinnie and his parents went to Pennsylvania to visit his grandmother for the weekend."

As she filled their glasses with iced tea Vivian remarked, "You know Rachel, I think your father actually likes Vinnie."

Larry wasted no time in twirling his first bite of spaghetti around the tines of his fork. "I've concluded that Vinnie's either the most likable teenage boy in the world, or he's the reincarnation of Eddie Haskel."

"Who's Eddie Haskel?" asked Rachel.

"Your father's trying to be cute. Eddie Haskel was a neighborhood kid on 'Leave It To Beaver' who acted like the perfect gentleman in front of Beaver's parents, but he was really a brat."

"Vinnie's no Eddie Haskel. He's for real," said Rachel.

"Yeah, I'm beginning to think maybe he is," Larry concurred with a smile.

All three of them were hungry and concentrated on their salads and spaghetti for the next few minutes. It was Rachel who resumed. "You know Vinnie never asked to read my essay. He knew about it all along, but never bugged me to see it."

"If he had, would you have let him?" asked Larry.

"No, I would never let anyone read it."

The unexpected discussion of the essay made Vivian uncomfortable, but she had a couple of perfect excuses to change the subject. "Rachel and I have a surprise for you. But before that, I have another surprise. This one's mostly for Rachel."

"Oh, goodee," exclaimed Rachel with equal measures of feigned and genuine excitement.

Vivian held up one finger and did her best Arnold Schwarzenegger imitation. "I'll be back."

Larry turned to Rachel. "I don't have a clue."

"Me neither."

True to her word Vivian quickly returned holding a large canvas, but with the back facing Rachel and Larry. "I guess you can tell it's a painting."

"Aaaah, yeah Mom, I think we figured that out."

"It's not finished yet. I've got quite a ways to go with it, but I'll definitely get it finished before your birthday. It'll be your eighteenth birthday present. That is, if you like it"

"Come on Mom, let me see it."

Vivian turned the canvas around. It was a painting of Rachel against a plain, pale blue background. Only partially finished, it consisted of a combination of preliminary soft, faint outlining brush strokes in some areas, and fully finished, rich, true-to-life tones and colors in other areas. Rachel stood smiling with her head held high, one foot crossed casually in front of the other, and her arms gently outstretched to the side. It was such a confident pose it looked as if she were about to take a bow in response to thunderous applause. A pair of unlaced running shoes peeked out beneath worn-out blue jeans with a gapping hole over the left knee. A simple, buttoned blouse was tucked neatly into her jeans. The only parts of the painting that were finished were her face and legs. Rachel looked like she had been dipped up to her waist in a vat of God's most glorious colors, and had then gone bobbing for apples in that same vat. The exquisite detail made you want to jump into the painting and tie up those slovenly laces dangling from her shoes. But more than anything the painting gave you no choice but to fall in love with that face. Without a trace of makeup, without a hint of pretentiousness, it was a face that exuded life, a face that looked anxiously to the future, a future with no limits.

Rachel's jaw fell, as she stood dumbfounded.

"Vivian, it's unbelievable. It's going to be the best piece you've ever done. It's going to be... no, no, it's already spectacular," said Larry.

Vivian turned to Rachel. "Well, what do you think pumpkin?"

Rachel crossed her hands against her chest. "It's totally awesome. I love it."

"Good. Then it'll make a nice birthday present."

"Oh no Mom, it's much more than just a nice present. It's the most wonderful gift ever."

"I decided to show it to you before I finished to see how you'd like me to do your hair."

Both Rachel and Larry only now realized that the edges of the face faded into the background without any trace of hair.

"I was so drawn into that face that I didn't even notice you hadn't started the hair," said Larry.

"So do you want black, blond, or black and blond?"

Rachel rubbed her hands through her hair. "Gee, I definitely don't want to have two-tone hair in such a beautiful painting. Make it blond I guess. I can't see myself staying with black hair all that long."

Larry pumped his fist in the air approvingly. "That young lady is an excellent decision."

"I agree with your father on that," said Vivian as she carefully leaned the painting against the wall. "And speaking of your father, let's get on to that second surprise."

"I'm all ears," said Larry.

"Rachel and I had so much fun skiing last Friday, we want to go on a real ski trip. So we've decided we're all going to Colorado over spring break. You'll have two good arms by then."

"Yeah Dad it'll be great! And Mom said it would be okay for Vinnie to go too."

Rachel looked hopefully at her father. Rather than consenting enthusiastically as she had expected, he appeared surprised and unsure as how to answer.

Larry ran his right hand up his face and over his head. "Skiing in Colorado?"

Vivian clapped her hands in front of her chest. "I've already made airline reservations, and I have us booked in a lodge right in the center of Breckenridge. I spoke with Vinnie's mother about him going."

Larry felt queasy and the smell of spaghetti, for the first time in his life, seemed somehow unpleasant. "When would this be?"

"We'll fly out on Saturday, the twenty-sixth of March, and return the following Saturday, the day before Easter. Rachel and Vinnie are off that week, so they won't miss any school."

"I wish you had checked with me first. I don't know what my work schedule is going to be," countered Larry, knowing that come March he would be in Chile.

"What's wrong, don't you want to go? For years you've tried to talk me into a ski vacation out west."

"It's not that I don't want to go, it's just that this is such a surprise."

"I thought you'd think it was a great surprise. I mean think about it, a week skiing in Colorado. It'll be a chance for all of us to get away from work and school and just have some fun together."

Larry got up from his chair, paced slowly about the kitchen, and stared down at the floor as he spoke. "There's something I have to tell you and it's not going to be easy."

The tone of his voice scared Vivian. "What is it? Is something wrong?"

"I won't be able to go on the ski trip. I've accepted a one year assignment as a Visiting Senior Scientist with the European Space Agency."

"You're going to spend a year in Europe?" screeched Rachel.

"No, in Chile."

"Chile!" Vivian shouted back in disbelief.

In a very subdued voice Larry explained, "The Europeans are building four large telescopes on a mountain top in Chile, and I'm going to be a member of the science team overseeing the construction."

Vivian's voice was choked with emotion as she sputtered, "I can't believe this."

"I'm sorry about the ski trip."

Vivian pounded her fists on the table. "To hell with the ski trip, I'm not talking about the stupid ski trip. I'm talking about you leaving Rachel and me for a year."

"This is a real opportunity for me."

"A real opportunity? My God Larry, things are getting so much better between us." Vivian turned to Rachel who was sitting next to her. "Between all of us." Then she returned her attention to Larry. "Why do you have to do this now?"

"It's not something I can schedule. I'll never get another chance like this. I'm tired of being a bureaucrat and this is my chance to be a real scientist again. By taking this assignment I'll have guaranteed observing rights for as long as I want."

"And you've already accepted this position?"

"Yes."

"There's no way you can delay it or reschedule it."

"No, I really can't, it's a one time deal and the schedule is out of my control."

Vivian sighed, and then straightened her back. "All right then, if this is something you feel you really have to do, I'll support you. When does this assignment start?"

"The seventh of February, but I'll need to fly down a couple of weeks before that to make living arrangements. I'll be leaving on the twenty-second of January."

"My God, that's only two weeks away! Just when in the hell were you planning on letting me know about this?"

"I was going to tell you tomorrow. I'm sorry, I should have told you sooner. I was going to tell you before the holidays, but I just couldn't make myself do it."

"Do you get to come back home anytime during the year?" asked Vivian hopefully.

"Yes, the way the schedule is set up I'll be off the first three weeks of August."

Vivian forced a smile. "Well, I have an idea as to how we can help make this work. The three weeks in August is good timing, that's when Rachel starts freshmen orientation at Harvard. Right Rachel?"

Rachel, her jaw tightly set, glared at her father, but turned away to direct her response to Vivian. "Right, freshman orientation begins the thirteenth of August, and parents are invited for the first two days."

"That's perfect, your father and I can be there with you for those two days. And then I can go down and spend some time with your father in Chile. You'll be okay at Harvard by yourself for a couple of months, won't you?"

"No Mom, I was expecting you to come up every weekend and wash my clothes. Of course I'll be okay."

Vivian got up and stood eye-to-eye with Larry. "So I guess you'll have to figure out how to put up with me for a couple months in Chile."

"Are you sure you really want to do that?"

Vivian backed away several steps. "My God, you don't want me to be there. Do you?"

"It's not that at all. It's just that August is the middle of winter in Chile and I expect the living conditions to be rather Spartan."

"I'll wear warm clothes and won't bother bringing any make up," Vivian replied defiantly.

With a nervous hitch in his voice Larry replied, "Okay, that's what we'll do then."

Vivian sat back down next to Rachel. "I know this is as big a surprise to you as it is to me. How do you feel about it?"

"This is between you and Dad, how I feel isn't important."

"Why that's not true. Is it Larry?"

Larry, his head throbbing and his stomach churning, wanted desperately to end the conversation. He wanted to go upstairs, collapse on the bed and not think about when and how he was going to tell the entire story, the part about Barbara Reilly. "Of course I want to hear how you feel about this."

"No, I don't think you do," Rachel barked.

"But I do."

"If you insist." Rachel paused for a moment to organize her thoughts. "This really stinks. I can't believe you made this decision without talking it over with Mom. And as for your job, I think your job is bullshit...... You study stars, right?"

"It's not just stars. We're concerned with..."

"Don't give me a bunch of horseshit. You know what I mean."

"Yes, I study stars."

"Well, I think it's a disgrace this nation spends hundreds of millions of dollars a year for a wimpy bunch of elitist snobs to wring their hands over whether we live in an open or a closed universe."

"Rachel, that's not fair," defended Larry.

With a steely determination, her voice rising in intensity and pitch, Rachel blasted back. "Not fair? Remember two summers ago in Kentucky when we hiked into that hollow near where you were raised. Go tell that to the mother of that little boy who had gone blind because the government wouldn't pay for a simple operation. Tell her how we can spend millions studying stupid-ass stars, and how we couldn't afford a couple thousand bucks to save her son's sight."

As Rachel paused to let her comments sink in, Larry started to speak, but she thrust the palm of her hand directly in his face, a clear message she wasn't finished. "And we don't have to go all the way to Kentucky. We can just drive a few miles into Baltimore to find thousands of kids who don't get enough to eat and who live in rat-infested housing. You tell them about fair....... So what do I think? I think it doesn't matter where you do your job. Either place, Washington or Chile, it's a waste of money that could be better spent to deal with real problems."

Having just stuck the dagger in her father's heart, Rachel got up and stormed away.

"She's just upset, she didn't mean what she said," said Vivian.

"No, she meant it."

"I need to know more about this whole thing, but I'm tired and I know you are too. So my questions can wait 'til tomorrow, but there is something I have to ask now....... When I suggested spending a couple months in Chile with you, I sensed you weren't telling me everything. Is there anything else I should know?   Do you have any more surprises for me?"

Larry shook his head back and forth emphatically. "No, there are no more surprises."

Chapter 17

Over the weekend Larry decided to delay telling Vivian about Barbara as long as possible, until August when he returned from Chile during his mid-year break. By then Vivian would have established her independence and become accustomed to life without him. And in August, Rachel would be off to Harvard and shortly consumed by academic life. She was a resilient girl and would be able to cope with the separation, and ultimate divorce of her parents. He worked hard at rationalizing this logic, but deep down inside he just couldn't bring himself to tell Vivian about Barbara, not yet anyway.

On Sunday afternoon he and Vivian cozied up in front of the fireplace. With a view of the snow falling outside the large picture window of their family room, they began planning for his departure. Vivian, now much more comfortable with the idea of him being away, did so in the context of joining him in Chile in September. He did so in the context of beginning his life anew with Barbara Reilly.

Since he always paid the household bills, they discussed payment procedures and schedules for the mortgage, car loans, credit cards and insurance policies. They also identified a number of long overdue household maintenance items that Vivian would have taken care of in the spring. But they spent most of the time discussing preparations that would need to be made for Rachel to go away to college.

Later that evening Larry and Rachel had a long talk. She apologized, indicating that what she had said about his work and his decision to go to Chile did reflect her true feelings, but that she was wrong to pass judgment on him.

He admitted that while he truly loved the beauty and wonder of astronomy, he also struggled with the question of its true worth to society. In discussing his career he raised the subject of her plans for a college major. Expecting to hear the answer she had always given in the past, "I'm not going to select a major until my sophomore year," he was surprised when she said, "Psychology." When she was evasive as to how she had come to that decision, he dropped the subject.

On Monday evening, Larry stopped at Barbara's apartment in Laurel on his way home from work. At first, she became upset when he told her his strategy for dealing with Vivian. But after hearing his arguments, she realized waiting until August would lessen the impact on his wife and daughter, and she sincerely wanted to minimize the pain his desertion would cause them, they had already suffered enough.

Larry was greatly relieved to learn that Barbara's husband wasn't going to cause any problems. He was planning to sell their Columbia house and move to Philadelphia, an option the airline had been pressing him on for quite some time. As for losing his third wife his only comment to Barbara was, "Maybe I'll get it right on the fourth try. Time to try out a younger model anyway."

Larry and Barbara spent the better part of an hour coordinating their plans, two round trip tickets to Chile with a departing flight from Baltimore Washington International on the morning of Saturday, the twenty-second of January, with the return flight left open. Barbara repeated over and over, "I can't believe it's less than two weeks away." They talked about how once inside the airplane, seated next to one another, their new life together would begin. In Chile they would stay in a hotel in the town of Santiago for the first week. The lead Chilean scientist, Dr. Jesus Ramirez, had provided information on three different rental apartments. During that first week they would pick out an apartment and shop for the necessities of setting up a new household.

After this meeting there would be few opportunities for Larry and Barbara to see one another before they left for Chile. Each would have many things to attend to and projects to wrap up at work. The one remaining weekend would be devoted to organizing and packing their belongings, and Larry would have to spend time with Vivian and Rachel. They agreed to meet one more time before they left, the following Monday evening, their last chance to double-check plans.

Fully committed to one another, they made love with passion and intensity. Afterward they nestled comfortingly in each other's arms discussing their future and their past.

As he was leaving, Larry chirped, "See ya in a week." Barbara lifted his right hand to her lips, kissed it gently and then silently mouthed the words, "I love you." He did likewise as he backed out of the front door, keeping his eyes on hers until the very last second as he pulled the door closed.

Barbara started toward the kitchen, but pirouetted in her tracks, hurried to the door and flung it open. "Larry, wait."

"What is it?"

"Does your cast come off before we leave?"

"Only two more days, I can't wait."

He arrived home in less than fifteen minutes. Vivian, Rachel and Vinnie were at the kitchen table finishing up the last of a large Domino's pizza.

"Hi," Vivian said, her cheeks stuffed full like a hamster.

"Thanks for saving me some pizza," Larry chided.

"There's a whole vegetarian pizza for you sitting warm on the stove," countered Vivian.

"Oh."

"Yeah Dad, we knew you wouldn't want any of this one, it's got pepperoni on it."

"We need to get crankin' or we're gonna be late," said Vinnie as he gathered up some papers from the table.

"Where are you going this late on a school night?" Larry asked Rachel.

"Us and some other dudes from school are starting a program to spend time with the kids in the pediatrics ward at Howard County General. We'll play board games, read them stories, stuff like that, a couple of times a week. Tonight we're having a planning meeting to get things organized, our first visit to the hospital is in a few days."

"It was Rachel's idea, she's organizing the whole deal," said Vinnie.

Larry wanted to convey how impressed he was with the idea, how proud he was of Rachel, but he couldn't elicit the words. All he could think of was the inconsistency between the maturity of Rachel's actions and his own selfishness. Finally, he managed a feeble, "How ya doing Vinnie?"

"I'm doing fine."

As Rachel and Vinnie headed toward the front door Rachel said, "Give me a minute. I need to make a pit stop."

Vinnie waited in the foyer as Rachel closed the door of the hallway bathroom behind her. In idle curiosity, he noticed the weights in the grandfather clock were nearly at the bottom of their travel, so he opened the door and carefully tugged the chain to raise the first of the three weights. As he reached for the second chain, Vivian came running down the hallway, and screamed, "What do you think you're doing!"

Startled, Vinnie sprang back from the clock. "I was just raising the weights."

Having heard Vivian's scream, Larry and Rachel both rushed to the foyer, Rachel still zipping up her jeans. Vivian, embarrassed and upset with herself, embraced Vinnie. "I'm so sorry. I didn't mean to yell at you like that, please forgive me."

"The clock is very special to Mom. It belonged to her grandmother and she's the only one who ever raises the weights," Rachel explained to Vinnie.

"I'm sorry Mrs. Webster, I didn't know."

"No Vinnie, I'm the one who's sorry. Please forgive me," Vivian pleaded again.

"It's no big deal Mom. Right, Vinnie?"

"Right. It's no big deal Mrs. Webster," said Vinnie as he and Rachel scooted out the door.

As soon as the door closed, Larry put his arm around Vivian. "Are you okay?"

Vivian bit her lower lip, but shook her head affirmatively.

"Rachel is something, starting that program at the hospital. She's turning into such a wonderful young lady, isn't she?" Larry said as he held Vivian tightly.

"No thanks to me," said Vivian deprecatingly.

"Vivian don't get started on that. Let's not look back, we need to look to the future," Larry counseled, immediately feeling pangs of guilt as he imagined how his future actions would affect his family.

"You're right. And speaking of looking to the future, I've got to run over to the office."

"What's up?"

"I have a late appointment with a young couple who are in the market for a townhouse. I think they're going to make an offer on a house I showed them over the weekend."

"You're really going great guns, aren't you?"

"Two sales and eight listings in less than a month," Vivian bragged.

"Eight?"

"I got another one today. A gorgeous two-story in the village of Harpers Choice. It's going to move quickly."

Vivian took a final bite of her pizza and jammed a stack of papers in her briefcase. "This is probably going to take a while. They're first time buyers and a real pair of 'Nervous Willies'. So stay up, I don't want you petering out on me." She kissed him on the neck and intimated, "Know what I mean?"

"Um-hm," Larry replied with a wink.

As soon as Vivian left, Larry devoured the vegetarian pizza, then bounded up the stairs to take a shower, only to make a quick detour to Rachel's room to turn off a blaring radio she had left on. As he reached for the radio on the bottom shelf of Rachel's stereo cabinet, he saw a computer disk lying on the plastic dust cover of her CD player. Aggravated that she wasn't taking better care of her disks he went to pick it up, only to realize that what he saw was actually the reflection of a computer disk in the dust cover. He dropped to one knee and found the disk taped to the underneath side of the next shelf, barely illuminated by a small night-light plugged into an electrical socket behind the stereo cabinet.

Carefully peeling the tape off, he removed the disk, its label marked in bold letters with a single word, "HARVARD." He skipped down the stairs to the study, turned on his computer, inserted the disk, and clicked on the icon for the disk. The file contents of the disk consisted of a single folder entitled, "Hail Mary," the meaning of which was immediately clear to him. Rachel was conversant with jargon from the sporting world and knew a Hail Mary pass was the last gasp play in football in which the quarterback lofts the ball toward his receiver surrounded by a crowd of defenders and prays for a miracle touchdown. The disk obviously contained Rachel's essay, the Hail Mary pass she had completed to score her miracle touchdown with Harvard.

Clicking on the Hail Mary folder, revealed two documents, the first entitled "Intro Letter", and the second entitled "Other." Another click and the letter appeared on the screen.

Dear Sir or Madam,

My application to Harvard University is enclosed. I realize it is unlikely your evaluation of my application alone will result in my acceptance to Harvard. Therefore, I am going to do the only thing in my power to try to convince you of my worthiness. I'm going to tell you about myself. That's right, I'm simply going to tell you about myself. I'm going to tell you things no one knows, not my mother or father, nor any of my therapists or psychologists.

I believe you will conclude my life experience is extremely rare, if not unique. More importantly, I hope you will conclude, as I have, that if combined with a Harvard education this experience will uniquely qualify me to pursue fundamental advances in the field of child psychology.

It was with enormous difficulty and pain that I wrote the enclosed paper. I trust you will treat it with the sensitivity it deserves. I respectfully request that under no circumstances is this paper to be shown to anyone other than those individuals directly involved with the evaluation of my application.

Sincerely,
Rachel B. Webster

Larry read the letter over and over, analyzing every word, sending chills the length of his spine. With a shaking right hand he pressed the control button that would open the document entitled "Other." He desperately wanted to know the secrets Rachel kept locked inside her soul, but he knew she wanted those secrets protected from the outside world. He released the control button, ejected the disk from the computer, took it back to Rachel's room and taped it back to the bottom of the shelf of the stereo cabinet.

Chapter 18

Larry discussed his planned leave of absence with NSF management weeks earlier, but had kept mum on the subject with his staff. However, with the well-oiled office rumor mill in high gear, everyone knew all about Chile. The cat out of the bag, there was no choice but to make it official with a memo to his staff. With that taken care of, he called a meeting with his management team to discuss plans for the Department during his yearlong absence.

His nervousness surprised him as he headed down the hallway toward the Astronomy Department's conference room. With all of his emotional energy focused on his private life, until now, he hadn't realized how much he was going to miss the gang at work.

Seated around the table were four men and two women, all of whom had worked for him for more than four years. "Sorry I'm late," he apologized, plopping a stack of papers and vu-graphs on the table. Normally a rowdy bunch, they were suspiciously stoic. "So, what's going on here?"

"What do you mean?" asked Linda Gilman the department's budget analyst.

"I mean those shit-eating expressions on your faces. Something's up."

"We do have a little surprise planned for you after the meeting."

"I can hardly wait, but first I want to discuss how this department is going to survive a full year without my vision, my inspiration, my leadership, my aaahh….., I forget what the next thing is."

"Your bullshit," replied Linda, igniting a roomful of laughter.

"Yes, that's it, my bullshit," Larry concurred, softly clapping his hands and realizing how good it felt to have the use of both of them again - his cast having been removed only a few hours earlier. "Let's get serious for a few minutes so we can get to that big surprise you have planned for me."

The change in his facial expression sent the message that it was time to stop the horsing around and get down to business. "I want to go over some organizational adjustments that will allow things to run smoothly while I'm away." Observing no reaction from the six faces around the table he plucked a vu-graph from the pile.

"Before I put this chart up on the screen, I'm going to cover the three factors I considered in developing the changes to......." He stopped in mid-sentence as the door of the conference room opened and Kathy, his secretary, tentatively inched her way into the room.

"Excuse me Dr. Webster, you have a phone call."

"Just take a message."

"I'm sorry, but I think you should take the call."

Larry puffed his cheeks out in disgust. Kathy had a habit of taking things a bit too seriously. Only yesterday she had phoned him at home and ear-banged him for twenty minutes about a visit by a Congressional staffer that was of no significance whatsoever. "Okay folks, give me a few minutes..... and no fair peeking at that chart while I'm gone."

Kathy backed out of the conference room into the hallway with Larry following close behind.

"Who is it?

"It's a woman and she's terribly upset?"

"Is it Vivian?"

"I don't know who she is, but it's not your wife or your daughter. I'll transfer the call into your office."

Larry darted down the hallway and slipped into his office, the phone was already ringing.

"Hello."

"I'll transfer the call now," said Kathy.

"Hello," he said again.

"Larry, I'm so scared," came the barely audible reply.

"Barbara?"

There was no reply just a sharp clanging sound as the phone on the other end of the line was dropped, then the muffled sound of weeping.

"What's wrong?"

Her only reply was a frighteningly, faint, breathless whine.

"Barbara, what is it? Please tell me what's wrong."

Her composure momentarily restored, Barbara mumbled with a pathetic unevenness in her voice, "I'm sorry, just give me a minute."

The minute seemed like an hour as chaotic thoughts cascaded through his mind. Was she in an accident? No, someone else would be calling if she had been in an accident. Did Vivian find out about them? Oh my God, is that what this is about?

"Larry, are you there?"

"Yes, I'm here."

"I've got cancer," Barbara sobbed.

Larry's knees weakened, his vision blurred, and he clutched the arm of his chair to steady himself. "Oh God Barbara."

"I'm having the lump removed from my breast tomorrow. The surgeon wants to see me at four o'clock today."

"Tomorrow!...... When did this happen? I just saw you on Monday."

"I had my annual appointment with the gynecologist last week. He did an exam and felt something..... said he didn't think it was anything, but sent me to a lab for a mammogram right then. He called me into his office on Tuesday - the mammogram showed a lump, but he still thought it was just a benign cyst. He used some kind of needle and took a tiny piece of tissue or maybe it was just fluid, I don't even know what he did."

"It's going to be okay."

"He just called me and said it was cancer.... told me what kind of cancer it was, but I couldn't understand him. My mind went blank, all I heard him say was I need to deal with it quickly."

"Which breast is it?" Larry asked, immediately realizing the stupidity of the remark.

"It's my..." Barbara struggled to catch her breath. "It's my left breast. Oh God, I can't believe this is happening."

"Everything's going to be all right."

"Can you come and get me, I don't think I can drive home?"

"Sure, where are you?"

"I'm in my office."

"I'll be there in thirty minutes. I love you."

"Please hurry."

Larry grabbed his coat and briefcase, and rushed from his office and past Kathy's desk. "Tell the staff I'll have to reschedule the meeting."

It began to drizzle just as Larry sped into the parking lot of the University of Maryland Administration Building. It had taken him forty-five minutes because of road construction on Route 1. He was fortunate that it didn't take longer - his needless horn blowing caused an irritated driver from the car in front of him to yell, "What the hell do you want me to do, drive over the top of that Toyota in front of me?"

As he jumped out of his Taurus, Barbara came running into his arms. He held her tightly against his chest, gently caressing the back of her head. "I'm sorry it took me so long."

"I'm just glad you're here. I'm okay to drive, just follow me to my apartment."

"Are you sure?"

She forced a smile and shook her head up and down.

Thirty minutes later they arrived at Barbara's Laurel apartment, her hands shaking violently as she fumbled to insert the key into the lock.

"I can't do this," she admitted helplessly.

"Here, let me."

As Larry opened the door, Barbara said, "I need to take a shower. I know I just took one this morning, but I feel like I'm covered with grime and I want to change clothes."

Larry sat at the kitchen table gazing out the window at passing traffic on Route 1, his mind numb, not even trying to think. It seemed surreal, like a dream where nothing happens, just sitting there in a dream superimposed on the drumbeat of his heart and the whistling of his raspy breathing. His thought processes were so sluggish he didn't even realize it was the phone until the third or fourth ring. Instinctively, he just let it ring – you don't answer the phone at your lover's apartment. But then he quickly realized it might be the doctor's office.

"Hello."

"Could I speak with Mrs. Reilly, please."

"She's not available right now. Would you like to leave a message?"

"This is Father Campbell. Let her know I'm going to be having dinner with an elderly parishioner, but I'll be available any time after nine tonight."

He wanted to know what this was about, even wondered if the Father had the right Mrs. Reilly, but he just said, "I'll tell her."

Concluding it had to be a call for a different Mrs. Reilly, he returned to his mind-numbing surveillance of Route1 traffic patterns. After another ten minutes or so – he wasn't sure – Barbara finally shuffled out of her bedroom.

"I feel a little better now," Barbara said as she sat down, dressed in a fresh pair of jeans and plain white cotton blouse.

"Good."

"Will you come to the doctor's office with me and then to the hospital tomorrow for the surgery?"

"Of course I will."

"Thanks."

"Don't be ridiculous, you don't have to thank me."

He glanced at his wristwatch. It was one-thirty. "What time is your appointment with the gynecologist?"

"Four o'clock, but it's with the surgeon, not the gynecologist. His name is Dr. Pointe. He removed a cyst from my uterus a few years ago."

"You never told me about that."

"It was no big deal."

"I can't believe you didn't tell me."

"Remember when we had that stupid fight and stopped seeing one another for four or five weeks? It all happened during that period."

"I think I conveniently forgot about that..... I can really be a jerk, can't I?"

She tilted her head against his shoulder. "Yes you can, but you're not being a jerk now."

He lifted her hand to his lips and kissed it.

"This ruins everything. After all these years, we were finally going to be together, now it will never happen," Barbara groaned as she buried her head against his chest.

"Yes, it will happen," Larry replied with forced confidence.

"But I won't be able to go to Chile with you."

"You're jumping to conclusions without any facts. Let's wait and see what the doctor says, then we can consider our options. As for Chile, you're a hell of a lot more important to me."

"But at first you were going to Chile by yourself. You just wanted to get away from everything, my coming along was just an afterthought."

"That's not true. At first I didn't think it was possible that you could come with me, but as soon as I realized that it was, I knew that was what I wanted. The biggest mistake of my life was not taking action years ago.... and I don't mean going to Chile, I mean being with you. No matter what happens we're going to be together, it doesn't have to be in Chile, it can be anywhere."

Barbara didn't have an appetite, but Larry was able to convince her to eat something. It would be foolish not to keep her strength up for the operation. As she packed a travel bag to take to the hospital the next morning, he made tuna fish sandwiches, opened a jar of three-bean-salad, and retrieved two bottles of soda from the pantry. They ate without speaking, as Larry forced down his sandwich to show he was confident things would turn out okay, while his insides boiled.

"Oh, I almost forgot. While you were taking a shower there was a call from a Father Campbell asking for Mrs. Reilly. I think he got the wrong Mrs. Reilly somehow."

"No he didn't. What did he say?"

"Since when did you start palin' around with priests?"

"Maybe, since I found out I have cancer. Now, what did he say?" said Barbara with more than a hint of irritation.

"I'm sorry. He said he was available tonight after nine. But why would he be telling you that."

Barbara closed her eyes and massaged her temples. "Because I want him to hear my confession."

"Hear your confession? You're not Catholic."

"Yes, I am. Or at least I used to be."

Larry cocked his head to the side and dropped his jaw in disbelief. "What's going on? You've always told me you're an agnostic. How can you be a Catholic?"

Barbara contorted her face to try to keep from crying, but it was no use as the tears came in a flood. "I'm sorry, Larry. There are just some things I need to...."

He took her in his arms and held her close as her crying went on and on. Catholic, Muslim, or whatever, he didn't care. He just wanted her hurting to stop, wanted to somehow detour her away from her morbid frame of mind. "You're not a KGB agent are you?"

She shook her head "no" as she sobbed into his chest.

"Good, as long as you're not a KGB agent, that's all I care about."

Dr. Pointe's office was in a building complex adjacent to Howard County General Hospital. They rode together in Larry's Taurus, the radio tuned to the oldies station, a convenient excuse for neither of them to talk.

"How are you doing?" he asked, turning off the ignition.

"A little better. I'm starting to think more clearly. I'm scared to death, but I'm certainly not the first woman to have breast cancer. I'll get through this somehow. It's just that this whole thing has hit me like a ton of bricks, everything happening so fast."

"Maybe you should wait a few days before having the surgery, give yourself time to think things through."

"Let me see what the doctor says, but I'm inclined not to screw around. He had a last minute cancellation and can do it tomorrow. If I don't have it done then, it'll be another week."

"Okay, but let's see what he says."

Larry opened the car door and started to get out, but stopped as Barbara placed her hand on his knee.

"What should I say to the doctor about you? Who should I say you are?"

His accompanying her placed them at risk of being discovered. Through all their years together, they took great pains to protect the secrecy of their relationship, knowing just one little mistake could cause the world to cave in around them. Rarely were they ever together in public, certainly never in Columbia where either of them might easily be recognized.

"I don't want Vivian to find out about you any sooner than she has to, but right now I'm not worried about that. You're the most important thing in my life....... Just tell him I'm a close friend, I don't care what he thinks."

"Should I use your real name?"

"Yes, now let's go."

Dr. Pointe's office was on the fourth floor. Both of them health zealots, they automatically took the stairs without even so much as a comment between them. The waiting room was empty. Barbara quickly scratched in the information on the insurance form and handed it to the nurse behind the desk.

The nurse, not looking old enough to be out of high school, much less college, took a moment to scan the form. "Dr. Pointe just returned from surgery. You can go in now, you're his only appointment this afternoon."

The nurse led Barbara along a hallway and into an examining room with Larry following behind. Barbara climbed on the examining table as Larry found a chair next to the wall, the nurse glancing at him without expression. Within a matter of seconds, the doctor, wearing a white lab coat and carrying a large folder, appeared. He was tall, well over six feet, had long blond curly hair, and as was the case with the nurse, looked too young to be a doctor, probably not much over thirty. Larry had reached that point in his life when many of society's authority figures, doctors, policemen, and the like, were younger than him, and he had a hard time getting used to it.

"Hello Mrs. Reilly, I'm Dr. Pointe. You look familiar, were you ever my patient before?"

"Yes, you removed a cyst from my uterus in 1990, but I wasn't Mrs. Reilly then, I was Miss Serelis."

"Oh, yes. You had some abnormal bleeding afterwards."

"I'm amazed that you could remember."

A vision of Barbara's nude body flashed through Larry's mind, he wasn't at all amazed Dr. Pointe remembered her.

Dr. Pointe turned to Larry and extended his hand. "You must be Mr. Reilly."

"No, my name is Larry Webster."

Dr. Pointe didn't seem the least bit phased, but Barbara felt an urgent need to explain. "I'm in the process of getting a divorce. Dr. Webster is a very close friend of mine, he'll be with me at the hospital."

Dr. Pointe's face remained expressionless. "That's fine. Are you a medical doctor?"

"No, I'm a scientist."

Larry expected a follow-up question as to what field of science, but the question was not forthcoming.

"Mrs. Reilly, is that what you want me to call you?"

"How about just Barbara."

"Okay Barbara. I've reviewed the results of the tissue analysis and have compared your mammogram with the one you had taken a year ago. You definitely have a cancerous lump, a medullary cancer. It's not really a rare form of cancer, but it's not the most frequent type we encounter either."

"Is it especially dangerous?" Barbara asked, unconsciously lifting her hand to her chest.

"No, not especially, but any cancer is serious."

"Is the cancer confined to just the lump?"

"There's no real way of knowing until we perform the surgery, but there are some encouraging signs. The size of the lump doesn't appear to be unusually large, and there was no indication of the lump in the mammogram from a year ago."

"Good, I'll take any kind of encouraging news I can get," Barbara sighed.

As he leafed through the papers in the folder, Dr. Pointe commented, "You've been getting a yearly mammogram. That's not routine for a woman your age."

Barbara glanced at Larry without intending to. "There's a family history."

"Did your mother have breast cancer?"

Barbara paused for a few seconds, consciously keeping her eyes locked on Dr. Pointe and away from Larry. "No my sister."

"But..." Larry blurted out in surprise, but quickly checked himself. He'd known Barbara more than seventeen years, and had always thought she was an only child.

"Do you know any of the particulars of her case?" asked Dr. Pointe.

"She had a radical mastectomy two years ago, but died of cancer a year later. That's about all I know. Is it important that you have her information?"

"Not really, at this stage we can only deal with your specific situation..... Now I need to examine you. Please take off your blouse and bra."

Dr. Pointe turned his attention to the mammogram X-ray, placed it on a light box and studied it closely while Barbara undressed. Barbara fought the impulse to shield her breasts in modesty, and left her arms dangling at her sides.

The doctor rubbed his hands together vigorously. "I have a tendency toward cold hands, not the best thing for a surgeon."

"Ooooh, you're right," Barbara yelped, jumping as he began manipulating her left breast.

Larry sat motionless, almost mummified, as the doctor moved his hands over her left breast, and then her right, and then the left again. It made absolutely no sense, but he could feel jealous anger building inside of him. Finally, he chose to look away until the doctor finished.

"You can get dressed now."

"Could you feel the lump?"

"Oh yes, I could feel it. I just wanted to confirm the size and location."

"What happens now?" Barbara asked, buttoning her blouse.

"You may have read about the debate going on in the medical community concerning the most appropriate treatments for breast cancer. There has been a lot of criticism of what many, including myself, feel are unnecessary surgeries. But in your case there is no question in my mind that surgery is necessary."

"Am I going to lose my entire breast?"

"No. The appropriate course of action is to remove the lump and the lymph nodes, there will be some deformation of the breast, but I don't expect it to be severe. If you feel reconstructive surgery is needed, that can be dealt with after completion of your treatment."

"Treatment?"

"Chemotherapy almost certainly will be required, but I won't be in a position to determine the precise dosage level and duration until after the surgery."

"How long will it take me to recover from this, how long until I'm back to .....", Barbara struggled to mouth the word "normal."

"I can't make any promises, but a four to six month recovery period would be typical."

"Including the chemotherapy?"

"Yes. Now Barbara, we have surgery scheduled for tomorrow morning. That's only possible because we had to reschedule another operation, the patient came down with the flu. If you prefer, we can wait until next Friday, that would give you a week to get mentally prepared."

"I'll never be mentally prepared for this. I want to get it over with as soon as possible."

"A lot of people feel more comfortable about something like this after they've sought a second opinion."

"I don't need a second opinion."

"Then I'll see you tomorrow morning." Dr. Pointe paused and then added, measuring his words carefully, "There are no certainties in this type of situation, but I think this tumor has been detected at a relatively early stage."

"Thank you, I hope so."

Barbara and Larry walked hand in hand - their hands ice cold - down the stairs, letting go of one another before they came into the view of others. They didn't speak until they were back in the car.

"Do you think I should have gotten a second opinion?"

"A second opinion never hurts, but I don't think you need one. The facts seem unambiguous in your case."

"I'm glad you were there with me."

"I didn't do anything."

"Just being there helped me."

The ride back to Barbara's apartment wasn't pleasant, but it was less tense than the ride to the doctor's office. Just having the facts, and having committed to the operation the next day, gave them a sense of progress in their fight to beat this thing. They left the radio turned off and talked about the logistics for tomorrow morning, and about delaying the Chile trip. It wasn't long before they were back in Barbara's apartment, standing just inside the door facing one another. He considered asking her about having a sister, but quickly concluded it best to delay that discussion until a later time.

"Are you going to be okay by yourself? I could stay with you tonight."

"I'll be all right, but I want you to make love to me before you leave."

"Are you sure?"

She closed the distance between them and draped her arms around him. "Yes, I'm sure. I don't know when or even if we will ever make love again."

"Don't talk that way, I don't want to hear any more of that. Understand?"

Barbara nodded her head up and down.

At first their lovemaking was tentative, even awkward, but the awkwardness was soon overcome by explosive passion. They made love as if it really might be their last time, finishing with her lying on top of him, both of them taking measured, deep breaths in unison. They stayed that way for so long their bodies seemed glued together. Barbara finally rolled off and retrieved something from the drawer of the nightstand next to the bed.

She held up a Hallmark card in front of him. On the cover of the card was a man and woman holding hands as they strolled down a country lane. "Do you remember this?"

"No, but I get the feeling I'm supposed to," he concluded with a smile.

"You gave me this a long time ago, 1981 I think. I had been trying to convince you to leave Vivian. We were lying together in my old apartment, just like this, when you told me you wanted to be with me more than anything in the world, but that you couldn't leave her. Then you gave me this card."

Larry took the card, and read the note he had written many years earlier.

"You ask where our relationship is going and what I want from it. I love you more than I could ever love anyone, but I can't undo the impossibility of our situation. I'm not sure where our relationship will lead us, but there is one thing of which I am certain. Ten years from now, if you need help, if you are feeling hurt, if you need someone to hold you or just to talk to, I want you to turn to me. No matter the circumstances of our lives at that time, no matter if it has been ten hours, ten days, ten months, or even ten years since we have last made love, I want you to turn to me. You are the love of my lifetime."

"I remember it now," Larry said softly.

Barbara pressed the side of her body against Larry, getting as close as she could. Not looking him in the face, she stared up at the ceiling and whispered, "I need to talk to you about something."

"What is it?" he said as he tenderly twisted her head on the pillow until their eyes met.

He waited patiently as he watched her eyes fill with tears and her lips quiver. She wanted to say something, but she just couldn't get the words out.

Finally, Larry said, "I once asked my mom why she never had another man in her life after Dad died. She was an attractive woman and I remember plenty of guys being interested, but she never so much as had a cup of coffee with any of 'em. You know what she said to me?"

"No," said Barbara as she shook her head ever so slightly.

"She said, 'Your daddy was the one man for me. Maybe the good Lord took him from me too soon, but He gave me eighteen wonderful years with him. So with your daddy and me, it was forever – it wasn't just 'til death do us part.'"

"What a wonderful thing to say about another human being."

Larry gently rolled on top of Barbara and lovingly wrapped his arms around her. "That's the way I feel about you. I don't know how to explain it, I just know we were meant to be together. I'm going to hold on to you forever. We're never going to be apart again, no matter what happens." He squeezed her tightly, but spoke softly, "What is it you need to talk to me about?"

Barbara buried her face into Larry's chest and sobbed, "Not now."

Chapter 19

Six o'clock the following morning Larry crawled out of bed. He was exhausted both physically and mentally, having spent the entire night trying to sort through what might happen after Barbara's operation. How long would it take for her to recover? How long should he delay going to Chile? Maybe he should just forget the whole damn thing, it no longer seemed very appealing. But the worst thing about his sleepless night was the haunting fear that Barbara might die. The doctor had been reassuring, but Barbara's long-term survival wasn't a certainty. It was in dealing with this fear that any vestige of doubt about his true feelings for this woman was purged from his thoughts once and for all. He cared for Barbara above all else and was prepared to place her in the center of his world and deal with the consequences. This simple conclusion, one he had struggled with for years, was nothing short of a defining moment in his life.

He lifted the razor to his face, but his hand was so unsteady he gave up any thought of shaving. A hot shower, well-worn jeans and a flannel shirt were the best he could do to ready himself for a long draining day at the hospital. Vivian, still sleeping soundly, was curled fetal-like with the blanket pulled up to her chin. He tried not to look at her, pretend she wasn't there, but a rush of sadness leaped into his thoughts as he began to reminisce about how their life together might have turned out so differently. The hell with it; he dismissed the possibilities; things are the way they are.

Expecting to slip out of the house before anyone else was up, having not given any thought to what he would say about this day, it was a surprise to see Rachel at the kitchen table gobbling down a bowl of Wheaties.

"Aren't you going to work?" asked Rachel.

"Aaah......., yeah I'm going to work."

"Dressed like that?"

Self consciously inspecting his shirt and pants, rubbing his hand across his unshaven chin, he fumbled, "Oh you mean this...... Today is casual day at work, we do it every once in a while to loosen things up."

"That's cool. Guess what I'm doing this evening?" quizzed Rachel.

Regaining his cool, he joked, "Let me see, you and a bunch of kids from school are going to take the principal hostage and demand more humane treatment for graduating seniors."

"Aaaah, no, that's not what we're gonna do."

"I give up. What are you up to?"

"After school, we have our first session with the kids in the pediatrics ward. Then I'm going out to dinner with three other seniors from Columbia schools who will be freshmen at Harvard next year. This dude from Wilde Lake High called me up earlier in the week. He found out the names of all of us going to Harvard and suggested we get together and hang out some. Pretty neat, huh?"

The dread of his daughter being at the hospital this afternoon tightened his jaw. "Yeah, pretty neat. What time are you going to be at the hospital?"

"Late afternoon. Why?"

"No reason, just curious."

He poured himself a glass of orange juice, guzzled it down in record time, kissed Rachel on the cheek, and bolted out the door. Catching just about every red light, made it seem like an hour, but it barely took him twenty minutes to get to Barbara's apartment. His panic over being late was totally unwarranted; she wasn't due for in-patient processing until eight o'clock with surgery scheduled to begin at nine.

"Good morning," Barbara, suitcase in hand, hailed with a strong voice as she opened the door before he had time to press the doorbell.

"Hi. How are you?"

"I'm good."

"Were you able to sleep?"

"Like a rock. I didn't expect to, but I was out like a light and the next thing I knew the alarm was going off."

"That's great."

"I'm scared, but I've decided I can't let the fear take control of me. I'm going to be positive about things, having you with me makes all the difference in the world."

"You look like you're all set to go."

"All set except for one thing," she said as she dropped the suitcase to the floor, wrapped her arms around him and kissed him. Several times one of them would attempt to end the kiss, but then the other would reignite the process. Finally their lips parted.

"Did I ever tell you, you're a great kisser?" said Larry.

Raising her eyebrows until they looked like two perfectly shaped Roman arches, she replied, "Yes, I seem to recall you saying that before, more than a few times actually."

"I don't think I've ever looked forward to anything as much as our first kiss when this is all over."

"Me too," she replied, the arches replaced by a furrow in her brow.

Larry released Barbara and picked up her travel bag. "Now come on, let's get going."

Barbara complied and grabbed the knob to open the door, only to spin around and squeal, "I can't do this!"

Larry placed his hands on her shoulders with a firm grip. "Now listen to me. Yes, you are going to do this. We're going to go the hospital. You're going to have this surgery and everything is going to be fine."

Barbara burst into tears and wailed, "That's not what I'm talking about. I can't leave here without being honest with you."

As her crying became more violent Barbara slumped onto the sofa and hid her face in her hands as her whole body shook uncontrollably. Larry plopped on the sofa and wrapped his arm around her. Barbara tried to speak, but all she could do was gasp for air. Again and again she tried to speak, but each effort only caused her sobbing to worsen.

"You've got to get control of yourself."

"I can't, I can't," she whined pathetically.

"Is this the same thing you wanted to talk to me about yesterday?"

Barbara continued to hide her face in her hands as she shook her head up and down.

Larry dropped to his knees in front of her and took hold of her hands and forcefully pried them from her face. "Barbara, look at me." When her eyes met his, he continued. "Whatever it is that you think you have to tell me can wait 'til this is over. You've got to calm down or else they won't do the surgery. I don't care what it is. It can wait. Do you understand?"

She looked at him, but didn't respond.

He squeezed her hands even more tightly, "Damn it, do you understand?"

Barbara clamped her eyes shut and bit her lower lip, but finally shook her head up and down.

Larry took her in his arms and held her comfortingly, "Everything's going to turn out fine. It's only natural for you to be upset." Larry had a good idea what this was all about and knew that Barbara was getting herself all worked up needlessly, making a mountain out of a molehill. "We can work this out after the surgery. Okay?"

"Okay," whimpered Barbara.

It took almost twenty minutes for Barbara to get herself sufficiently composed that they could leave for the hospital.

Despite the unexpected delay caused by Barbara's emotional outburst they still made it to the hospital in plenty of time. After some initial confusion over which office to report to, the admitting process went smoothly. Barbara was taken to a changing room where she slipped into a plain cloth gown. The room was chilly, the cold of the tile floor going right through the paper-thin hospital slippers she wore, and her gown providing very little protection from the icy bite of the metal chair. She sat there shivering, her confidence and optimism vanishing chunk by chunk, like a chocolate cake at a church social.

Larry was allowed to join Barbara a few minutes later. He had organized a last minute speech in his head, declaring his love for her, expressing his confidence in what the future held for them, but before he could get started a young black doctor, Dr. Willis, the anesthesiologist, walked in. He questioned Barbara about her medical history, then took great pains to explain each step of the process, indicating Dr. Pointe had requested a general anesthetic so Barbara would be asleep during the procedure. As Dr. Willis was finishing up his explanation, Dr. Pointe, dressed in operating garb and whistling, of all things "The Blue Danube," waltzed into the room waving his outstretched arms, looking more like a middle linebacker than a ballerina.

"Watched my tape of '2001' last night, and can't get it out of my head.... So Barbara, how are you doing today?"

"Nervous as heck."

"You'll do just fine, look at Dr. Pointe, he's not nervous," Dr. Willis reassured, as he patted her on the shoulder before departing.

"Have any last questions?" Dr. Pointe asked as an expression of seriousness returned to his face.

"A couple. How long is the operation going to take? And how long will I be in the hospital?"

Dr. Pointe dragged a classroom-type-chair across the floor, straddled it with his large frame, his chest against the back of the chair, and sat directly in front of Barbara. "I'm sorry, I should have discussed those concerns with you yesterday - guess I was just tired, performed two procedures in one day..... From the time you're under, the surgery should take about an hour and a half, so about two hours all together. As far as going home, two days should do it. I expect you to be out of here on Sunday."

"When will I get to talk to you?"

"I'll come see Dr. Webster in the waiting room as soon as the operation is over. I'll look in on you this afternoon, but I don't think we'll be doing much talking, you'll still be pretty groggy. I'll come see you tomorrow morning and we can talk then. Anything else you need to know?"

"I guess not."

"Okay, I'll see you in a few minutes. The nurse will be in to …, here she is now."

The no-nonsense nurse, a weathered face with no hint of a smile, didn't waste any time wheeling her out of the room, stopping only for a moment at Barbara's request. Larry bent over and kissed her on the cheek, wanting to say something reassuring but unable to find the words, his well-organized little speech of just a few minutes ago erased from his memory bank. She gave him a wink then said to the nurse, "Let's get this show on the road." The nurse pushed her about twenty yards then made a sharp left at an intersecting hallway. As Barbara turned her head at the last instance, it only took that tiny glimpse to see the fear on her face.

It was going to be an agonizing day, he didn't do well in situations over which he had no control and this was clearly that kind of situation. The next two hours would be the worst part, once he knew the results of the operation he would know what he had to deal with, but for now all he could do was wait.

The waiting room was disgusting, littered with cigarette butts despite a no-smoking sign, and thick with the odor of stale smoke. This just wasn't the place he was going to spend the next two hours, he needed to get outside and clear his head. His initial inclination was to get in the car and drive, but it would be stupid to chance having car problems and being stranded away from the hospital, so he opted for a walk instead. A crisp clear day with the temperature in the thirties, he headed east letting the sun's rays warm his face. With no particular destination in mind, he wandered through the hospital parking lot to the grounds of Howard Community College, located on an adjacent parcel of land.

Strolling along, he played out in his mind how he would break the news to Vivian, how he would break her heart. No easing into the subject, no delicate selection of words was going to make it right. There was no choice but to just tell her the truth, tell her he loved another woman, loved this woman more than he had ever loved her. Until now he had intended to put it off as long as possible, but depending on how the operation turned out he would likely do it sooner rather than later. In a way he looked forward to getting it over with, freeing himself of the enormous burden strapped to his back all these years.

He knew that telling Vivian would be the hardest thing he would ever have to do in his life. Just thinking about it for these past few minutes was causing his stomach to sour. He needed to focus on something different or else he feared he might vomit. He forced his brain to shift gears and considered how he was going to deal with Barbara's upcoming confession. That was what her little emotional tirade back at the apartment was all about; she wanted to come clean with him about something that had happened between them over five years ago. He had been having lunch with a couple of faculty members from the Maryland physics department at a restaurant in College Park when he happened upon Barbara with a nice looking guy sitting quietly in a corner booth. When he confronted her about it later that evening she insisted that it had been nothing but a working lunch and that the guy didn't mean anything to her. But he'd zeroed in on the look on the guy's face as he peered across the table at her – it was anything but a working lunch.

They had argued violently. He had repeatedly challenged her, "All I want you to do is to be honest with me…. Just be honest with me." But Barbara just wouldn't, or maybe couldn't, admit that she had lied to him. They bickered constantly for over a month. With no resolution in sight, they knew they had to stop their quarreling or else it would be the end of their relationship. Finally, they kissed and made up – well they did a bit more than kiss – because neither of them could bear the thought of losing the other. After that, neither of them ever brought the subject up again. But now with cancer staring her in the face, Barbara was going to finally set things right. She was going to "be honest with him," she was going to tell him she had lied. Damn, he hoped he didn't hear that she had been intimate with the guy. What the hell, it happened over five years ago. Nonetheless, this subject wasn't doing much for the sourness in his stomach either.

Slowly circling the entire campus, he headed back toward the hospital, quickening his pace once the sun was to his back. It was half past ten o'clock when he re-entered the waiting room. Thankfully it had been cleaned, the floor swept and mopped, magazines neatly stacked up, and the stale odor replaced with the sweet scent of air freshener. An hour and a half had passed since he last saw Barbara; hopefully the operation wouldn't last much longer.

He paged through an old issue of Sports Illustrated, trying to keep from constantly checking the wall clock, but he couldn't help himself. The second hand advanced in slow motion, sticking for just an instant each time it passed the 7. A talkative old woman limped into the room, occupying him with a non-stop description of her granddaughter's injury, "My precious little baby broke her ankle playing dodge-ball at recess." Fortunately, the old woman stayed for less than ten minutes, proclaiming, "I can't stand this God-darned sitting around any longer." He clicked on the television, but shut it off after a few minutes; there was no way a talk show featuring a group of supposedly reformed rapists could hold his interest. By eleven o'clock he became concerned that things were not going well. Twenty minutes later he was so frazzled he had to lock his hands together to keep them from shaking.

Just as he got up to go to the nurse's station - he had to find out what was happening - Dr. Pointe whirled around the corner and wasted no time dispelling his anxiety. "The operation went extremely well, she's going to be fine. She's in the recovery room, you should be able to see her in an hour or so."

"Whew, what a relief. But what about the cancer?"

"I won't know for sure until I have the biopsy results, but I feel there's a good chance the disease was confined to the tumor. I did detect some slightly abnormal cellular structure in her lymph nodes, a pre-cancerous condition, but we caught this thing early. Her prospects are excellent."

"What does that mean exactly?"

"I'm sure you realize making a prognosis for cancer patients isn't an exact science. In your wife's case," he quickly caught himself, "I'm sorry, I mean in Barbara's case, I believe there's a good chance we removed all of the cancer from her body, but she should probably still undergo some limited therapy."

"So her life is no longer in danger?"

"No, it's not. The major risk is that the disease could flare up again somewhere down the line."

"What's the probability of that?"

"I know you want a precise answer, but I just can't provide one. There's a good chance, certainly better than fifty-fifty I suspect, she will remain disease free."

Larry's jaw slackened, his fists unclenched and his shoulders dropped as relief flooded his body. "It sounds like it went as well as we could have hoped for."

"I think so. The tumor was tightly embedded in her breast tissue and I had to remove a bit more healthy tissue than I had expected, but the deformation of the breast isn't going to be significant. I don't feel reconstructive surgery is needed, but she will have to be the judge of that."

He sensed that Dr. Pointe was tired and wanted to move on to other matters, probably lunch, and knew it was time to let him go. "When will you speak to her?"

"My colleague, Dr. Dolan, will check on her this afternoon. Something has come up and I won't be available, but I'll see her tomorrow morning. I expect her to go home on Sunday and then I'll see her on Tuesday, we'll have all the test results by then."

"Thank you so much Dr. Pointe, she's a very special person."

"One last thing, I expect her to be in a great deal of pain, especially for the next twenty-four hours or so. We'll keep her medicated, but she's in for a tough time."

"Thanks again," Larry said as he extended his hand to Dr. Pointe who shook it and left, only to spin around again.

"What kind of scientist are you?"

"I'm an astrophysicist."

"An astrophysicist, oh my." Dr. Pointe's eyes brightened, he began whistling "The Blue Danube," pointed his hands straight up in the air and pirouetted out of the room.

Larry sat down and inhaled the deepest breath of his life, rubbing both hands up his face and back over his head, before he exhaled. Not a religious person, he nonetheless, bowed his head and whispered, "Thank you dear God."

He was anxious to see Barbara and didn't want to wait the hour suggested by Dr. Pointe. Just outside the waiting room he spied a young orderly pushing a cart, piled high with linens.

"Excuse me, where's the recovery room? "

The orderly glanced back over his shoulder. "Down the hall, first right and then the second left."

A young nurse eating a sandwich sat at the recovery room desk, absorbed in the crossword puzzle from the Baltimore Sun. The room consisted of two rows of beds, about a dozen in all, the curtains drawn around four of them, the others empty.

"Hi, I'm with Barbara Reilly. Can I see her now?"

She kept her face buried in the newspaper. "Know a seven letter word for Nature's Colorful Arch?"

"Ahaa.... rainbow."

"How could I not get that?" The nurse scribbled down the answer and looked up. "We just got her in, she's not awake yet. Come back in an hour, you can see her then. Go get a bite to eat, I bet you haven't had lunch."

The nurse was right, hunger was hitting him in the stomach like a two-by-four now that he knew Barbara was okay. "Lunch? I haven't even had breakfast. How's the cafeteria food?"

The nurse held up her half eaten sandwich and grimaced. "Stay clear of the chicken salad."

Skipping breakfast and getting no sleep had thrown Larry's system out of kilter. Normally a big breakfast eater and a snacker for lunch, today he was starving from a combination of real hunger and tremendous psychological relief. Filing through the hospital's cafeteria line he filled his tray with copious amounts of food - a cheeseburger, a large order of French fries, cole slaw, and a large soda. Usually a health conscious eater, today he thought, "The hell with it." He ravenously consumed everything on his plate then went back for a second soda, another cheeseburger, plus a big slice of chocolate cake.

Bloated and uncomfortable, he wished he hadn't eaten so much. Adding to his discomfort was an ache to be with Barbara, but he resisted the urge knowing a full hour had not yet elapsed. A discarded newspaper at the adjacent table helped kill the next twenty minutes. When he returned to the recovery room, the same young nurse was working at her desk pounding away on her computer.

"You're right on time, aren't ya?"

"Can I see her now?"

"Yes, I'll take you back. She's been asking for you."

The nurse led Larry through the recovery room to the very last bed. The curtains were pulled closed around it making it seem more like a tent than a bed.

"She's experiencing considerable discomfort and she's nauseous from the anesthetic. Dr. Pointe prescribed some pain medication, but we have to let her stomach settle first."

The nurse slid the curtain open. Barbara, her head propped up with two large pillows, was lying on the bed raised at about a thirty-degree angle. A small plastic U-shaped pan, partially filled with an ugly yellowish phlegm, rested on the right side of her chest just below her chin. She was dressed in the same gown she wore when he had last seen her. A blanket she had kicked off was rumpled at her feet. An "IV" contraption stood next to the bed with a bag of clear fluid oozing into her left arm. Tears streaked her cheeks from the corners of her closed eyes.

The nurse offered, "Let me get you a clean one of these," as she removed the pan from Barbara's chest.

The strong odor of betadiene, smeared on Barbara before the surgery, blended with the fading remnants of a flatulent expulsion. An orange stain discolored the inside of her left arm and neck. The nurse bent down close to her and pulled an errant strand of hair away from her face. "Barbara, your friend is here. Wake up now, try to open your eyes."

Barbara's eyelids quivered as she struggled to open her eyes. The nurse tried again. "Barbara, can you hear me?"

Barbara shook her head in assent, whimpering, "Um hm."

"Would you like to try a sip of juice?"

Barbara shook her head emphatically from side to side. "Feel too sick."

The nurse turned to Larry. "She starts to wake up and then falls back to sleep. Would you like to stay with her for a while?"

"Yes, thank you."

"Try to get her to take some sips of the juice, we need to get some fluids in her. If she needs anything just give me a yell."

Larry dragged a folding chair up to the bed, sat down close to Barbara, and took hold of her right hand. "Barbara it's me, it's Larry."

She squeezed his hand and her eyelids quivered again, her right eye opening slightly. With considerable effort, but barely above a whisper, she slurred, "Larry, have to tell you, have to tell you something."

"What is it?"

Rolling her head to the side in an attempt to face him, both eyes now slightly open, she tried to speak, but her body convulsed as she started to gag. He quickly grabbed a clean plastic pan from the small table beside the bed, placed his hand behind her head and assisted her up as he held the plastic pan below her mouth. She didn't vomit, but moaned pathetically as her body retched violently, clutching her left breast and crying out, "oooohhh hurts, hurts bad."

Her nausea momentarily checked, he sat the plastic pan on her lap and pried her hand away from her breast. "Try not to touch it. I know it must hurt, but grabbing it is only going to make it hurt more." Once again her body retched painfully. He reached for the pan just in time as she vomited forcefully. Holding her until she went limp, he carefully lowered her head to the pillow. Again she moaned, "Have to tell you."

"Barbara listen, I spoke to Dr. Pointe. The operation went very well, he removed all of the diseased tissue. You're going to be okay, everything's going to be fine."

"Is cancer all gone?"

"Yes, it's gone." There was no need to pass along any of the doctor's qualifying statements about getting the final test results or the risk of the disease recurring. Soothe her as much as possible now, give her the details tomorrow when she can think clearly.

Her eyes fluttered, but closed once again. "Thirsty, I'm real thirsty."

He held a large cup of juice close to her, the straw touching her lips. "Take a sip of this." She sucked hard, making dimples in her cheeks. "No more..... Must tell you. Adrian's okay. Adrian's alive."

"Of course Adrian's alive, I stopped by to see him earlier this week. He's almost fully recovered. He's even coming back to work in a few weeks."

Adrian Hall was their only mutual friend, but he knew nothing of their relationship. A senior official in the personnel department at NSF, he had been a mentor for Barbara many years ago when she worked there. Their friendship continued over the years after she left NSF, with Barbara frequently being a dinner guest of Adrian's and his wife. Larry was also a close friend of Adrian's, with the two of them occasionally going for a lunchtime jog together when their schedules allowed, which wasn't very often anymore. About four months ago, Adrian had been severely injured in a car accident, but was now nearly recovered from a punctured lung, two broken legs and a fractured skull. Adrian's friendship was the only piece of the outside world -that part of the world beyond the motel rooms - that Larry and Barbara shared in common.

In her drugged condition Barbara was obviously reliving her horrible shock upon hearing of Adrian's accident. Or was it something else..... A bizarre thought rocketed through his mind, "Could her relationship with Adrian have been something different. Could they have been ..." He quickly discarded the notion, it was just too ridiculous.

Barbara licked her chapped lips. "More juice."

Larry brought the straw to her lips. "How do you feel?"

Barbara looked pathetic, like a newborn puppy fighting to open its eyes. "Hurts sooooo bad."

"Let me get the nurse. She said they would start you on some pain medication soon."

He started to get up, but she motioned for him to stay.

"Don't understand. I mean Adrian, not Adrian," she whimpered.

"Barbara you're not making sense," he chuckled.

Larry was startled as the nurse yanked the curtain back and stuck her smiling face in. "If she was making sense, she'd be the first person in recovery who ever did. I had a guy in here last week, insisted he was late for a boxing match with President Clinton. How's she doing?"

"She threw up before, but then she drank some juice and has kept it down so far."

"Good, I think we can start the pain medication." The nurse stroked her hand across Barbara's forehead. "Would you like that dear?"

"Um hm."

"She's doing fine. We're going to get her ready to go upstairs, so we need you to get out of here." The nurse glanced at her clipboard. "She'll be in room 340. We'll have her up there in about thirty minutes, you can come on up then."

"Are you sure she's ready to go up?"

"Yes, I'm sure. We just keep them here until they're stabilized. Her vitals are all normal, she's ready to go."

Larry leaned over and whispered in Barbara's ear, "I love you."

"Love you too."

Larry thanked the nurse and left quickly, the two large sodas from lunch were making their effects known and he needed relief in a hurry. His stop in the men's room was enormously refreshing - peeing for so long he thought of Adrian Hall, their mutual friend, who had boasted of once peeing for two minutes without stopping. Until now he had never thought it possible to pee for two minutes, but he just kept peeing and peeing. He'd be seeing Adrian again in a week or so and planned on telling him that he'd broken his record.

Needing to kill some more time he wandered outside again. The cold January air was invigorating, the sun against his face was an even more potent tonic, but all of a sudden something was very strange. People coming and going from the hospital, cars jockeying for spaces in the parking lot, an airplane zooming overhead, all seemed like normal happenings, but something wasn't right, something was very different. He couldn't see it, hear it, smell it or sense it in any normal fashion, but he just somehow knew that something about his world had changed in a fundamental way. It was as if he had suddenly fallen into an alternate universe - like being in a crowded room one moment and the next moment riding an empty bus. No smooth transition between universes, no leaving the crowded room, no waiting for the bus - just bam you're on the bus. "What the hell is going on?" he said aloud to himself. He wasn't on a bus, he was outside the hospital, the same hospital he had walked out of a couple of minutes ago...... But how could he have pissed for so long, how could he have pissed for twenty minutes without stopping. No, no, he didn't piss for twenty minutes....... it was Adrian Hall who had done that, and he only pissed for two minutes, not twenty minutes. No, he did just piss for a long time because he just broke Adrian's record.

Stumbling along he came to a bench, flopped on to it, and mumbled to himself. "Why in the hell am I worrying about Adrian Hall taking a piss? What does

Adrian have to do with anything? My mind's playing tricks on me, that's all it is. I didn't sleep last night. Barbara had a tumor cut out of her tit. I just need to clear my head, that's all." He leaned his head back, stretched his arms along the top of the bench, closed his eyes, and took long deep breaths as the sun baked his face. "That's better," he thought, "this is just some kind of emotional reaction to Barbara's surgery. God, how I love that woman, how I love that woman."

After a few minutes of meditation, concentrating on his love for Barbara, he felt better, but despite the warmth of the sun on his face he began to shiver. He had left his coat in the hospital, but didn't want to go back inside, at least not for a few more minutes, not until Barbara was in her room. Even though the operation was a success, it depressed him to be in the hospital. The aura of the place, the smell, the sounds, everything about the place, despite their well-intentioned efforts to disguise it with bright colors, was depressing. Most depressing of all was seeing his Barbara in such pain.

Feeling a bit better, he decided to take one more short jaunt around the grounds of Howard Community College. At first he thought everything was back to normal - if Barbara being sliced up could be thought of as normal - but after covering a few hundred yards it hit him like a Greyhound bus, stopping him dead in his tracks. The strangeness was back in full force, only this time it was slowly beginning to take shape, like a slide projected on a blank wall, fuzzy at first, then gradually coming into sharp focus.

He now realized what was happening to him - he was becoming aware of something, something he never understood before. It was the sensation of a developing awareness not yet completely formed, not yet fully defined. The sensation was oozing up his body, starting at his feet, gurgling up his legs and then spilling into his torso. A fluid of understanding was being poured into him, and his body was behaving like some oddly shaped vase being filled from an unseen font.

When his body was brim full of insight, he knew! He knew! She wasn't going to confess about having lunch with some guy five years ago! That's not what this is about. No wonder she needed to see a priest!

He turned and sprinted as hard and as fast as he could, the gluttonous lunch bouncing heavily in his stomach. The normal feedback signals from the brain that moderate the actions of one's body didn't kick in, the burning of his lungs didn't slow him down, the aching in his thighs had no effect. He sprinted the half-mile back to the hospital faster than he had done as a member of the Princeton track team, faster than he had run in his entire life. Bursting through the hospital door, he dashed to the elevator and pounded his fist against the up-button. Spotting the door to the stairway, he rushed to it and flung it open, blasted up the stairs, taking the steps three at a time to the third floor. Room 328 then 326...... no, he was heading the wrong way, spinning around he charged off in the other direction, skidding to a halt at room 340.

From inside came a soft voice with a southern accent, "Now if you need me, just push this button." Seconds later an elderly nurse smiled as she walked out of the room.

Larry Webster - hunched over, hands on his knees and gasping for air - paused to let his body recover from the physical overload to which it had just been subjected. He straightened up, pulled back his shoulders, set his jaw, and went in. It was a private room with a single bed. Pillows propping up her head, Barbara was in much the same position she had been in the recovery room. She spotted

Larry as he came toward her. Her eyes were now wide open, and tears trickled down her cheeks.

"You weren't talking about Adrian Hall, were you?"

In a sluggish, but much more coherent voice she replied, "No. I tried to tell you."

"Who were you talking about?"

She tried to speak, but couldn't as her lips twitched wildly. He reached to the bed for support as his knees buckled beneath him, his stern demeanor of just a moment ago completely gone. Letting go of the bed, he sprawled to the floor, covered his eyes with his hands. "Karen? My Karen's alive? My baby's alive?"

From above came the chilling reply, "Yes. Her name is Adrienne now."

Chapter 20

Larry pulled himself up from the floor and buried his face in the blanket lying on the edge of the bed. Barbara leaned forward to comfort him, but stopped short of making contact. Holding her hand just a few inches away from him for several seconds, she slowly pulled it back. He uncovered his face and their eyes met as he unsteadily regained his feet, and stumbled into the bathroom. Lifting the toilet seat, dropping to his knees, the vomiting came quickly, violently and with such force it splattered back onto his face. Wiping himself clean with a towel, he spotted Barbara's travel bag, found her toothbrush and toothpaste and brushed his teeth. Inspecting himself in the mirror, he expected to see some emotion in his face, some clue as to what he was feeling, but there was no clue because there was no feeling - no anger, no regret, no joy, nothing. He was thinking coherently, understood exactly what he had just heard, but there was no feeling. Surely, the feelings would come later.

Re-entering the room he noticed a small chair against the wall, scooted it next to the bed and sat down as close to Barbara as he could. "Who took her?"

"My sister."

"You were in on it?"

"Yes."

He leaned even closer, so close he could smell the thin layer of Vaseline smeared on her cracked lips, and spoke purposefully and calmly. "You were fucking me in the van so your sister could take my baby."

She closed her eyes and turned away.

"I said, you were fucking me so your sister could take my baby."

"Yes."

His teeth made a screeching sound as he ground them together. "You know what is so incredible? The idea you could have been involved never crossed my mind, not one time in seventeen years." Now he could begin to feel something, anger. "I've got my two babies with me, a woman lures me into my van to fuck me, my baby disappears, and not once does the thought cross my mind she may have had something to do with it. That's pretty fucking amazing, isn't it?"

Barbara couldn't move. Frozen stiff. Submerged in concrete.

"Why did you do it?"

She wanted to speak, but she couldn't form a coherent thought.

"Damn it, why did you do it?"

Barbara's paralysis faded. "There's nothing I can say to explain it. It was a horrible act, I've regretted it every day of my life."

With a steely determination he demanded, "I want to know why you did it."

"Larry, it doesn't make any sense, but at that point in my life...." she paused as her voice faltered. "I worshipped my sister, she wanted a baby so desperately, and she had two miscarriages. After the second one she tried to kill herself, that was only one week before I met you. That day you came to see me about your health coverage was my first day back after being with her."

"So you had this idea from the beginning?"

"When you came to see me for help, one of the first things out of your mouth was something like...... 'this wouldn't be so hard if I didn't have twins.' I came up with the idea right then and drove up to Philadelphia to see my sister and her husband that night. I was terrified she was going to kill herself. "

"Did I seem so weak, so pathetic, that you thought you could take one of my babies away from me? "

She held her reply.

"Damn it, did I seem that weak?"

Not daring to look at him, she reluctantly conceded, "Yes, I thought I could do it."

"That was April. Why did you wait until December?"

"We didn't wait. We tried two times before that, but each time something went wrong. We didn't know what we were doing, and worst of all, while I was trying to set you up to get just the right opportunity, I was falling in love with you. I wanted to call the whole thing off, but my sister wouldn't let me."

"She wouldn't let you!"

"I know it sounds ridiculous now, but I was so young and so stupid then."

"Where's my daughter?"

Barbara moaned as she rolled onto her side. "Oh Larry, why do you need to know, she has a wonderful life?"

He gritted his teeth, recoiled from her, and fumed, "If you'd ever had a child of your own, you couldn't possibly ask that question. Now tell me where she is?"

Having phrased the question that way left no doubt in Barbara's mind as to where she stood with him. Like her sister, she had also wanted children very badly, but due to the turns and twists in her life it was never to be. Larry knew the deep hurt this caused her, had always been sensitive to it, but obviously no longer cared.

"She lives in Jackson Hole, Wyoming. My sister...... my sister died over a year ago."

With all the insincerity he could muster, he sniped, "Gee, that's too bad."

" She was not a bad person."

"I'm sure she was a wonderful person, just had a nasty habit of stealing babies..... What was her name?"

"Cynthia Sullivan. Her husband is Hank, he's a nice man."

"Oh, another nice person who happens to steal babies."

"It wasn't him. Cynthia's first husband was a jerk, he left her over twelve years ago. She married Hank a few years later, he thinks Cynthia was Adrienne's mother. I met him November before last."

"You just met him less than two years ago?"

"I hadn't seen my sister since my father's funeral, thirteen years ago. She ran away and hid from me. She knew I was in love with you and was afraid I was going to tell you everything....... I guess she was right."

"How did you find her?"

"She finally contacted me when she knew she was going to die. I immediately went to be with her..... She died two days later."

Without a trace of sympathy he simply said, "Now, where did you say my daughter lives?"

She had no choice but to tell him. "Hank and Adrienne live right in the center of Jackson Hole on Hansen Avenue. I don't remember the exact address. Hank owns an outdoor sporting store in town called Teton Adventures."

"What's", he paused to compose himself, "What's Adrienne like?"

The tone of Barbara's voice brightened ever so slightly. "She's the most wonderful girl, a fantastic student. She's going to Stanford next year on a full scholarship. And you won't believe this - she just missed making the Olympic Ski Team. She's a fantastic athlete."

"The Olympics?" he mumbled.

"No one else her age even came close. They think she's a cinch to make it in four years."

Larry pushed the chair away from the bed and stood up. "You said Hank Sullivan, Hansen Avenue, Teton Adventures. Right?"

"Oh my God, you're going there, aren't you?"

Towering over her, he demanded, "What made you decide to tell me?"

She wrapped her arms around herself as if suddenly chilled. "This one terrible thing turned my life into a nightmare. I wanted to tell you so many times, but I was too afraid. When I found out I had cancer, I knew I couldn't live with this lie any longer. I decided that no matter what happened I would tell you."

Seemingly unmoved by her response, he commented, "One last thing. Around the time Karen was taken, two other babies were abducted from the area and then found dead, the police lumped all three cases together, they....."

Barbara quickly interrupted. "Oh my God, you don't think we had anything to do with that. That was just a horrible coincidence."

Kicking the chair to the side, he turned to leave.

"Larry wait!" Barbara pleaded.

He stopped, but didn't turn around to acknowledge her.

"Larry don't tell her. Think of what it will do to her if you tell her. She's such a beautiful girl. She has such beautiful ...." Before she could finish he started walking away. "I think I have a pretty good idea of what she looks like."

As he left and headed to his car, a group of teenagers approached the hospital from the other side of the parking lot.   One of them, a young man with a black ponytail, turned to the girl next to him. "Isn't that your dad?"

"Looks like him, but I'm not sure. What would he be doing here?"

"See, it is him, that's his Taurus, " said Vinnie as the car pulled out of the parking lot.

Chapter 21

It was as if the car had a mind of its own. Larry could see his hands on the steering wheel, could feel his foot on the gas pedal, but he wasn't in control of the car, at least not consciously. Buildings, trees, pedestrians, other cars, just zoomed by, the way they do in one of those low-budget amusement park rides where you sit behind the controls of a futuristic vehicle staring at a screen of on-rushing scenes.

The car didn't take him far from the hospital, only about a mile before turning into the parking lot of an office building adjacent to Clyde's Restaurant where he and Vivian had brunch not long ago. It came to an abrupt stop in a handicapped parking space, but Larry didn't seem to notice. Directly in front of the car was Lake Kitimakundi, similar in size and character to Lake Elkhorn, only about two miles away to the southeast. With the unavoidable view of the lake right in his face, he couldn't help but think of that day seventeen years ago, couldn't help but think of the pain he had caused Vivian and Rachel. Nausea overtook him again. Flinging the door open just in time, he barely avoided vomiting in the car.

"Young man, do you need help?"

A woman, about sixty years old, dressed incongruously in a waist-length mink jacket, an outrageously short leather mini-skirt, black fish net stockings, and spiked heels came waddling toward the car. She smacked her lips on a big wad of gum, lips so red they looked like they were covered with metallic paint.

"Oh, you're probably wondering why I'm dressed like this.... My company won this big government contract and we just had a party to celebrate. Some of the other girls and I decided to get dressed up like hookers. It's perfectly okay, I own the company so I can dress however I choose.... I make a pretty good looking hooker, don't I?" She turned her head from side to side, looked suspiciously in both directions, hunched her shoulders forward and whispered, "Actually, I really am a hooker. No one suspects 'cause I'm filthy rich. Interested?"

She looked more like a five year old guilty of raiding her mother's closet and make-up tray than a hooker. Actually, she looked much better than any hooker he'd ever seen. He'd been tempted twice, but never took the leap, his conscience getting the better of him each time. He was never quite sure whether it was Vivian or Barbara he couldn't bring himself to cheat on. Of course he cheated on Vivian with Barbara all the time, but that seemed different, somehow not quite as bad if it was with a woman you loved. But what if it was with a woman who stole your baby?

This lady looked better than the two hookers because she had beautiful eyes, ancient eyes but beautiful eyes, eyes that were full of life. And she was cute, ridiculous looking and old as dirt, but somehow cute. The two hookers, both encountered on business trips years earlier, had nice bodies, but their eyes were dead. Had either of them not had dead eyes, he probably would have gone through with it, conscience or no conscience.

"How much do you charge?"

"Five hundred a night, but I'm worth it."

"Do you take Visa?"

"Cash only."

What would she say if he told her to follow him to an automatic teller to get the money...... maybe she was worth it. "I'm a little short on cash."

"It's just as well, you look like a sick puppy, white as a sheet. Did ya see a ghost or something?"

"In a way I did...... I just have a mild stomach virus, that's all."

"Would you like me to drive you home or to a drugstore? My car's right over there."

" Really I'm fine, I feel much better already."

"Suit yourself." She zipped up her mink jacket, started walking away, swinging her butt from side to side, and yelled back over her shoulder. "If you ever come across five hundred bucks, look me up. By the way, was it a good ghost or a bad ghost?"

"It's a terrific ghost."

This goofy lady, who obviously packed her life full of fun, had somehow made Larry feel better. Their brief, playful interaction had totally reversed his way of thinking. Only half an hour earlier he had received the biggest shock of his life and reacted to that shock with horror. He always blamed himself for Karen's abduction, but discovering Barbara had taken her made it even worse. It wasn't just a random thing that had happened to him, he had let it happen, had unknowingly been a part of it. He had never thought it possible to feel more ashamed, but now he did.

But the foolishness with Zelda - he had no idea what her real name was, she just seemed like a Zelda - made him focus on the other dimension of that shock, the glorious, stupendous dimension. Karen hadn't been raped, hadn't been burned with an iron, hadn't been dismembered, hadn't had her eyes punctured with a screw driver, hadn't been beaten with a baseball bat - none of the horrific images he tortured himself with on sleepless nights, images he shared with no one, none of those images were real, none of it had happened. Karen was alive and, according to Barbara, quite happy.

He trotted past the Columbia People Tree into a white stone office building, checked the listings in the lobby, took the elevator to the fourth floor and located the office of Columbia Travel. The travel agent, a cheerful young woman in her early twenties with short dark hair, worked with him for almost thirty minutes to satisfy his requirements - a round trip flight to Jackson Hole with a departure as soon as possible, but with the return flight held open; and motel and rental car reservations for two days with the option to add extra days. After checking and then checking again, at his insistence, she convinced him there was no hope of booking a flight any sooner than the next morning. He opted for an American Airline flight departing at 7:40 a.m. from Baltimore Washington International, with connections in Chicago, and Denver, arriving at 2:15 p.m. He reserved a room at the Antler Motel in the heart of Jackson Hole and a Ford Mustang from Budget Rental Car.

The agent handed him a confirmation statement with his itinerary. "You'll have to pick up your ticket at the counter tomorrow morning, we're all out of ticket forms.... Are you going skiing?"

He popped open his briefcase and stuffed the confirmation statement in the back pocket. "Why else would anyone go to Jackson Hole in January?"

Larry needed some time to think before going home to pack, so he drove to Patapsco State Park, and pulled off the road at the top of River View Trail. He quickly descended the half-mile to the river then walked north alongside the railroad track. The river was silent, barely more than a trickle. He hadn't been back to the tunnel since the day he broke his arm. Stopping at the entrance and looking up, he saw the numbers and letters "19-Union Dam-02" chiseled into the stone at the top of the tunnel opening. Despite all the times he'd been in the tunnel he had never noticed the lettering before. Penetrating deeper and deeper, he challenged the tunnel's darkness. The rustling of the gravel stones beneath his feet echoed all around him. When he stopped, there was complete silence except for his breathing. Holding his breath, he thought he could hear the beating of his heart, but he wasn't sure.

It struck him as odd that mixed in with his feelings was concern for Barbara's well being. The initial anger he felt towards her earlier in the day had been replaced with confusion, and embedded within this confusion was concern. Surely he should be feeling hatred, but it wasn't there, at least not yet.

And what of Vivian and Rachel, how would they react to learning of Adrienne Sullivan? Would it destroy the new found equilibrium in their lives? Maybe they would be best served by not knowing of the young woman in Wyoming. Did he really believe this or was he just rationalizing his intent to keep the existence of Adrienne Sullivan a secret - for to know of Adrienne Sullivan would be to know the details of that December day at the lake.

Sitting on the cold damp gravel, he couldn't remember having sat down, nor did he have any idea how long he'd been there. The tunnel was especially dark - he had never been in the tunnel at night. His thinking was no more coherent in the solitude of the tunnel than it had been outside, he needed to get home and pack his things.

He tramped down the tracks until he reached River View Trail then began negotiating its steep slopes, more by rote than sight. He gauged his steps and didn't rush, the last thing he wanted to deal with was another injury. Finally, a break in the clouds revealed a sliver of a moon that helped light the way.

The house was dark when he arrived home. Flicking on the lights, he realized how filthy he was. Fortunately, no one was home so he wouldn't have to explain his soiled appearance. Rachel was having dinner with her Harvard-to-be friends, but he didn't know Vivian's whereabouts.

He showered, donned clean clothes, and slipped a TV dinner in the microwave. It was thrown away half eaten, his appetite having not fully recovered from his bouts with nausea earlier in the day.

As he spread out his clothes for the trip on the bed Vivian startled him from behind. "What are you doing?"

"Ahhaa..., I'm packing."

"But you're not leaving for another week."

"I'm not packing for Chile. Something has come up and I have to go to Flagstaff tomorrow. Flagstaff, Arizona."

"Flagstaff!"

"Yes, they've had a major failure in the drive system of the main telescope at the Lowell Observatory. They want a hundred thousand dollars from NSF to help fix it. With our budget problems we don't have that kind of money. I've got to go out there and see exactly what's going on."

"How long are you going to be away?"

"Probably just a few days, maybe a week."

"A week! My God Larry, you're leaving for Chile in a week."

"This is much more important than Chile. Don't worry, I'll delay the Chile trip."

"Here, let me help you get packed, you'll forget something important," Vivian said as she began rearranging the piles of clothing. "Looks like you're expecting it to be cold in Flagstaff."

"Yeah, it's cold there," he replied, lucky the lie he fabricated with absolutely no forethought seemed reasonably credible.

With Vivian's suggestions the packing went smoothly. Finishing up, they went down stairs to have some hot tea. Just as they were sitting down at the kitchen table Rachel came in the front door.

"Hi Mom, hi Dad. Dad, what were you doing at…."

Before she could finish Vivian interrupted, "Rachel, what are the other Harvard kids like?"

Rachel opened the refrigerator to fetch a soda. "The kids are great, a little nerdy, but I like 'em. We're going to keep hanging out together on a regular basis."

Vivian turned her attention back to Larry. "What time is your flight tomorrow?"

"Tomorrow! You're not supposed to leave until next week," bristled Rachel.

"Calm down now. I just explained everything to your mother. I'm going to Arizona, not Chile. I have to go there for a few days, they've had a serious mechanical problem with a telescope at the Lowell Observatory. So I'll probably have to delay the trip to Chile."

Rachel scrunched up her face. "When did you find out about this?"

"Just this afternoon."

"Why do you have to go out there? It's not like you're going to be the one to actually take a wrench and fix the thing. Isn't this something you can work out over the phone?"

"There's only so much you can accomplish over the phone. In fact, we were on the phone with them all afternoon, but didn't make much progress."

Rachel studied her father curiously. He seemed to be acting normal, but something didn't jibe, she knew he hadn't spent the entire day at the office. "I thought you said today was casual day at work."

"It was. What's that got to do with anything?"

Rachel nonchalantly poured soda into a glass of ice. "So even on casual day you spent the whole afternoon downtown in your office, you didn't even knock off early or anything?"

"Nope, put in a full day just like any other day."

227

Rachel took two gulps of her soda and then stretched her arms over her head and yawned. "I'm really tired, I'm going to bed. What time are you leaving tomorrow morning?"

"I'll be leaving the house around six."

Rachel kissed her father on the cheek. "Wake me up so I can say good-bye."

"Okay."

At the top of the stairway Rachel glanced into her parent's bedroom - a suitcase and her father's briefcase rested on the floor at the foot of the bed. She cocked her head - quietly listening as her parents continued their conversation in the kitchen - tiptoed into the bedroom, kneeled on the floor, popped open the briefcase and hurriedly went through the main compartment - a magazine, several office memos and a super bowl pool with the box marked Dallas 2 and Buffalo 5 circled..... what a loser score. She unzipped the back pocket of the briefcase, fished out the computer printout with her father's trip itinerary, and studied it carefully.

Chapter 22

Larry set his watch back two hours to 2:05 pm, Rocky Mountain time, and adjusted his seat to its upright position as the gravelly voice of the pilot crackled over the plane's intercom. "We'll be landing in about five minutes. As you can see the weather in Wyoming today is sunny and clear, temperature in Jackson Hole is 37 degrees."

"Wow, that's a real heat wave for Jackson Hole in January," remarked the pretty redheaded flight attendant as she took an empty diet Pepsi can from Larry.

"Meeting friends in Jackson Hole?" asked the stewardess.

She was talking to him, but her words just didn't register. He was not usually guilty of ignoring an attractive woman. "I'm sorry, what did you say?"

"I asked if you're meeting friends in Jackson Hole."

Awkwardly clearing his throat he replied, "Yes, I hope to meet up with an old friend."

As the plane banked to the left, beginning its approach to the airport, the Grand Tetons came into view. Normally, Larry would have been in awe of these imposing mountains jutting ramrod straight above the valley floor, but not today. With his senses worn numb, his only reaction was to wonder where one could ski on such rocky, steep slopes.

Stepping out of the plane onto the landing of the portable stairway, he was blinded by the brightness of the sun and its reflection from the snow - the airport, a small island in an ocean of white. He had forgotten to bring sunglasses, buying a pair was an immediate priority.

From the makeup of the happy crowd that scurried toward the terminal it was clear everyone coming to Jackson Hole had only one thing in mind, skiing. It was a small airport, one you could process through in a hurry. Picking up keys for the rental car, locating his luggage, and buying a pair of sunglasses from a small gift shop took less than fifteen minutes. Coming out of the gift shop he spotted a pay phone. The phone book was small, about the size of a TV Guide. With trembling hands, he found the number and address of Henry Sullivan, and then the number and address of Teton Adventures, and scribbled the information on the back of a Washington Metro fare card, the only thing in his wallet to write on.

The temperature may have been in the upper 30's, but with no wind and a bright sun it felt more like 60 degrees. Budget Rental space #22 was just outside the terminal. He tossed his luggage into the trunk of the sporty silver Ford Mustang and took off.

The directions from the car rental agent led him out the airport exit road and then right on Route 191, heading south toward Jackson Hole. Off to the right, a departing Boeing 727 was about a thousand feet off the ground. Only now could the true grandeur of the Tetons be fully appreciated. The 727 appeared to be a tiny model airplane against the backdrop of these enormous, beautiful mountains. To the left in the foreground were low, rolling morainal hills with more substantial mountains behind, although not nearly the size of the Tetons. Everything but the blue sky was white, covered with several feet of snow.

On the left side of the road about a half-mile in front of him, a line of people were coming north, marching in single file, and wildly swinging their arms in locomotion fashion. Closing the gap, he discerned it to be a group of about twenty cross-country skiers, dressed in brightly colored body suits, loaded down with large backpacks.

In just a few miles he entered the town of Jackson Hole, Route 191 having turned into North Cache Street. Motel parking lots were jammed with arriving and departing skiers, their cars jockeying for parking spaces. Only a couple of blocks farther he came to the intersection of North Cache and West Broadway, the street where Teton Adventures was located. Stopped at a red light, he gripped the steering wheel so tightly he could feel the pulsing beats of his heart in his fingertips.

This was happening much too fast. He wasn't ready to see Adrienne Sullivan, he needed time to think, time to get ready to look into her eyes. The startling blare from the horn of a Jeep Cherokee caused him to stomp abruptly on the gas pedal and speed through the intersection, sending a small group of pedestrians scurrying. "Calm down, calm down," he said aloud. Only one block beyond the intersection he came to the Antler Motel.

Hefting his bags from the Mustang trunk, he peered to the south of town and was surprised to see ski slopes not more than a half-mile away. More surprising was the fact that the mountain didn't look all that threatening, not much more impressive than WhiteTail back east. Maybe western skiing was overrated.

"Hi," said the young man behind the counter.

"I should have a reservation, my name is Webster."

The clerk shuffled through a pile of index cards. "Here it is. Larry Webster, Columbia, Maryland. Is that near Baltimore?"

"West of Baltimore about fifteen miles."

"And how long are you going to be staying with us?"

"Two nights for sure, but I might decide to stay longer. The reservation should have been set up that way."

"Yep, that's what it says. Would you prefer a room with two double beds or one queen size?"

"I'll take the queen. It's a non-smoking room isn't it?"

"Yes it is. Now if you decide to keep the room after Monday night, you need to tell us a day in advance. Here's your key, room 212. Anything else I can help you with?"

"Yeah, do you have a map of town?" The affable clerk reached below the counter and picked up a map. "Here ya go."

"Oh, one other thing. Where's a good place to rent skis?"

"There's a list of rental places on the flip side of the map. They're all about the same. Also a bunch of other info is on the map, restaurants and stuff like that."

Larry studied the back of the map. "Oh yeah, Teton Adventures, a guy at the airport said that was a good place to rent skis. Where's that located?"

"One block up on Cache, right on Broadway, then a block and a half down the street on the right."

"This guy at the airport said a young girl there was some kind of champion skier or something."

"That would be the owner's daughter, Adrienne Sullivan. She's definitely the best woman skier in this town, only a senior in high school too."

"How did she get to be so expert that young ?"

"She's a natural athlete, good at everything she tries."

Larry wanted to know more, but felt self-conscious and decided to divert attention away from his interest in Adrienne Sullivan. He pointed out the large picture window. "The ski slope doesn't look nearly as big as I thought it would be. Actually, it looks pretty easy."

The young man slapped the counter with both hands. "You gotta be kidding man! That's just Snow King, only old ladies ski there. The real skiing is at Teton Village west of town. Let me know if it looks easy when you get to the top of Rendezvous Peak."

Feeling foolish Larry replied, "Okay, I'll let you know."

Huffing and puffing up the steps to the second floor - it was going to take a while to acclimate to the altitude - he found his room, flopped down on the bed and repeatedly ran his hands up his face and back over his hair. He had come all this way to see his daughter, but now found the prospect absolutely terrifying.

How would he find Adrienne, he certainly wasn't about to go knock on her front door - "Hi, you probably don't remember me, but I'm your real father.   Tell me about yourself." Maybe Barbara had said she helped out at the store, but he wasn't sure. The store was the place to start, but he just wasn't ready to barge in there and possibly see his daughter within the next ten minutes.

He hadn't eaten anything since leaving his house this morning, eleven hours earlier. Normally a big eater when traveling, he was unable to stomach the idea of airline food on this day. Right out his window, directly across the street was a Sizzler Steak House. A t-bone steak, baked potato, ear of corn, and a large slice of apple pie should fill his anxious stomach.   Usually guilty of gobbling down his food, he took small bites and chewed slowly, stretching out the time as long as possible. Finally, he pushed himself away from the table. There was no sense in delaying things any longer; the time had come.

The days were short in January and it was already getting dark outside. He could see his breath in the cold evening air, the temperature having dropped twenty degrees since the afternoon. Almost before he knew it, he stood at the entrance to Teton Adventures. He closed his eyes, took a deep breath for courage, and then swung open the door. The first sensation was the sound of soothing music, a

Beatles song, "Nowhere Man." The next sensation was that of color, the store was wildly colorful and filled with every conceivable type of outdoor equipment and clothing - against the walls, in the aisles, and hanging from the ceiling.

The wall to the right was adorned with a dizzying array of skis. The first section devoted to downhill skis and the next to cross-country skis. Beside the skis were circular platforms displaying ski boots. Toward the back of the store and down several steps was an area with a half dozen fully erected tents. Surrounding the tents were sleeping bags, stoves, lanterns, shelves of freeze-dried food, and other camping paraphernalia. A blizzard of backpacks dangled from the ceiling.

Walking to the back of the store, he heard voices coming from his left, but he wouldn't allow his head to turn. With his peripheral vision, he could make out a checkout counter with two people behind it, a man and a young woman. As he edged past the counter, gazing fixedly at the rear of the store, a young female voice said, "If there's anything I can help you with just give me a yell." The voice seemed familiar in an odd sort of way.

"Okay," he replied without turning his head.

He continued in a beeline toward the rear of the store, stumbling on two unexpected steps leading down to the tents, but somehow regaining his balance without drawing attention. Further back in the store were racks of outdoor clothing and several kayaks propped against the rear wall. Another room, filled with rental skis, led off to the right. He dawdled there trying to summon the courage to venture back to the front of the store, to approach the girl with that strangely familiar voice. Only now did he become aware of the seven or eight shoppers meandering throughout the store. The music had changed, still the Beatles, but now it was Paul McCartney singing

"Michelle." This wasn't a radio station that just happened to be broadcasting a Beatles' song. No, someone in this store was playing his favorite album, "Rubber Soul."

Mustering his resolve, he boldly marched back toward the front of the store. There were three employees dressed in dark green vests, all wearing nametags. One, a rugged man of about thirty with a shaved head and a large gold earring, was fitting a young black woman with ski boots. The other two were the man and the young woman behind the counter. The man looked in his direction, but Larry's eyes were fixed on the young woman who was turned with her back to him. She had long blond hair, tied back in a ponytail, and looked to be of the same height and build as Rachel.

The man, whose nametag identified him as "Hank" asked, "Getting ready to do some skiing?"

Larry heard the question, but paid no attention. He camped in front of the counter staring at the form of the young woman who was rearranging knives in a glass case. The man behind the counter looked at Larry quizzically.

"Excuse me miss."

As she spun around, his knees buckled. Clutching the counter was the only thing that enabled him to stay on his feet.

"Yes sir. What can I do for you?"

He bore in on her face and then the nametag on her vest. It read "Sue". It wasn't her, it wasn't her. He stared at the young woman for several seconds, unable to speak.

"Mister, are you okay?" the man asked with concern.

He needed to regain his composure quickly. "I'm sorry. Practically dead on my feet........ up all last night and then flew in today from the east coast. The combination of no sleep, altitude, and jet lag is doing me in. I must look like a zombie walking around here."

Hank Sullivan laughed a deep warm laugh, a Fred Flintstone kind of laugh. "I wasn't going to say it, but that's exactly what I was thinking." He extended his hand and introduced himself. "My name's Hank Sullivan. In theory, I'm the boss around here."

Larry clasped his hand and they exchanged a firm friendly handshake. "My name's Larry." Larry studied this man who had become the father of his daughter. He appeared to be in his late forties, about 5'10", thin but solidly built, dark brown eyes, long thinning black hair with just a smidge of gray around his temples, and a big genuine smile. He was prepared to dislike, even hate this man, but realized instantly this would be a man who would be hard to hate.

"Where you from Larry?"

"Maryland."

"That's a mighty long way away. Are you in Jackson Hole by yourself?"

"Yeah, my wife and daughter are at home. I'm going to try to get some skiing in on the front end of a business trip."

"How old is your daughter?"

"She's seventeen."

Hank smiled a big friendly smile. "So's mine." He maintained his smile and slowly shook his head from side to side. "Seventeen, I can't believe my little girl is seventeen years old."

"So does she help you around the store?"

"She sure does. She opened up the store this morning and worked until around one. Then she took off with a group of cross-country skiers to spend the night at Jenny Lake."

"Where's that?"

"Oh, about seventeen or eighteen miles to the north."

Larry's eyes widened as he pictured the group of cross-country skiers he had passed earlier in the day. "Were they traveling north on the road that goes by the airport?"

"Yep, that's the way to Jenny Lake."

"Would they have been near the airport at about three o'clock? About twenty skiers."

He scratched his chin, as he thought for a moment. "That's about where they would have been around that time."

Larry felt a chill tingle his body, realizing he had passed within a few feet of his daughter without knowing it. He tried not to let the emotional knot in his stomach affect his expression. "Is there a lodge up there?"

"Up where?"

"At Jenny Lake."

"There's a lodge there, but they won't be staying in it."

"Where are they staying?"

"Outside."

"You mean they're going to be camping out in this weather."

"They do it three or four times every winter. If you've got the right gear, it's not a big deal."

"When will she, I mean... when will they be coming back?"

"They dropped off their cars yesterday evening. Adrienne will be driving straight to Teton Village in the morning. She'll be teaching tomorrow, she's a ski instructor there."

"When does this daughter of yours ever do her school work?"

"I don't know how she fits everything in, but she does. She's the most organized person I know. Got that from her mother."

"I'm taking up a lot of your time here. Can you help me with some rental skis?"

"That's why I'm in business."

Hank Sullivan led Larry through the store to the back room, filled with rental skis and boots. The store now echoed with the sounds of John Lennon singing "In My Life."

"Who's the Beatles fan around here?"

"I am. How 'bout you?"

Larry could feel himself being torn between liking, yet resenting this man. "Yeah, me too."

"What kind of skier are you?"

"Well, I used to be pretty good, but I haven't skied seriously in almost twenty years. Went one time earlier this year and caught the bug again."

"You gonna want to ski the bumps?"

"Yeah, I want to. Whether I'll be able to is another question."

Hank selected a pair of multi-colored skis from the wall. "This Atomic Premiere is a real nice all purpose ski. I'd also recommend these Nordica boots, they feature an adjustment to change the amount of forward lean."

"Sounds good to me, but anything would sound good to me. I lost track of skiing equipment a long time ago."

For the next fifteen minutes Hank assisted Larry in obtaining a snug boot fit, adjusted the release settings on the bindings, and measured him for poles.

"How many days do you want to keep the equipment?"

"I'm not sure. I'll just rent the gear on a day-to-day basis."

"That's fine, but it's $25 a day, and only $15 a day if you rent for four days."

"I don't think I'll be here that long."

Hank carried the equipment to the front counter and Larry followed. "How do you want to pay for this?"

"Visa."

"I'll just take an impression now and we'll fill in the amount when you return the equipment. Have fun skiing, but take it easy at the beginning."

"Okay, I will. Thanks a lot."

Larry shouldered the skis, snatched the boots and poles, and started leaving the store, but turned around after only a few steps. "You know my skiing is going to be pretty rusty. I could probably use a refresher lesson. Does your daughter give private lessons?"

"She sure does, she'd much rather teach a private lesson than a group lesson. Just ask for Adrienne Sullivan at the Teton Village Ski School. The first class time is 9:30."

"I'll do that. Thanks."

Chapter 23

Larry expected to have difficulty sleeping, but he slept well, his physical fatigue overwhelming the anxiety of this approaching day. Awaking at 6:00 a.m., he felt surprisingly rested. A fresh shave and a hot shower made him feel even better.

Toweling down after the shower, he felt the tingling in every part of his body, just like when he was a little boy on the verge of experiencing something fantastic. He remembered a summer morning more than thirty-five years ago, being awakened by his father to drive the 160 miles to Cincinnati to watch the Reds play the Pirates that afternoon. Attending a major league baseball game just wasn't possible, it couldn't be happening. Maybe it was possible for the kids who lived in the big cities like New York and Philadelphia, but it wasn't possible for a little boy who had never been out of the hills of southeastern Kentucky. No, a major league baseball game was a mystical event that one was only allowed access to through the static filled sounds of a radio in your living room. But there was his father, rubbing the sleep from his eyes with a damp cloth and saying, "Come on Larry Joe. They ain't about to hold up the start of the Reds game just for us."

And now this couldn't be happening. A father just doesn't get a chance to see his daughter who has been dead for seventeen years. Maybe you can envision her in your dreams, maybe you can meet her in heaven, but you don't actually see her alive in a beautiful place like Jackson Hole. It just wasn't possible.

Outside everything was black and white. The morning sky was still black, but filled with shimmering white stars. The streets and buildings, hidden from light, were black. Beneath the lampposts everything was white from the thin blanket of snow that had fallen during the night. Crossing the street, he ran several quick strides and slid about ten feet with his arms stretched out like a surfer to keep his balance. After a filling breakfast at the Sizzler of French toast and fruit, he was back in his room changing into ski clothes - a pair of black bibbed insulated pants worn over long johns, a white cotton turtle neck pullover, a gray knit sweater, and a heavy pair of wool socks beneath hiking boots. A hooded parka, wool hat, ski gloves, and goggles were tossed on the floor next to ski boots.

Brushing his teeth, he stared into the bathroom mirror. There should be feelings reflected in his face, feelings of sadness, regret, anger, and guilt. But he didn't see any of these emotions. What he saw instead was childish excitement. And he could feel it - his whole body tingled. Maybe it was impossible, but today he was a little boy again, going to Cincinnati to see the Reds play the Pirates.

Chapter 24

The green 1980 Ford Maverick swerved off Interstate 80 in western Iowa and followed the signs to McDonalds.

"Just go through the drive-thru lane," Rachel Webster directed.

Vinnie Carolla drove past the drive-thru window to the parking lot. "We're stopping, I've got to take a dump."

"That's not possible, you just took one four hours ago."

"Believe me, it's possible. Anyway that was Illinois, this is Iowa."

"What does that have to do with anything?"

"I'm working on my goal of defecating in all of the 48 contiguous United States."

"You never mentioned this goal before."

"Oh yeah, it's been a life long ambition of mine. I've now dropped dung in 31 of them."

"Why didn't you stop in Ohio or Indiana?"

"I'll get Indiana on the way back. As for Ohio, I have relatives there. I've crapped there a bunch of times."

Vinnie steered the car into a parking space. They sat there gawking into the restaurant filled with mid-western, Sunday morning churchgoers. As soon as they turned to face one another they burst into laughter. When the laughing stopped, Rachel moaned, "I want to get out of this car so badly, but I think my body is permanently molded into a sitting position."

"Tell me about it," Vinnie whined.

"Come on Vincent, you go take your Iowa shit and I'll get us a mess of pancakes."

The Other Part Of Me

Walking like robots without their hinges oiled, they made their way inside. Rachel bought two orders of pancakes, two orange juices, and a jelly-filled donut they would split. She wandered around the eating area, instinctively looking for the non-smoking section only to realize that McDonalds had recently declared most of their restaurants completely smoke free. Finding an open table, she began eating, foregoing the normal courtesy of waiting for Vinnie. If she finished first he could eat in the car, it was her turn to drive anyway.

Vinnie plopped down with a thud in the seat across the table. "You know I expected Iowa to have the cleanest toilets in the world and they do."

"Why did you expect that?"

"I just expect Iowans to place a high value on the cleanliness of their johns."

An elderly lady in the next booth, overhearing Vinnie, reached over and tapped him on the shoulder. "We do."

Vinnie and Rachel just looked at one another, both of them too tired to react.

Cramming her cheeks full of pancakes, Rachel mumbled, "Only two more stupid states to go."

"Yeah right, but they're the states from hell. You know those maps where they superimpose Alaska on the lower 48 states. Alaska fits inside of Nebraska........ hell, you can fit three Alaskas in Nebraska. And as for Wyoming, forget it, you can fit a dozen Alaskas in Wyoming. And we gotta go all the way across Wyoming. We're never going to get there."

Rachel resigned herself to the ordeal. "This is taking longer than we thought, isn't it?"

Vinnie rubbed his eyes and yawned. "Well, your original prediction that we would be there tonight doesn't look very good, does it?"

Rachel strained to focus her eyes on the AAA Road Atlas spread out on the table in front of her. "We're just about half way and we've driven almost a thousand miles, I think." She looked up. "You know, it would be nice if you had a car with an odometer that worked."

Vinnie did a Steve Martin comeback. "Well, excuuuuse me!"

Rachel ignored him and checked her watch. "Half way and we've been driving for twenty-five hours."

"Twenty-six," corrected Vinnie with a yawn.

"Oh yeah, I forgot the hour we set our watches back. We should get there sometime tomorrow morning."

"If we don't drop dead first," Vinnie groused.

"What are you complaining about, it's your turn to sleep."

They finished their pancakes and then argued over who would get the biggest piece of the donut. In the end, Rachel took the smaller piece in exchange for the last gulp of Vinnie's orange juice.

Vinnie rested his elbows on the table, propped up his chin, and struggled to keep his eyes open. "Are you going to call your mother? You promised her you would call this morning."

"Oh God, do I have to?"

"Yes, you have to. There's a pay phone outside."

Rachel slipped her coat on, slowly trudged to the phone, and punched in the MCI access code and her home phone number. The phone rang only one time before Vivian answered, "Hello."

"Hi, Mom."

"Oh Rachel, are you okay?"

"I'm fine. I told you there's absolutely nothing for you to worry about. Vinnie is with me, and we're perfectly okay."

"Rachel, please tell me what this is all about. Tell me where you are."

"I'm sorry. Like I said last night, you're just going to have to trust me."

"How can I trust you when you do something like this?"

"I'm sorry Mom, but you don't have any choice. Did Dad call?"

"Not yet."

"Now remember you can't say anything to him," Rachel replied sternly.

"Oh Rachel, I don't know what I want to do most, hug you, or wring your neck."

"I have to get going now."

"Please don't hang up. When are you going to be home?"

"Like I told you last night, it'll take a few days before I know exactly how long we're going to be away. But it's not going to be that long, not much more than a week or so."

"I hope to God you're not screwing up your life."

"It's nothing like that. Call Vinnie's mom and tell her everything is okay."

"How can I tell her everything is okay?"

"Please just do it. I gotta go. Bye."

Rachel hung up the phone and reeled around to face Vinnie who had been listening over her shoulder. Vinnie squared his shoulders, folded his arms in front of him and tilted his head back. "Mothers! We run away from home, we don't tell them where we're going or how long we'll be gone...... and they get all worked up. They are just so damned unreasonable, aren't they?"

"Funny guy, aren't you?"

Vinnie scrunched up his face. "You wanna tell me one more time why we're doing this?"

"I know there's something very important going on. I feel it in the bottom of my soul, I really do."

"The only thing you know is your father lied about being at the hospital and he lied about going to Arizona instead of Wyoming. So what?"

"How many times are we going to have this same stupid conversation? Remember, now you're supposed to say -- Rachel why didn't you just confront your father. And then I say because I saw something in his eyes that makes me know I have to do this. I know he's involved with something that could change his life forever and maybe mine."

"What do you mean yours? You never said that before."

"I don't know what I mean, it's just a premonition I have." Rachel frowned at Vinnie. "If you want to turn around and go home, just take me to a bus station."

Vinnie reached into his coat pocket, fingered the car keys and dangled them in front of Rachel's nose. "Make sure you wake me up before we get to Wyoming. I gotta take my Nebraska crap."

Chapter 25

Larry motored out of the Antler Motel parking lot and headed west, and in less than ten minutes was driving north on Teton Village Road. The Grand Tetons towered on his left. Snow was everywhere, more snow than he'd ever seen before. The early morning light rendered everything a dull gray making it impossible to distinguish discrete objects or features of the land, everything blending into a gray nothingness. But to the left and up high, the first rays of the sun were just catching the very peaks of the Tetons causing them to glow a soft pink. As the sun continued to rise, the peaks began to take on their natural colors, brilliant white snow laced between the dark gray rocky outcroppings that were too steep to hold the snow. The pink glow marched slowly but steadily down the face of the mountain, only to be transformed into brilliant white a few minutes later.

It was a little after eight o'clock when Larry arrived at Teton Village. The dullness of just twenty minutes earlier was now replaced with the vivid colors of Teton Village and of the arriving skiers, most dressed in flamboyant attire. Glancing around at the other skiers, Larry chuckled to himself that the blandness of his ski clothes actually made him stand out.

Having arrived early - the slopes didn't open until nine o'clock - he was able to park in the front of the lot and didn't have to trudge very far. Nonetheless, the 150 yards to the ticket window was still a pain given the awkwardness of clomping around in ski boots. Only three people were in line when he reached the ticket window and they quickly bought lift tickets.

"Can I pay for both lifts and lessons here?"

The young woman behind the window scratched her nose with a pencil. "Yes, you can. How many days do you want for your lift ticket?"

"I'm not sure how many days I'm going to be skiing so I just want a single day ticket."

"You get a big break if you buy one of the multiple day packages, the prices are listed on that sign just to your right."

"I'll just take a single day ticket and a lesson."

With a hint of irritation the woman gruffed, "That'll be seventy dollars, forty for the lift and thirty for the group lesson."

"No, I want a private lesson from Adrienne Sullivan."

"A private lesson costs sixty dollars for an hour and a half, or one hundred dollars for three hours."

Even with the enormity of what he was about to experience, his cost-conscious instincts surfaced niggardly as he momentarily debated his options. But he quickly startled himself back to reality. He wasn't buying time with a ski instructor; he was buying time with his daughter. "I'll take the three hour lesson."

"One hundred and forty dollars please."

"How do you arrange it so Adrienne Sullivan will be my instructor?"

"I don't have anything to do with that. You'll have to work that out with the ski school. Their office is just around the corner, they open at eight-thirty."

Just around the corner turned out be fifty yards. The door was locked and it was eleven minutes until eight-thirty. He thought about looking around the village for a few minutes, but didn't want to chance having someone get in line ahead of him. The minutes passed agonizingly slowly and it wasn't until eight-thirty-five that a stout man with unruly hair and a gray beard who looked to be in his mid-fifties opened the door. The line behind Larry was now fifteen or so people long. He quickly stepped up to the counter.

"Hi, I'm here to take a three hour lesson from Adrienne Sullivan."

With a surprising soft, southern accent the man replied, "Adrienne doesn't teach on Sundays, only on Saturdays."

"But I spoke to her father," Larry countered nervously.

"Look, Adrienne's a fantastic skier, but she's not one of our more experienced instructors. Let me see who else might be available," the man said, tracing his finger down a clipboard.

Larry tried to calm himself. "I really do want to have the lesson with Adrienne."

"All I can say is come back next Saturday when she'll be here."

A young woman behind the counter to the man's left who was serving a second line interjected, "Major." The bearded man replied, "Yo."

"Adrienne is working today. She took off yesterday. She switched days with Dave."

The bearded man grimaced at Larry and sputtered, "What the hell do I know; I'm only the boss around here. You want Adrienne Sullivan, you got her. Give this ticket to her, she'll be at the ski school station on top of the mountain at nine-thirty. It's about twenty-five yards to the left of where you step off the gondola. It takes twenty minutes for the ride up, so be on the gondola no later than nine-ten."

"Thanks."

The man added helpfully, "If you'd like to ride up with her, you might be able to catch her when she picks up her equipment, if she hasn't already gone up. The instructors keep their gear in a locker room at the bottom of the steps leading up to the gondola. Some people like to get an early start on their lesson by picking their instructor's brain on the ride up."

"Okay thanks," replied Larry with a teenage like cracking in his voice.

Larry jostled his way out of the now very crowded room, hefted his skis and poles, followed a sign pointing to the gondola, and located the locker room. Almost immediately, three instructors, two men and one woman, wearing dark blue stretch pants, light blue parkas, and dark blue knit hats came out carrying their skis and poles. The woman was very tall, taller than both of the men, and certainly wasn't the one he was looking for. He found a convenient place to stand on the other side of the steps only about fifteen feet from the door of the locker room.

A steady horde of skiers plodded by him up the steps to the gondola. The pounding of their boots against the concrete steps sounded like an invading army. Mixed in among the skiers were another seven or eight instructors who stopped to pick up their skis. Every time an instructor went into the locker room the door emitted an annoying creaking sound as it closed behind them. Two of the instructors had been young women. The sight of each had started his heart racing, but neither was the one he was waiting for. At five after nine he decided he had to go, it was going to take him at least five minutes to climb the steps and board the gondola. Adrienne Sullivan must already be at the top of the mountain, having a hot chocolate or maybe even sneaking in a quick run down one of the slopes. He hoisted his skis over his right shoulder, snatched up his poles with his left hand and joined the marching army of skiers trudging up the steps.

After about twenty steps he came to a small landing and stopped to reposition his skis, which were cutting into his shoulder. Hearing the creaking sound of the locker room door closing at the bottom of the steps, he quickly turned to look, but no one was there. Someone must have just gone inside. The steady stream of skiers had momentarily abated so his view was unobstructed. How long would it take for someone to go inside, open her locker, take off her shoes, slip into her ski boots, pick up her skis and poles, and then .... Before he could visualize the end of the process the door swung open and Karen Webster, now known as Adrienne Sullivan, walked out.

She looked up and her eyes met those of the man standing on the landing above her. Her hat was pulled over her forehead and ears, hiding her hair and revealing only about two-thirds of her face. It was the face of Rachel Webster, there was no difference, it was the same face. The eyes, the nose, the lips, the chin, everything was identical. He was stunned by the beauty of this face - oval shaped with bright blue eyes, perfectly formed lips and a slightly upturned nose. It was the same face he saw every day, but the beauty of which, until now, he had never fully appreciated.

She paused momentarily, conscious of the man's unwavering scrutiny. She lowered her head to check her footing on the icy steps and began climbing. After four more steps she glanced up, his undue attention was now cause for concern. Uneasiness was beginning to show on her face.

With the young woman, again having averted her gaze away from him, now only a few steps below, Larry politely inquired, "Excuse me, are you Adrienne?"

"Yes," she replied tentatively.

He forced a smile. "Hi, my name is Larry. I signed up for a private lesson with you this morning."

"You did?"

"I rented equipment from your father last night and he said you liked giving private lessons...... and I need a private lesson."

"Oh, great." The relief in her voice was obvious.

"I'm sorry I kept staring at you like that. I had my eyes examined a couple of months ago and I need glasses. Haven't been able to make myself go get them yet, just can't accept the fact that I'm getting old."

"You sound like my father."

Thunderstruck, he steadied himself against the railing. A piercing chill surged through his body and a rush of heat flushed his face. He thought of a hundred things he wanted to say, but couldn't.

"Are you okay?"

He gasped several deep breaths. "Yes, I'm fine."

"Are you sure?"

"I'm good, really. Let's get going. I'm anxious to get started with my lesson."

"That's why they pay me the big bucks," Adrienne joked.

Adrienne bounded up the steps ahead of him. He wanted to walk beside her, but was unable to catch up. She negotiated the steps with such ease it didn't seem possible she was wearing ski boots. Nearing the top of the stairs Larry yanked down the zipper of his parka to cool off, the steep climb was stoking his internal furnace a bit too much. Feeling the same effect, Adrienne whipped off her hat and a thick shock of long, shiny blond hair cascaded down her back and gently swished back and forth in rhythm with her strides. At the top of the landing Adrienne turned to check Larry's progress. With her hat off, her face was fully revealed for the first time. She was beautiful - dazzling golden blond hair her most striking feature - but what shocked Larry the most was her resemblance to Vivian. It didn't seem possible that he had never recognized the intense resemblance between Rachel and her mother. It had to be the hair. The combination of Rachel's short black hair and Vivian's long, premature gray hair produced a camouflaging effect that hid the similarity of their facial features. But with Vivian's youthful blond color having been recently restored and with Adrienne's long blond hair worn in the same style, the resemblance was incredible.

"That's quite a climb," Larry panted, feeling the effects of Jackson Hole's altitude.

"Yes it is," Adrienne agreed without a trace of breathlessness in her voice.

"Let's hustle, we can still make this car," she urged, nodding in the direction of the bright blue gondola car filling up with skiers.

Larry was surprised to see a large gondola car holding fifty or sixty people. He had expected a small car that carried only a few skiers.

"Hi Tim. Can you fit us in?" Adrienne asked the young attendant helping skiers into the gondola.

With exaggerated concern the young attendant, who looked to be about Adrienne's age, replied, "For you Adrienne, anything." Larry detected an unmistakable element of seriousness buried within the young man's jovial reply.

As the gondola inched along, they squeezed on board the crowded car. All the seats around the perimeter of the car were occupied and dozens of people stood grasping a variety of handholds. Adrienne and Larry managed to reach two available looped straps hanging from the ceiling near the back of the car just before the car connected to the main cable and lurched forward gaining speed. Sandwiched together like sardines, their faces were only inches apart. While the other passengers gaped out the windows at the majestic scenery and clamored excitedly, Larry peered directly into Adrienne's eyes. It had been more than seventeen years since he had been this close to his daughter. They stood there quietly, neither of them speaking. Feeling his eyes begin to moisten, he had to do something, say something, or else he was going to go to pieces.

But before he could speak Adrienne said with obvious nervousness, "Are you, I mean, have you skied Jackson Hole before?" Clearly, she found his actions disconcerting - the last thing in the world he wanted. Somehow, he had to put her at ease.

"No, I haven't. Just about all of my skiing has been back east. I skied at Steamboat in Colorado one time, but that was twenty years ago. To be honest, I'm a little scared."

"There's no need to be scared. We just have to make sure you stay within your capabilities."

"Sounds good to me."

"So what level of skier are you?"

"I guess I'm an advanced intermediate....... at least I think that's what I used to be."

"That's cool. After I watch you ski, I'll tell you what I think, and we can go from there."

Thinking it must seem odd that he hadn't even glanced out at the spectacular scenery, he diverted his attention to the rear window of the gondola, which was now well up the mountain. In the floor of the vast valley below, the Snake River frozen in most sections, but free flowing where there were rapids, wound its way southward.

"Wow, it really is beautiful here."

"My mother used to say that Jackson Hole is the most beautiful place in the world."

The Other Part Of Me

Reflexively, he almost asked her about her mother, the woman who had stolen her away from him, but he caught himself and stayed the impulse.

"Adrienne........ is it okay if I call you that ?"

"Sure, that's my name."

"I'm curious about what you're going to major in at Stanford?"

Again a strain of uneasiness returned to her face. "How do you know that I'm going to Stanford?"

"Your father told me last night. We had an interesting conversation while he was helping me pick out ski equipment."

"About what?"

"Lots of things."

"How is it that you were talking about me going to Stanford?"

"We were talking about our daughters. I have one too."

"What's her name?"

"Rachel."

"How old?"

"Same age as you."

"Senior in high school? "

"Yep."

"Is she going to college?"

"Yep."

"Where?"

"Harvard."

"Really?"

"Really."

"What's she gonna major in?"

Larry raised his free hand to his chin, rubbed it contemplatively, and smiled. "Oh, I don't think I should answer that question......... you didn't answer me when I asked you the very same thing just a minute ago."

The gondola abruptly slowed as it neared the top of the mountain. Not expecting the change in speed, Larry lost his balance and bumped into a man in a bright red ski outfit standing in front of him.

"Sorry."

"No problem," the man replied.

In regaining his balance Larry happened to look out the rear window again. Skiers were tentatively navigating their way down the steepest ski slope he had ever seen. "Oh my God," he nearly shouted.

Sensing his awe, Adrienne tapped him on the shoulder and wisecracked, "Welcome to Jackson Hole skiing."

The gondola came to a complete stop, the doors opened and the mass of skiers began slowly oozing out. Swept along with the tide of skiers they began to get pushed apart. Adrienne yelled, "We need to go over to the Ski School Hut and check in. Try to follow me."

Exiting the gondola station Larry again experienced the blinding intensity of a bright sunny day in Jackson Hole. He dropped his skis to the snow and hurriedly searched his pockets for his sunglasses. With his vision restored he spotted Adrienne up ahead, shouldered his skis, and hustled to catch up with her for the short walk to the Ski School Hut. Adrienne slowed to match his pace, calling out over her shoulder, "I just have to sign in. Do you have your lesson ticket?"

"Here," he complied as he handed her the ticket.

She reached back to take the ticket without bothering to turn around. "This should just take a minute. Go ahead and put your skis on."

By the time he buckled and adjusted his boots and stepped into his ski bindings, Adrienne was ready to go. She checked her watch and said, "It's a few minutes after nine-thirty. We've got three hours to have some fun, and help make you a better skier. But before I start a lesson I always like to ask one question."

"Shoot."

"Of all the lessons you've taken in the past, what's the single most important thing you've learned?"

"I've never taken a lesson before."

"I'm your first ski instructor?"

"You'll be the best ski instructor I've ever had."

"And the worst," she added with a smile.

Adrienne jammed her poles into the snow and then pulled a bright red and black scarf from her pocket. She removed her hat, gathered her hair and neatly tied it into a ponytail with the scarf.

"How 'bout we take one practice run on an intermediate slope to loosen up. I'll watch you ski, and when we get to the bottom we'll figure out what we want to accomplish with this lesson."

"Sounds like a sensible plan," said Larry as he slipped on his gloves.

Shoving off with her poles and taking a few smooth skating strides Adrienne yelled over her shoulder, "Follow me."

She led him over a slight rise and then across a wide open area with a gently pitching slope, stopping at a small cluster of pine trees at the top of a trail marked with a blue square, the symbol for an intermediate run.

"This is Upper Gros Ventre. It's a nice smooth run, practically no bumps at all."

"Gros Ventre? As in French for big belly?"

"Yeah, it's a Wyoming thing....... and don't ask me about the Tetons, " she cautioned, pointing with one of her poles to suggest her intended route. "We'll cut off to the right down there and ski over to the Thunder Chair Lift. See the lift through the trees?"

"Yep."

"Just take off whenever you're set. I'll follow you."

"First you have to answer my question."

"What question?"

"Your major at Stanford?"

"Physics. I'm gonna major in physics."

"That's great. Why did you pick physics?"

"Listen Mister....... I'm sorry, I don't know your last name."

"It's Webster."

"Listen Mister Webster. You paid a lot of money for this lesson. We can either spend our time chatting about my academic aspirations or we can have some fun and try to improve your skiing. Which will it be?"

"Skiing. But I prefer that you call me Larry. If you don't feel comfortable with that, then please call me Dr. Webster."

Adrienne's eyes brightened with curiosity. "You're a doctor?"

"Not a medical doctor, I'm a scientist."

"In what field?"

As he lunged forward with his poles, quickly picking up speed, he turned and shouted, "Physics, I have a Ph.D. in physics."

Larry concentrated on the trail in front of him. About fifty yards wide, bordered by pine trees on both sides, and nearly deserted, it was covered with a five-inch layer of fresh snow. After a few awkward turns, he got into a reasonably smooth rhythm. As his confidence rose he began carving tighter turns and increasing his speed. But with the increased speed he sensed a gradual loss of control. His skis chattered back and forth and his turns became mechanical and less smooth. Unable to see or hear her, he knew Adrienne was skiing in his tracks, close behind. In a strange way it was important that he make a positive impression on her. He wanted her to like him, and recognize his intelligence. He even wanted her to think of him as a good skier. His poor skiing was embarrassing. He made several skidding turns to slow his speed and gain control of his form. As the slope leveled out just above another steep pitch, he came to a clumsy skidding stop. Within a couple of seconds, Adrienne gracefully came to a smooth stop right beside him, her skies locked together as if they were one.

With a forced grin Larry admitted sheepishly, "You know, maybe I'm not an advanced intermediate."

"Actually, you're a much better skier than that, but you have some absolutely terrible habits," Adrienne replied in an analytic manner.

Larry's spirits brightened, in a confused way. "I am? I do?" He took several deep, gasping breaths. "I'm not sure what you mean."

"You've got a tremendous amount of natural athletic ability. Just on the basis of that ability alone, you've made yourself a very good skier, but you've got any number of flaws in your technique." She began chuckling. "In fact you've got so many flaws I'll have to watch you ski quite a bit just to get them sorted out. We'll never correct them all in three hours, but I think we can make some good progress."

Larry replied enthusiastically, "So where do we start?"

"Well, the biggest problem is your upper body, it's much too busy."

"Busy?"

"Your arms and shoulders are swinging all over the place, and your head is bouncing around like one of those stupid dolls people put on their car dashboards. You need to keep your upper body very quiet. Make your turns with your legs, not your arms."

"I hear what you're saying, but I'm not sure what it means."

"We've only got a few hundred yards to go until we catch the lift. Ski behind me and watch what I do."

"What should I be looking for?"

"Just watch and you'll figure it out."

"Here we go," Adrienne said as she let her skis glide down the increasingly steep slope.

Larry followed in her path and observed silky smooth turns. She was obviously an excellent skier, but he couldn't relate what he was seeing to what she had just said. Then all of a sudden she changed from being just an excellent skier to a ballerina on skis. Her skiing was no longer merely impressive, it had become a thing of beauty, as if she were floating down the mountain without touching the ground. A few turns later the ballerina disappeared, she was just a skier again. And then the ballerina was back. Now he got it. The ballerina's upper body stayed very still, remaining in perfect harmony with the rhythm of the gentle swiveling action of her lower body; whereas, the skier's shoulders were constantly twisting back and forth and her arms swung with each turn. These unnecessary motions resisted each turn, requiring effort and energy that served no purpose. The ballerina had no wasted motion; her skiing reminded him of the smooth flowing Beatles' music he had listened to the night before with the man who was now her father. The ballerina reached the bottom of the trail and skied right up to the empty line for the lift. Larry followed her to the chair-lift loading point.

"Since when are you working on Sundays?" a young attendant with long black hair and a golden tan remarked.

"Just today. I switched with Dave," replied Adrienne as she and Larry hopped onto the chair that began whisking them back to the top of the mountain.

"I saw what you meant about keeping your upper body quiet. I saw it, now all I need is to figure out how to do it," joked Larry.

"We'll start working on that on our next run. Now tell me about where you got your physics degree and what you do."

Larry peeled his gloves off and stashed them in the pocket of his parka, scratched his chin affectedly and kidded, "Now wait a minute. I paid for a ski lesson, not to discuss my academic background."

Adrienne covered her mouth as she laughed. "You really set me up for that one."

"I did that quite nicely, didn't I? Here's the deal, I'll answer your questions and then you can answer mine. I earned my B.S. in physics from Princeton and my doctorate from Johns Hopkins. My doctorate is actually in astrophysics, I'm an astronomer."

"That must be exciting."

"It can be. At least it was when I was involved more directly with the science."

"Where do you work?"

"The National Science Foundation. I'm the head of the Foundation's astronomy department. We manage most of the country's ground-based telescopes."

"That sounds like you're involved with the science."

"I'm involved, but from a distance. I hardly ever get the opportunity to perform actual research anymore. That's what I used to do, that's when it really was exciting."

"Why did you decide to stop doing research?"

"I never really decided to stop, it just kinda happened. Every time I climbed another step up the career ladder, I further distanced myself from research. Then one day, you look around and discover you've traveled so far you can't go back."

"Hmm," Adrienne replied with a frown.

"Hey, it's not all that bad, my job does have its good points...... Now it's your turn. Why did you decide to major in physics?"

"I just love learning about how things click and how the forces of nature cause things to happen. This may sound goofy, but I especially love studying about how things move, whether it's a satellite orbiting the Earth, the spinning of a tornado, or a skier racing down a mountain."

"Do you know what field you want to specialize in after college?"

"Not really. Technology is changing so rapidly, I figure if I decide prematurely I could miss the boat. Right now, I just want to build a solid foundation in physics."

"You'll certainly get that at Stanford. You must have done really well in school to get accepted at Stanford."

"I guess so," Adrienne replied modestly. "What about your daughter?"

Larry just looked at her.

"What's she going to major in at Harvard?"

"Psychology."

"How did she pick that?"

"I'm really not sure. Actually, it came as a surprise to me."

"You must be really proud of her. I mean Harvard, that's a big time wow."

"I am proud of her. Harvard is a big time wow, but so is Stanford. I'm sure your mother and father are proud of you."

Adrienne fidgeted in her seat as the chair continued its slow ascent up the mountain. She rearranged her ski poles, wedging them on the chair beside her, freeing her hands. She removed her sunglasses and momentarily bowed her head and rubbed her face with both hands, then lifted her head and put her hands together in a prayer-like position against her chest. Larry sensed the emotional aura of the situation and decided to change to a lighter subject, but Adrienne began speaking before he could do it.

"My mom died of cancer a little over a year ago. She was a wonderful person, the greatest mother in the world. She was very proud of me and that makes me happy. My dad, Hank, adopted me when I was seven. He's proud of me and that pleases me, but it bothers him that he's not my real father. I couldn't possibly love him any more than I do, and I tell him that and I try to show him. But he thinks that because both of my real parents are dead, that somehow I have this horrible emptiness in my life. I miss my mom terribly, but there's no emptiness. It makes me very sad that he feels that way. I tell him he's all I need, but he just can't accept it."

Larry desperately wanted to put his arms around Adrienne and pull her to his chest. His body tingled with the pricks of a thousand little needles as she continued.

"My real dad was a jerk, he deserted us when I was four. I can just barely remember him..........He'd throw tantrums and hit my mom. He got drunk and was killed in a car accident. It was his fault, I don't feel sorry for him."

Larry didn't know how to react. He was glad he was wearing sunglasses because tears were welling up in his eyes. Still preoccupied with her memories, Adrienne sighed heavily. "This is crazy. I can't believe I'm saying these things. I just met you an hour ago. At first you scared me. Now I'm telling you things I don't even talk about with my closest friends. This is absolutely nuts."

"Adrienne..." Larry's reply was interrupted by the chair lift arriving at the unloading point. As they skied down the ramp from the chair, Adrienne tried to mask her discomfort. "I have to go to the bathroom. I'll be back in just a minute."

She took a series of rapid skating strides with her skis and then poled herself over to the mountain top restaurant, only fifty yards or so away from the lift. She deftly shed her skis and disappeared inside. Larry waited at the ski rack where she had stowed her skis. It was almost fifteen minutes before she reappeared from the restaurant. One glimpse at her eyes before she put on her sunglasses revealed that she had been crying.

"Sorry I took so long. I have a slight case of indigestion," she fibbed as she located her skis in the rack.

"Adrienne, I'm sorry I scared you when we first met. I aahh .....," he stopped momentarily to clear his throat and to keep his voice from cracking. "I'm going to buy those glasses as soon as I get home. I can't keep going around staring at people like that. I feel terrible, I'm very sorry."

Adrienne responded with a slight smile, but didn't say anything.

"Listen, if you're not feeling well let's forget the lesson."

"Oh, no, no, no. I'm fine now. Really."

"Are you sure?"

"Yes, I'm sure and I'm sorry about taking so long in there...... Don't worry about getting your full three hours. I don't have an afternoon lesson. They don't have very many classes this afternoon, and I'm the low guy on the totem pole."

"I'm not worried about getting my three hours. I just want to know for sure that you're okay."

"I'm okay, and I really feel like skiing," said Adrienne with genuine enthusiasm.

"Okay, teach me how to keep my upper body quiet."

For the next three hours Larry focused his attention on Adrienne's instructions and made considerable progress in ridding his upper body of its unnecessary movement. He developed a better rhythm and technique for his pole plants, and began handling more difficult terrain by turning his skies with a smoother motion, rather than always raising up to "unweight" his skies. This greatly improved his ability to ski the most difficult trails with their large moguls, bumps that a skier must either ski around or over.

Larry was amazed at Adrienne's ability to analyze his skiing, identify very subtle deficiencies, and to effectively communicate the necessary corrective actions in a way he could understand and implement. He had known she would be an outstanding skier, but hadn't expected her to possess the level of maturity needed to be such an excellent instructor.

At twenty minutes after one o'clock they stood together on the side of Avalanche Trail. Larry didn't want this brief period with his daughter to end, but he knew it had to.

"You certainly gave me my three hours worth, more like four actually. I had a lot of fun," Larry said, fighting to dispel any hint of sadness from his voice.

"Good, I had fun too. But I need to get home, there's this term paper I've got to finish. Tomorrow's a holiday so there's no school, but I'm going to be helping Dad in the store all day."

"Tomorrow's a holiday?"

"It's Martin Luther King's birthday."

"How could I possibly forget? My mom and I went to Washington for Dr. King's march back in the sixties."

"You really are a neat person. I wish I had more time to spend with you."

"Me too."

"Let's make one last run together down Beaver Tooth. It's a beautiful slope and we haven't skied it," Adrienne suggested as she whacked her pole against the sides of her boots to knock off the snow caked on the buckles.

"Sounds good to me."

Adrienne pointed off to the left. "We just follow South Pass Traverse. It cuts over to Beaver Tooth.....I hope you feel that you've had a good lesson."

"It was a great lesson. I feel like my skiing has definitely improved. What do you think?"

Adrienne blushed. "Well, since you asked........ I've never seen anyone's skiing improve so much during the course of a single lesson."

"It's because you're such a great instructor."

"No. You were a good skier just crying out for a lesson. Don't wait twenty years for your next one."

Larry laughed. "I disagree. It's because you're the best instructor I've ever had."

Adrienne joined in his laughter and reminded, "And the worst."

She bent over and inspected her left boot. "Go ahead. Wait for me at the end of the traverse. I need to adjust my buckles."

Larry skied along the traverse, a short, narrow trail about 100 yards long and only about twenty feet wide with large pine trees on both sides. At the end of the trail he waited for Adrienne. Just as she started down the trail, the sun came out from behind a cloud and shafts of sunlight broke through the pine trees. With her hat and scarf both removed, her hair flowed freely behind her and flashed a brilliant golden blond as she skied in and out of the shafts of sunlight. Her arms held straight out to the side, it looked as if she were flying instead of skiing.

He came to Jackson Hole to find his daughter, to take just the smallest peek at the young woman she had become, to assure himself that she was okay, that she had a good life. He had not come expecting to fall in love with her, but that was what happened. This young woman was his, just as if she had lived every day of the last seventeen years in his house. He wanted to cuddle her in his arms and tell her everything, tell her he was sorry, that he would make everything up to her. But he couldn't.

She zoomed to a stop beside him. "No teaching this time, just the two of us skiing down the mountain together." He wanted to say something significant, something profound that she might carry with her through the years, but all he dared was a muted, "Okay."

"You can ski over to the Apres Vous lift off to the left. It'll take you up to a side of the mountain we didn't even get to."

He nodded in acknowledgement as his eyes brimmed with tears behind his sunglasses.

"I'm going to cut off to the right to drop off my gear. Have a great time on the rest of your trip. I really enjoyed the lesson."

All he could evoke was a torturous, "Thanks."

"Let's roll," Adrienne shouted as she took off.

Larry followed immediately, Adrienne slowing her speed until he caught up. They began skiing side-by-side, turning in perfect unison as if tethered together by some secret force of nature - which of course they were. Larry's skiing was effortless, seemingly floating down the mountain without touching the ground, his head directed toward the bottom of the slope, only seeing his daughter as a graceful blur out of the corner of his eye. When he did glance aside to catch sight of her for just an instant, he saw her beautiful flowing hair and glorious smile. He turned away as tears streamed from his eyes in a torrent.

As they approached the bottom of the slope she screamed, "Your skiing is fantastic! Keep it up!" Then as she peeled off to the right and out of his life she shouted, "Goodbye."

Chapter 26

"Vinnie, wake up."

No response, not even a twitch. Frustrated, Rachel grabbed him by the shoulder and shook vigorously. "Come on, wake up. We're almost there."

"Huh," muttered Vinnie as his head rolled forward jarring his eyes open for an instant.

"Wake up!" Rachel screamed hysterically.

Startled from his near comatose state, Vinnie snapped his head back like a timid private reacting to an angry drill sergeant. He surveyed the landscape with confusion, seeing nothing but white in every direction. "Where are we, the North Pole?"

"Hoback Junction."

"Where?"

"Hoback Junction, about ten miles south of Jackson Hole."

"I can't believe we're actually going to make it. What time is it?"

"Five of nine."

"Monday morning?"

"Yes Vinnie, it's Monday morning," barked Rachel. They had been driving for fifty-two hours, stopping only to eat and to go to the bathroom. Their nerves were worn paper-thin.

Vinnie rubbed the stubble on his unshaven face. "I feel like shit. No, I feel much worse than shit, feeling like shit would be a big improvement."

Ignoring his childish ranting, Rachel squeezed the steering wheel tightly. Overwhelmed with fatigue her arms began to quiver.

"What's wrong?"

Oblivious to his concerns, Rachel clutched the wheel even tighter and began shaking more violently.

"Pull over, pull over!"

"No, we're almost there," Rachel replied, her words slurred like a drunk.

"I said pull over! You're going to get us killed," Vinnie yelled as he shook her by the arm.

"Okay, okay, there's a spot up there."

Rachel swerved the car off the side of the road onto the shoulder and skidded into a mound of snow. She leaned forward, resting her head against the steering wheel, and sobbed. "Why the hell did I make us do this? This is so stupid. We came all this way, and now I don't know why."

"You just need some sleep. I feel like hell, and I've been able to sleep much more than you." He stroked the back of her neck. "You've hardly slept at all, have you?"

Her head still planted against the steering wheel, she whimpered, "I think I slept two hours one time, but I can't remember when."

"I can't imagine how badly you must feel."

"I feel awful."

"Scoot over here and I'll drive," said Vinnie as he tugged her away from the steering wheel. He slipped into his boots and plodded around the car through knee-deep snow, catching a glimpse of the Snake River through the trees as he slid behind the wheel. Ten minutes later they entered the southern outskirts of Jackson Hole. Vinnie spotted a run-down motel with a "Vacancy" sign and turned into the parking lot.

"What are you doing?" Rachel asked, her words slurred even worse than before.

"I'm getting us a motel room."

Rachel's head wobbled pathetically. "We've got to find my father first."

"You're nuts. You've got to get some sleep."

Rachel began sobbing again. "I've got to find him."

"You're going to bed lady. I'll go look for him."

Unable to keep her eyes open, Rachel relented. "Okay, I guess you're right. How are we going to do this room thing, tell them we're married?" Vinnie shook his head at the absurdity of their circumstances. "Can you believe it? We've been driving for a million hours and we don't have a plan. No plan for the motel, no plan for anything."

Surrendering to her fatigue, Rachel moaned, "Just get the room."

Vinnie decided to register as a single and sneak Rachel into the room. Having never checked into a motel by himself, he was concerned the desk clerk would ask for proof they were married. His fears proved unwarranted, the clerk hardly bothered to look up from the Penthouse magazine he was ogling.

The room was on the ground floor in the back of the motel, so slipping Rachel in without drawing attention wasn't going to be a problem. He draped her arm around his shoulders, dragged her from the car and coaxed her in the general direction of the door - the two of them weaving back and forth like drunken sailors. Fidgeting to get the key out of his pocket, he propped her against the door, then strained to keep her upright as the door swung open. Stumbling blindly, he dropped her unceremoniously on the bed, yanked off her coat and boots, and then covered her with a blanket.

A hot shower and clean clothes pumped a small dose of vitality into his body, but exhaustion and stiffness from two straight days in that wretched Maverick remained. He slumped in the hard wooden chair sandwiched between the bed and clothes chest, the only three pieces of furniture in the room. A pamphlet lying on the chest provided a map of Jackson Hole and a list of motel addresses and phone numbers. The Antler Motel was second on the list. Should he go to the Antler Motel? What in the world would he say if he actually came upon Larry Webster? Maybe he should park in the lot and set up a stakeout like the private detectives did in the movies.

The unaccommodating wooden chair dug into his back. Sitting down on the edge of the bed, careful not to disturb Rachel, he felt her warm butt against his back. How he would love to lie down, pull himself against her, and drift off to sleep. Instead he picked up the phone.

"Antler Motel," a gruff voice answered.

"Is Larry Webster staying at the motel?"

"Yes, Dr. Webster just passed by the desk, said he's going to be checking out in a few minutes. He should be back in his room by now, I'll put you through."

Vinnie hurriedly improvised. "No, that's not necessary. I'll be seeing him in a little while. Thanks."

Vinnie hung up, conscious of the rhythm of Rachel's breathing against his back. Gingerly stroking her hair, he started to wake her, but then thought better of it. Stuffing the pamphlet in his coat pocket, he searched the room for a notepad, finding one in the chest. With a trembling hand he left her a message - "Rachel, It's now 10:35 a.m. Going to look for your wild and crazy father. Back soon. Love you. Vin"

The general aesthetics of Jackson Hole improved dramatically closer to town - nicer looking motels, ski shops decked out in western motif, and expensive restaurants. Holding the pamphlet with the map in one hand and the steering wheel with the other, Vinnie went about a mile and turned into the heart of town. Before he knew it, he had gone past the Antler Motel. Circling the block, with three sequential right turns, brought him back to the motel parking lot.

The entire trip had a make believe feel to it, like when you're playing Monopoly and get caught up in the game, but still realize all your wheeling and dealing is just a bunch of bullshit. He came looking for Rachel's father with his heart, but somewhere inside his head he knew Larry Webster wasn't actually in Jackson Hole, knew the guy on the phone at the Antler Motel was just part of the game. That's the way the trip seemed, until now. "Holy shit, there he is!" Vinnie exclaimed aloud to himself.

Larry opened the trunk of his Mustang as the Maverick drove right behind him. Scooting down in the seat, barely able to peer over the dashboard, Vinnie pulled into a parking spot two spots away, with a Toyota Camry in between him and the Mustang. Squinting through the windows of the Camry he watched as Larry opened the passenger door, stashed something in the glove compartment, and then headed away on foot. Instinctively, he sprang from the Maverick and followed as Larry scampered out of the parking lot and up South Cache Street. Vinnie yanked the hood from his coat over his head, pulled the drawstring as tight as it would go, and left only his eyes and nose exposed. After only one block Larry turned the corner and headed right on Broadway. Vinnie broke into a jog and then slowed to nearly a stop as he came to the corner and peeked around. The sidewalk was mobbed, people walking three and four abreast in most places, but Vinnie was able to zero in on Larry just as he popped into a store about half way down the block. With his insides thrashing wildly, Vinnie moseyed down the sidewalk trying to look nonchalant, passing Teton Adventures with only a glance. Just inside the door, not more than twenty feet from him, Larry was at the counter being helped by a girl with long blond hair.

At the end of the block Vinnie crossed the street to the Town Square park, opposite Teton Adventures. The entrance to the square was a large arch, about fifteen feet high, and looked like it was constructed of white driftwood. Upon closer inspection, the arch turned out to be an interlocked maze of elk antlers bleached white from the sun. A bench just to the side of the arch provided a good surveillance spot. Vinnie unzipped the front of his coat, but kept the hood cinched tightly around his face. Across the street, Larry was still talking to the girl behind the counter.

Ten minutes later - which seemed like an awfully long time to buy something - Larry emerged from the store and started back in the direction from which he had come. Keeping a discreet distance between them, Vinnie followed him back to the parking lot. Obviously in a hurry to get somewhere, Larry jumped in his car, raced out of the parking lot, and headed north. As the silver Mustang zipped past him, Vinnie shielded his face then jerked the hood off his head and ran to his car.

By the time Vinnie fishtailed the Maverick out of the parking lot he had lost sight of the Mustang. After just one block he came to the intersection of Broadway, the light was red. Having no idea whether the Mustang had turned or gone straight, he looked left and right then desperately ran the red light, much to the dismay of several dodging pedestrians. Stomping the gas pedal to the floor and running another red light brought the Mustang back into sight.

A few minutes later Jackson Hole disappeared behind the speeding Mustang and the straining Maverick. The Mustang kept bearing north for another eight miles until it turned off the main road, following signs to the Jackson Hole Airport.

Larry squealed the Mustang to a stop in a space designated for Budget Rental Cars almost directly in front of the entrance to the terminal. Quickly parking the Maverick, securing the hood tightly around his face once again, Vinnie hustled as Larry sprinted into the terminal. The terminal was small. The only activity was at an American Airlines counter where a final few passengers - the last being Larry - were being rushed to catch a departing flight. Just above the door through which they were rushed, a flashing light read, "DENVER FLIGHT 662 NOW BOARDING."

Vinnie stood in the center of the terminal, dumbfounded. To his left several kids were gawking out a large window that faced the airport runway. He joined them and watched as Larry ascended a set of portable steps and boarded a medium-sized plane. An attendant closed the door as the steps were pulled away from the plane by a strange looking towing vehicle. Vinnie, pressing his forehead against the window and smudging it with his nose, held his vigil as the plane taxied out to the runway, accelerated, and took off.

"Excuse me."

"How can I help you?" replied the ticket agent at the American Airlines counter.

Realizing the hood was still drawn tightly around his face, Vinnie loosened the string and swept the hood off of his head.

"I'd like to know if my uncle made the flight that just departed for Denver."

The agent frowned at Vinnie expectantly.

"Well, what's his name?"

"Oh, I'm sorry. His name's Larry Webster."

The attendant glanced at the computer screen in front of her. "Yes, he made it."

Not used to lying, Vinnie smiled crookedly. "Good. I didn't get to talk to him this morning, and I wasn't sure if he was going to Flagstaff now or at the end of his trip."

"I don't remember a Flagstaff, let me check."

After punching a few keys the agent looked up. "Your uncle is connecting to a Baltimore flight, he'll arrive there a little after ten tonight. He has no flight reservations beyond that."

Vinnie mumbled, "thanks" and retreated in confusion.

On the drive back to Jackson Hole, Vinnie tried to make sense out of what was happening, but nothing he could come up with would explain why Rachel's father had flown to Jackson Hole on a Saturday and was now flying back to Baltimore on Monday. And whatever it was he was doing certainly had nothing to do with Flagstaff, Arizona. He dreaded the idea of telling Rachel. What in the world were they to do now? There was no way they could turn around and start the drive back to Maryland, not without a couple of days rest. Drive back hell, maybe they should just junk the car and fly back, he doubted the Maverick could make it anyway, the clutch was starting to slip on steep hills. As he approached the intersection of Cache and Broadway, the light he had run not more than an hour earlier turned red. As he idled behind three other cars, a man entered a car parked at the curb just in front of him. When the light turned green Vinnie motioned to the driver to go and then impulsively steered into the vacated parking space. Not yet ready to confront Rachel - she might be awake when he got back - he locked the car and ambled half a block to Teton Adventures.

Hank Sullivan stood behind the counter, ringing up a pair of ski gloves for a customer. Fighting overwhelming fatigue, Vinnie wobbled past the counter to the back of the store. Other than the one customer buying the gloves, the store was deserted. Moving past skis, camping equipment, and outdoor clothing brought him to the far end of the store where he turned right, aimlessly following an arrow pointing to rental skies.

Just as Vinnie turned the corner, he collided with the girl with the long blond hair, their eyes meeting no more than six inches apart. He froze! It seemed as if he had walked into an amusement park fun house, everything outside of him strangely distorted and everything inside of him spinning askew. This girl couldn't be real - maybe she was some kind of new state-of-the-art holographic projection or something. No, you didn't bump into holographic images, you couldn't touch one, and they didn't come with such a dreamy hint of perfume. Dreamy, that's it. You can feel things in dreams, you can smell things in dreams...... this must be a dream!

"I'm sorry, please excuse me," Adrienne Sullivan offered.

"Rach ....," Vinnie blurted instinctively.

Adrienne smiled back quizzically.

Agape, all Vinnie could manage was an autistic stare.

"Is there something I can help you with?"

"I don't know. I mean....."

After several awkward backward steps Vinnie started running away, but then turned to take one last look. The girl, hands on hips, head cocked to the side, was still there. It wasn't possible, but she was still there.

The motel room was oppressively hot. Beads of sweat covered Rachel's forehead. The blanket he had covered her with lay on the floor next to the bed. Turning off the heat and cracking the window brought a welcomed rush of coolness. Vinnie stripped down to his briefs and settled in the chair next to the bed - too tired and too stunned to notice its hard edges - and watched as Rachel's chest rose and fell. He mentally compared her sweet face with the face of the girl in the store, imagining the two faces together. He smiled as tears dripped into his mouth, the taste of salt causing him to lick his lips. Fatigue attacked his body, slowly consuming him. Fixated on the movement of Rachel's chest, his breathing slowed until it was perfectly synchronized with that of the girl he loved.

Very soon he would tell this lovely young girl about a miracle, and he would tell her she was right - coming to Jackson Hole was going to change her life forever.

Chapter 27

Larry hustled off the airplane and up the enclosed ramp, a cold winter wind whistling outside causing the ramp to shake.

"Connecting flight destination?" asked the elderly male attendant waiting just inside the terminal.

"Baltimore."

The attendant's eyes lit up. "Gate G28. To your left, then take the first right. Departure time is six-fifteen....... And go O's."

"Huh ?" ·

"Used to live in Baltimore, next to Patterson Park."

Larry looked at him with a puzzled expression.

"O's, as in the Baltimore Orioles. I'm a big fan."

"Oh....... Yeah, me too. Gate G28, right ?"

"Yeah, G28."

After a stop in the men's room, Larry spotted a large bank of pay phones, all of them in use. Waiting impatiently, he paced back and forth until a teenage girl with brilliant red hair slammed down one of the phones and stormed away. He darted to the free phone, just barely getting there before a man in an expensive looking blue pinstriped suit. He mentally congratulated himself - the guy was probably a Mercedes or BMW driver.

He punched in the code from his long distance card and a phone number, tapping his foot anxiously as the phone rang six, seven, and then eight times. Ready to hang up, a weak reply came from the other end of the line. "Hello."

"Hello Barbara."

"Larry, is that you?"

"Yes, it's me. How are you?"

"Do you really care?"

"I wouldn't be calling if I didn't care. Now please tell me if you're okay."

"Well......... from what I can see beneath these bandages, about half of my breast is gone."

"You're not going to be able to tell anything until the bandages are off and the swelling goes down."

With mock enthusiasm Barbara bellowed, "Oh, you're right Larry. Everything is absolutely wonderful, that is, of course, if you don't mind having half of a tit."

"Barbara, I'm sorry. But what did the doctor say?"

"He said he had to remove more of the breast than he expected. He's very sorry."

Conscious of the two people on either side of him - so close their shoulders brushed against him - Larry lowered his voice and leaned his forehead against the phone. "You're over-reacting. When I spoke to him right after the operation, he said he had to remove more tissue than expected, but he also said the deformation wouldn't be that severe. You're just upset now, you have to give it a chance to heal and let the swelling go down......... Now, what did he say about the cancer?"

"He thinks he got it all. He didn't find any in the lymph nodes."

"That's wonderful."

There was a long silence before Barbara spoke. "Do you hate me for what I did?"

"I don't know."

"What does that mean?"

"It means I don't know. I'm horribly conflicted. I've loved you so much for so long … and then to find out that you took my baby. I just don't know what to do, what to feel. But I am worried about you, I guess I just can't help myself."

He could hear her uneven breathing and knew she was trying not to cry.

"When did you come home from the hospital?"

"This morning."

"Are you in much pain?"

"It's getting a little better. The painkillers help, but they make me sick to my stomach. The doctor said in another day or two I should be feeling okay."

"When do you see him again?"

"Friday. He'll tell me about the chemo treatments then."

"Treatments? I thought you said he got it all."

"He said it's a precaution. I don't want to take the treatments. He said we can talk about it on Friday."

"I don't want to, but I have to hang up or else I'll miss my flight."

"Where are you?"

"I'm in Chicago, between flights."

She let out a slight moan. "You're on your way to see her now, aren't you?"

"I'm on my way back. I've already seen her."

"Oh my God!"

"I've got to go now. I'll come see you tomorrow."

"Larry, don't hang up. There are so many things I need to talk to you about, so many things I need to tell you."

"I'm sorry. I don't have time now."

"Please at least tell me what happened."

"I didn't tell her if that's what you mean. I've got to go now, I'll come see you tomorrow."

He hung up the phone just long enough to break the connection, then punched in another number. The phone rang only one time.

"Hello."

"Hi Viv, it's me."

"Where the hell are you?" came Vivian's nearly hysterical reply.

"What's wrong?"

"Rachel has run away!"

"What?"

"She's run away with Vinnie."

"Damn, I knew she was getting in over her head with him."

"It wasn't him. It was her idea. I think she made him go with her."

"How do you know that?"

"She called. I can't remember exactly what she said, but it was pretty obvious it was her idea."

"Where are they?"

"For God's sake, do you think if I knew where they were I would be this upset?"

"I'm sorry. This is such a shock. Just tell me what happened."

"The last time I saw her was early Saturday morning. She rushed out the door, and said she and Vinnie were going out for breakfast. She called that evening, said she had to do something and didn't know how long it was going to take. She said Vinnie was with her and not to worry, then she hung up."

"Vivian, wait a minute. What did she say exactly? Did she say where she was going and what it was that she had to do?"

"Stop treating me like an idiot! If she had said any of that, do you think I would leave it out? She called again yesterday. Both times all she said was that she had to do something, and she didn't know how long it was going to take."

"You don't have any idea what this is about?"

"No, I don't have the slightest idea."

"Did they take our car?"

"No, they drove Vinnie's car."

"Have you talked to his parents?"

"I've talked to his mother several times. Vinnie called her on Saturday night too and told her he was doing something for Rachel, told her there was nothing to worry about."

"That's all he said?"

"That's all. His mother's very worried, but she trusts him not to do something stupid."

Larry exploded. "That's just great. Her kid isn't the one who thought about committing suicide."

"Why are you yelling at me? You're the one who hasn't been here. Where have you been anyway?"

"I'm on my way home now. I'm in between flights. I'll be there around eleven."

"Why didn't you call?"

"I'm sorry, I should have. I just got so caught up in working on this problem."

"I called the Lowell Observatory."

"You did?"

"I got the number from information, but all I kept getting was a recording."

Larry moved the phone from his mouth and exhaled slowly. "You probably got the number for the administration building. No one was there over the weekend. We spent all of our time in the telescope building. We were...."

Before he could finish his fabrication, Vivian interrupted. "Never mind that now."

"You're right....... Now think, you don't have any ideas at all as to why Rachel would do this?"

"No, she's been so positive about things lately, so happy. I don't have a clue what this could possibly be about."

"Should you call the police?"

"What would I tell them? She's called home twice. Said she would call every day, but she hasn't called today."

"I know this sounds crazy, but they aren't eloping, are they?"

"No, it's nothing like that. I can't remember her exact words, but she said something like she had to go and find out about something and she didn't know how long it was going to take."

"Did she sound upset?"

"She didn't sound upset either time, but yesterday she sounded really tired."

"All right, listen. My flight arrives a little after ten, so I should be home by eleven. When I get there we can figure out what to do."

"I think the only thing we can do is what she said."

"What's that?"

"Trust her."

"Try not to worry. This is probably just some stupid teenage thing that's going to turn out to be nothing. I'll see you in a few hours. "

Chapter 28

Rachel curled her body up as tight as possible and groped in the darkness for the blanket, but couldn't find it. She rubbed her hands along her arms trying to warm herself.

"Vinnie, I'm cold. I'm real cold."

Rachel blinked her eyes open, and the room was black. There was no one next to her, but she could hear labored breathing.

"Vinnie! Vinnie, is that you?"

"Huh," came the reply from the darkness.

"Vinnie please. Tell me it's you."

Vinnie reached out, searching for her. He crawled onto the bed and wrapped himself around her. They fit together perfectly.

"It's me."

Rachel reached behind her and drew his body tighter against her.

"Are we in Jackson Hole?"

"Yeah, we're at the Stay Longer Motel."

"The last thing I remember was you making me pull off the road."

Vinnie felt the blanket at the bottom of the bed with his feet and tugged it over them.

"That was just to the south of here, about ten miles away."

"What time is it?"

"I don't know. I'm not even sure what day this is."

He reached for the nightstand, found the lamp, but had to run his hand up and down and then around it to find the switch. The light was blinding. He clicked the three-way switch to its lowest setting and dove back under the blanket with her.

"It's so cold in here," Rachel shivered.

"It was too hot before. I opened a window and turned the heat off."

"Go turn it back on."

"Let me just take a minute to wake up."

"Please, I'm freezing."

He snatched the blanket, wrapped himself in it and climbed out of bed.

"Hey," Rachel protested.

"You can't send me on a frigid expedition like this without a blanket."

Vinnie turned the heat up, belly-flopped into the bed, and wrapped himself around Rachel again.

"What time is it? "

Vinnie rolled over and picked up his watch from the nightstand.

"It's six-thirty. But I don't know if it's six-thirty Monday evening or six-thirty Tuesday morning."

"What time did we get here?"

"It was Monday morning, around nine or ten, I can't remember exactly."

"I'm starving," griped Rachel.

"Me too, but I have to find out if it's Monday night or Tuesday morning so I can decide if I want breakfast or dinner."

Vinnie slid out of bed to the window and drew back the curtain.

"What do you see?" said Rachel from beneath the blanket.

"A parking lot with a bunch of cars and huge piles of snow."

"Well, which is it, Monday night or Tuesday morning?"

"I can't tell."

"Turn on the TV."

The TV flashed on with a loud cracking sound just as the camera zoomed in on Peter Jennings, with the ABC nightly news music playing in the background. It took only a few minutes for positive confirmation that it was indeed Monday evening. Rachel cast the blanket off, sat up, and clicked the TV off.

"My God, I think my brain just kicked into gear. We need to find my father. I'm lying here like we drove all this way for no reason." She sprang out of bed, searching for her boots. "Come on, let's get going."

"Don't you want to take a shower first?"

"Hell no, I don't want to take a shower. I want to find my father."

"Let's go get somethin' to eat and we can decide what to do."

"Get serious, we can eat later. We've got to find him."

Vinnie slouched in the chair as Rachel hurriedly tied the laces of her boots.

"Come on Vinnie, let's go."

"He's not ...."

"He's not what?"

"Not here any more. Your father's not here."

Rachel slid onto the floor, her back braced against the bed. "You've got to be kidding?"

"He's on his way back to Baltimore now. He'll get there about ten o'clock. Heck, that's eight o'clock our time. He's almost there."

Rachel slammed her head against the bed and pounded her fist against the floor. "I can't believe it."

"You were dead on your feet this morning so I tucked you in bed and called the Antler Motel to see if your father was there. They said he was just getting ready to check out. I found him right off the bat, and started following him. He went into town to a ski shop, and then drove to the airport and boarded a plane to Denver. The ticket agent said he was connecting to a flight to Baltimore."

"And I slept through all of this?"

"It all happened so quickly. If I'd been five minutes later I would have missed him."

"Are you saying he came to Jackson Hole to go skiing?"

"I'm just tellin' you what happened. When you woke me up a few minutes ago, at first, I thought it was all a dream. But it's not a dream, he's gone."

Rachel covered her face with her hands in bewilderment. "I'm numb, completely numb."

"Take a hot shower and then we can get something to eat."

Rachel struggled to her feet and carried some clean clothes into the bathroom. After just a few seconds she poked her head out. "I don't know whether to laugh or cry, but in a way I'm relieved."

Vinnie heard the water from the sink running as Rachel brushed her teeth. A few minutes later the shower splashed noisily. He waited a short while, went into the bathroom and brushed his teeth. Rachel folded the shower curtain back and laughed. "Is this the stupidest thing you've ever done in your life or what?"

Vinnie was startled by the sight of Rachel's fully exposed breasts. They had made love three separate times, that first night in the back seat of his car and then two times at his house when his parents were out, but he hadn't yet gotten used to seeing her nude. He was immediately aroused.

"I guess so," he sputtered, the toothbrush wedged in his mouth.

He finished brushing his teeth, washed his face, and waited attentively on the bed. The shower continued to splatter for a little while longer then gurgled to a stop. Rachel waltzed out of the bathroom completely nude, paraded right up to him, and pulled his face to her chest. Cradling his head and gently stroking the nape of his neck she purred, "You know, we're like all alone in this motel room and nobody in the world has the slightest idea where we are."

He nibbled her breasts, delicately at first, but then more hungrily. Seizing her buttocks, he massaged them sensuously, fell backward, and pulled her on top of him. As she started to grind her body into his, he gently rolled her off.

"What's wrong?"

"Can we just wait 'til later?"

"Why?"

"Please don't ask me to explain right now."

"Did I do something wrong? Don't I turn you on?"

"Are you crazy, you're so sexy I can't stand it. But can we just wait a while?"

"Are you sick?"

"I'm fine, I just want to get something to eat first."

She snatched a pillow and covered his face. "You'd rather have a Big Mac than me, wouldn't you? Wouldn't you?" She removed the pillow from his face and laughed. "Don't answer that."

He clutched her to his chest. "I love you."

Rachel rose up on her palms, above him. "I'm sorry I made you travel all this way for nothing. I just had this stupid feeling we were going to find something really important. I should have just asked my father straight out what he was up to. And that's exactly what I intend to do when we get home."

Vinnie looked up, resisting an overpowering urge to fondle her breasts. "Let's go eat."

They were dressed, out the door, and in the car in less than five minutes.

"There's a McDonalds on the right about a mile away," Vinnie said as he headed north in the direction of town.

Rachel folded her arms across her chest with emphasis. "Hmmh, I was right, you do want a Big Mac instead of me."

As they swung through the door into McDonalds, Rachel said, "Go get us a table. What do you want?"

"Mac, fries, coke, apple pie."

Vinnie chose a table farthest removed from a rowdy group of men in their late twenties loudly boasting about their feats of daring on the slopes earlier in the day. He kept his eyes fixed on Rachel as she waited in line about twenty feet away. He struggled to keep his eyes from tearing, not wanting to reveal any clue to the emotional time bomb lodged inside of him. Time seemed to stand still as he watched her wait in line patiently, the woman at the head of the line changing her order three separate times. He wasn't sure whether he wanted things to speed up or slow down.

"That was funny," Rachel said as she sat the tray of food on the table.

"What was funny?"

"That girl behind the counter kept lookin' at me in the strangest way, like she knew me or somethin'," said Rachel, stuffing fries in her mouth. "I guess they're not used to seein' two tone hair in Jackson Hole. I'm gonna have it dyed when we get back home."

"Which color, black or blond?" asked Vinnie, his head bowed, his eyes not meeting Rachel's.

She reached across the table and lifted his chin. "Which color would you like?"

"Blond. Dye it back to your natural blond, and don't ever dye it black again."

"Vinnie, is everything okay?"

He halfheartedly nodded yes, scooped his food off the tray and began working on his Big Mac. Despite the emotions slashing through his insides, he was famished.

Sensing that something was troubling him, she chirped, "What should we do now? I'm sure not up for startin' the drive back tomorrow." She took a gulp of her soda and answered her own question. "It's obvious. There's only one thing for us to do." She chomped on her hamburger, and with her mouth half full continued. "We're in Jackson Hole. We gotta go skiing, we can't possibly go home without skiing at least one day."

Vinnie put his food back on the tray and pushed it away. The time had come, he couldn't put it off any longer. His voice was methodical and much deeper than normal. "Did the police find your sister's body?"

Rachel stiffened in her chair and swallowed her food prematurely. "What?"

His voice still had an unnatural robotic quality. "Did they find your sister's body?"

Rachel clenched her fists on the table, knocking her soda to the floor but paid no attention.

"I know you don't like to talk about it, but I need to know. You've never told me anything other than she was taken and killed."

Rachel remained mute. Tears began running down his face, as Vinnie reached across the table, cupped Rachel's clenched fists in his hands, and now in his normal voice, repeated, "Did they find her body?"

Rachel's face was expressionless, her reply barely a whisper. "No."

One at a time, Vinnie pried Rachel's fingers free from their clenched position. He leaned across the table and delicately lifted her hands to his lips, kissing her left hand lightly and then her right hand. His lips trembled as he spoke. "She's not dead. She's here in Jackson Hole."

Rachel's face remained devoid of emotion as she slowly rocked back and forth in her seat. Then there was a sliver of emotion, as her chin quivered and she bit her lower lip.

He leaned closer. "Do you understand what I'm telling you?"

Still rocking back and forth she tried to nod her head up and down, but it went sideways as much as it went up and down.

"Please tell me if you understand."

Rachel tried to free her hands. "Let me go, I need to get to the bathroom."

"I can't let you leave until I'm sure you're okay."

"Please, I wet my pants. Now let me go, I'll be right back."

Rachel flung open the door of the rest room, yanked a stack of paper towels from the dispenser on the wall and waddled into one of the stalls, her wet jeans sticking to her thighs. She removed her boots, slipped out of her jeans and panties, and dried the panties, jeans, and herself as best she could.

Washing her hands in one of the rest room sinks, she purposefully gazed in the mirror. She examined her reflection and tentatively lifted her hand, trying to touch the face of the girl in the mirror. She couldn't touch the girl's face because her hand met the hand of the girl in the mirror who was reaching out to touch her. Moving her hand in sweeping circles, she watched as the girl in the mirror mimicked the gesture. The two girls both retracted their hands and leaned toward one another, staring into each other's eyes as their faces inched closer and closer. Just as their noses were about to touch, the door opened and a young girl, about twelve years old, bounded in. Startled, Rachel jumped away from the mirror. The girl in the mirror jumped further back into the mirror exactly at the same time.

"Had something in my eye," explained Rachel.

"Oh," the young girl replied, stepping aside to let Rachel out the door.

Vinnie was wiping Rachel's seat clean with napkins. Rachel sat down next to him, leaning her head against his shoulder. "Thanks for cleaning that up for me."

"Are you gonna be okay?" asked Vinnie, giving her a reassuring squeeze.

"I think so, but I have to know if you are absolutely sure?"

"I've never been more sure of anything in my entire life."

"Was she the reason my father came here?"

"She has to be the reason. She was working in the ski shop he went into. They were in there together, but I really didn't get a good look at her. When I came back from the airport, I went back to the store."

"Why?"

"I'm not sure.......... guess I just wasn't ready to come back to the room and tell you he was gone."

"Exactly where did you see her?"

"I went into the store, and was turning the corner to the room where the rental skis are kept, and we bumped into one another. I couldn't believe my eyes. It was you - she looks exactly like you. Even her voice, it's different, but it's your voice."

"What did she say?"

"She said excuse me or something like that."

"What did you say?"

"I have no idea what I said. I was in a state of complete shock."

"I've got to go see her."

"Now?"

"Yes, now."

"Are you sure you're ready for this? Don't you at least want to go back to the motel and change your pants?"

"I've got to see her now."

"What about her? She doesn't even know you exist. What will this do to her?"

"I want to see her, but I don't want her to see me."

Vinnie parked the Maverick in the lot behind the Town Square. As they took a shortcut on a small path through the square, Vinnie stopped and grabbed Rachel's arm. "The store might be closed now."

"It's only a few minutes after eight o'clock. I'm sure they stay open 'til nine or ten."

"Maybe she doesn't work at night."

"Damn it Vinnie, I wanna see her."

"I know you do. I'm just trying to prepare you for the possibility that she might not be there."

Emerging from a large stand of pine trees at the edge of the square, they stopped across the street from Teton Adventures. "It's the store with the green and white lights above the door. See the girl through the big window just to the left of the door, that's her."

"She has long blond hair," mumbled Rachel.

"Did you expect her to have black hair?"

Rachel moved close to Vinnie. "I'm so scared."

"Maybe you should wait 'til tomorrow to do this? Give yourself some time."

"I have to see her now........... but how can we do this so she won't see me?"

"Your coat doesn't have a hood. Let's switch."

"What for?"

Vinnie demonstrated his technique by pulling the hood over his head and cinching the drawstring tight, just as he had when he followed her father earlier. Only his eyes and nose peeked out.

"I see what you mean."

While donning Vinnie's coat, Rachel outlined her strategy. "You go in the store first and start talking to her. I'll come in after you."

"What should I talk about?"

Rachel stomped the snow with her boots anxiously. "I don't know, just ask her about rental skis. No, buy something...... buy a hat and take it up to the counter and pay for it. Go ahead now, I can't wait another minute."

Snow flurries began drifting from the sky as Vinnie jaywalked across the street. The instant he opened the door his eyes met those of Adrienne Sullivan.

"I see you're back. Anything I can help you with this time?"

Vinnie stopped dead in his tracks, once again mesmerized by the face of Rachel Webster on another girl. Even though mentally prepared to see her, it still took him several seconds to snap out of it.

"I want to buy a hat."

"What kind?" she replied helpfully.

Incongruously, Vinnie replied, "What kind of what?"

"What kind of hat? We have all kinds."

"Oh. Maybe, like a baseball cap that says Jackson Hole."

Adrienne pointed to a shelf no more than twenty feet past the checkout counter. "There's a whole bunch you can choose from."

Vinnie quickly made his way to the shelf, as Rachel came in the door, the drawstring of her hood so tight that

294

only her eyes were exposed. She walked straight up to the counter. Adrienne Sullivan finished punching in a few items on a computer keyboard and looked up.

"Hi. Is it snowing out there?"

Rachel nodded her head affirmatively as she paced past the checkout counter. Vinnie grabbed a hat off the shelf, and walked by Rachel back to the counter. As he approached the counter he could glimpse Rachel out of the corner of his eye, standing just a few feet away gawking at Adrienne.

"I'll take this one."

"I thought you wanted one that said Jackson Hole."

Vinnie glanced at the hat he held in his hand - a dull solid green with no design or logo. He had taken it from the shelf without even looking.

"I like this one."

"Ten dollars and fifty cents with tax. How will you be paying?"

Rachel came right up next to Vinnie. It felt like he was clamped in a vise with Adrienne as one jaw and Rachel the other.

"How would you like to pay?" Adrienne repeated.

Vinnie fished his wallet from his pocket. "With money...... I mean cash." He handed her a twenty-dollar bill. As Adrienne counted change out of the cash register, Rachel zoomed past him and out the door.

Vinnie dashed across the street to where Rachel was waiting at the edge of the Town Square. She had removed the hood from her head, but it was too dark to see her face. She didn't say anything, just reached out, clasped his hand and led him diagonally across the Town Square. As they slogged their way through the snow, she asked, "Do you want to make love now?"

"If you insist."

Rachel searched in the darkness, found Vinnie's head, drew him to her and kissed him tenderly. "I insist...... I'll never forget what you've done for me. Thank you for finding Karen, thank you for making me whole."

Chapter 29

Vinnie rushed into the motel room, tossed a McDonalds take-out bag on the bed, and kicked the door shut behind him. His teeth chattered as he rubbed his hands together. "Boy, it's a lot colder today than it was yesterday. Don't go out without your gloves."

"Did it snow much last night?" asked Rachel.

"Just a couple of inches."

"Well, did you find out about the high school?"

"I bought you pancakes, it was going to be a long wait for an Egg McMuffin, so I ....."

Rachel interrupted, "I don't care about the Egg McMuffin. What about the school?"

Vinnie devoured a blueberry muffin as he took the food from the large McDonalds bag and spread it on the bed. "Only one high school in town. Of course it's called Jackson High."

"Where is it?"

"Less than a mile from here. South on 191, turn right on, what else, High School Road and it's right there. Classes start at eight o' clock. Only three buses and they all arrive at about ten of eight."

"How did you discover all this?"

"I saw a guy at McDonalds reading a physics textbook, same one I had last year. So I started talking to him."

Giving in to their hunger, they gulped down their breakfast. Vinnie slipped on an extra sweater and Rachel dressed warmly wearing both a hooded sweatshirt and a thick wool sweater under her coat.

It was seven-thirty when the Maverick rolled to a stop in front of Jackson High - a small school, only about the size of a typical elementary school back in Maryland. Vinnie turned off the ignition and puffed out his cheeks, then let out a soft whistling sound to calm himself. "Just wait and make sure I get in the door."

"Thanks for doing this Vinnie."

Vinnie set the emergency brake and hopped out. Trying to act natural, like any other student, he bounded up the steps to the double door entrance of the school and went in. Rachel slid over to the driver's seat and drove back to the motel.

It was warm inside the school. Vinnie shed his gloves and coat, and laid them on a small table in the main hallway just inside the door. Two teachers - he assumed they were teachers - passed by, but paid him no attention. Peering out the glass panels of the door provided a view of vehicles approaching the school. At about twenty minutes before eight o'clock more teachers began arriving as did an occasional student, but not the blond girl.

It seemed logical that Rachel's sister attended this school. She was seventeen and should be a senior in high school. The guy at McDonalds indicated the next closest high school was more than thirty miles away. He thought about asking the guy if he knew a blond girl who worked at Teton Adventures, but then thought better of it. Any doubts about the blond girl's whereabouts disappeared when the first school bus pulled up to the curb. She was sitting next to the window near the back of the bus. The bus spilled its contents, kids that looked a lot like those back at Howard High where Vinnie and Rachel went to school, with only one exception - no black students. The blond girl wore running shoes, black jeans, and a bright blue ski coat and carried a backpack. She, just like Vinnie a few minutes earlier, bounded up the steps, opened the door, and zipped down the hallway.

Vinnie bolted down the hallway, right on her heels. "Excuse me." But with the noise from the stampede of kids rushing to their first class, she didn't hear him. Vinnie reached out and grabbed her arm causing her to spin around and drop her backpack.

"Hey, what are you doing?"

"I'm sorry. I shouldn't have touched you like that. Please, I'm really sorry," Vinnie pleaded as he picked up the backpack.

The girl scowled at him. "You're the guy from the store yesterday. What are you doing here? Are you a new student?"

"No."

"Well, what do you want?"

"Look, I'm sorry about startling you."

"You already said that."

As Vinnie tried to collect his thoughts, a tall girl with short black hair approached the blond girl. "Yo Adrienne."

"Hi Bonnie," the blond girl replied.

As the tall girl continued down the hallway, she asked, "Who's the new dude?" The blond girl shrugged her shoulders.

"My name's Vinnie Carolla. I need to talk to you. It's important."

"I don't have time. I've got a biology test in less than five minutes."

"What I have to tell you is more important than any test."

The blond girl hoisted the backpack over her shoulder and took off. "Maybe to you."

Vinnie jumped in front of her, retracting his hands to make sure he didn't touch her. "I've got to talk to you."

The blond girl sidestepped him and picked up her pace. "Look, I've got a regular guy. And even if I wasn't going steady I wouldn't be interested, you're just too weird."

"You think I'm trying to come onto you? Well, I'm not. I've already got a girl friend. And you know what, she's just as beautiful as you."

"I'm very happy for the two of you."

"Wait please, what I've got to tell you is going to change your life forever."

She veered into a classroom door and laughed. "Thanks, but no thanks. My life's just fine."

Vinnie dawdled at the door of the classroom and watched in disappointment as the blond girl took her seat. He trudged dejectedly a few feet farther down the hallway and flopped down on the floor, propping his back against the wall.

It had been a very late night for him and Rachel and it was a struggle to keep his eyes open - a struggle he couldn't sustain. Many minutes later he was startled awake by an announcement over the public address system about tickets for an upcoming basketball game at another school. Realizing he had fallen asleep, he sprang to his feet and rushed to the door of the classroom. The door was closed, but it had a small window. The blond girl was still working away at her test. He stood at the door until the bell rang. A parade of kids immediately burst through the door, the blond girl was in the middle of the pack. Her eyes met those of the guy with the long curly black hair and the cute, but scraggly unshaven face.

"Are you for real? I mean what is your story?"

"I told you what my story is. I've got to talk to you. Please, it's very important."

"I'm not going to cut class because some guy appears out of the blue and says he has something important to talk about."

"Okay, when can we talk?"

"Can you run?"

"Run? Yeah, I can run."

"I have a free period today right before lunch, and I'm going on a training run. I'm leaving from the gym door at eleven-fifteen. It's around back. You can talk to me for as long as you can keep up."

"I don't have running shoes with me."

"That's your problem," snapped the blond girl.

Vinnie double-timed it back to the motel, occasionally detouring onto the road in stretches where the sidewalk wasn't plowed. Rachel was standing at the window of the motel room and rushed outside to meet him.

"Did you find her? Did you tell her?"

"I found her, but didn't tell her."

"Why not?"

"I haven't had a decent chance to talk to her yet, but I'm going to."

"When?"

"Soon. Grab your coat, I've got to buy some running shoes."

"Running shoes?"

"Her highness has granted me the opportunity to talk with her while she goes on a training run......... if I can keep up. I'm looking forward to running her ass into the ground."

"Why are you upset with her?"

"She thinks I'm an idiot. I shouldn't blame her, but this is so frustrating. I just want to get it over with."

"So the two of you are going running together, huh. What's next, dinner and a movie?"

"Very funny."

They drove into town and found a shopping center with a small sporting goods store. The selection of running shoes was minimal, but Vinnie found a pair that was marginally acceptable. He also bought sweat suit pants, a jock strap, a knit pullover hat, and thin cotton gloves. With very little time to spare, Vinnie gunned the Maverick back to the motel and began changing into his running clothes.

Rummaging through his suitcase, Vinnie muttered, "I should have bought a pair of white socks. I hate wearing black socks with running shoes."

Rachel handed him a pair of white socks from her suitcase. "Here, I wouldn't want your girl friend to think you're a geek."

It was ten minutes after eleven o'clock when Rachel pulled the Maverick up to the front of the school. Vinnie sat beside her in the passenger's seat.

"Good luck," encouraged Rachel, squeezing Vinnie's hand.

"I need it, I'm scared shitless."

"You know she's not going to believe any of what you tell her."

Vinnie kissed Rachel on the cheek. "Not until she sees you anyway."

She reached into her pocket and retrieved a sealed envelope and handed it to him. "Give this to her."

"What is it?"

"It's just something I keep with me."

Vinnie jogged around to the back of the school and waited next to the gym door. It was cold - in the upper teens - but sunny and no wind, reasonable conditions for running. Exactly at eleven-fifteen the door swung open and out came a muscular young man wearing a gray sweat suit, with the school emblem - an elk - blazoned across the shirt. He was big, over six feet tall and well over two hundred pounds. The blond girl was right behind him. She wore the same style sweat suit.

"I see you're all set for our run. This is my friend Jake. You don't mind if Jake comes along with us, do you?"

Jake extended his hand. Vinnie reluctantly grasped his hand and Jake clamped down hard, outrageously hard.

"Nice meeting you Vinnie. That is your real name, isn't it?"

"Actually my name is Vincent, but my friends call me Vinnie. You can call me Vincent."

"You're a real smart ass, aren't you?" growled Jake.

"Could you give me back my hand please."

"Sure," Jake said as he gave Vinnie's hand one last crushing squeeze.

Vinnie turned to the blond girl. "You know it would be easier to talk to you if I knew your name."

"Adrienne."

"Thanks Adrienne. I know it must seem like I'm from outer space or something, but you don't need a bodyguard for protection."

"I'm not convinced of that. And just so you make no mistake about how good of a bodyguard Jake is, you should know he's captain of the football and basketball teams."

Vinnie resisted the urge to utter any number of appropriate cutting replies. Adrienne and Jake did some stretching exercises, as Vinnie stood and watched. Then without a word they took off jogging around to the front of the school and out to Route 191. Vinnie galloped along beside them.

"Remember our deal Vinnie, we can talk as long as you can keep up," Adrienne reminded as she increased the pace slightly.

"How far are we going?" asked Vinnie.

"We're going out Route 22 to the Snake River and back. It's about eight miles round trip."

Panting heavily, Jake taunted, "Think you can run eight miles?"

Vinnie remained silent, mentally chuckling to himself.

They ran past the Stay Longer Motel, turned left and headed west on Route 22, as the shops and stores of Jackson Hole disappeared behind them. They stayed on the road, occasionally swerving to the side to avoid a passing car or truck. The three of them ran side by side with Adrienne in the middle. Adrienne ran comfortably, Jake labored, and Vinnie felt very awkward having to run so slow.

After about five minutes of silence Adrienne said, "So I take it you're a runner." Vinnie didn't reply and ever so slightly increased the pace. Jake's breathing became more uneven as he began dropping behind.

"Okay, what's the important thing you have to tell me?"

"Listen Adrienne, there's no need for you to be afraid of me. I'm not a rapist or a murderer. In fact, I'm the most non-violent person I know. I'm just a guy who drove two thousand miles over the weekend with a friend to find you. And I'd like to talk to you, not to you and Jake."

"You drove two thousand miles to find me? What are you talking about?"

Vinnie upped the pace another notch. Adrienne kept with it, but Jake lagged farther behind. Vinnie turned his head and yelled back, "Nice running with you Jake." Jake wobbled to a stop, doubled over and grabbed his knees, straining to suck air into his burning lungs.

"That wasn't very nice."

"Yeah, and it wasn't very nice when that gorilla tried to break my hand either. Is he your regular guy?"

"I don't have a regular guy, I just said that when I wanted to get rid of you. Jake's a good friend, a very cool person. Now cut the bullshit, and just tell me what you want...... And please slow down some."

Vinnie reduced the pace considerably.

"There's a girl back at the Stay Longer Motel. She's my girl friend and I love her."

"And?"

"And she's your sister."

"Get real! I don't have a sister."

They kept running for another two minutes in silence, Adrienne finally saying, "Look to your right, you can see the Tetons."

"Wow, I've never seen anything like that before."

"Why in the world would you say your girlfriend is my sister?"

"Because she is."

"Don't you think I would know if I had a sister? I'm an only child."

"Adrienne can we stop running. This is so hard for me to explain and I just want to be able to look you in the face."

"The bridge over the Snake is less than a mile away. We can stop there."

They ran the next mile, slowing to a walk at the bridge. Vinnie leaned against the bridge railing and gazed up the Snake River. "How much faster can you run?" Adrienne asked.

"A lot faster. I expect to win the Maryland high school cross-country championship this spring. Do you believe that?"

"Yes, that I believe."

"Good, and you should believe everything I'm about to tell you."

Adrienne met his eyes unflinchingly and waited for his explanation.

"I don't know anything about the last seventeen years of your life, but I know a lot about the first year. You were born in Columbia, Maryland. Your real name is Karen. Your sister's name is Rachel. You were kidnapped, taken from your family when you were less than a year old."

"This is ridiculous. Why are you saying these things?"

Vinnie needed to clear his head. He let himself be momentarily distracted by a splashing trout, fighting to hold its place in an eddy in the clear water below. "That's quite a fish."

"I bet you'd be some fisherman, the way you can lie."

"I'm telling you the truth."

"And this girlfriend of yours, Rachel, she believes this?"

"Yes."

Adrienne combed her fingers through her hair and shook her head wildly. "One or both of you is a con artist. I think she must be the con artist."

"I don't understand."

"Sometimes, I can be very gullible. And maybe that's what I'm being right now, because I believe you."

"You do?" Vinnie replied with surprise.

"Yes, I believe you think it's true. But it's not true, none of it. Somehow this Rachel is deceiving you, tricking you into believing this. I don't know why, but that's what she's doing."

"That's not what's happening at all. She didn't find you, I did. I know it's true beyond a shadow of a doubt. I swear to God it's true."

"Then you're the con artist."

Vinnie reached out and gently placed his hand on her shoulder. Perceiving no signal to remove it, he left it there.

"I haven't told you everything. Rachel isn't just your sister?"

"What do you mean, not just my sister?"

"She's your twin sister, your identical twin sister. That's how I know it's true."

Adrienne turned away from him, looking north up the river toward the Tetons. "I can't imagine what this must be like for you to hear this. Rachel and I were up almost all night while she was trying to decide whether you should be told or not. She knows this is going to turn your world upside down. Finding you is turning her world upside down too, but it's much worse for you. She at least knew she had a sister." Vinnie took his hand and turned Adrienne until she faced him. "Rachel decided she would want to know if the situation were reversed. And I agree with her. I think eventually you'll be glad you know the truth."

"And why is it you here telling me all this and not this twin sister of mine? Am I ever going to meet her in person or will she have to leave town unexpectedly?"

Vinnie, now having gotten everything out, felt a sense of relief. "Yes, you're going to meet her. She wanted me to tell you so you can get used to the idea before you see her. I know you're not going to really believe this until you see her." Vinnie reached into the pocket of his sweatshirt and produced the envelope Rachel had given him.

"Rachel said to give you this."

"What is it?"

"I don't know, she wouldn't tell me."

"I don't believe any of this. But if this is all true, how did you find me?"

"Rachel wants to tell you that part."

"When do I get to see this Rachel?"

Vinnie smiled eagerly. "That's up to you. We're at the Stay Longer Motel, Room 124. The phone number's on the envelope. Call us after school and then you name the time and place."

For the first time Adrienne smiled back. "You really are quite cute, but you're the biggest bullshitter I've ever met in my life. I have this incredibly strong feeling this Rachel is going to have blown town unexpectedly if I call."

The smile disappeared from Vinnie's face. "She'll be there."

Vinnie pointed to the east, back in the direction from which they had come. "Hey look, it's Jake coming to your rescue. You know, that must be a hell of a football team you have if Jake is the captain." Seriousness returned to his voice. "Rachel and I will wait for your call."

Vinnie started running at his normal training pace back to Jackson Hole. As he whizzed past the exhausted young man slogging toward the bridge, he waved and jabbed, "Hey Jake, your fly is open."

There was no doubt in his mind that Jake had fallen for it. He didn't even bother to turn around and watch. He just shouted back over his shoulder.

"Made ya look."

Chapter 30

A cracked flowerpot with two dying cactus plants was perched on the windowsill in front of faded curtains. Paint peeling from the front door added to the overall lifeless appearance of the apartment. "She said it was a dump and she was right," he thought. He pushed the doorbell, but heard no sound. The metal door felt like stone as he pounded it with freezing knuckles.

"Who is it?" she asked in a weak voice.

"Barbara, it's me."

She wore a bright red University of Maryland sweatshirt that initially diverted attention from her face. But when Larry looked at her face, a face that normally glowed, it appeared swollen and rubbery.

"You don't have the duck in the window."

"No husband, no reason for a duck."

"You look pretty good, all things considered."

"You're lying."

Larry didn't argue. "How do you feel?"

"Much better today, but I'm still really sore."

Larry crept a few steps into the apartment. Barbara backed up, maintaining the separation between them. "I thought you were going to be here this morning."

"I can't stay."

"Oh, I see."

"No, you don't see. I've got a real problem. Rachel has run away with her boyfriend."

"I'm sorry. What made her do that? It sounded like everything was going so well for her."

"We don't have the slightest idea why they did it or where they went."

"When did this happen?"

"Saturday. This is the fourth day they've been gone. Rachel called Vivian on Sunday and that was the last we heard from her."

"At least tell me about Adrienne. What did you say to her?"

"I didn't tell her anything. She's a wonderful girl, but I don't have time to talk about her now."

"What are you going to do about Chile?"

"I called the Europeans and told them I have to delay my plans. I can't worry about that until I find Rachel."

"John called me."

"What did he want?"

"He wants me to come back to him...... swore he would never take another drink. He joined Alcoholics Anonymous."

Larry's expression soured, confusion tinged with a touch of disappointment. "What are you going to do?"

"What do you want me to do?"

"I don't know."

Desperate for things to be as they were, Barbara moved close and leaned her head against his chest. Her left arm hung limply at her side. "Please don't hate me."

Larry put his arms around her and gave her a tentative hug, but then backed away. "I have to go. Vivian is nearly out of her mind over Rachel, and so am I."

She wiped her eyes on her sleeve. "I'm almost forty-one years old, and I'm fighting cancer. I don't want to be alone. My husband wants me back, but it's you I want. Is there any hope for us?"

"Too much is happening right now. I need some time. I can't even begin to think about what to do until I know Rachel is okay. I'll call you later in the week. You've just got to give me some time to deal with things."

"I need you now. I'm not sure I can wait."
"That's your decision."

Larry sped back to Columbia, oblivious to the speed trap on Route 1. He offered no explanation as the trooper handed him a $125 ticket, but felt like ranting about the trooper's misplaced priorities - wasting time catching speeders while Rachel is missing. As he turned into the driveway his thoughts flashed back to another January day twelve years earlier. He and Rachel were sleigh riding down the snow packed driveway. He went into the house to go to the bathroom, leaving strict instructions for her to stay put until he returned. Just as he came out the door, Rachel took off on the sleigh down the driveway and into the street. Cruising down the street - at just the wrong moment - was a car driven by an elderly woman. As Rachel slid into the street, the woman veered sharply to the left and crashed into Larry's Chevy Citation parked on the street. His view of Rachel blocked by the Citation, he feared the worst as he bounded across the front yard in foot-deep snow. The elderly woman jumped out of the car and shouted hysterically, the front of her car having ridden over top of Rachel's sleigh. He could remember his heart stopping as he heard Rachel's screams, only to discover they weren't screams at all, but rather shrieks of joy. As she was dragged out from under the car she looked up and yelled, "That was fun." He and the old woman stood there bawling as Rachel laughed with delight.

Vivian was half snoozing at the kitchen table when he startled her awake.
"Did she call?"
Vivian shook her head no.
"Did the phone company come and hook up the caller ID box?"

"They just left about twenty minutes ago."

"Does it work?"

"Yeah. I called Vinnie's mother and had her call back, her number popped up on the display after just a few ......"

The phone rang unexpectedly. Vivian and Larry both reacted as if someone had just tossed a live grenade in the house. Vivian was the first to grab the phone from the kitchen wall.

"Hello." She listened intently for about ten seconds. "I'm not interested." Larry watched as Vivian became aggravated. "I said I'm not interested," she shouted, slamming the phone down. Vivian slumped down at the table and started crying. In between sobs she explained, "He couldn't understand why I'm not interested in having my carpets cleaned at half the regular price."

Larry draped his arm around her. "She's going to be all right. Vinnie's with her, he's not going to let her do anything stupid."

"This is my fault. I know it's my fault," sobbed Vivian.

Larry caressed the back of her neck. "You're being too hard on yourself. If this is anybody's fault, it's Rachel's. She said it herself, she's got to start taking responsibility for her own life."

"But she carries all those scars on the inside. And I'm the one who gave her those scars. If only I had ....."

Larry spun Vivian around, took hold of her shoulders and got right in her face. "Listen to me. I want you to stop blaming yourself for everything. Do you hear me, I want ..... "

The phone rang, startling them once again. This time Larry jumped to get it.

"No, let me," Vivian said as she thrust her arm out like a traffic cop to impede his movement toward the phone. She clasped her hands together, closed her eyes, took a deep breath, and picked up the phone after the fourth ring. "Hello."

"Mom it's me," came the reply from the other end of the line.

"Rachel, are you okay?"

"I'm fine mom. Everything is fine."

Vivian's voice trembled. "Why didn't you call me yesterday? You said you would call me every day."

"I'm sorry. I didn't get a chance."

"Please tell me where are you?"

"You know I'm not gonna do that. Mom, I've gotta go. I should know in a couple of days when I'll be home. Now don't worry."

Larry motioned to Vivian to give him the phone.

"Don't hang up, your father wants to talk to you."

"But I don't want to talk to him, not now anyway. Goodbye."

"Rachel, no. Please don't hang up." Vivian stared at the phone and then slowly hung it up. "This is insane. It's absolutely insane."

Larry shook his head in bewilderment. "I've racked my brain and I can't come up with anything to explain why she would do this."

Vivian smacked her cheeks, and shrieked, "The caller ID box! Did we get the number? .... We got the number!" she shouted, scribbling 307-555-9949 on a pad of paper. "It's area code 307, she's calling from Virginia. She can't be all that far away."

Larry shook his head. "That's not Virginia. Virginia is 703, not 307."

Vivian raced to the hallway closet, grabbed the phone book off the top shelf, ran back to the kitchen table, and turned the pages furiously. "Where the hell is the map with all the area codes?"

"Take your time, you'll find it."

"Here's the map. 307, where is 307?   I found it." Her mouth dropped open.   "Wyoming, she's in Wyoming........ What in the world could she possibly be doing in Wyoming?"

Larry retreated several steps and clumsily lowered himself on to a kitchen chair. With absolutely no emotion, he said, "I don't know."

Chapter 31

Adrienne Sullivan followed her best friend, Bonnie Pierman, into the school library. They marched past the front desk and down an aisle between two long stacks of bookshelves.

"Good, this one's empty," Bonnie whispered, opening the door to a small study room.

Adrienne sat down at the wooden table in the center of the room, dropping her backpack to the floor. Bonnie closed the door and perched herself on the edge of the table. She blew a big pink bubble, popped it, sucked it back into her mouth and started chomping away. "Now tell me why Jake was so pissed off at lunch. I've never seen him like that before."

"It was nothing, really."

"Come on Adrienne, since when did we start keeping secrets from one another? You're upset, I can tell."

"I'm fine, really."

"I've known you since the fourth grade. I know when you're fine and when you're not. It's about that guy I saw you with in the hallway this morning, isn't it?"

"Kinda."

"Come on, fess up," prodded Bonnie as she leaned closer.

"Well this guy....... he's just so weird." Adrienne pushed herself away from the table and away from Bonnie. "Look, it's nothing. I've got a calculus test next period and I'm not prepared. I spent most of my time studying for a biology test I had this morning."

"Oh bullshit. If you are so unprepared, why did you and Jake go running during your free period? And when was the last time you got anything other than an A on a test anyway?" ˙

Adrienne's hands trembled as she scooped up her backpack and stood up. "Really, I gotta go."

Bonnie took hold of Adrienne's arm. "You're scared. You're afraid of that guy aren't you?"

Adrienne fell back into her chair. "Yes."

"Why? What did he do?"

"When I was with him, I wasn't afraid of him at all, I even found myself liking him. But at lunch I started thinking about what he's been doing and I got really scared."

"What? What did he do?" asked Bonnie, quietly pounding the table with her fist.

"He came into the store twice yesterday and acted totally lame both times. The second time he bought a hat and I could tell he never even looked at it until he paid for it. And he was here this morning waiting for me."

"That's not so scary. It just sounds like this guy has a serious case of the hots for you."

Adrienne covered her face with her hands. "Yeah, I think he's got the hots for me, but I'm afraid he's some kind of psycho or something."

"Why? Why would you think that?"

"This morning he said he had to talk to me about something important, said it would change my life forever. I knew he was hitting on me, but I just couldn't get rid of him. Finally, I told him he could go running with me and talk to me then."

Bonnie tilted her head and scrunched up her face. "You asked him to go running with you?"

"Yeah, I wanted him to see Jake. I thought that would get rid of him."

"Well, what happened?"

"He went."

"Went what?"

"Running. But he turned out to be some kind of champion runner or something and Jake couldn't keep up."

"You left Jake? That was bogus, why did you do that?"

"I don't know, it was like he just sucked me along with him. Like I said, when I was with him I wasn't scared." Bonnie swept her hands in circles toward her body, motioning for Adrienne to continue. "Well, we get way ahead of Jake, stop at the Route 22 bridge and he makes up the most ridiculous story."

Bonnie clenched her fists and leaned so close to Adrienne that their noses bumped together. "What ridiculous story?"

"Do you mind?" Adrienne softly pushed her away, restoring a modest amount of personal space. "He said he drove two thousand miles to find me." Bonnie jerked her head back with a snarl as Adrienne went on. "And here's the best part...... He said he came with my sister."

"You don't have a sister."

"No shit Sherlock. He said I was kidnapped seventeen years ago and my sister is with him and wants to see me. And, oh yeah, one other little detail?"

"What?"

"She's my twin sister."

"Incredible. Was this guy joking or was he acting serious when he said this crap?"

"He was acting dead serious all the time. I kept waiting for him to say it was all a joke, but he didn't."

"Wow, this guy is a psycho. No wonder Jake was so pissed off."

"No, I didn't tell Jake what he said. I just said he wanted to go out with me. I'm afraid if I told Jake, he would hurt him."

"Maybe you ought to let him."

"I think I've seen the last of him. And you know what the craziest part is?"

"No, what?"

"On the bridge, if he would have just asked me to go out with him I would have said yes. Instead, he tells me to come to his motel room after school to meet my sister. When I was out there with him, I was even thinking that I would go see him."

"You're nuts."

"I know. But like I said, he didn't seem scary until I got away from him and could think about things."

"What are you going to do if he comes back?"

"I don't think he will. If he does, I guess I'll tell Jake."

Bonnie placed her hand on Adrienne's arm. "Did you take the bus today?" Adrienne bit her lower lip and nodded yes. "Let me drive you home today. I brought my bother's car."

Adrienne stood up and gave Bonnie a hug. "Thanks...... Now I do need to go over my notes for that calculus test."

"I can take a hint. I'll leave you alone so you can study for your dumb ass test. I have to get my history book from my locker anyway. See you at the front door at three."

Bonnie left only to stick her head back in the door a few seconds later with a big grin plastered across her face. "Hey, maybe this explains how you ended up with blond hair and blue eyes."

Adrienne glared back at her friend. She was afraid of this Vinnie character and in no mood for jokes.

"I think I need to learn when to keep my mouth shut," said Bonnie.

"Don't worry about it. Just leave me alone so I can get some studying done."

The Other Part Of Me

Adrienne opened her calculus textbook to the chapter on derivatives for geometric expressions, tried to concentrate, but couldn't. She reached for her loose-leaf binder and pulled out the envelope the strange young man had given her - she had thrown it in the trash after lunch, but excused herself from history class twenty minutes later to retrieve it. She flipped the envelope in her hand, turning it over and over. It was a plain sealed envelope with nothing written on it except a phone number. Resisting the urge to open it, she put it back in the binder and tried concentrating on calculus again.

But it was no use, she had to open the envelope and risk whatever mind games that Vinnie Carolla - or whatever his real name was - had in store for her. Inside were four typed pages, stapled in the upper left corner. She placed the pages on the table in front of her and began to read. On the top of the first page, in bold letters, were the words, "THE OTHER PART OF ME."

She carefully read the first paragraph and the first four sentences of the second paragraph, and then read those four sentences again and again.

"When I was a little girl, I had a recurring and terrifying dream. I dreamt I was not whole. I dreamt that my right leg was missing, that it was not there. Even sometimes when I was awake I would find myself reaching to feel for my leg, afraid to look down to see if it was really there."

Icy chills raced through Adrienne Sullivan and goose bumps peppered her skin. Feeling as if she were engulfed in a suffocating cloud of noxious fumes, she gasped for air. Unable to control her breathing she became light-headed and the room began to spin. She gripped the edge of the table with both hands, but couldn't stop the room from spinning. She pushed away from the table, closed her eyes, and lowered her wobbly head to her knees. Remaining perfectly still, she slowed her breathing and felt the room slow down and finally come to a stop. Eyes closed, she returned to a normal sitting position, lifted her right hand to her face and rubbed her fingers across her sweaty forehead. She gingerly placed her palms on the table far apart. Were those four pages really there on the table in front of her? Did they really exist? She tentatively inched her hands inward toward one another. Yes, she felt the pages. But were the words as she had read them? She opened her eyes, but everything was a blur. She blinked her eyes tight and opened them again. This time the words gyrated into focus.

The first and second paragraphs were the same as before. She continued to read, but was no longer sure if the words were originating from the paper to her eyes and being relayed to her brain - or if instead, the words were being transmitted from her brain to her eyes and then being projected down onto the paper. Was she reading the words, or was she causing the words?

When finished, she carefully folded the four pages, put them back into the envelope, and zipped it in a side pocket of her backpack. From another pocket she pulled out several tissues and wiped the sweat from her face. She tossed the tissues in a small garbage can in the corner of the room and then placed her hands on the table.

Closing her eyes, she withdrew her hands from the table and slowly lowered them until they were less than an inch above where her left thigh should be. Slowly, almost imperceptibly, she moved her fingers until they finally touched her thigh then clutched it tightly with both hands. Her hands moved forward to her knee and then down the front of her leg until she felt her foot.

Having performed this ritual, as she had done so many thousands of times before, she once again assured herself that her left leg was there, and that she was whole. But for the first time in her life, unlike all the other times, she now understood what the ritual meant and why she did it.

Chapter 32

Rachel impatiently shifted her weight from one foot to the other as she leaned against the pay phone and prepared to sever the electrical umbilical cord to her mother. It was time to end their conversation. "But I don't want to talk to him, not now anyway. Goodbye."

Vinnie trotted out of McDonalds, a carry out bag in each hand, just as she hung up. "You know, the next time we go on one of these trips I'm gonna buy stock in McDonalds."

Rachel countered, "Actually, I already own stock in McDonalds. This whole trip is just one big scam to drive up the price. Everybody's in on it, except you - Adrienne, Jake, my father, everybody."

"So what did you say to your mother?"

"Told her I should know in a couple of days when we would be coming back."

"That's all?"

"My father was there. He wanted to talk to me, but I told Mom I didn't want to talk to him."

"So I take it he hasn't told her about Karen."

"No, I think he intends to keep that his little secret. Some secret, huh ?"

"How did your mother seem? Is she still freaking out?" asked Vinnie as he climbed behind the steering wheel.

Rachel slammed her door shut. "Yeah, I think you could say that."

Pulling out of the parking lot, the Maverick sputtered even more than usual. "I've absolutely got to get gas right now. We're running on fumes."

Rachel squirmed in her seat. "Let me off first. I gotta go bad."

"You should have gone in McDonalds."

"You guys have it so easy. If I had a......... never mind, just get me back to the room."

Vinnie pulled right up to the motel door and dangled the key in front of Rachel's nose - throughout the ordeal of this trip Vinnie was proving himself to be a wonderful companion, but this was one little habit of his that was starting to wear thin. She jerked the key away and hustled to the room, the McDonalds bags tucked under her arms like footballs. Vinnie rolled down the window of the Maverick. "I'll be back in a few minutes. Don't eat all the fries."

Rachel didn't bother replying, she was much too interested in getting to the bathroom. Sitting on the toilet, it dawned on her; not only was she in love with Vinnie, she wanted to spend the rest of her life with him. It was much too early to make such a decision, much too early to cement such a commitment. She certainly wasn't about to say anything to him - just telling him she loved him was enough pressure - but she couldn't imagine ever finding anyone as wonderful as him. Odd, she realized, to be having such thoughts while she was wiping her butt.

She washed her hands and rinsed her face with cold water, then ran her fingers through her hair just like her father always did. Drying her face with a threadbare towel, she tripped over a pair of Vinnie's discarded jeans as she came out of the bathroom - neatness wasn't one of his endearing qualities, but then it wasn't one of hers either. She demonstrated as much by flinging the towel back over her shoulder in the general direction of the bathroom. Looking about the room, littered with random piles of clothing, she thought, "Mom would go nuts if she saw this place." She cleared some space on the bed and spread the food out, dividing it into two equal piles. She took a bite of her cheeseburger just as Vinnie knocked on the door.

"Just a minute." She forced the cheeseburger down her throat. "That was quick, " she said to Vinnie as she opened the door.

But it wasn't Vinnie. It was Adrienne Sullivan.

They stood there less than two feet apart, one in the cold of a Wyoming winter and the other in the warmth of a dimly lit motel room, neither knowing what to say. Adrienne's golden blond hair, made even brighter by the fading sunlight, was pulled back neatly into a ponytail. Rachel's short black hair with an inch of blond roots was wet and disheveled.

Their two sets of blue eyes became lost in each other. Without thought, almost robotically, Rachel lifted her right hand, the palm facing Adrienne. Adrienne immediately responded by lifting her gloved left hand, but pulled it away before their hands touched. Their first touch had to be skin against skin, there could be no artificial barrier between them. Adrienne took her gloves off, dropped them to the ground, slowly raised her left hand and put it against her sister's right hand. The two hands, Rachel's right and Adrienne's left, were exact mirror images of one another.

"I've never seen the ocean," whispered Adrienne.

"What?"

"Your shirt, it says Ocean City. I've never seen the ocean before."

Rachel glanced down at her tattered green sweatshirt, the words Ocean City, Maryland written across her chest. "Yes you have, you just don't remember. We went to the beach when we were five months old."

"How did you find me?"

"I followed my father. I had no idea you were here. I had no idea you were even alive."

"Your father was here?" puzzled Adrienne.

"Yes, I think he came to find you."

"Well, he didn't."

"Yes he did."

Adrienne pulled her hand away and covered her mouth. "Oh my God, is your last name Webster?" Rachel shook her head up and down. "That man, Larry Webster, I knew something was strange about him. He's your father."

"He's your father too."

"He was crying," said Adrienne, more to herself than to Rachel. "I thought he was crying when he skied away from me, but I wasn't sure."

"You went skiing with him?"

"I gave him a lesson on Sunday. I don't understand any of this. Why did he come here to see me now?"

"I don't understand it either. I followed him here, because he was lying about something and I just knew it was something really important."

Adrienne's eyes began to fill and then a single tear ran from each eye.

"Karen, come in here where it's warm."

"Don't call me that. My name's Adrienne."

Rachel took hold of her sister's hand. "I'm sorry. It's just that even though I thought you were dead, you've been with me my entire life. You've been inside of me, and I've always thought of you as Karen."

They both turned as Vinnie pulled the Maverick into the parking space right in front of them. He eased out of the car, an expression of uncertainty on his face, and took a couple of tentative steps forward and stopped.

"Vinnie, why don't you go for a ride or something for a while," Rachel suggested.

"Sure," replied Vinnie thankfully as he started backing up.

"Wait, get some food. I know you're hungry," Rachel said as she motioned for him to come inside.

"That's okay, I can wait 'til later."

"Don't be ridiculous. Twenty minutes ago you were starving," insisted Rachel.

Vinnie lowered his head, not looking either girl in the face, and walked past them into the room. He stuffed a cheeseburger in his pocket and started to leave. Adrienne stepped in front of him, blocking his way.

"I'm sorry I didn't believe you."

He looked her in the face, still not used to the sight of her. "How could you believe me? I see the two of you together right now and it still seems impossible. I'm sorry I upset you, I just didn't know how to tell you."

Vinnie bolted out the door, but didn't get in his car. Both girls watched as he jogged across the parking lot, climbed over a ten-foot high pile of snow for no apparent reason, and continued heading in the direction of town.

"Are you in love with him?"

Rachel nodded her head and confided, "I fell in love with him the day I met him."

"I can understand how that could happen."

With the two of them still sharing the doorway Rachel said, "Adrienne, please come in. I'd like to close the door, I'm getting cold."

Adrienne inched her way into the room and took off her coat. Rachel opened the curtains and the room brightened considerably. "Would you like some of this McDonalds stuff?" asked Rachel.

"I'm not hungry."

"Me neither, not now anyway."

Rachel cleared off the bed and sat down. Adrienne sat beside her, but looked straight ahead out the window. Rachel studied the side of Adrienne's face.

"I'm sorry about the room. We don't even have a decent place to sit and talk to one another."

Adrienne continued to stare out the window, not wanting to turn away from the familiar view of Jackson Hole, a view she could understand, a view that made sense. She shook her head slowly from side to side, as her voice trembled. "I'm a different person. I'm not who I think I am. I'm someone I don't even know."

No longer able to contain the impact of what was happening, Adrienne covered her face with her hands and broke down. Her sobs shook her body and escalated into a high-pitched wailing as she grabbed a pillow from the bed and brought it to her chest. She buried her face in the pillow and pressed her chest against her thighs, the pillow sandwiched in between. Even in this position, and despite the muffling effect of the pillow, her wails sounded pathetic, like a wounded animal. Rachel reached out to touch her sister, but pulled back and began pacing wildly about the room. "Adrienne, I'm sorry. I should have never told you about any of this." Adrienne's wailing shrilled unabated. Rachel continued chaotically scurrying about the room, as if the motion of her body could somehow extract the pain from her sister. Finally, Rachel couldn't stand it any longer. She climbed on the bed behind her sister, laid her chest on Adrienne's back, and cradled her arms around her. "I'm sorry Adrienne, I'm sorry, I'm sorry ...." she whispered over and over as Adrienne's body shook in her arms.

Feeling the warmth and comfort of her sister, both the frequency and intensity of Adrienne's sobs gradually waned. When the sobs had subsided to just an occasional gasp for air, Adrienne straightened up and shoved the pillow aside. She leaned into Rachel, who began softly stroking her hand over Adrienne's long blond hair. Then with neither knowing which one of them initiated the motion, they fell back onto the bed and rested side by side wrapped in each other's arms. Adrienne's head was against Rachel's chest.

"I can hear your heart beating."

"What does it sound like?"

"Like a great big drum inside of a cave that's far away."

"Adrienne, why did you come to the motel if you didn't believe Vinnie?"

"Your essay."

"Huh?"

Still speaking into Rachel's chest, Adrienne explained. "Your essay, when I read it I knew everything Vinnie told me was true."

Together they adjusted their positions so they could look in each other's eyes.

"I don't understand. The essay's about me," whispered Rachel.

"It's about me too."

"What do you mean?"

"The dream about your leg, it's my dream too. I've had the same dream all of my life, but unlike you, I still have it. And the make believe friend you had when you were little, who you named Rachel because you couldn't tell the difference between her and yourself - it was exactly the same for me. My make believe friend was named Adrienne."

Rachel's eyes widened. "My God, how can this be possible? I've read strange stuff about twins before, but to think we could be experiencing the same things is unbelievable. I mean we were less than a year old when we were separated."

"I don't know how it's possible, but I know your essay is about me too. It's almost as if I wrote it."

"I've read every book in the library about twins. Have you ever read anything about twins?" asked Rachel.

"No."

"I guess not. Why would you?"

"Tell me something about twins, anything," Adrienne implored.

"Well, monozygotic twins, that is identical twins like us, come from one egg and one sperm."

"I know that. Not the monozygotic part, but the one egg, one sperm part."

"The odds of having identical twins are about 5 in a 1000. And guess what?"

"What?" Adrienne replied anxiously.

"My mother, I mean our mother, just told me this a couple of months ago. We're monoamnionic twins. That's the rarest type of all, only about 1 percent of identical twins are monoamnionic."

"What does that mean?"

"We were in the same sac together, we shared the same placenta. Most twins have their own sac with separate placentas."

"So does that mean we're about as identical as identical twins can be?" asked Adrienne.

"I think so. Dad told me that when we were babies he would have to look at the bottom of your foot to tell us apart. You still have the birthmark, don't you?"

"Yes. On my left foot."

Rachel raised her hand to Adrienne's face and carefully ran her finger down the bridge of her nose. "You do have the bump on your nose, don't you? I couldn't tell if you had it or not." Adrienne took her finger and ran it down Rachel's nose. "Your nose feels just like mine."

Adrienne sprang to an erect sitting position and started ripping off her shoes and socks. "Let me see your feet. Do you have goofy toes where your little toes kinda tuck underneath the ones next to them?"

Following her sister's lead Rachel also took off her shoes and socks. Sitting side by side with their backs against the headboard of the bed, Rachel and Adrienne gaped down at their twenty toes, with all four of the little toes trying to hide behind the toes next to them. They stared at the toes, then slowly turned to face one another, and for the very first time they smiled. Their smiles got bigger and bigger, until they erupted into laughter - not just, hey that's funny kind of laughter, but uproarious, body retching laughter where you want to stop just so you can catch a breath. But they couldn't stop.

With both of them rollicking around on the bed and laughing uncontrollably, Rachel struggled to get out the words, "Stop it, please stop it."

Laughing even harder, Adrienne screeched, "You stop it, you're going to make me pee my pants."

Rachel doubled over in pain, "I thought I was the only one who still did that."

Adrienne stopped gyrating about and came to rest lying on her back. She reached out and took hold of Rachel's hand. "Really let's stop, I can't breathe."

In between gasps for air, Rachel pleaded, "Okay, okay, let's stop, let's stop."

Adrienne matched Rachel's breathless cadence. "Okay, we're stopping now, we're stopping now......... I mean what's so funny about me having better looking toes than you anyway?"

And with that the riot started anew, both sisters laughing as they had never laughed before, laughing so hard tears flowed from their eyes and their insides hurt.

Finally, fatigue set in and the laughter ebbed to intermittent spurts and then subsided completely. They laid beside one another with their eyes closed for several minutes in complete silence, silence brought on by physical, and even more so, by mental exhaustion.

With her eyes still closed, Adrienne whispered, "Tell me how it happened."

Rachel knew exactly what Adrienne meant. "It was December 4th, 1976. Dad took us to Lake Elkhorn. That's a lake in Columbia, Maryland, near where we lived. We still live there in the same house. He pulled the van right up to the dock. It was one of those vans like the hippies used to drive. The two of us were in front of the van sitting in one of those side-by-side strollers they make for twins, throwing Cheerios to the ducks. Dad went around to the back of the van to get some juice and mix up some baby food for us. He was only back there for a couple of minutes. When he came around to the front of the van you were gone. The police never had any suspects, no leads, nothing. Two other baby girls disappeared from the Baltimore area over the next month. Their bodies were discovered a few weeks later. The police were convinced you were dead too. Everyone accepted what the police said except for Mom, she wouldn't give up hope."

Adrienne moved close to Rachel. "What's she like?"

Rachel cleared her throat and stared up at the ceiling. "She's very pretty. I can't believe how much you look like her."

Adrienne gently turned Rachel's face toward her. "But what's she like?"

"I hate her and I love her. She went to pieces emotionally after the abduction. She became an alcoholic. When she was sober, she was okay. But when she drank, she was terrible."

"But she's not still like that, is she?"

"No, she hasn't taken a drink in three years. I take that back, we got into a horrible fight last month on the anniversary of your abduction...... that's always a terrible day for us. We got into this fight and she got drunk, but she promised me that she would never drink again. And I believe her. Things are the best they've ever been between us. At least they were until I took off on this trip to Wyoming."

"What did you fight about?"

"I can't even remember how it started, what we pretended it was about."

"What do you mean?" Adrienne said as she squeezed Rachel's hand.

"We both knew what it was really about. All those years that she drank she was very mean to me. It was as if she blamed me for you not being there. She treated me terribly. But after she stopped drinking, she has tried so hard to be a good mother. I'm the one who has been terrible since then. All she wanted was for me to forgive her, and I would never do it. I rejected every little act of kindness from her."

"But you just said things between the two of you are good now."

"They're good in the sense that we agreed not to fight anymore. But I've never forgiven her." Rachel paused to compose herself. "And I've never told her that I love her, but ..."

"But what?" Adrienne implored as she tenderly wiped the tears from Rachel's eyes with the edge of the blanket.

Rachel bit her lower lip. "Looking at you right now, I do forgive her. I want to tell her I forgive her, tell her I love her. I'm gonna tell her the minute I see her."

As the intensity of Rachel's crying increased Adrienne hugged her tighter. "It's okay." Cradling Rachel even closer, Adrienne said, "In your essay you wrote that you used to hate me. Do you still hate me?"

Rachel lifted her head so she could look Adrienne in the eyes. "Oh no Adrienne, I don't hate you. I'm not sure I ever really hated you. I just hated the feeling of not being whole."

They lay silently entwined in each other's arms. Without either of them noticing, twilight's grayness was upon them; only a flicker of light filtered into the room from the final rays of the weakening sun.

"We had the same dream," murmured Adrienne.

"When we were..." Rachel started to speak, but before she could finish Adrienne interrupted her.

"You don't have to tell me, I know the reason why we had the same dream."

"You couldn't possibly know. I really didn't explain it in my essay."

Adrienne spoke in the darkness, the sun now completely extinguished for the day. "The way our legs are wrapped around each other right now, your right leg and my left leg, this is the way we slept together when we were babies, isn't it? I know it shouldn't be possible, but I think I can remember lying together with you just like this when we were babies. It was as if your leg was mine and my leg was yours. That's why we had the dream, isn't it?"

An icy chill poured through Rachel. "Yes, I've seen the pictures of us sleeping like that."

The mention of the word 'picture' immediately triggered a question from Adrienne. "Do you have a picture of your mother?"

Rachel thought for a moment. "Yes, I think I do. In my purse." She grabbed her purse from the nightstand and began rummaging through its contents. "I'm sure I have one in here somewhere…Here it is. It's of Mom and Dad. I took it a couple of years ago." She handed the picture to her sister. "So is he your skiing buddy?"

Adrienne held the picture under the lamp, looked at Larry's face and ever so slightly, almost reluctantly, nodded her head up and down. Then she looked at Vivian's face and spoke in a whisper. "God, Bonnie was right."

"Who's Bonnie?"

"She's just a friend." Adrienne fought to maintain her composure. "It's just that…. I don't look anything like my mother. She had dark hair and dark eyes."

"She had?" Rachel said softly with emphasis on the word 'had.'

"She died of cancer a year ago."

Rachel didn't say anything.

"My mother always told me I looked like my father."

"What do you mean, she told you?"

"My father left us when I was four. I can hardly remember him."

"Didn't you ever see a picture of him?"

"My mother threw all of them away. She said she never wanted to see his face again. I…" Adrienne began crying. "I guess what she really meant was she never wanted me to see his face….. There's a million things I want to know, but right now I need to be with my dad."

Rachel correctly assumed Adrienne must be referring to a stepfather, but chose not to ask – her sister's emotions were already rubbed raw.

"Take your time. I'll be here waiting for you when you want to see me again."

Adrienne loosened her sister's embrace enough that their eyes were a few inches apart. "Rachel, what do you want to happen now?"

"There's only one thing I want."

"What?"

"I just want to be your sister."

Chapter 33

Larry slumped at the kitchen table concentrating solicitously on Vivian who was sitting on the floor, leaning against the kitchen counter. Her face was tired, her hair matted and greasy. On the floor beside her was a cup that had been knocked over. Neither of them seemed concerned about the small puddle of spilled coffee. Vivian's head tilted back against the counter with the phone balanced between her neck and shoulder.

Larry rested his face in his hands and slurred, "Try again later. You've been letting it ring for over five minutes. No one's going to answer."

"I can't believe they drove all the way to Wyoming. What in the world is my baby doing in Wyoming?" Vivian stared vacantly at the cup, watching the final drop of coffee struggling to cling to the rim before it spilled onto the floor. "It's no wonder she sounded so tired...... How far is Wyoming anyway, 2500 miles?"

"It's not that far, more like 2000." Larry got up and dabbed the spilled coffee with a paper towel. As he reached to pick up the cup he said, "Please just hang up. You can call ...."

"Hello, hello!" Vivian shouted into the phone as she sprang to her feet.

Her body grew taut, while Larry's went limp as he flopped down in the kitchen chair.

"Is my daughter there? Her name is Rachel Webster." She wildly twisted the phone cord around her free hand as she listened. "Who are you?" Her hand continued to snake itself inside the cord. "Are you in Wyoming?" She continued to twist the cord. "Where exactly?" Larry restrained Vivian's hand as the cord became so taut it started to dislodge from the connector plate on the wall. "Please, would you go in the restaurant and see if my daughter is there?" With her hand now somewhat under control she squeezed Larry's arm. "I see," she said and then hung up the phone, her movements taking place in slow motion. She tried to move toward the kitchen table to sit down, but felt the resistance of the cord. "Did I do that?"

"Who answered?" Larry asked with a cracking voice.

"Some man. It was a pay phone in a McDonalds parking lot."

"In Wyoming?" Larry asked, even more strain in his voice.

"Yes, Jackson Hole, Wyoming."

Larry deftly unwrapped the cord from Vivian's arm and embraced her. "Let's sit down. There's something I need to tell you."

They sat across from one another, their hands meeting at the center of the table. "Should we call the Jackson Hole police department?" Vivian asked in a raspy voice.

"No, I don't think we need to do that." Larry licked his lips and tried to smile, but couldn't. "I didn't go to Flagstaff. I was in Jackson Hole."

Vivian shrieked, "Rachel was with you in Jackson Hole!"

"No, no, I didn't know she was there. She must have followed me."

"What the hell is going on?"

Larry cracked his knuckles trying to buy time to collect his thoughts. "Last Friday, I got a call in the office from some man. I don't know who he was. He said he had something important to tell me." He paused, hoping that a few more seconds would somehow help prepare Vivian for what he was about to say. "He said our daughter was alive."

The comment didn't register with Vivian. She cocked her head to the side in a puzzled fashion. "What are you talking about......... Rachel wasn't even missing on Friday."

"He wasn't talking about Rachel."

Vivian stiffened, her face paled as she transformed into a department store mannequin, not moving a muscle, not blinking an eye.

"He said Karen was alive and living in Jackson Hole, Wyoming."

Vivian moved her lips to form the words, "Is she?" but no sound came out.

Chapter 34

Vinnie buckled his belt as he sidestepped out of the stall of the men's room in O'Hare Airport. He sauntered over to the long bank of sinks, disdaining the first five, until he came to one that was only marginally disgusting. Adjusting the faucet he gingerly tested the temperature until it was just right - hot, but not too hot. Surprisingly, the soap dispenser responded with a generous supply of pink soap after only three or four pumps. Clean hands and a clean face made him feel a bit better, but he was tired and wanted to get home.

Gazing in the mirror, he was pleased with his respectable growth of facial hair. He backed away for another perspective - even from ten feet away it really looked like a beard, not just a dirty face. It made him look much older, twenty or twenty-one, he thought. And distinguished..... yes, it added a touch of distinction. Maybe he would let it grow. If it looked this presentable after only a week, imagine how great it would look after a full month. He couldn't believe it had been only a week since he had shaved - last Friday morning before going to school. School, how in the world were his teachers going to respond to a week of unexcused absences?

Cruising past the bank of sinks, he stole an occasional glance in the mirror, disappointed to notice that the quality of his beard appeared to fluctuate as he passed in and out of the full intensity of the overhead lighting. Maybe he could solve that problem by staying out from under bright lights for the next couple of weeks until some of the thin spots filled in a little better. Hell, that wasn't necessary. Even though she hadn't remarked about it, it was clear Rachel liked his beard. More important than that, he could tell it turned her on.

He strolled out of the men's room to Gate C-3 where Rachel and Adrienne were sitting side by side in the waiting area. Just as he located them among the crowd, they simultaneously looked down. At first he thought they had seen him, but obviously they hadn't since neither acknowledged him. They were oblivious to his approach, helping themselves to generous handfuls of popcorn from a box on Adrienne's lap.

As he came closer, they appeared to be trembling. "Oh no," he thought, what's happened this time to torpedo their spirits. Just ten minutes earlier they were almost giddy with happiness. How long could two people stay on such an emotional roller coaster? Wait a minute, they weren't struggling to hold back the tears. No, not at all.

"What's so funny?" asked Vinnie.

Without looking up, Rachel muttered, "nothing," and then shoveled a handful of popcorn into her mouth. He turned his attention to Adrienne who was shaking uncontrollably. "And I guess you don't think anything is funny either?" Adrienne crammed some more popcorn into her mouth and looked up at Vinnie. Immediately upon making eye contact, popcorn came spewing out of her mouth. She erupted into maniacal laughter, collapsing from her seat to the floor. The popcorn box was launched from her lap into the next isle of seats, showering popcorn on two elderly women. Rachel followed Adrienne to the floor, laughing hysterically. As their bodies writhed about, occasionally a mouth would open and eject several pieces of popcorn. And every once in a while, one of the girls would attempt to calm herself and try to speak; but instead of words coming out of her mouth, it would be just more popcorn.

Vinnie was embarrassed by the chuckling crowd of people gathered around these two girls behaving as if they were seven years old instead of seventeen. One of the elderly women who had been hit with the initial barrage of popcorn kneeled down next to Adrienne. "Young lady, young lady, please tell me what is so funny." With tears drenching her face and her mouth, somehow still stuffed with popcorn, Adrienne pointed up at Vinnie. "He keeps a record of every state he poops in. He just did it in Illinois."

From somewhere beneath Adrienne came Rachel's shrieking rejoinder, "He wants to poop in all fifty of 'em." With deadpan seriousness, the woman inquired of Vinnie. "Well young man, how many states have you done your business in?"

The crowd, which now numbered a dozen or so, exploded with laughter. Vinnie could feel the heat in his face as he blushed the mother of all blushes. The two girls sprawled side by side on the dirty floor, with identical giggling faces, one framed with long yellow hair and the other framed with short black and yellow hair. Vinnie retreated across the open area in front of the check-in counter to another row of seats and sat down next to Hank Sullivan.

Hank put his hand on Vinnie's shoulder. "Watching the two of them together is the most amazing thing I have ever seen. On Tuesday night, when Adrienne told me she had a twin sister, it seemed like the most impossible thing in the world. But seeing them together these past few days I can't imagine..." his voice trailed off as his expression betrayed his sadness.

Vinnie shook his head in wonderment. "Here they are having this same unbelievable experience, but it must be so different for each of them. Adrienne not knowing she had a sister, and Rachel haunted by a sister she thought was dead."

Hank pulled a handkerchief from his pocket and wiped his eyes. "I'm glad my Cynthia can't see them together now. I don't know how, or why she took Adrienne. But anyone who sees them knows they were meant to be together."

"Mr. Sullivan, I don't know what to say, but I think the key for them is to look to the future. How it happened and why it happened, I don't think make any difference now." When Hank didn't reply, Vinnie spoke again. "I just don't feel right about you paying me a thousand dollars for my car. It's not worth anywhere near that much. And paying for my airfare on top of that, I just..."

Before Vinnie could finish, Hank interrupted. "I'll get good use out of the car. I don't want to hear any more about it."

"Vinnie you're not mad at us, are you?"

Vinnie looked up. Rachel and Adrienne were standing in front of him. Unable at times to distinguish between their voices, he wasn't sure which one had spoken, so he directed his response to the small space between them. "Of course I'm not mad. I actually enjoy being humiliated in front of a bunch of strangers."

"We're sorry Vinnie," said Adrienne. "It's just that when Rachel started telling me about........ you know, your goal of doing it in every state. Well, she started laughing and then I cracked up. When we did stop laughing, we promised each other we wouldn't laugh when you came back from the men's room. But we couldn't help it."

Just as Vinnie started to respond there was an announcement over the loudspeaker. "Flight 67 to Baltimore, now boarding at Gate C-3."

'That's our flight," Rachel said excitedly.

"I can't believe this is really happening," Adrienne quietly mumbled.

Walking down the aisle of the Boeing 727, they came to Row 18 and took their seats. Adrienne sat in between Rachel and Hank, and Vinnie sat across the aisle from Hank. The two seats next to Vinnie were not occupied. Once they were airborne, Hank moved across the aisle and sat in the window seat, two seats away from Vinnie, knowing Adrienne and Rachel would want to share some private thoughts during the next two hours.

"Did Rachel phone her parents this morning before we left for the airport?" asked Hank.

"Yes, she talked to them for quite a while."

"Did her father say any more about the call he received explaining about Adrienne?"

Vinnie leaned across the empty seat between them. "No, he told her basically the same thing he did the other night....... that a man, whose voice he had never heard before, called him at work and told him his daughter was alive and living in Jackson Hole."

Hank shook his head in bewilderment. "That is so strange. Why would someone wait seventeen years to tell? And who in the world could it possibly be?"

"Sir, I guess it had to be someone who helped your wife and her first husband take Adrienne." Vinnie paused for a moment. "I'm sorry Mr. Sullivan, but they had to be the ones who took her. You don't doubt that do you?"

Hank turned away from Vinnie and tried to conceal his expression. "My wife was a wonderful woman, but no, I don't have any doubt. I've tried to figure out some other plausible explanation, but there just isn't any." Hank sighed and cleared his throat. "On the night before she died, Cynthia said she had to tell me about something terrible she had done a long time ago. She was holding a picture of Adrienne and got real upset. The nurse came into the room and gave her a sedative that put her to sleep.

The next day she didn't say anything and I didn't ask about it. She died that afternoon."

"Do you think she was about to tell you she took Adrienne?"

"Yes. I told Adrienne about it last night. You know what she said?"

Vinnie shook his head no.

Hank fought not to cry. He reclined his seat, hiding behind Vinnie, so Adrienne couldn't see him. "She said Cynthia had been the most wonderful mother in the world."

Vinnie started to console Hank, but he just couldn't make himself do it. He wanted to be sympathetic to this man, but there was just no way he could condone what his wife had done. Turning his attention from Hank, he sneaked a peek at Adrienne and Rachel holding hands and quietly conversing.

"Do you think your mother is upset because I didn't want to talk to her on the phone?" asked Adrienne.

"She's not upset. I don't think she was ready to talk to you either. Anyway, the two of you talking for the first time is much too important to do over the phone."

Adrienne's mouth was so dry it felt like it was filled with cotton. "I've never been so scared in my entire life."

"You shouldn't be. There's nothing to be afraid of."

"I keep telling myself that, but it's not working. I know it sounds crazy, but somehow I feel guilty about all of this."

"How could you possibly feel guilty about what happened?"

"I feel like I deserted my family and had this wonderful life, but my disappearance turned my family's life into a nightmare."

"You were only nine months old. None of this is your fault, none of it."

"I know that all sounds logical, but maybe I'm just feeling my..." Adrienne's voice trailed off.

"Feeling your what?"

"Nothing."

"I want to know what you started to say."

Adrienne covered her face. "Maybe I'm feeling my mother's guilt. She's not alive to feel it for herself, so maybe I'm feeling it for her. She was a wonderful person, I want you to understand that."

"That's something I'm not sure I'll ever be able to understand. I know I have to respect your right to feel that way, but I'm going to need some time."

Rachel hugged her sister, as she motioned across the aisle. "Hey Vinnie, come over here for a minute." Vinnie lifted up his tray, secured it to the seat in front of him, slid across the aisle and sat next to Adrienne, then leaned forward so he could talk to Rachel. "What's up?"

"I wanna talk to you about your beard."

Vinnie raised his eyebrows. "Really."

"Do you have a razor in your carry-on bag?"

"A razor?"

"Yeah, a razor. Shave that thing off before we land. You look ridiculous."

His eyebrows dropped and his smile evaporated into a painful grimace. "Oh sure, I was going to shave, but I forgot. I'll go do that now. Thanks for reminding me."

Vinnie got up and pulled his travel case out of his carry-on bag and headed down the aisle toward the restroom at the aft end of the plane.

Adrienne was surprised by Rachel's lack of tact. "I think he thought his beard looked good."

"I don't see how that's possible, but I think you're right. I'll have to make it up to him somehow," Rachel said with a coy smile.

Adrienne glanced at her watch. "Oh no, we're going to be there in less than half an hour. What should I say to her? I was awake all night trying to figure out what to say."

"Don't worry about what you're going to say, just let it happen."

"But what should I call her? I don't even know what to call her."

"Call her Mom."

"I can't do that."

Chapter 35

Larry turned from the pay phone at Baltimore Washington International Airport and scanned the noisy parade of arriving passengers passing behind him.

"I've got to go now. Their plane is going to be landing in just a few minutes."

"Please call me as soon as you get a chance," pleaded Barbara.

"Okay, but I don't know when that'll be. Now stop worrying, there is nothing to worry about. I've got to go. I love you."

"Oh Larry, do you really mean that? Do you still love me?"

"Yes. Now goodbye."

He hung up the phone, checked his watch and started running toward the arrival gates, stopping at the metal detector, but passing through quickly. He jogged down the large hallway leading to Gate B until he neared B-16, and then walked the last hundred feet. Vivian, and Joe and Debra Carolla, Vinnie's parents, were standing at the front of a reception area for arriving passengers.

He tapped Vivian on the shoulder. "Is the flight still on time?"

"Yes. What took you so long?" Vivian barked, miffed at his absence.

"You're not the only one who's nervous about this. I had a little problem in the men's room," Larry lied convincingly.

"I'm sorry. The plane is already on the ground. They should be coming through that door in just a few minutes."

On the plane most passengers were still collecting their belongings, while some of the more anxious ones had already scrambled up the servicing walkway into the terminal. The passengers further aft waited in patient resignation for those in front to clear out. Hank, lugging a duffel bag, and Vinnie, wearing a backpack, stood in the aisle. Adrienne and Rachel remained in their seats.

"Well kitten, I guess this is it," said Hank.

"Daddy, you and Vinnie go ahead. Rachel and I want to sit here for just a few more minutes."

"Are you going to be able to do this?"

"Yes Daddy, I'm okay. I love you."

Hank leaned over and kissed his daughter, wanting to tell her he loved her too, but reluctant to risk an overload of emotions just before greeting Rachel's parents. He joined the slow processional filing toward the front of the plane. Vinnie swayed back and forth in the aisle, not wanting to go, but knowing that he must.

"Rachel, my parents are going to be out there waiting for me. I think it would be best if I just left with them right away. Call me tomorrow when things settle down."

Rachel motioned to him with her index finger. "Okay, but come here first."

Leaning in front of Adrienne, Rachel grabbed the shoulder strap of his backpack and drew him to her and kissed him on the lips. As he withdrew Adrienne unexpectedly caught his arm to stop him. Still doubled over and his face just a few inches in front of hers, Adrienne moved her lips toward him. She stopped momentarily. "It's okay, I have Rachel's approval." As he turned to check with Rachel, Adrienne kissed him deeply on the lips, holding it for four or five seconds. "Thank you for what you've done for my sister and me. And by the way, I think you should change your mind and go to Stanford instead of Duke."

Rachel mockingly punched Adrienne on the arm. "Hey, you said no more than three seconds."

"Sorry, I forgot to count."

"And what's this Stanford crap?" Rachel laughed.

Vinnie, his face flushed with embarrassment, stood up and surveyed the two sisters who stared back at him with identical smiles. Completely flustered, he bolted up the isle, the human gridlock having disappeared with most of the passengers now off the plane. Halfway up the servicing walkway, Vinnie came upon Hank who had stopped.

"Thought I'd wait for you. I don't particularly want to walk out there by myself. Hope you don't mind."

"No sir, I don't mind."

Vinnie and Hank advanced up the walkway and into the terminal. Vinnie spotted Rachel's parents and his parents immediately.

"That's Mrs. Webster, the one in the red sweater with the blond hair."

"Jimminy Cricket, I see why Rachel and Adrienne ended up being so beautiful," Hank observed, immediately feeling embarrassed he had done so.

They moved forward with Vinnie in the lead. Vinnie walked directly up to Vivian and Larry, Hank stopping about ten feet behind.

"Hi, Mrs. Webster. I hope you're not too mad at me."

Vivian gave Vinnie a stern look, broke into a big smile, and then hugged him. "How could I possibly be mad at you? Just don't ever run away with my daughter again."

"Don't worry, I won't. At least not any time soon."

"You did bring Rachel home, didn't you? I can't believe anyone's still left on that plane."

"She's on there."

Vivian released Vinnie who turned to face his parents and smiled sheepishly.

"Vincent, what in the world did you do to your face?" Vinnie's mother asked.

"I kinda nicked it shaving on the plane. We were flying through some turbulence and everything was bouncing around."

Vinnie linked arms with his parents, said goodbye to Vivian and Larry, then started walking away, but stopped and turned around. "Goodbye Mr. Sullivan. Thanks for everything."

"Goodbye Vinnie."

Larry stepped forward. "Hank, I thought about you on my return flight from Jackson Hole. I was reading an article about the three remaining Beatles getting together to make a new album."

"I just heard that yesterday. I kinda wish they wouldn't. The memories are too perfect; they shouldn't be disturbed."

"That's the way I feel," Larry said as he extended his hand to Hank.

They exchanged a firm handshake. "Hank, this is my wife Vivian. Vivian, this is Hank Sullivan." Hank took a step closer.

"Mrs. Webster..."

Vivian extended her hand. "Please call me Vivian."

"Thank you," he replied as he took her hand in both of his. "Vivian, I wish I knew the appropriate words to express the sorrow I feel for the heartaches you've suffered."

"Mr. Sullivan..."

"Call me Hank, please."

"Hank, I know you had no hand in any part of this. Larry has told me what a wonderful girl Adrienne is. That

349

never would have happened without you. I have no reason whatsoever to blame ....."

Vivian stopped in mid-sentence, her face paled, and she started to tremble as she gasped, "Oh my God."

Standing side by side, holding hands at the entrance to the terminal, not more than twenty feet away, were Rachel and Adrienne. They stood there stiffly, like two identical paper cutout dolls, the kind that you clip on different outfits and hairdos - Rachel with black jeans and a gray sweatshirt, and Adrienne with light blue jeans and a blue sweater imprinted with two large white snowflakes. They came forward together, moving with a common rhythm.

Vivian lifted her hands to her face as they came closer. Hank and Larry instinctively moved to the side, both knowing there was no place for either of them in this most special and precious of human triangles.

Rachel and Adrienne continued hand in hand until they stopped not more than five feet in front of their mother. Vivian lowered her hands revealing trembling lips. She looked first into Rachel's eyes, then into Adrienne's eyes, and then back to Rachel. She reached forward to embrace Rachel, taking her in her arms and squeezing her tightly.

Rachel sobbed, "Mommy, I love you. I love you. Please forgive me for never letting you know that."

Vivian rocked back and forth with Rachel in her arms. "That's the most wonderful thing I've ever heard."

After several seconds they stopped swaying and slowly released one another. Rachel took a step to the side and Vivian turned to face Adrienne, who stood with clenched white-knuckled fists held tightly against her chest. Mother and daughter stared at one another for the first time in more than seventeen years, both trembling, both with tears quietly running down their faces.

Vivian tentatively extended her right hand, the palm facing up and the fingers gently bent. Adrienne looked down at the hand, stared at it for several seconds, and then raised her head and looked into her mother's eyes. As Vivian painfully withdrew her hand, Adrienne said, "No don't," and gently laid her hand on top of her mother's.

Vivian took hold of her daughter's hand and with a soft, but shaking voice asked, "Would it be okay if I gave you a hug?"

Unable to speak, Adrienne shook her head with an unmistakable yes.

Vivian stepped forward and took her daughter tenderly in her arms, looked upward and whispered, "Oh dear God, thank you, thank you."

As Vivian cried unashamedly and buried her face against her daughter's neck, Adrienne raised her arms and returned her mother's embrace. When her crying subsided, Vivian released her daughter and took a step backward.

"Over these past three days I've thought of a thousand things I wanted to say to you and ask you, but right now I can't remember any of them."

Adrienne took hold of her mother's hand and held out her free hand to Rachel who stepped forward and closed the circle by joining hands with her sister and mother. The two sisters and their mother moved inward, shrinking the circle smaller and smaller until they were engulfed in each other's arms. People in the airport stopped and watched, sensing that something very special was happening.

With their three faces pressed together Adrienne whimpered, "You have all the time in the world to say and ask me those thousand things."

The three Websters and the two Sullivans left the airport and drove back to the house Adrienne had lived in for the first nine months of her life. The five of them sat around the kitchen table eating pizza, oohing at pictures of the girls when they were babies, and talking well into the night. Rachel made a point of showing Adrienne a picture of the two of them asleep on the family room rug with their legs interlocked. Neither of the girls said anything about their dreams. With just a glance, they sent one another the message that their dreams would be but one of many intimate secrets they would share.

A little after eleven o'clock Hank excused himself and went to bed. Adrienne followed a few minutes later leaving only Rachel and her parents. As soon as Adrienne had gone upstairs, Rachel turned to her father. "The man who called you and told you about Adrienne, who do you think he could possibly be?"

Even though Rachel had directed the question to her father, it was Vivian who answered. "Your father and I have talked about that and we can't come up with anything that makes sense. The only man who would have definitely known about the abduction was Cynthia Sullivan's first husband, but he's dead."

"Daddy, what did the man say?"

Larry shook his head in feigned befuddlement. "I was in such a state of shock I can't remember very many details. He started by saying he had something important to say, told me to be quiet and not ask any questions. Then he said my daughter, who was taken seventeen years ago, was alive and her name was Adrienne Sullivan. Then he told me where I could find her."

"Did he ask for money or anything?"

"No."

"Why did you believe him?"

"I really didn't believe him, but he sounded convincing enough that I had to find out."

"He called you at work?"

"Yeah, he called me at work last Friday afternoon."

Rachel jerked back in her chair. "But I saw you at the hospital last Friday afternoon."

Larry, sensing his fabrication was unraveling, unconsciously combed his hair with his fingers. "You're mistaken, you must have seen someone else. I wasn't at the hospital on Friday."

"But Dad, Vinnie saw you too. We saw you drive away in your Taurus."

Larry glanced quickly at Vivian and then slapped his forehead with the palm of his hand. "You're right, I completely forgot. I was at the hospital. After I got the call at work I drove straight to the travel agent's office....... you know, the one near the mall. She made all the reservations, but couldn't print out the airline tickets because her computer was down. She said to come back in an hour to get them. I remembered this guy at work was in the hospital, and I went over to see him for a few minutes."

Vivian put her arm around Larry. "Your father is tired; we're all tired. This last week has been a blur for all of us. As for the man who called your father, I don't think we will ever find out anything about him."

"I guess you're right. What's important now is the future, not the past."

Larry tried to remember how to breathe.

Chapter 36

Two thin shafts of early morning sunlight sliced through the openings of the partially drawn curtains, piercing the gentle softness of Rachel's room. The single bed was neatly made, covered with a light blue flowered spread and matching pillow. The floor was a heap of stuffed animals, pillows, sleeping bags, and exposed arms and legs. Rachel's hair, protruding from beneath a sleeping bag, looked almost phosphorescent as it was highlighted by one of the shafts of sunlight. Adrienne was submerged beneath another sleeping bag. Stepping over several bears, a lion, and a monkey, Vivian reached down and gently shook Rachel's shoulder.

"Rachel, wake up. It's almost nine o'clock."

Rachel looked up at her mother through squinting eyelids. Instinctively, she reached back over her head and groped with her hand until she found Adrienne's foot sticking out of the unzipped sleeping bag.

"That's her, isn't it? That's really my sister sleeping next to me."

Vivian got down on her knees and smiled. "It seems impossible, but yes, that's really your sister."

Rachel rose to a sitting position and surveyed the ocean of keepsakes floating around her. "I forgot how many stuffed animals I've accumulated over the years."

"How late were you girls up talking?"

Stretching her arms over her head, Rachel yawned, "About two-thirty, I think."

"Go ahead and wake Adrienne. I'm sure she doesn't want to spend her only full day here sleeping."

"No Mom, you wake her."

The Other Part Of Me

Vivian bit her lower lip as she visually traced the outline of Adrienne's body beneath the sleeping bag. She bent over and tentatively pulled the sleeping bag off of Adrienne's face. Still half asleep, Adrienne jerked the bag back over her. Vivian nudged her and slowly peeled the sleeping bag off once again. "Adrienne, it's time to get up." This time Adrienne rolled over and opened her eyes just as her face moved into a blinding beam of sunlight. She immediately sprang to a sitting position, the sunlight now at her back setting her hair ablaze.

"I had the strangest dream," Adrienne said stoically.

"What was it about?" Rachel asked.

Adrienne stared blankly straight ahead, not looking either Vivian or Rachel in the face. "The two of you were on a merry-go-round, riding on horses, the kind that go up and down. I was running alongside trying to catch up. It was cold and there was snow on the ground, but both of you were wearing bathing suits, the old-fashioned kind. Vivian was reaching out to me, but no matter how fast I ran I just couldn't grasp her hand. It seemed so real. Even now it feels like this room is spinning, just like the merry-go-round."

Vivian picked up a tattered Miss Piggy doll and moved it aside so she could sit facing both girls. "I've never been one to place much credence in dreams, but I know your feelings have to be all mixed up. Your dream is probably some sort of reflection of what's going on inside of you."

Adrienne picked up a small fluffy bear and turned it end-over-end in her lap. The bear continued its somersaulting as she spoke. "When I met Rachel on Tuesday and realized she was my sister, it was the strangest feeling I ever had. I didn't think it was possible to feel so strange, but I was wrong. Being here with you, knowing that you're my mother, that's much stranger. Strange isn't even the right word. It's only been four days and I know it doesn't seem possible, but the idea that Rachel is my sister seems so natural, so normal. But I don't think I'll ever be able to get used to the idea that you're my mother."

Vivian placed one hand on Adrienne's knee and the other on Rachel's. "I wish I could push a magic button and make both of you nine months old again and we could live our lives all over. I wish I........" Vivian stopped to cover her face with her hands.

Adrienne touched her mother's shoulder. "I'm sorry, I didn't mean to upset you."

Vivian composed herself, and with a resurgent voice said, "It's okay, I'll get over it." She reached out and tenderly ran her hand down the side of Adrienne's face. "You're here, you're alive, that's the only thing that matters to me...... Now come on, you girls get dressed and come downstairs. I made blueberry pancakes. Rachel loves blueberry pancakes. How 'bout you?"

Adrienne grinned from ear to ear and yummied, "I love 'em too."

As Rachel and Adrienne shuffled past Hank, reading the morning newspaper in the family room, they heard the muffled conversation of Vivian and Larry from behind the closed door of the den. The scent of pancakes from the kitchen caused them to quicken their pace and dive into their breakfast. Just as they were dividing the last pancake in half, Vivian poked her head into the kitchen.

"We'd like you girls to join the rest of us in the family room when you're finished."

"We're finished," they replied in perfect unison.

As the girls walked into the family room, Vivian put her hand on Adrienne's shoulder and ushered her to the middle seat of the sofa next to Hank, then she had Rachel sit in the final seat of the sofa next to Adrienne. She and Larry sat in two chairs on the opposite side of the coffee table. After several awkward seconds, Larry tried to break the ice. "Adrienne certainly is a terrific ski instructor."

"Yes she is," came the obligatory response from Hank.

Larry rubbed his hands up his face and back over his head. "Vivian and I have been talking and we want to make something clear. It's pretty obvious the five of us being here together is not a normal situation. There's no guidebook to tell us how to deal with this. " Feeling the ever building tension in the room, Larry entreated Vivian for moral support, "Hey, jump in any time you want."

"Okay, I will." Vivian, summoning her courage, coughed nervously. "This past week has been an unbelievable experience for all of us. We've all been on a roller coaster of emotions. But each of us has been on a separate roller coaster because this experience is different for each of us. I can't describe the joy I feel seeing Rachel and Adrienne sitting next to one another."

Adrienne linked hands with Rachel and Hank on either side of her as Larry picked up where Vivian left off.

"What Vivian and I want to say is we may be Adrienne's biological parents, but you Hank have become Adrienne's real father. It's very clear to us that the two of you have a special relationship, and we don't want to change or replace that relationship in any way."

"Thank you so much," came the barely audible reply from Hank as he squeezed Adrienne's hand.

Vivian spoke next. "We just want to have a chance to be part of Adrienne's life in some way. And more importantly, we want Rachel and Adrienne to have the chance to be sisters, very special sisters."

"Can I ask you something?" said Adrienne.

"Of course," Vivian replied.

"I don't know what to call you. Please tell me what I should call you."

Vivian smiled. "Just call me Vivian."

Larry waved, grinned like a Cheshire cat, and said, "And I'm Larry."

"As in Larry, Moe and Curly," chirped Rachel.

For the first time, the tension in the room eased as everyone laughed. "So Dad is this the end of yours and Mom's speech?" asked Rachel. Larry checked with Vivian. "Yeah, I think that's the end of our speech." Vivian nodded in agreement.

"It was a very nice speech, I liked it a lot," Adrienne said.

"Me too, and thank you again," Hank added.

Rachel sprang to her feet. "If that's the end of our little group therapy session, Adrienne and I are going to see a little of Columbia and then meet Vinnie at the mall for lunch."

"Hank, do you like to shoot pool?" Larry asked.

"As a matter of fact I do."

"Great, I have a table in the basement. We can listen to some Beatles tapes."

"Sounds good."

Vivian checked her watch. "Listen up everyone. I have to go to the office for a few hours this afternoon, but I want everybody back here no later than five. We have reservations at Phillips Crab House at the Inner Harbor this evening."

"That's in Baltimore. They have great seafood," Rachel added.

Rachel and Adrienne slipped on their coats and headed to the door. "Dad, I'm taking the Taurus. Okay?" By the time he could reply, "okay," they were out the door.

As Rachel backed the car out of the driveway she said, "Wanna go see my high school, it's open on Saturdays? It's a lot bigger than yours."

"No."

"Okay, wanna just go straight to the mall?"

"No."

"What then?"

"Take me to where it happened."

About ten minutes later, Rachel pulled off Cradlerock Way into the parking lot next to Lake Elkhorn. They got out of the car and started toward the lake.

"These retaining posts weren't here then, so Dad drove his van right up to the dock."

"How do you know?"

"When I was thirteen, I had Dad bring me here and show me where everything happened. We never came back here together after that."

"It's just a regular looking place, isn't it?" Adrienne commented almost unconsciously as she surveyed the surroundings, trying to make a connection with this place that was so pivotal in her life.

"I come here every once in a while when I want to talk to you."

"You talk to me?"

Rachel shook her head up and down. "I used to ride my bike. I can come all the way on the bike path that runs behind our house, but now I only come if I have one of the cars."

"What do you talk to me about?"

"Everything........ school, boys, everything."

"Boys, as in more than one boy?"

"No, it's just Vinnie," Rachel said as she stooped to pick up a stone and skim it across the lake. "The Christmas when I was fourteen, I walked here. Mom and Dad had no idea where I was."

"You walked all this way."

"It took me almost two hours to get here. I didn't get home until after dark. I never told them where I went."

Rachel found a dry spot on the wooden dock and Adrienne sat down next to her.

"The way Dad described it, right where we're sitting is exactly where our stroller was when it happened." Rachel joined hands with her sister. "You know, you were born first, and weighed almost a pound more than me. You did everything before me. You had already started walking when you were taken, you were only nine months old. I didn't walk until I was a year old."

"And you used to let that kind of stuff bother you? That's ridiculous, we're exactly the same."

"Sitting here it seems ridiculous, but when I was little and Mom would say that kind of stuff, it really hurt. She only did it when she was drinking."

"She seems like such a wonderful person now."

"I know. She stopped drinking that Christmas I came here, and she's been a changed person ever since. It's taken me a long time to accept it."

Adrienne retrieved a wool hat from the pocket of her coat and yanked it down over her ears. "How long does it take to drive here from Philadelphia?"

"About two hours, I think. Why?"

"That's where my mother lived seventeen years ago. I always thought I was born there. I wonder if she and her first husband - I used to call him my first dad, but I don't know what to call him now - I wonder if they did it themselves or if they paid someone to do it. And I wonder how they picked this place to do it; and how they picked me."

"We'll never know any of that stuff."

Adrienne rubbed her hands together. "Somehow I feel a little better having seen this place, but I'm ready to go. I'm getting cold and I'm anxious to see Vinnie......" she smiled, "I mean I'm anxious to see this fancy shopping mall."

Rachel made a fist and shook it in front of Adrienne's face. Adrienne held up her hands as if a gun was being pointed at her. "No more kisses, no more kisses. I promise." Rachel put her arm around Adrienne, and the two sisters sitting in the exact spot where they had been separated seventeen years earlier, leaned against each other.

"I think I love you," whispered Adrienne.

"Me too."

At the Columbia Mall they did some shopping and pulled a practical joke on Vinnie who had been dropped off by his mother. Over lunch at the Taco Maker, the three of them discussed what kind of car Vinnie should buy - a used Toyota Celica was the final consensus. A conversation about their upcoming freshmen years at college touched off a heated debate over the relative superiority of Stanford, Duke and Harvard. No one argued persuasively enough to change anyone else's mind.

After a few burritos too many, the three of them piled into the Taurus and headed to the east side of Columbia. They stopped at an office complex on Route 175, and went into the offices of Columbia Realtors. The door to Vivian's office was open. She was having a conversation with a very large man wearing a baseball hat.

"I'll get back to you with a preliminary report as soon as I can," the man said as he rose to leave.

"Thanks so much Ted."

Vinnie and Rachel appeared in the doorway, holding hands, as the man walked past them. Rachel had on a black turtleneck sweater, and a big floppy black beret that engulfed her entire head.

"Hi! Is that hat and sweater new?" said Vivian.

"Yeah, I just bought them at the mall."

"Where's Adrienne?"

Just then, Adrienne skipped around the corner, wearing the exact style sweater and hat, and screeched, "Got ya." She yanked the beret off, revealing short black hair. The other girl, the one with Vinnie, simultaneously pulled off her beret to reveal long blond hair. Vivian had just been fooled with the oldest twin trick in the book. Rachel was really Adrienne and Adrienne was really Rachel.

"They did the same thing to me in the mall. I couldn't believe I fell for it," said Vinnie.

Vivian crumpled up a letter she had in her hand and tossed it over her shoulder in disbelief. "When the two of you were babies, I was the only one who could tell you apart. Now, even I can't do it."

That evening everyone had a festive time at dinner. It was agreed that Adrienne would fly back to Columbia for a weeklong visit over the Easter holidays, and that Rachel and Vivian would spend the entire month of July in Jackson Hole. Larry made known his decision to go to Chile for a one-year assignment with the international science team developing the four large telescopes. He would be leaving in two weeks. A three-week break in August would allow him to spend a few days in Jackson Hole and then return to Columbia to see Rachel off to college.

Vivian indicated that once Rachel was settled at Harvard, she would spend several months with Larry in Chile. Larry seemed reluctant to commit to Vivian's plan, indicating they should discuss the subject at a later time.

It was late - a few minutes before midnight - when they arrived home after dropping off Vinnie. Vivian asked Hank if he minded if Adrienne spent a few minutes alone with the three Websters. He didn't mind at all, seeing how he could barely keep his eyes open. Once Rachel,

Adrienne, and Larry gathered in the family room, Vivian got to the point quickly.

"Adrienne, I'm sure Rachel has told you about my drinking problem, and how terribly I treated her when she was a little girl. I did plenty of horrible things, and I'm ashamed of them."

"Mom, you don't have to do this," Rachel pleaded.

"Yes, I do. Please just listen."

Rachel rocked back stiffly on the sofa as Vivian continued.

"There's one thing I've always been more ashamed of than anything else. Did Rachel tell you about the Mickey and Minnie dolls?"

"Yes, she told me."

Larry fidgeted uncomfortably in his chair and rubbed his hands up his face, but catching himself, stopped short of completing his nervous habit. Relieved that no one seemed to notice his discomfort, he locked his hands together in front of him.

Vivian moved closer to her daughters. "When the two of you were four months old, Larry came home one day with Mickey and Minnie Mouse dolls. Adrienne, you reached out and chose the Mickey doll, and Rachel, you picked the Minnie doll. Both of you were inseparable from your dolls, so much so we started calling you Minnie and Mickey as often as Rachel and Karen."

Vivian instinctively reached across the table and put her hand on Adrienne's knee. "I'm sorry I said that."

"That's okay. I realize my name was Karen, but Adrienne is all I've ever known."

Vivian forced a painful, but appreciative smile. "When you were abducted, you were taken without your doll. Actually the dolls caused a lot of confusion when you were taken."

"Rachel told me about that."

Ronnie Kinsley

The smile faded from Vivian's face. "On Rachel's second birthday, I got drunk and bought her a stuffed bear, but I took Minnie away from her. She cried and cried, but I never gave it back. I told Larry I had thrown away both dolls. I told him if Karen couldn't have Mickey, then it wasn't fair for Rachel to have Minnie. I don't think I've ever seen him get so angry."

Vivian snatched a tissue from her purse and wiped her eyes. "I never threw them away. All these years I have kept those dolls hidden."

She turned to Rachel. "I wanted to give Minnie back to you so many times, but I was so ashamed. I knew it would reopen all the old hurts. But so many of my memories of the two of you together are with those dolls."

Rachel stepped around the coffee table to her mother's side and wrapped her arms around her.

"I want you girls to have your dolls back....... if you want them." Vivian pressed her face into Rachel's chest. "Do you want Minnie back?"

Unable to speak, Rachel nodded her head. Vivian released herself from Rachel's grasp and asked Adrienne. "Do you want Mickey?"

"Yes," whispered Adrienne.

Vivian disappeared into the laundry room and returned carrying the dolls with the care one would apply to the handling of a crystal menagerie. She timidly handed Minnie to Rachel and Mickey to Adrienne.

"Thank you .... Mother," said Adrienne, her face turning red from the awkwardness of acknowledging Vivian as her mother.

Recognizing Adrienne's discomfort, Vivian turned her attention to Rachel.

"I don't know what to say," Rachel said softly.

"You don't have to say anything."

364

Larry remained glued to his chair, as still as a statue, a statue with raindrops slowly dripping down its face.

Rachel hugged Minnie to her chest. "Mom, I do have something I want to say. Actually, it's something I want to ask you to do for me?"

"I'll do anything. What is it?"

"The painting you're gonna give me for my birthday – could you put Adrienne in the painting with me."

Vivian's eyes widened and her mouth opened into a perfect circle. "What a wonderful idea. There's plenty of extra canvas wrapped around the back. I could easily…" she stopped herself in mid-sentence and turned to Adrienne. "I'm sorry Adrienne. I need to know how you feel about this. Has Rachel shown you the painting?"

Adrienne shook her head up and down. "It's beautiful."

"Would you like to be in the painting?"

"That would be wonderful."

"Great. I can't wait to get started on it."

"Do you need to take a picture of me to use for the painting."

Vivian leaned over and kissed Adrienne on the cheek. "I definitely want to get some pictures before you head back to Wyoming, but the only picture I need to paint you is up here," Vivian said as she tapped her temple with her index finger.

"We should probably get to bed," Rachel said as she took Adrienne's hand. The two of them hugged Vivian and went upstairs.

Hours later Vivian was still up, long after everyone else had retired for the night. As she tiptoed up the stairs the grandfather clock chimed three times behind her, causing a chill to run down her spine. She continued up the stairs and peeked into Rachel's room. The soft glow of a tiny nightlight was just enough to reveal the outlines of the girls lying on the floor amongst the jungle of stuffed animals. In the shadowy darkness she saw a face turn in her direction. It was Adrienne, her long blond hair giving her away. Vivian held out her hand and motioned to Adrienne to get up. Adrienne took a series of tiny steps, careful not to awaken Rachel. She emerged into the light of the hallway, dressed in an oversized tee shirt and clutching Mickey.

"Please come downstairs with me."

Adrienne pulled her hair from her face to wipe the sleep from her eyes and followed Vivian down the steps. They stopped at the bottom of the stairs in the hallway foyer. Vivian took hold of her daughter's free hand.

"I've had a special secret for more than seventeen years. I want to share that secret with someone, and you're the only person in the whole world with whom I could ever share it."

Adrienne - her eyes now wide open - stared at Vivian anxiously, but couldn't imagine what to expect. Vivian reached out and traced her hand down the side of the grandfather clock that stood in the foyer.

"This clock belonged to my grandmother. It's very old, over seventy years old. I've had it since before you were born. When I first got it, it didn't work and we just used it as a decoration. A month after you were taken, I had it repaired. See the pendulum, how it swings to and fro."

"Um hmm."

"That's your heartbeat."

"My heartbeat?"

"That's my secret."

Vivian inhaled an enormous breath and slowly let it out. "Every time I lift the weights.... I do it every week.

I'm the only one who does it, no one else is allowed." She glanced upstairs in the direction of the bedrooms. "I tell them it's because the clock belonged to my grandmother........ Well, every time I lift the weights I say a prayer. I tell God I'll raise the weights to keep the pendulum swinging, and I ask Him to keep your heart beating in return. I've done it every week for seventeen years."

Vivian took Adrienne in her arms. Adrienne let Mickey drop to the floor as she returned the embrace.

"All these years I never really thought He was listening, but I kept reciting the prayer anyway. Would you raise the weights for me this time?"

Adrienne opened the door of the clock and lovingly pulled the chains to lift the weights.

Chapter 37

Vivian pounded away on her computer with jittery fingers. "Lovely Starter Home. 3 Bedroom Townhouse. Within Walking Distance of Village Center and Elementary School…….."

What else can I possibly say? Maybe I should just tell it like it is. She deleted what she had typed and started over. "3 Bedroom Townhouse. $175K – Non-negotiable. Fully equipped with a 40 Foot High Power-Line Stanchion in your backyard.… "

Her heart was racing, and she could feel it thumping away – when is he going to get here? She lifted her hands from the keyboard, closed her eyes, and tried to relax. Several cycles of breathing exercises she had picked up from one of Dr. Weil's holistic health books helped calm her a bit.

She'd gotten the listing a couple of days ago, and had promised the sellers, a young African-American couple, that she would have an ad in the Columbia Flier by the end of the week. She should have never taken the listing. There was no way in the world that anyone was going to pay $175,000 with that metal monstrosity right next to the house. She'd try to reason with the sellers, told them $150,000 was the most they could possibly hope for. But they were insistent, "We won't take a penny less than 175." Ultimately, she knew they would have to face facts and come down on the price, but they were going to be a royal pain in the butt until that happened.

God, when is he going to get here? Damn, I've got to get this ad written. "3 Bedroom Townhouse. Less than 2 years old. Convenient Location – Walk to…..

The office doorbell buzzed.

She leaped from her chair and rushed out of her office past the receptionist's desk to the front door. There he was decked out in his normal garb – jeans, sweatshirt, and Baltimore Orioles baseball cap. An old, beaten-up brief case dangled at the end of a long arm.

"The parkin' lot's empty. You here by yourself?" he asked in a soft voice that belied his imposing 250-pound frame.

"The office doesn't open 'til ten. We'll be able to talk without being interrupted."

"Sorry, I'm late. I stopped to help an old guy change a flat. Said he didn't need any help, that is, until he threw his back out."

"It's no big deal," she lied. It most certainly was a big deal. She hadn't gotten so much as a minute of sleep. Awake all night agonizing over what he might tell her.

"Coffee?" she asked in obligatory fashion as she led him to her office.

"No thanks, I'm fine," he said, closing the door behind them, and somehow squeezing in the chair next to her desk.

The effects of her breathing exercises had evaporated, and it once again felt like someone was playing a set of bongos inside her chest. Trying to disguise her anxiousness she interlocked her fingers behind her head, and casually leaned back in her desk chair. "So aaaaaah, how was Wyoming?

He pushed the bill of his Oriole hat up a couple of inches. "Snowy."

She just looked at him.

"I got lucky. I found out quite a bit."

"That's good...... I think."

"Since you're sittin' there lookin' like you might have a stroke any minute, let me put you at ease right off the bat…. I didn't discover anything that I think you'll find especially upsetting…. That is nothing that's any more upsetting than what you already know."

"What do you mean, you got lucky?

"My cousin I told you about who lives in Casper, one of his old school buddies is a Wyoming State trooper. That made things a lot easier."

Vivian brought her hands together in prayer like fashion just below her chin.

"All right, let me show you what I got," he said as he popped open his briefcase and placed a single piece of paper on the desk in front of Vivian.

"How did you get this? I told you I didn't want you to do anything that would upset Adrienne or Hank."

"You made that perfectly clear to me, and I listened good. Neither one of them has the slightest idea I was ever even in Wyoming. You don't have to worry. Okay?"

"All right, but how'd you get this thing?" she said, waving the sheet of paper in her hand.

"I got it in Cheyenne at the Wyoming Department of Transportation. That's where I got a lot of the info I'll be giving you. Like I said, it helps to have a state trooper taggin' along with you."

"Is Cheyenne near Jackson Hole?"

"Oooohhh, it's only about 400 miles away….. Got a bunch of stuff in Casper also where they keep the state tax records. Casper's way the hell away from Jackson Hole too. Wyoming's one big state."

Vivian smiled appreciatively and then began studying the copy of Adrienne's phony birth certificate.

"They had it from when Adrienne applied for her driver's permit in 1991 when she was fifteen."

Vivian began reading aloud, "Adrienne Jean Sarsfield, Date of Birth: March 26, 1976."

The Other Part Of Me

Vivian looked up at Ted McAlister, private detective - $75 per hour, plus expenses. "The bastards didn't even get her birthday right. How did they get this thing? It looks so official."

"Today, they're a piece of cake, probably buy one for a hundred bucks what with the things crooks can do with computers. Back then they probably had to pay ten times that much."

Vivian started reading again. "Father: James Sarsfield, Mother: Cynthia Sarsfield, Place of Birth: Philadelphia, Pennsylvania."

"I spent the day in Philly yesterday. Didn't find much there….. now take a look at this," Ted said as he put another piece of paper in front of Vivian. "They had this on record too with Adrienne's driver's application. She had to give them this because her last name had changed."

Again Vivian read out loud. "Wyoming Record of Adoption. June 23, 1983. Father (adoptive): Henry Sullivan. Mother (biological): Cynthia Sullivan…….. biological, my ass."

"Let me try to give you the whole picture as best I can, puttin' things in order."

Vivian nodded in approval and anticipation.

"You just jump in if you have a question about anything…. Okay, here goes. I think James and Cynthia Sarsfield must have met at Temple University, at least they were both students there in the '60s. She graduated in '67, but he dropped out in '65. They got married in '70. They lived in Philly from the time they got married until the end of '76. Sometime in '77 – I couldn't find out exactly when, probably right after they took your daughter I suspect. They took her in December of '76, didn't they?"

"Yes."

"As I was about to say, sometime in 1977 they showed up in West Yellowstone, Montana."

"Montana?"

"West Yellowstone's just across the Wyoming state line, right at the west entrance to Yellowstone National Park. They both worked for one of the concessionaires in the park. Then a couple of years later, Cynthia Sarsfield took her daughter ...... I'm sorry, I shouldn't of said it that way. She took the girl and moved to Jackson Hole in 1980. Jackson Hole's about a hundred miles to the south. She kept her job with the same outfit, only in Grand Teton National Park. Teton's just outside of Jackson Hole."

"What about the husband?"

"Sometime in 1981, sorry about my lack of accuracy on this date stuff,.... he moved to Mammoth Hot Springs, Wyoming. Mammoth's the north entrance to Yellowstone."

"Sounds like they liked national parks."

"Yeah it does, doesn't it?.....Well, on July 6, 1982 good old James Sarsfield ran his car off the road and slammed into a telephone pole. Autopsy report said his blood alcohol level was 0.18."

Ted reached into his briefcase and tossed a 5x7 black and white photograph on the desk. "I got his Wyoming driver's license picture blown up at Kinkos. I was surprised they had a Kinkos in Wyoming."

Vivian jerked away and let out a loud whimpering moan.

"I'm sorry. I shouldn't of startled you like that."

She took a deep breath and picked up the picture.

"That was taken in 1981 when he got his Wyoming license. The only reason they still had it on file was because he was in a fatal accident."

Vivian studied the face. Sharp features. Dimpled chin. Thin, tight mouth. Long sideburns. Wild, dark hair.

"I need to ask. You ever see this man before, or does he look familiar at all in any way?"

Vivian turned the picture over hiding the man's face from view and said, "No."

"Movin' right along here.... Cynthia Sarsfield married Henry Sullivan on October 14, 1982. Henry Sullivan has lived in Jackson Hole his whole life. I didn't bother gettin' a picture of him. Suspect you got some pictures of him yourself when he and Adrienne visited last week."

"Yeah, I got a bunch of them."

McAlister paused for a moment, thinking Vivian might say something else, but she didn't.

"Cynthia Sullivan died of cancer on November 2, 1991. I had a copy of her obituary, but somehow I lost it."

"That's just as well. I don't think I would want to see it anyway."

"You might not want to see what else I have in my briefcase here either."

Vivian crossed her arms in front of her chest.

"I got a picture of Cynthia Sullivan. Same deal as with her first husband. It's a blow-up from the last time she had her license renewed."

Vivian stood up and turned her back to McAlister. She stared out the window, pulling the strings that open and close the blinds; she did it several times. She left them in the open position, and then quickly spun around.

"Let me see it."

"It was taken in '88," he said as he handed it to her.

Long, thick, wavy hair pulled back from her forehead; dark black with a single streak of gray. Dark eyes. Full lips. Thick, really thick, black eyebrows.

Vivian expected to feel a surge of hatred, but she felt nothing. "I've never seen this woman before."

"Me neither. But it's the damndest thing. Somethin' about her looks familiar to me.... I guess I'm just lettin' my mind play tricks on me. Hell, I'd never even been to Wyoming until a week ago."

"You said you went to Philadelphia yesterday."

"I found the apartment where James and Cynthia Sarsfield lived. It was seventeen years ago, I really didn't expect to find anyone who knew them, but I did."

Vivian instinctively initiated a Dr. Weil breathing cycle.

"It was an old woman. She said she didn't really know 'em, but she remembered 'em. When I asked her how she could remember that long ago she said, 'You don't tend to forget people who try to kill themselves'."

Vivian squeezed her lips into a tight little circle.

"She remembered Cynthia Sarsfield bein' taken away in an ambulance. Word around the neighborhood back then was she took a bottle of sleeping pills 'cause she had a miscarriage; they got her stomach pumped out just in time. The old woman said the two of 'em moved away real quick like later that year, sometime in December. Said she remembered them putting up Christmas decorations and then moving away a few days later. That's how she remembered it was December. Said they were in such a hurry, they left with the decorations still up."

"She couldn't have her own baby so she took mine."

"That's what it sounds like."

Vivian leaned her head back as if she were counting ceiling tiles. After ten seconds or so she slowly lowered her head. "What did you find out about my husband?"

McAlister rubbed his large, meaty hand across his chin. "Everything seems to jibe with the story he gave you. He bought his airline ticket on Friday afternoon at that place near the mall, and flew to Jackson Hole the next morning. Rented a car from Budget, spent two nights at a motel, and flew back on Monday. No phone calls billed to his room. Clerk said he was by himself, remembered him asking about a place to rent skis."

"What about the call to his office from the man who told him about Adrienne?"

"There's nothin' I can really do on that. Even if I went ahead and got the record of calls to his office I wouldn't know what to look for. A big government agency like his probably gets a hundred calls a day. Only the police with cooperation from your husband could do anything there. And I doubt they could either. The guy who made the call, if there was a guy, would of used a pay phone."

"What do mean, if there was a guy?"

"Like I said, everything that I found out seems to jibe with what your husband told you, but somethin' don't smell right to me…. As for the hospital, I checked the visitor log for that Friday and your husband didn't sign it. But that doesn't mean anything, most people don't sign those things, I never do….. Your husband said he was seein' a friend from work, right?"

"That's right."

"Do you know the person's name?"

"No, I don't."

"I know a guy who can get me the list of patient names, but he's on vacation this week. You get the name and I can check it against the list."

Vivian replied with a comfortable voice. "That won't be necessary. What you have found out has been extremely beneficial to me, Ted. It's really helped to put my mind at ease. I truly appreciate it."

McAlister took off his Orioles hat and began turning it around and around. "Mrs. Webster……."

"Since when did I become Mrs. Webster?"

"Since I started getting ready to stick my nose where maybe it don't belong."

Vivian didn't say anything.

"Mrs. Webster, when you hired me three years ago to find out if your husband was cheatin' on you, why'd ya never do anything about it?"

"Well Ted, you did find out that he was seeing that woman, but you also found out he stopped seeing her when she got married."

"It just don't make no sense. A nice, beautiful woman like you."

"I wasn't always so nice. I'm not saying I deserved it, but I think my husband needed a way to escape my drinking. Once I got sober, he stopped doing it."

"You sure you don't want me to check that patient list?"

"Yes, I'm sure."

"Okay Mrs. Webster, I mean Vivian. I'll work up my final report tonight. It'll cover everything we went over today."

Vivian swept up everything on her desk with the picture of Cynthia Sullivan on top of the pile. She handed it back to McAlister and chuckled, "She sure has bushy eyebrows. You know, in a stupid kind of way it feels good to be able to laugh about that."

"I'll drop off your copy of my final report tomorrow," he said.

"No Ted, you just keep the report. I've got my daughter back. In a way, I've got both of my daughters back. I'm not going to worry about what happened in the past any longer."

Chapter 38

It was early morning, Saturday, the fifth of February. Barbara rested her head on Larry's bare chest and pulled the sheet over top of them.

"So you're a Catholic, huh?" said Larry.

"Yes."

"Well?"

"Well what?"

"Well, I want the rest of the story – you know, like that Paul Harvey guy gives you at the end of his radio show."

"Are you sure?"

Larry just stared at her expectantly.

"I grew up a devout Catholic. Went to Catholic schools all the way through high school. Never missed mass. You know, the whole nine yards." She tried to force a smile, but it didn't work. "When I was little I even wanted to become a nun."

Larry felt an ever so slight giggle beginning to build in his stomach at the thought of Barbara decked out in a nun's habit, but quickly caught himself, realizing this was not a laughing matter. If anything, he suspected it was a crying matter.

"How could I not know any of these things? Whenever we talked about what it was like when we were growing up, you never told me any of this stuff."

"I lied."

"Why?"

She just looked at him and didn't say anything.

"How could you be a Catholic all these years and me not know it?"

"I stopped being a Catholic."

"When?"

"The day I met you."

"Maybe, I shouldn't have asked for the rest of the story."

"I stopped being a Catholic the instant I decided to take your baby. I stopped being me." She paused to lick her lips. "You know, when I was little….. we had to go to confession once a month. I would always lie to the priest. I never had anything to confess, so I would make up something. I would tell him I disobeyed my mom or that I told a dirty joke, just so I would have something to say… But I never cheated, stole, or did anything bad. I didn't even curse then."

"How can that be? You always told me you were a bit of a hell-raiser. You said…."

She interrupted, "I lied."

"Why?"

"I don't know. I guess I just didn't want you to know about what I had been like."

"I'm sorry."

"There's nothing for you to be sorry about. I did it to myself."

"Help me understand how you could take my baby?" Larry whispered.

"Like I told you, my sister had two miscarriages. She was suicidal. If she hadn't gotten a baby she was going to kill herself. I believed that then and I believe it now."

"Even if that's true, it doesn't justify the act."

"I know that."

"Why didn't she get help from a doctor or someone?"

"She was seeing a priest, but it wasn't helping. I felt I had to do something."

"Why did you have to do something? Why you?"

"Cynthia was only four years older than me, but sometimes she seemed more like a mother than a sister to me. Mom was sick so much that Cynthia ended up taking care of me most of the time. I leaned on her for everything. She always took care of me."

"And then you had to do something to take care of her?"

"That's right."

"Even at the risk of ruining your life?"

"Taking your baby did more than ruin my life, in a way it ended my life. Up until that point I had a positive self-image. I liked myself, but afterwards I was ashamed. I stopped going to church. I stopped being me."

She waited for Larry to respond, but he didn't.

"I tried to fill my life with my job and doing volunteer work to compensate for my shame. I became compulsive about those things. In a way it worked. I still hate myself for what I did, but I know I have helped a lot of people."

"How did I fit into all of this? Didn't I just make things more complicated for you?"

"Along with being a baby stealer, I was an adulterer with the baby's father. How could it get any more complicated?"

"Then why did you stay with me all these years?" Larry asked as he softly stroked her cheek.

"I couldn't help myself. You know how upsetting it was for me whenever you would start saying how we were meant for one another, how I was the one woman in the whole world for you. I got upset because I knew it was true. I felt the same way, but I didn't dare ever say it – not after what I had done to you."

Barbara took several uneven breaths and went on. "I knew that robbing you from your family was wrong, I'd already hurt them more than enough. I tried to make myself stop seeing you so many times, but I just couldn't do it. When we would stop seeing one another for a while I missed you so much I thought I was going to go crazy. I thought marrying John would force me to stop seeing you, but even that didn't work."

Barbara began sobbing and Larry took her in his arms, inadvertently placing his hand on her scarred and tender breast.

"Does it bother you?" asked Barbara.

"Does what bother me?"

"My breast, the way it looks, does it bother you?"

"Have I been acting like it bothers me?"

"No, but should I have the reconstructive surgery?"

"That's up to you. But if you're asking me if I want you to have it done, my answer is no."

Barbara rolled over on her back and seized Larry's hand, pressing it to her lips. "Just a couple of weeks ago there was so much blackness in my life. I never thought I could ever be happy again. But now everything seems so bright....... the doctor changing his mind about the chemo treatments." She paused to kiss his hand again. "More importantly, you still wanting to have me, still wanting me to go to Chile with you."

Larry brought their interlocked hands against his naked body. "I want you to be happy. I want us to be happy together."

"Do you really think we can?"

"Despite everything that has happened, I still believe we were meant to be together. It's as if us being together is some kind of cosmic inevitability."

"But what about leaving your family?"

"For so long I've been the one in the middle, the one trying to keep peace between Vivian and Rachel. But now there is no middle."

"What do you mean?"

"They don't need me any more. They've done more than make peace - they depend on one another. And Karen... I mean Adrienne - I've got to stop calling her that. She just magnifies the love between Vivian and Rachel. But you know what all this has made me realize?"

"No, I don't."

"I realize I don't really love Vivian. I know I must have loved her at one time, but I can't remember what it felt like. All this time I've been confusing my guilt with love. But now that she doesn't need me any more, now that the pain has gone from her life, I realize I don't love her. I care for her, but I don't love her. It's you I love."

"You must be terribly angry at me."

"I remember feeling anger, intense anger, but it went away. And when it went away it was like everything was happening to someone else. Like I was watching a movie or something."

"How long did it stay that way?"

"Things didn't seem real until I got on the plane to leave Jackson Hole. You know, I hardly thought of you during those first few days. And for the past seventeen years, I honestly don't believe I've gone one waking hour without thinking of you. You know those split-screen televisions?"

"Huh?"

"A split-screen television, the kind where you can watch a second channel in a little box in the corner of the screen."

"What about them?"

"That's what my life has been like since I first met you, a split screen television. I could be doing anything, seeing anything, feeling anything, and this little image of you would always be there in the corner of my consciousness........ For those first few days after you told me about taking Karen, you weren't there; your image was gone. It was as if you no longer existed......... But then you reappeared."

"Why didn't you start hating me then?"

"I knew I was supposed to hate you; you had taken my baby. I tried to make myself hate you, but I couldn't."

"What were you feeling?" whispered Barbara.

"I was feeling what I always felt. I was worried about you. I missed you. I wanted to be with you."

Barbara closed her eyes. "It's only been a short time. Are you sure the hatred won't come later, that you won't grow to detest me once you're away from your family?"

"I'm not sure of anything. That's just the chance we'll have to take if we want to be together."

"I want to take that chance."

Chapter 39

She pushed the hands-free speaker button on the phone and answered, "Columbia Reality, Vivian Webster speaking."

"Hello Vivian, this is Ted McAlister."

"Hi Ted."

"I was hopin' you'd be workin' today."

"Saturday's the biggest day of the week in the real estate business."

"You gonna be there for a while? I need to drop off your copy of my final report."

"Like I told you a few days ago, I don't need the report."

"Yes you do. I got a whole bunch of new information to give ya."

"What is it?"

"I hope you're sittin' down."

Vivian picked up the receiver and put it to her ear, but didn't say anything.

"Remember how I told ya Cynthia Sullivan looked familiar to me? I finally figured it out. It was those bushy eyebrows."

Chapter 40

It was shortly before noon when Larry left Barbara's apartment. He arrived home just as Vivian was putting on her coat to walk out the front door. Before they could exchange greetings they were startled by Rachel bounding down the steps.

"Mom, Dad!"

"What is it?" Larry asked.

"I just got this message from Adrienne. The remodeling at her school is going to be more extensive than she thought. She's going to be able to stay three extra days with us over Easter break."

Larry jokingly complained, "How many e-mail messages can you two girls send each other?"

"We have a lot of catching up to do."

"I guess you do," Larry said with a smile.

"Rachel, if you still want me to drop you off at Vinnie's, let's go. I need to run a couple of errands and then get back here. An old friend is coming by to see me in a little while."

"Mom, is something wrong? You look real pale, like you just saw a ghost or somethin'."

Vivian didn't respond to Rachel's question. Instead she said, "Come on, I don't have much time."

"Viv, Rachel's right. You do look pale," said Larry as Vivian sped past him without so much as an acknowledging glance.

Mother and daughter were out the door and gone in a flash. Larry shrugged his shoulders, and went upstairs to the bedroom. He changed into running clothes, picked up his Sony Walkman from the nightstand, and inserted the Beatles' "Sergeant Pepper" tape.

Heading for the stairway, he noticed the door to the spare room had been left open; Vivian normally kept the door closed. She had recently converted the room into a workspace. He could see the back legs of the easel that held the painting of Rachel and Adrienne. After Rachel's request that she add Adrienne to the painting, Vivian had been emphatic about Rachel not seeing it again until it was finished. She didn't want him looking either, but hadn't made nearly as big a deal of it as she had done with Rachel. Sneaking a quick peek couldn't do any harm. Even so, he tiptoed into the room – despite being home alone.

Just one glance was all it took. His knees wobbled so badly he immediately fell into the only seat in the room – a wooden, classroom-type chair. His eyes jumped back and forth from Rachel to Adrienne to Rachel to….. The faces were the same, but somehow different. Rachel was untouched from the last time he'd seen her with the exception of her hair. She was now adorned with a short crop of golden blond hair. With Rachel having dyed her hair back to its natural color only a few days earlier, the painting was true to life in every respect.

Most of Vivian's recent efforts had been devoted to introducing Adrienne into the painting. Adrienne stood next to her sister, and was turned ever so slightly toward her. Whereas Rachel seemed ready to leap off of the canvas into the three-dimensional world, Adrienne looked as if she was content to sink further into the canvas. Adrienne was reaching out to touch Rachel and appeared a little unsure of herself, but not afraid or the least bit sad; in fact, she was smiling, although not quite as radiantly as Rachel was. And while Rachel's smile was directed at the viewer of the painting, Adrienne's smile was directed at Rachel.

The message was unmistakable. Adrienne was saying to Rachel, "You're my sister, I love you, and I need you. Please lead the way for me, I'm right beside you." It was the most empowering message Rachel could possibly receive from the only person capable of delivering that message, her sister.

He now knew what Vivian had meant when he asked, "Whose birthday present is it anyway?" and she had replied, "This painting is for Rachel. When I'm finished, I'll paint a different one for Adrienne."

Vivian had done something wondrous, something truly astonishing. The painting was no longer "just" a gift of love to Rachel from Vivian, it was now also an expression of love to Rachel from Adrienne.

The painting held him like a magnet. It was as if he had to consciously will himself out of the chair. He escaped the room and again headed to the stairway, but instead was drawn into Rachel's room by the hum of her computer. There was a message on the screen, an email from Adrienne. The last line of the message jumped out at him: "Love Adrienne, P.S. Every time I read your Harvard essay I learn something new about myself."

He could not stop himself. He dropped to his knees, and with his head at floor level, searched the underside of the shelf holding Rachel's stereo components. The computer disk he had replaced was still taped to the bottom of the shelf. He peeled away one edge of the tape and removed the disk.

He inserted the disk in the computer and opened its contents, a single folder entitled "Hail Mary". A double click on the folder, revealed two documents - "Intro Letter" and "Other". He read the "Intro Letter" addressed to the Harvard Admissions Office that he had read previously, several weeks earlier. Two sentences near the end of the letter made his stomach tighten. *"It was with enormous difficulty and pain that I wrote the enclosed paper. I trust you will treat it with the sensitivity it deserves."*

A double click on the document entitled "Other" caused its contents to spill onto the screen in front of him. It seemed as if he was underwater wearing scuba gear. He leaned over the desk until the limited field of view of his scuba mask was completely filled by the computer screen. The persistent low hum of the computer was the engine of the boat on the ocean's surface a hundred feet above him. His breathing was heavy and loud, like the noise made by the regulator as it released air from his tank. He became cotton-mouthed as he sucked in the air through the regulator and read the words through his scuba mask.

The Other Part of Me

My name is Rachel Webster and I am seventeen years old. During my seventeen years I have gained a depth of understanding of the human psyche that most people never realize during an entire lifetime. I have gained this understanding through a spectra of emotional experiences that are extremely rare, if not unique. Let me take you back with me, so that I might share some of my experiences with you.

When I was a little girl I had a recurring and terrifying dream. I dreamt that I was not whole. I dreamt that my right leg was missing, that it was not there. Even sometimes when I was awake, I would find myself reaching to feel for my leg, afraid to look down to see if it was really there.

I never played with other children. I only had one friend. My parents said she was a make believe friend, but she was real. Some of the time my friend was with me, but most of the time it seemed like she was inside of me. When I closed my eyes tight and pressed my hands against my ears real hard, I could hear both of our hearts beating together inside of me. I could always see my friend in my dreams and sometimes I could see her when I was awake. She looked just like me. My friend's name was Rachel, just like mine. Sometimes I would get Rachel and me mixed up. I wasn't sure if I was me or if I was my friend Rachel.

I liked my friend very much, but my mother and father didn't like her. If they could have seen her, I think they would have liked her, but they could never see her. Every time one of them would come near us, Rachel would jump back inside of me.

One time my father took me to a place where two women had me play with some funny looking toys, and then they started asking me questions about my friend. It scared me a lot, and from that time on I told everyone my friend had gone away, but she hadn't.

My mother used to get drunk all the time. When she was drunk, she would yell and throw things and cry a lot. She would tell me I was bad, and lock me in the closet where it was real dark, but she never did that when my father was there. One time my father came home when I was locked in the closet. He hit my mother real hard and made her mouth bleed. After that she never did it again. Being locked in the closet wasn't nearly as bad as it sounds. I never cried or got scared because Rachel would always be in there with me, but it made me very, very angry.

Many times when my mother was crying she would say things about some girl named Karen. One time I asked her who Karen was and she hit me, so I didn't ask her about Karen any more.

Then another time when I was eight years old, I was playing with the contents of my mother's purse, and I found a picture of two babies who looked exactly alike. I asked my mother who the babies were, and she started crying even though she wasn't drunk. That night my mother and father had me sit on the sofa between them, and they told me I was one of the babies in the picture. The other baby was Karen, the girl I had heard my mother talking about.

It was at this point in my life that I discovered I had a twin sister, Karen. She was abducted when she was nine months old. Karen was killed, but the police never found her body so my parents never got to bury her. My mother was unable to deal with Karen's death and this turned her into an evil person. I believe it would have been much better had my mother been able to bury Karen.

After I found out about Karen, I stopped having the dream about my leg not being there. And my friend, Rachel, told me she was changing her name to Karen. I still liked Rachel a lot, I did not care if she changed her name. But something terrible started to happen. Now that I knew about Karen (my sister, Karen, not my friend, Karen) my mother started telling me about her. She always told me how Karen was better than I. Just like locking me in the closet, she only told me these things when she was drunk and would almost never say them when my father was there. She told me Karen was bigger, smarter, prettier, and nicer than me. At first my mother was just talking about when Karen and I were babies, but then she started talking about the way Karen was then, as if she were the same age as I. This was very confusing to me because my sister was dead.

I began to hate my sister because she was so much better than I and because my mother loved her more than she loved me. I also began disliking my friend Rachel who had changed her name to Karen, so I made her go away. But worst of all, I started hating my mother. When I was little, before I knew about my sister, I had loved my mother even though she was mean to me. But now I hated her.

My father was always wonderful. He would play with me and take me places. My mother blamed my father

Ronnie Kinsley

for Karen's abduction, but she never told him that, she only told me. My sister and I had been under my father's care when she was taken. My mother told me my father was lying about something, that the abduction could not have happened the way he said it did. As I have gotten older and have analyzed the details of the abduction myself, details that need not be presented here, I often wonder if there might not be some truth to my mother's assertion. The depth of guilt my father carries with him, a guilt he unsuccessfully tries to hide, is clearly out of proportion with the circumstances of the abduction as he asserts them to be. As he tells the story, he was essentially in the wrong place at the wrong time. But the guilt he attempts to camouflage tells a different story.

So this is the parental foundation on which I have matured into a young adult: a mother obsessed with a baby taken from her; and a father burdened with guilt over that baby's disappearance. My maturation process was, and continues to be, dominated by one fundamental personal relationship – a personal relationship that has been hidden from my parents and from everyone else. (There is one exception: over the past year I have begun to share my innermost feelings with my boyfriend who has helped me greatly in my efforts to deal with these feelings.) The personal relationship of which I speak is the relationship between my dead sister and me.

The evolution of our relationship began with nine months in my mother's womb, continued for nine months out of the womb, and was then harshly terminated when she was abducted. The next phase of the evolution consisted of my unknowing attempts (e.g., my dreams, my make-believe friend) to re-establish our relationship. Once re-established (when I found out I had a sister), my relationship with her consisted primarily of my attempts to deal with her superiority, her superiority over me when she

Ronnie Kinsley

for Karen's abduction, but she never told him that, she only told me. My sister and I had been under my father's care when she was taken. My mother told me my father was lying about something, that the abduction could not have happened the way he said it did. As I have gotten older and have analyzed the details of the abduction myself, details that need not be presented here, I often wonder if there might not be some truth to my mother's assertion. The depth of guilt my father carries with him, a guilt he unsuccessfully tries to hide, is clearly out of proportion with the circumstances of the abduction as he asserts them to be. As he tells the story, he was essentially in the wrong place at the wrong time. But the guilt he attempts to camouflage tells a different story.

So this is the parental foundation on which I have matured into a young adult: a mother obsessed with a baby taken from her; and a father burdened with guilt over that baby's disappearance. My maturation process was, and continues to be, dominated by one fundamental personal relationship – a personal relationship that has been hidden from my parents and from everyone else. (There is one exception: over the past year I have begun to share my innermost feelings with my boyfriend who has helped me greatly in my efforts to deal with these feelings.) The personal relationship of which I speak is the relationship between my dead sister and me.

The evolution of our relationship began with nine months in my mother's womb, continued for nine months out of the womb, and was then harshly terminated when she was abducted. The next phase of the evolution consisted of my unknowing attempts (e.g., my dreams, my make-believe friend) to re-establish our relationship. Once re-established (when I found out I had a sister), my relationship with her consisted primarily of my attempts to deal with her superiority, her superiority over me when she

390

was a baby, and the superiority she would have held over me throughout our lives had she been able to live.

It was this phase of my relationship with my sister that was most damaging to me. It was during this phase that I grew to hate my sister. It was during this phase that I tried to compete with her, but always unsuccessfully. No matter how well I did in school, or in sports, I knew she would have done better had she been given the opportunity. It was during this phase that I began to cheat and lie in an attempt to offset her superiority and exaggerate my own accomplishments. And most damaging of all, it was during this phase, that I finally gave up and stopped caring. It made no difference how hard I tried or how hard I worked, my sister would have done better. So I stopped trying. Instead of a motivational force to do better, my sister became an emotional excuse not to care, not to try. I became, in the words of the school counselor, "the worst underachiever she had ever encountered."

The final phase of my relationship with my sister is the one I am in now. I do not know exactly when I entered this phase, but I suspect it began with the transformation of my mother. She stopped drinking several years ago, and ever so slowly she has begun to gain my respect and love. As a result, I began to feel much more comfortable with my sister. I stopped hating her. I stopped trying to compete with her. Most significantly, I began to grieve for her. I grieve for the life she was denied. I feel sad that she will never see a rainbow, will never look up into a night sky full of stars, will never experience the tender kiss of someone she loves, and will never do or be able to feel the things I will get to do and feel.

I now realize I am living for both myself and for my sister. My sister is The Other Part of Me. I miss my sister. I love my sister.

Acknowledging my love for my sister has been the most significant step in my lifelong struggle for personal wholeness. There is one final step I know I must take in order to realize a full sense of personal wholeness. I must acknowledge the respect and love I now feel for my mother. I have not told my mother I love her since I was eight years old. To achieve wholeness, I must say three words to my mother, "I love you." I am not yet ready to say those words. I do not know if I will ever be able to say those words. In many respects, I am still that angry little girl locked in the closet.

Larry's hands trembled as he entered the command to eject the disk. He knelt down and taped the disk back to the bottom of the shelf. Light-headed, he stumbled out of Rachel's room. He felt stiff and uncoordinated as he went down the stairs, each step jarring his body. At the bottom of the stairs, he was startled as the door opened. It was Vivian and a man with a bushy, gray mustache wearing a dark blue overcoat. He inspected the man's face, a face hidden deep within his memories. The mustache used to be black.

"Larry, you remember Detective Mathias don't you?"

Before Larry could respond the man extended his hand. "Why Dr. Webster, it's been a long time. How many years ago was it, fifteen or sixteen?"

"Seventeen, why it's been seventeen years," Vivian replied enthusiastically as she placed her hand on the man's back to guide him down the hallway. "Would you like some iced tea Detective?"

"No thank you."

"How about you Larry?"

"No," replied Larry uncertainly.

"Well, I'm going to help myself to some."

"Mrs. Webster, I can't tell you how happy I am to hear that Karen is alive."

"Yes, it's absolutely wonderful," Vivian said gleefully as she poured herself a glass of iced tea. "Please, let's all sit down at the table. Now Detective, you told me on the phone how pressed for time you are, so let me get right to the point. "

"Please do."

"I want you to reopen the case. I have a report from a private detective, Ted McAlister. I believe you know him."

Larry, feeling an overwhelming rush of helplessness, clenched his fists on the table in front of him.

"I know him very well. Worked with him when he was on the force. Whatever he gave you is first rate, you can count on that."

Vivian slid a notebook binder across the table. "Here's his report. It gives you more than enough information to reopen the case. I know you don't have time to read it now, so let me just give you the highlights. I used Ted about three years ago. I think it was his very first case after he left the Howard County Police Department. Well, back then he discovered that my husband was having an affair with a woman named Barbara Serelis; her name is Barbara Reilly now. She got married shortly after that. I thought that the affair had ended, but it seems they have started up again."

Detective Mathias glanced at Larry who sat dejectedly with his face in his hands.

"It turns out that my Karen was raised in Wyoming by Barbara Reilly's sister, Cynthia Sullivan. This woman, Cynthia Sullivan, died over a year ago and her first husband was killed in a car accident a long time ago. Karen's current father is a wonderful man and didn't marry Cynthia Sullivan until Karen was six years old. He never knew anything about the abduction. Until very recently he thought his wife was Karen's biological mother."

Vivian paused to sip her tea. "I think I put too much sugar in this. Now where was I, oh yes........ I suspect that the only people alive who know the details of the abduction are my husband's lover, Barbara Reilly, and possibly my husband. My husband was with her this morning at her apartment. And I have a strong suspicion that they both have airline tickets on the same flight to Chile, a week from today. I know this is a lot to throw at you, but it's all in the report."

Detective Mathias patted the binder in front of him. "Whew, that was a lot to throw at me and I'm not sure all of it sank in. Let me try to get a few things straight."

Larry stood up and started walking away.

"Dr. Webster, don't go anywhere. I'll want a word with you before I leave."

"I'll be in the living room," Larry said without turning his head.

The Detective turned his attention back to Vivian. "Now, where was I? Oh yes, help me to understand some things,"

"Of course."

"Did you say your husband had an affair with this Cynthia Sullivan?"

"No, with Cynthia Sullivan's sister, Barbara Reilly."

"And when did you find this out?"

Vivian steadied herself and wiped her eyes with her fingers. "I'm sorry Detective Mathias."

"That's okay, take your time."

Vivian took a relaxing breath. "Detective, I'm an alcoholic. I stopped drinking three years ago. That's when I had it confirmed that my husband was having an affair. Before that I had suspicions but I didn't care, at least I had myself convinced I didn't care. But once I sobered up I did care, and I had to find out if my suspicions were justified. It took Ted McAlister less than a week to verify that it was true."

Detective Mathias scratched his chin. "And your husband has been having this affair with this woman Barbara Reilly since the abduction."

"I'm not sure when it started, but my guess is that it did start back then. All I know is that only two weeks after Ted found out about them, my husband's lover got married. They stopped seeing one another after that. At least they stopped seeing one another for the next two months. That's when I took Ted off the case. I thought it was over and......." Vivian stopped in mid-sentence as she fought to keep from crying. "I thought my husband wouldn't cheat on me anymore once he believed I was going to stay sober, but obviously I was wrong."

"And when did you discover the affair had started again?"

"I didn't find out until this morning, right before I called you. That's when I found out everything I just told you."

"And you hired McAlister because you suspected your husband was having the affair again?"

"Oh no, I didn't think that at all. I hired Ted because I knew my husband was lying about something concerning the way he found out about Karen. Rachel, my other daughter, saw him at the hospital the day before he went to Wyoming to find Karen. At first, he said he wasn't at the hospital, and then he said he forgot he had been there. It was so obvious he was lying."

"What does the hospital have to do with any of this?"

"Ted just explained that to me too. It turns out he was with Barbara Reilly. She had some type of surgery that day."

"Because your husband lied about being at the hospital you hired McAlister again?"

Vivian leaned her head back and closed her eyes for a moment. "Larry lied about the hospital which meant to me he was probably lying about how he found out about Karen, and I've always known he lied about some aspect of the abduction. It was the combination of those two lies that made me call Ted again."

"Well Mrs. Webster, this is an incredible development. I'll review this report thoroughly later today, but I do need to get going. Like I told you on the phone, I have to pick up my wife at the airport. But tell me, how did McAlister piece all of this together?"

"About two weeks ago he went to Wyoming to see what he could find out. One of the things he came back with was this picture of Cynthia Sullivan," Vivian said as she opened the loose-leaf binder containing McAlister's report. "He said she looked familiar, but he didn't know why. Said it kept driving him crazy. Then one night when he couldn't sleep, it hit him like a ton of bricks. It was her eyebrows."

"She certainly has big ones," said the Detective.

"Yes, she does. And Ted remembered that Barbara Reilly has them too. He said he knew right then that they were sisters, so all he had to do was prove it."

Vivian began rapidly flipping the pages in the binder. "And look at this. It's the fake birth certificate they had made up for Adrienne….. See it says Mother's Name: Cynthia Sarsfield, but look down here in the corner. The type is so small and so faint because it's a copy of a copy. Neither of us even noticed it at first."

"I'll be damn. Mother's Maiden Surname: Serelis," said the Detective.

"Ted spent the last couple of days confirming everything and tying up the loose ends. And to top it off, he followed my husband to Barbara Reilly's apartment this morning."

Detective Mathias slowly got up from his chair. "Mrs. Webster, I do need to get going now." A large smile came across his face as he reached out and took Vivian's hand in his. "I'm so happy your daughter is alive. I can't wait to tell my wife, she'll remember this case very well. It broke her heart when it happened."

"It broke everyone's heart."

The Detective found Larry in the living room. "Dr. Webster, I want to see you in my office tomorrow morning at nine o'clock. Same office as seventeen years ago."

"I'll be there," came the muffled reply.

Vivian let the detective out the front door and came back to the living room.

"You know Larry, finding out three years ago that you were having an affair was the best thing that could have happened to me. I had always thought you were the good parent, the one Rachel could count on. But when I found out about you, I realized you couldn't be counted on for anything. I knew then I had to become the parent Rachel could depend on. That's what has kept me sober these last three years."

Larry Webster got up, and trudged slowly past Vivian and out the front door. He started running and he kept on running. It took him an hour and fifteen minutes to run the nine miles to the railroad tunnel in Patapsco State Park. It was late in the afternoon on a cold winter day when he entered the tunnel.

"Lucy In The Sky With Diamonds" was playing on his Walkman.

The End

About The Author

Ronnie Kinsley was born in West Virginia. His family moved to Baltimore when he was in the second grade, and he has lived in Maryland ever since. He has an undergraduate degree and a graduate degree in aerospace engineering from the University of Maryland, and he has a graduate degree in management from George Washington University. His most noteworthy accomplishment: "I once swam naked across the Potomac River."

"The Other Part of Me" is Ronnie's first novel. He is currently working on his second novel.

To order this book or to provide comments to the author contact: ronniekinsley@hotmail.com